The John Morano Eco-Adventure Series

FLOCKS OF ONE

A NOVEL
BY JOHN MORANO

grey gecko press

Published by Grey Gecko Press

www.greygeckopress.com

Printed in the United States of America

Library of Congress Cataloging-in-Publication Data
Morano, John
Flocks of one / John Morano
Library of Congress Control Number: 2018951379
ISBN   978-1-9457601-3-6
First Edition

"You really feel like you are that petrel or octopus struggling in a dying world. But the stories aren't depressing either. They spin magical tales made all the better by learning real ocean facts along the way."
— Martha Sorren, *Azula Magazine*

"Beyond his efforts at highlighting incredible, endangered species in his novels, John has also built a universe for his characters that is inclusive, diverse, and speaks to all readers."
— Sarah Evans, *Junto Magazine*

"A completely new approach to writing . . . like many animated classics, this is a story the whole family can enjoy."
— Terry Lipshetz, *Home News Tribune*

" . . . so well researched, so tightly written, at times it's difficult to tell where fact ends and fantasy begins."
— Roger Caras, best selling author & former President of ASPCA

" . . . delightful . . . powerful . . . perfect . . . good science within a clever story."
— Dr. Joan Ruddiman, *The Messenger Press*

" . . . astonishingly real . . . an educational lesson inside a very good read."
— *Ocean County Observer*

"Morano does something few writers do. He provides us with a unique perspective - that of the exploited animal. In doing so, he demonstrates just how profound and pervasive humans' effect on the ocean is."
— Roger Rufe, President of The Ocean Conservancy

" . . . [Morano has] creatively touched upon major subjects of contemporary interest, and I trust that [his] work will remain in print and discover a very large and appreciative audience."
— Gay Talese, best selling author

"Morano has the talent to connect with readers through prose that both informs and delights . . . He has great range as a writer . . . His books are delights: well researched and beautifully written, they contain powerful and important messages. He spins tales that have meaning . . . written in creative, stylistic verve."
— Dr. Douglas Anderson, Dean, Penn State College of Communication

" . . . a warm story . . . a great deal of imagination . . . a good job of pulling the reader into the story . . . I can see these novels some day as possible Disney movies."
— Dr. Will Norton, Jr., Dean, University of Nebraska College of Journalism and Mass Communications

"Morano has a clear, light style and can say a lot directly. He also has a fine sense of humor and makes you laugh out loud."
— B. A. Sweeny, *The Herald* (NJ)

"Morano challenges the reader to think, feel, and enjoy. I hope that no one passes up the opportunity to experience the message."
— Jason Chavez, *Albuquerque Journal*

"Morano redefines a classic genre. His eco-adventures speak to the young readers of today and allow them to look at the world around them and actually care about it. There are no 'scare tactics' needed. Good writing is naturally engaging."
— Jennifer Anna, author and literary critic

For Kris,

You were my Blue Sky

when I wrote and dedicated *Wing* to you

over 25 years ago.

And you're still my Blue Sky . . . always.

Thank You

Kris, John, and Vincent for your help, for listening, for reading, for suggesting. As with all things, you make me better.

Jason Aydelotte, Gecko-in-Chief, for being committed to writers, readers, books, ideas, voices, and to making a difference.

Sarah Anderson, for giving your best to the words on these pages and for sharing what beautiful images dance in your mind.

Juan Jose Olivieri for capturing the soul of this story and designing the cover so that readers can see, from the moment they spot this book, just what it's all about.

Josh Mitchell for another beautiful job of refining and shining my words. Thanks for making me look better than I am.

Sarah Townsend for doing more than anyone expected, for going above and beyond. I'm thrilled that you are part of this story.

Michelle Vines for having my back and watching over the progress of this book with the care that only one Gecko can give to another.

Tara Ackaway, publicist, friend, and so much more. The fact that you believe in these stories so deeply helps me and so many others feel the same way. Always a joy to be with you.

Mark Ludak for taking the time to capture a portrait of me that truly belongs with the story on these pages. Your generosity is very much appreciated.

Nicole Klemas for being so supportive and for taking care of all the tech things I don't understand (which is basically everything). Thrilled that you are a part of this adventure, my friend.

Monmouth University for supporting my work and making it possible for a journalism professor to apply the five Ws to characters, settings, and issues that are often underdiscussed, if they're discussed at all.

To everyone who turns these pages. It is one of the great honors of my life to be able to share these words with you.

Introduction

by Andrew Sharpless, CEO
Oceana

Pity the poor flounder.

Consider the plight of the unluckily named Patagonian toothfish, chased to near extinction.

Sea cucumbers, kelp, anchoveta, tainha—these are fascinating but unloved creatures. A fish is not a panda bear. Nobody hangs wall calendars of sea scallops on their office wall.

Most people will tell you they love the oceans. Whales, dolphins, seals, and sea lions evoke our sympathies. But extending empathy to the briny reality of most other sea life is another step entirely. They are cold, wet, and slippery—and, too often, forgotten.

The disfavor these creatures find themselves up against, it turns out, has real and dire consequences. You probably wouldn't want to eat an animal raised in a garbage heap, and yet an estimated 17.6 billion pounds of plastic enter the marine environment every year. We are dumping a garbage truck's worth of plastic into the oceans every minute.

If people went hunting for rabbits and accidentally killed another 25 percent of the creatures in the forest, we'd hear their cries, and people would demand that it stop. But when dirty fishing kills or damages countless sea creatures, their agony is distant and silent.

If someone decided the most efficient way to catch game was to tear through the forests with bulldozers, we'd hear the trees falling and make them stop. But when a bottom trawl wrecks a thousand-year-old coral garden that provides a nursery for young fish, there's no soundtrack to the violence.

The cost of our emotional distance has been high: overfishing, poor management, and the squandering of a tremendous resource. Our oceans have the potential to do so much more than most people can imagine. It has been estimated that a healthy, well-managed ocean could provide more than a billion people with a seafood meal every day, forever. That's a sustainable source of protein which, by the way, is also healthier for you than beef. Wild fish is also better for the planet, requiring no arable land or fresh water to cultivate, and generating only small amounts of greenhouse gasses compared to other animal protein sources. At Oceana, we say that if we save the oceans we can help feed the world.

Despite the challenges, we're making real progress. Oceana is winning victories in countries around the world. We've helped Brazil begin to manage its fisheries in line with science. We've stood alongside Chile's leaders as that country became a global leader in ocean conservation, banning bottom trawling in 98 percent of its territory and designating massive marine parks. Belize, after years of campaigning, protected its beautiful and unique barrier reef by banning offshore oil from the entirety of its ocean. We're fighting to protect sharks and whales—but also the Peruvian anchoveta.

Oceana now campaigns in Belize, Brazil, Canada, Chile, the European Union, Mexico, Peru, the Philippines, the United Kingdom, and the United States. Together with our allies, we have won more than 200 policy victories and protected more than 4.5 million square miles of ocean. We are winning the policies that will help restore our oceans to abundance.

But much work remains. And to enlist the world in the cause, we need to get people to think about how we treat even those bottom-dwelling fish and the oceans they call home.

It's been said the highest level of consciousness is learning empathy for other lifeforms. It gets harder the less they remind us of ourselves. And that's why John Morano's books are important. He puts us in the minds of some lesser-known, perhaps unloved creatures. The octopus we all know, of course, but how many of us spare daily thoughts for a coelacanth or a petrel?

The unique perspectives offered throughout the *Eco-Adventure Series* elevate our consciousness by forcing us to empathize with these creatures. We learn in a way that is only possible through fiction—a forced perspective that helps us understand how our fates entwine with theirs. These books bring us closer to ocean life and remind us that we may not be as different as we think. Fish get sick, just as we do. They breathe oxygen like we do. If we prick them, they will bleed. If we poison them, they will die.

You, as a reader of the latest addition to this series, have already taken the first steps. You've opened your mind to the possibility that a lifeform very different from your own is worth knowing, understanding, and saving. That's how, together, we will save the oceans.

Andrew Sharpless
CEO, Oceana
Washington, DC

Here Today, Gone Today

The Caatinga is a dry, arid, somewhat forgotten corner of Brazil. Much less well known than its sultry cousin, the Amazon, the Caatinga is still a fascinating environment, rife with secrets and jewels all its own. One of its most valuable treasures is large and blue. In fact, it's one of the rarest gems in all of nature. Neither sapphire nor sparkling mineral, it's often more desired, more collectible, and, to some, more enticing than any diamond. This treasure, however, is alive, at least for the moment. And while gold and silver can be tucked away for a lifetime, even buried for centuries, this jewel has a lifespan. One day, it will likely be gone, and sadly, for many, that reality only increases the desire to possess it.

Azul is a Spix's macaw—at least that's how the man-flock describes him. To the other inhabitants of the Caatinga, he's known as a sky parrot. They call him *Sky* because his kind is adorned with pale-blue feathers and soft white cheeks. Perched on a bare branch or soaring on the wing, they blend beautifully into the beyond, presenting the illusion that they're absorbed, unified with the heavens. Perhaps no other bird is colored so identically to the atmosphere and appears to be so one with the sky.

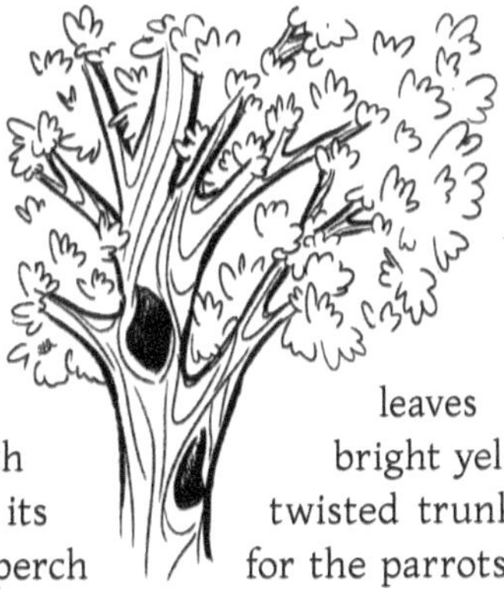

Azul perched alone in a caraiba tree. Its branches were brushed with silvery, oblong leaves that would soon be replaced with bright yellow flowers covering the limbs, its twisted trunk and furrowed bark a preferred perch for the parrots.

In its own way, the caraiba was as threatened as the bird it supported, at least in this corner of the Caatinga. This was Azul's favorite tree, especially when the dry, brown, elongated seedpods began to appear. The parrot relaxed by pulling pods from stems while the soft wood of the branches bobbed agreeably.

Although the Caatinga appears uninviting to many of the man-flock with its cacti, stunted trees, and thorny scrub, this largest dry, forested region in South America is home to some 350 bird species, 80 different mammals, another 50 lizard species, as well as 50 snakes, 49 amphibians, and even 3 types of crocodiles.

Within the dry Caatinga, Azul's flock gravitated to a unique woodland gallery of caraiba trees, the only tree they would nest in, clustered along a series of seasonal waterways. Many of the trees were 200 to 300 years old, having supported generations of the same families.

A smaller green maracana parrot watched from another tree close by. She'd recently taken an interest in Azul, and he'd begun to notice. The sky parrot dined alone, not what he naturally preferred. Before the spring arrived—in the midst of the rainy season, when all the creeks flowed briskly—he'd had a mate and two chicks in his nest.

The chicks were taken quickly before they could fledge. The man-flock had come in the night to the family's roosting hole in the caraiba tree. As the parrots slept, they placed a large, hard web over the exit hole, blocking the birds' escape. Then they poked down into the nest with sticks that were drenched in some type of sticky sap. The chicks were easily caught. While their young were being removed, Azul and Aura flew off, lest they disappear from the Caatinga as well.

The pair had lost young before. They knew the drill. Another tree was selected. Another nest in another roost hole was constructed. Other eggs would be laid, incubated, hatched. What else could they do? But again, the man-flock returned. They covered the entrance and plunged their sap-covered sticks into the cavity.

This time, however, the parrots roosted in a tree that had a second hole, smaller and lower than the main entrance.

Azul pushed Aura into the opening, squawking for her to fly. Aura hesitated. There were three healthy eggs—a clutch almost ready to hatch—but nothing could be done.

"You go, I'll follow you," she promised.

Thinking maybe he should go first in case the man-flock waited beyond the opening, Azul squeezed through the crack in the bark and flew above the narrow canopy, waiting for his mate to join him. She never arrived.

When the male returned to the tree, he saw the man-flock carrying Aura off. He didn't know it, but his mate was destined for another city, another country, another continent. What Azul did realize was that his mate was gone. It was the fate of most of their flock. Those not taken by the man-flock often succumbed to hawks, snakes, cats, rats, mongoose, disease, and, on very rare occasions, old age. But today, Aura had fallen prey to the man-flock, and every time she was passed from one hand to another, money would follow—lots of it.

Azul returned to the roost. He wondered if any of the eggs remained. Carefully, he climbed into the hole. The parrot avoided the sap that the sticks left on the walls. One of those sticks, left behind, protruded from the roost. If Azul slipped and got stuck to the hefty wood, it could easily cost him his life. Weighed down, he'd be stuck in the roost, unable to fly, unable to feed. He climbed around the sticky branch, descending into the den. There were feathers, egg shells, and blood. He studied the scene. The pale-blue parrot tasted the blood. It wasn't from Aura. It was from the man-flock.

On a limb outside the roost, he looked out at the quiet creek that split the small rise of trees, wondering what he'd do without his mate. Most of the caraibas had been cleared to provide pasture for cattle and goats. Others were felled and burned. A few sparse stands of the trees, however, clung to the creek and its small floodplain, flowering and fruiting to the best of their ability. The caraibas not only fed the parrot, they also provided good cover. Azul was always on the lookout for hawks, which were always on the lookout for him. And now, without his mate's eyes also on the lookout, he nervously shuffled deeper into the foliage.

Even though it had been a season since she was taken, and as rare as his kind was, Azul still couldn't get used to being without Aura. Often, his heart felt so heavy the parrot couldn't lift himself to fly, yet he realized deep within that same heavy heart that giving up would be another form of extinction. Azul was accustomed to relative isolation. He didn't need many companions. He just needed Aura.

When the trees were with seed, Azul ate well, but when the season passed and creeks dried up, life would become more difficult. A breeze blew through the branches. Azul stepped closer to the trunk, where the limb was more secure, where the leaves provided better cover. He grasped the wood and watched the caraiba's yellow flowers bounce on the tips of the branches.

The parrot nibbled at seeds while the wind whipped over his plumage. If he angled himself a certain way, his feathers lifted gently and the air crept in across his skin. It made him think of afternoons preening Aura and the simple joy it brought them. This was his favorite time of year—plenty of food, plenty of cover, plenty of fresh, clean water. Azul let the image, the memory, carry him away. He could feel the tug of Aura's beak pealing back his plumage. It was vivid. He hoped it would never fade. A sudden pinch, however, snapped him from his daydream. Azul smiled warmly. Aura would sometimes pluck a single small feather just when he was at the height of relaxation. She'd nuzzle her mate and whisper, "Outside the roost, one should never be too relaxed. It can be dangerous."

Azul would reply, "It's not too dangerous as long as I have you sitting next to me, because you don't know how to relax."

"I am here," Aura would whisper, ignoring the parrot's petulant peck, and Azul would relax again, knowing that together, they'd handle whatever life threw at them.

Azul felt another pinch, but instead of hearing echoes of his mate, he heard a raspy, squeaky, "I'm sorry. This is new to me. I mean, I've seen you and the female do this many times . . . not that I'm watching you! It's just that . . ."

A small green maracana parrot was perched on the branch next to him. It had a fluffy blue feather dangling from the corner of its mouth. Apparently, while his mind wandered off to Aura, it was the green who preened him. Azul was *screech*less.

The green continued, ". . . you see, we kind of live in the same trees, so I see, I mean saw . . . sorry . . . a lot of you and your mate. I'm just so fascinated by sky parrots, I couldn't help but stare . . . but it was purely out of admiration . . . and then you seemed so lonely. Who wouldn't be?"

*Screech*less, Azul listened.

"I'm kinda lonely myself, so I know how that feels. Not as lonely as you, but . . . oh, sorry. . . I should probably make myself scarce . . . ah, gee, bad choice of words . . . but I don't know, I just thought you were missing your companion, and the next thing I knew, I was perched right next to you . . . sorry."

"Don't be," Azul said as he shuffled a little farther away from the contrite green.

"No, it was wrong for me to preen you. I don't even know you . . . We've never actually met. That was just too presumptuous of me . . . I'm sorry."

"Stop apologizing so much. It's OK."

The green paused, filtering out an apology for apologizing so much. Shuffling closer, she asked, "Would you like me to con—"

"No, no, it's not *that* OK. Let's just slow down." Azul shuffled some more to regain the space the green had reclaimed and said, "How about a name? Let's start there."

"Nipiklee."

"Nipiklee?"

The green nodded *yes* several times.

"OK Nipi, my na—"

The smaller parrot raised a wing, interrupting Azul. She stuck out her black beak and, speaking slowly, said, "Ni-pi-klee. It's Ni-pi-klee," as if trying to explain thermal loft to a hatchling.

"Yes, of course, Nipiklee," Azul agreed, giving proper emphasis to all three syllables.

Suddenly, Nipiklee said, "I'm thirsty. Would you spot for me while I whet my whistle?"

"Certainly." Azul popped up to the crown of the caraiba, where his light-blue plumage made him disappear to anyone looking up into the tree and took a moment to scan the sky. A hawk could hang in a cloud or a ray of sun miles away and spot a parrot at a puddle quite easily. Azul watched the sky, studied the trees, and examined the bush for any signs of danger. When he was sure it was clear, he turned to Nipiklee, who was gone. Then Azul spotted the smaller parrot in a basin hidden by a green overhang. The impatient maracana had rushed off before Azul had given the signal. This was not the behavior of sky parrots, but perhaps the little greens didn't need to be as careful as Azul. In truth, he and his kind often used the green parrots as an alarm system.

The sky parrots generally liked to travel as a family while they gathered food over a range as large as forty miles. They regularly visited clay exposures along the banks of streams, eating mud to neutralize toxins from seeds and fruit that might upset their stomachs. The clay licks also added sodium and calcium to the parrots' diets. But visiting a clay exposure can be risky, and when your numbers are as low as the sky parrots', a little extra caution makes sense.

Azul's flock would always wait before they dropped down to the lick. Invariably, the green parrots would be there first, impatient to feed on the mud which certainly wasn't about to disappear. So, the sky parrots waited, using the green flock as an early warning system. Azul felt a little guilty watching his new friend sipping—somewhat recklessly, he judged—from the puddle. Azul figured it paid to be a little smarter, yet somehow, *smarter* resulted in almost no sky parrots, and *reckless* resulted in an endless number of greens.

Nipiklee drank her fill and then flew off. The shadows were growing long. It was time to roost. Azul liked to wait until dark was well on its way before he returned to roost. It was a little more dangerous to do so, as many predators became active at dusk, but if he entered his nesting hole when the sun was still shining, there were others—equally dangerous—who might see where he slept and then come for him with their sticky branches.

Instinctively, Azul rose into the sky, heading mindlessly toward the roost he and Aura had made a home. Realizing his error, he turned abruptly and flew off in another direction, upstream along the ribbon of trees that clung to the banks of the creek, where he'd found a hole in a tall, lifeless carnauba. It wasn't his favorite tree, but this also might throw off those who were surely watching for him.

Azul paused before entering. He perched in a living buriti palm and ate nuts while he watched the entrance to the hole in the carnauba, hoping that he wasn't being *parronoid*. He watched for anything. Even something as small as bees swarming near the opening could prove fatal if he wasn't careful. Aggressive African bees, an invasive species not native to the Caatinga, would claim nesting holes. Azul had seen birds who underestimated them stung to death.

The crevice was fairly high in the tree, which meant that it would be difficult for the man-flock to climb without Azul knowing, but the parrot had other dangers to fear. Although wild cats wouldn't climb the palm, marmosets and even snakes might scale it.

While he waited, Azul gazed at the running water of the stream below. He found its presence deeply satisfying. There was something so enriching about water flowing through such an arid land. He loved the sound as well. Without even taking a drink, he felt healthy, strong, and, on some level, secure.

When his roost looked clear and safe, Azul flew to the trunk of the palm. He'd gathered several green maracana feathers and spread them at the base of the tree. If the man-flock noticed the nesting hole and became curious, the little feathers would indicate that only a green parrot lived there, so it wouldn't be worth the climb. Azul ascended the tree and settled into the vacant hole.

He awoke in the night to scratching on the bark. He could hear it clearly. Something climbed along the trunk. Azul flew. This time, there were no eggs to worry about. No mate either, so there was no hesitation. And if a web caught him, so be it, but he wasn't waiting for any man-flock to spread it. He launched himself into the opening. As he passed through the portal, he knocked the intruder from the tree. It was nearly upon him. He flapped powerfully, lifting himself toward the shining moon. Behind him, he heard a guttural groan, "Aghhh." Was it pain or perhaps disgust?

"You made me drop them."

Azul glanced back over his wing and saw a green parrot drifting toward the ground. Nipiklee landed softly, shook out her feathers, and began searching for something. The sky parrot perched on a limb and then flew back into his hole. A moment later, the sound of scratching returned, and Nipiklee climbed into the crevice. At first, Azul was going to scold the bird for invading his privacy, but after a quick thought, he decided he liked the idea of the green parrot entering and exiting his roost—more disinformation for any who might be watching.

"I brought some nuts," the green said proudly, depositing a clutch of them in front of Azul. "Buriti palm nuts. I can't get enough of them. Nothing better when you're roosting than a foot full of these beauties."

Agreeing, Azul reached out and grabbed one. Most animals could do nothing with the rocklike nuts, but for macaws and maracanas, it was easy. It was a refreshing workout for their beaks that relieved stress and strengthened facial muscles as well. Nipiklee also seized one, using a raised foot and her tongue to position it perfectly and began to peel. The green cut at the nut with her lower beak until the morsel split in two, revealing the softer inside. Nipiklee polished off the halves, grinned, and moaned, "Oh, my . . ." Then she looked at the blue and said two words: "Nut me." Azul rolled another Nipiklee's way.

Azul had to admit that as good as the palm nuts were, having some company was even better. The larger parrot scratched through a bit of debris on the floor of the roost and selected a thick twig. He shaved it down and slipped it into the top of his beak. Then he placed a nut into his mouth. The wood pressed the nut against his lower beak so that it couldn't slip out or slide awkwardly. And then Azul ate with a fraction of the effort Nipiklee had expended.

"Nice technique," the green said admiringly, stripping down a piece of wood just as the sky parrot had done.

"The next time you pop in on me—"

"Yeah," Nipiklee interrupted, nut debris cascading from the corners of her beak. "You're a little nervous, aren't you? I understand."

"The next time you pop in on me," Azul continued, "would you give me a little whistle? Just let me know it's you?"

"Sure," the green agreed. "I'll do that when I come back tomorrow."

When all the nuts were eaten, Nipiklee went out and got more. And when all those nuts were eaten, Azul said, "It's nice to have met you, Nipiklee. I guess I'll see you . . . tomorrow."

"Yup," the green responded. She slid her head under her wing and leaned against Azul.

"I'm probably going to sleep now. I don't want to keep you out too late," the blue hinted.

As Nipiklee's breathing got heavier, although not officially a snore, Azul added, since it seemed necessary, "I wouldn't want anyone to be worried about you . . ."

Nipiklee raised her wing slightly, peered out from under it, and said, "No one's worried."

"Oh, come on, what about your family, your friends, your flock? Don't want them to think a mongoose got you."

"They won't."

"Did you tell them you'd be here?"

"Nope."

"You might want to be a little more thoughtful about others' feelings. Trust me, they will worry. I wish I had someone to worry about me. If I did, I wouldn't pop out and leave them alone all night." Azul prayed the parrot was picking up on the hint.

"You have someone."

"I used to, but not anymore . . . Maybe someday."

"You have someone now. You have me." Nipiklee snuggled against Azul, and in no time at all, a faint snore echoed from the hole in the tall tree.

Azul awoke thirsty, suffering from a bad case of dry beak. Late-night palm nuts will do that to a parrot. He flew down to his favorite pool and drank the cool morning water before the sun had risen high enough to bake the rocks and warm the liquid. He thought about the maracana as he drank. She wasn't there when he awoke, and Azul wondered if she ever actually was. Had he imagined the visits, the visitor?

Now that Nipiklee was on his mind, Azul guessed that she was the same parrot he and Aura had noticed following them around. The green had already admitted that she watched the pair. It wasn't anything creepy. Other animals were often curious about rare breeds like sky parrots. But they'd noticed Nipiklee specifically. Azul recalled his mate commenting that the bird looked like she didn't have many friends. Neither of them discussed it further. Today, however, the thought stuck with Azul. Nipiklee probably didn't have friends. And as if the little green could read Azul's thoughts, she popped up on a rock not far from him . . . alone.

"Palm nuts do make you thirsty," the petite parrot declared.

Azul nodded and waved her over. He studied the green and wondered why she might not have friends. Being in Azul's situation, it was sometimes difficult to understand social nuances. He was never really part of a society. At their healthiest, his flock numbered a fraction of what most birds experienced. He realized that sometimes birds would avoid others who had unproductive habits, especially those who flew on a bad breeze. But that didn't seem to describe Nipiklee. Birds, however, might also practice a degree of guilt by association. A friend or relative might be unappealing, and therefore so were you. Perhaps that was Nipiklee's problem.

Azul chirped, "Did you return to your family last night?"

"No, not really."

"Didn't they miss you? Weren't they worried?"

"No, no one worries about me. I told you."

"Really?"

"It's OK. It's a good thing. If no one worries about me, then I don't have to worry about anyone else. It's very liberating." Nipiklee bent low into the shimmering pool and swallowed.

"Yes," Azul said with a nod. "I'm familiar with the scenario, although I'm not sure I'd describe it as *liberating*. How about friends? Who do you fly with?"

"Just you . . . I guess you don't see it. That's one of the reasons I like you so much. It just doesn't make any difference to you."

"See what?" Azul asked. He bent low and took a drink.

"You really don't see it, do you? I'm surprised. I mean it's so obvious. All the other greens notice immediately. I understand why they don't want to be around me."

"I can't. What's the issue?"

"Look at me closely. Forget the hawks and the other stuff, just for a moment. Look at me closely."

"OK . . . not seeing it."

". . . I'm ugly."

"What! You're a green maracana! You could never be ugly!"

"Well, you're a sky parrot. You see the world differently. But pretend you're a green for a moment. Then you'll see what I mean. I shouldn't even be telling you this. You're, like, my only friend, and now I'm gonna ruin it."

"I'm still not seeing it."

"Look just above my beak. Right between my eyes."

"OK."

"All the greens have a patch of bright red feathers there. It might be our most striking feature. Well, I don't have any red there, nothing, not even down."

"So?"

"It's disgusting. Hideous."

"That's why you have no friends?"

"It's a good reason. Why would anyone want to look at me? It's depressing." Nipiklee lowered her head to take another drink from the puddle and caught her own reflection on the surface. She popped her beak into the still water and shook violently, trying to erase her image.

"I'll tell you what's disgusting, the idea that the feathers make the bird. One has nothing to do with the other. If I could only be friends with one other green, I'd choose you every time."

"That's nice, but you're really only saying that because you like my *bird*sonality. It doesn't mean I'm not ugly."

"OK, first, don't tell me what I mean. I know what I mean. I meant what I said, not something else. Secondly, you're wrong. You can look any way you do. It's nothing compared to who you are. Imagine the most beautiful green parrot you've ever seen. Got one in mind?"

Nipiklee grinned and nodded slowly. "Rolina."

"She's beautiful?"

"Beyond beautiful . . . enchanting, exquisite."

"Got it, OK. So, now, picture Blowina—"

"It's Rolina."

"OK, Rolina. Picture her, red patch and all. Now picture another green exactly like her. The only difference—and I mean *only* difference—no red patch. And this ravishing Rolina won't associate with her because there are no red feathers on her face. You're gonna tell me that Rolina is beautiful? Really? If you ask me, she's kind of ugly."

Nipiklee opened her eyes. "I know what you're trying to do, but thanks. You know, when I perch with you, sometimes I kind of feel pretty."

"Oh, you mean *I'm* so ugly, anyone sitting next to me must look beautiful?" Azul teased. He snickered but stopped abruptly, asking, "Why am I the only one laughing?"

Now Nipiklee giggled. "No, I'm kidding. Of course, you're striking. You're blue! Look at you!"

Azul shook his head. "Ah, you still don't get it. It's not a blue thing or a red thing. It's swag."

Nipiklee looked puzzled.

"You should always feel attractive. Other birds can believe whatever stupidness they want to, but the only time it means anything is when *you* believe it. That, my friend, is swag. It's when you feel good about you regardless of what anyone else thinks. Forget about them not wanting to be with you. You're the one who should not want to be with them. Are those really the kind of birds you want to be accepted by? There's nothing wrong with you. In fact, it's quite the opposite. You're different. You're special."

"Yes, but see," Nipiklee countered, "that's just as bad. You're saying I'm special because I don't have red. In the end, my value is based on my missing feathers. It's no different from *devaluing* me for the same reason."

"No, it doesn't mean that at all. Are you here with me because I'm blue? Am I here with you because you're green? We're both here for a nest full of reasons that have nothing to do with any of that. Why would I, or you for that matter, want to fly with a bunch of feathers? I'm looking for more than that. And you're way more than that."

Nipiklee mumbled, "Well, tell that to my flock."

"First, I need to tell you."

The smaller parrot smiled and nodded. The conversation was over. Her expression told Azul that his words were just words, that they really didn't mean much to her, that they really didn't solve her problem. The green was, however, deeply touched that she finally had a friend who cared enough to try to make her feel better. It was nice.

Azul had been busy. Before he knew it, the day was coming to a close. He could not only see it in the lengthening shadows, but he could hear it as well. The chorus of dusk has a different timbre, different players than the chorus of day. One orchestra was becoming muted while another was just warming up. Azul ate one last cara-iba seed and returned to his roost. He hadn't seen Nipiklee since their early morning discussion and hoped that the green might make another palm nut delivery later in the evening.

As he'd done ever since Aura was taken, Azul landed on a long branch that overlooked the carnauba. He used the same branch every night because its vantage point was perfect. Azul settled on the wood, grasping it tightly, effortlessly, with his unique toes—two in front, two in back for added stability. But as soon as his feet touched the bark, he knew something was wrong ... very wrong.

While his roosting tree looked fine, something had been done to the branch he perched on. Azul couldn't move his feet. They were held tightly to the tree. Looking beneath him, he could see short, spiky stubs running up the trunk. They were not of the bush. They did not belong. The parrot flapped his wings and tugged with his legs. He threw his body from side to side but couldn't free himself from the branch. A sap-like substance confined him. It got on his wing, and he couldn't free the pinion from the branch. The parrot stopped struggling.

He saw him coming, one of the man-flock, teeth shining in the early night. Stepping on the spikes, he climbed the tree. Azul began to call. Hopelessly, he cried out for Aura, realized how desperate that was, and then he just cried. The parrot could smell the breath as the man-flock reached him. Azul could feel the heat coming off the intruder's body, so much bare flesh, dripping with fevered moisture. *No feathers at all*, the parrot thought. *As it should be—they are undeserving.*

Azul took one last look at the Caatinga, the ribbon of trees that guarded the stream, and then all was dark. The macaw felt a warm liquid wash over his feet and wings. It was pungent. It stung. A moment later, the sap let go, but the man-flock didn't. The parrot was wrapped in a binding darkness. There was nowhere to go. The man-flock carried him away.

What Azul didn't understand was that Pernambuco had been studying the bird's habits. When the parrot was away feeding, Pernambuco hammered nails into the lookout tree, climbed it, and covered the branch with lime glue used to trap wild birds. Once the adhesive captured the macaw, he slipped a burlap sack over Azul, exposed the feet and wing, poured a mixture of vegetable oil over the glue to dissolve it, and then pried the bird from the branch just as he was prying the parrot from the Caatinga.

Pernambuco placed Azul in a wire mesh cage, the same cage that had contained Aura and others. He tied it to the fender of his motorbike and began his migration toward a different stream, a green stream, a money stream. The parrot would feed his hungry family, provide schooling, fuel his motorbike, and satisfy many other needs. He didn't enjoy removing the bird, but it would solve so many of his problems. Pernambuco wasn't an evil man by nature, but there are times when even good men might do evil deeds. For some, good and evil might differ, defined by whether one lives in the trees or stands beneath them.

The trapper headed south. Normally, he'd take his birds to one of the wildlife markets in the city, but this bird was special. He was already spoken for. Pernambuco would take Azul directly to a dealer who would pay him $5,000 for the parrot. Perhaps he'd show him the parrot and then ask for $7,000. The ploy had worked before.

The trapper's main concern now was keeping the bird alive so he could collect the money. Too often, his catches would die before they could be sold. He was torn between getting his parrot to the dealer quickly and taking it slower so the bird wouldn't be tossed and bounced in the crude cage. The poacher knew his business, knew that up to 70 percent of trafficked birds die in transport from the wild. He also knew that no one pays for dead birds.

Once the dealer got his "blue" alive, he made a quick phone call. Papers had already been forged, and the flight was ready to leave. Carefully drugged and strapped into the hollow of a spare truck tire, Azul was smuggled into Paraguay. There, a "mule" carried papers documenting Azul as a more common, captive-bred hyacinth macaw. Most customs agents would likely neither know nor care. If, for some reason, the South American agent raised concern, a modest payment would usually move things along. From Paraguay, the bird was flown to Newark Airport in New Jersey, hidden in a shipment of green Quaker parrots routinely imported for the pet trade.

Once in the United States, new papers were substituted that claimed the bird was captive bred in Paraguay for a zoo in Switzerland. It all looked very official. A customs agent would never connect a Spix's macaw to what the shipping information reported, if he checked at all. In the end, if Azul survived, the Brazilian dealer would be paid $150,000 from his Swiss client for the parrot. After all his expenses were covered, he'd pocket over $125,000 for what was likely the last wild Spix's macaw on the planet.

But things don't always go the way they're planned.

When it came time to examine the shipment destined for Switzerland via Newark, the customs agent on duty, Evelyn Florez, scanned the paperwork. Seeing that it was a shipment of parrots, she thought she'd take a look. Her daughter, Maria, had just spent every evening of the previous week sketching and profiling a variety of parrots for her term paper in biology. Evelyn helped print the captions for Maria.

As the customs agent looked the birds over—some breathing a bit too softly, others panting pathetically—she thought that the parrots in her daughter's illustrations seemed more alive, more vibrant than the ones in front of her, packed for shipping. Evelyn was disappointed. She had intended to take a photo of the parrots and show it to her daughter when she got home, but these poor birds weren't worth recording. The customs agent remembered reading that one-third of all wild parrots were endangered.

"Evelyn, break time in ten minutes!" her supervisor called.

Startled, Evelyn dropped her pen into the shipping crate. She reached in and worked her hand between the individual canisters until she felt the plastic pen. With two fingers, she grasped it and lifted it from the box. As Evelyn stuffed the pen into her pocket, thinking of what she'd eat on break, a sticky blue feather clung to her finger. The customs agent looked at the feather. The gooey glue was on her pen as well. Evelyn became curious. This was a shipment of green Quaker parrots. Green. Where did this feather come from?

Evelyn searched the shipment, finding the lone pale-blue macaw. The bird was barely alive, possibly drugged, and clearly distressed. Remnants of sticky goo cleaved to its feet, wings, and belly feathers. Evelyn looked at the shipping papers. It was listed as a hyacinth macaw, the only one in the shipment. The customs agent thought back to the labels she wrote for her daughter's biology project. It didn't look like any of those parrots.

She remembered the two blue parrot labels she'd printed. This one was smaller and the wrong color blue. Evelyn wondered if it was, perhaps, an immature bird and would grow into the image of the ones in Maria's report. But something didn't feel right. The customs agent seized the shipment. Calls were made. Evelyn would have a good story to tell her daughter over dinner that night.

When you're hungry, there's nothing like a big, dead cypress tree. Gonzo grasped the bark easily. His long toes tipped with curved claws had evolved for just such a purpose, designed to spread and hold. His elongated tail feathers not only balanced him in flight, but did the same when he held on to a tree, like a built-in tripod. But that was only the tip of the talon. Gonzo could actually hear the meal within the tree.

Of the three hundred thousand species of insects on the planet, Gonzo preferred three, and he could hear two of them inside this dead cypress. Those who have a taste for grubs and larvae generally need to be more patient to get to the insects. Even those special few who are capable of drilling into bark wouldn't be able to reach this meal. When a tree is freshly deceased and the bark still clings tightly to the trunk, others might need to wait. Gonzo, how-ever, eats.

Convinced that fine fare lurked within, Gonzo went to work. His most conspicuous attribute, his ivory bill, singular among all the Creator's creations, glistened in the sun. Gonzo's flock, the ivory-billed woodpecker, is named for it, and with good reason.

Gonzo gripped the bark firmly. He angled his head, focusing his striking yellow eyes on the target. And *strike* was exactly what he had in mind. The woodpecker aimed the chisel attached to his face and began his onslaught on the tree. *Ke-bam! Ke-bam! Ke-bam!* The ivory-bill's unique double-rap drumming echoed through the swamp. His long, curved, crimson crest shimmered with each blow. Instantly, the bark began to split and peel. Gonzo then used his beak like a crowbar to pry long sheets of bark from the cypress.

He snapped up the white, flat-headed grubs that wiggled against the exposed wood. They would've molted into pupae in a few weeks, but the woodpecker needed to eat today. And if too many of the larvae made it to the next stage, they could wreak havoc on the balance of the ecosystem. Gonzo was doing more than just feeding. He was playing a vital role in the delicate web of life that kept the swamps healthy, so that they could keep all that depended on them healthy, and so on.

The woodpecker possessed another weapon that helped him feed. His tongue had a hard tip lined with needle-like barbs. Gonzo would thrust the long muscle into holes and cracks, and when he retracted it, it would return with larvae ready to be swallowed.

After the tree was peeled and the meal was eaten, if he was still hungry, Gonzo would descend to the base and poke through the bark at the foot of the tree. This, however, could be a danger-ous activity. Other animals were attracted to the woodpecker's debris. They, too, were looking for a meal of grubs or other dis-lodged insects. Often, there were plenty of morsels within the pile of stripped bark. Gonzo wasn't nearly as cautious as one would ex-pect a member of a flock on the verge of extinction to be, especially when feeding. He wasn't exactly reckless. He tried to be responsible without being obsessed. He had faith.

There was something else about Gonzo—he was a bit of a phantom. Other birds usually only heard him or perhaps were lucky enough to catch a fleeting look, but rarely for very long. The man-flock almost never even caught a glimpse of him. One reason was that whatever Gonzo did, he did it quickly, never dawdling. He was a master at keeping the trunk of a tree between him and whatever looked at him, rarely allowing anything to get too close. It was his way.

Those of the swamp accepted that the Creator watched this species with interest, feeling a connection to the birds, intrigued by their nickname, "Lord God Bird," granted because when they were spotted, either by man-flock or forest dweller, the witness often proclaimed, "Lord God, what a bird!" If this bird, hovering near extinction, evoked the image of the Creator's best work, it would truly be a sin, a most heinous transgression, to allow the ivory-bill to disappear. But that, in a manner of speaking, is exactly what the Creator did. It allowed the bird to disappear.

The lore proclaimed that for those who might do it harm—predators and the man-flock—the bird would be virtually invisible. At best, one might be able to glimpse it, unless, of course, the ivory-bill was careless. The Creator watched with satisfaction as the bird evolved to be careful, stealthy, flighty—attributes that made it difficult for others to observe, study, or prey upon the woodpecker. It was being tested. If the ivory-bill really was worthy of its moniker, it would survive this challenge. It would defeat extinction and rightfully be called, Lord God Bird.

So, the large woodpecker with the massive ivory beak, the bright red crest topping the males, and the iridescent black crown adorning the females, had become an apparition, a quality that didn't guarantee the flock's survival, but certainly helped. And for the Creator, it made life in the swamp that much more interesting to behold.

Those who were pure, who admired or appreciated the bird, those who genuinely wished it no harm—man-flock included—

might be allowed to revel in the glory of the impressive fowl. But for most, the ivory-billed woodpecker would be a shadow in the flooded forest for as long as it could survive, according to the scripture of the swamp.

As he pecked up the last few grubs in the pile of bark, Gonzo heard the impatient call, the nasally *kint* that beckoned. It's easy to get distracted dining in the swamp, and no self-respecting woodpecker would ever turn his beak from fresh grubs, but there was no denying it. Gonzo was late. He took to the wing and hoped she would understand.

Near the top of a large dead cypress, a dark, rectangular hole waited. Gonzo landed on the bark outside the roost and rapped the wood. *Ke . . .*

Before he could tap the second strike, his mate appeared in the hole. She stared at him without saying a word. She didn't need to. This was a universal look that not only spanned gender and generations, it spanned species. Any creature—insect, fish, human, bird—who sees this look in their mate's eyes knows exactly what it means . . . and it's not good.

"Gonzo, darling, is that you out there? Or is it a hawk who has come to kill us all while you flap around the swamp? Is it you?"

"Very funny, Kwim. I wasn't gone *that* long."

"Wait. I hear a familiar voice, but I can't see you. Where are you, Gonzo?"

"Oh, how witty. Yes, I get it. You can't see me because I'm an ivory-bill and you wish to do me harm, so I'm invisible. Ha! You're actually a much better mockingbird than a woodpecker."

The female looked him dead in the eyes, pulled back her head, and said, "Harm? Do you harm? That's an understatement." Then she flew off.

A beak full of larvae fell from his mouth into the roost as Gonzo called, "But I brought grubs. I thought we'd preen . . ."

"Think again," he heard from the sky above.

Gonzo crawled into the crevice. It was his turn to sit on the eggs.

By morning, Kwim hadn't returned. Gonzo was nervous. He had a bad feeling. The woodpecker was in a tough spot. On the one wing, he wanted to look for his mate, felt he needed to. Had something happened to her? Was she in trouble? Or was she merely punishing him, trying to make a point, since he was habitually late from his foraging time? On the other wing, however, Gonzo couldn't leave the nest. To abandon the eggs, such important eggs, was unthinkable.

Gonzo was stuck. For the most part a loner, there was really no one in the swamp he could turn to. Occasionally, he'd chat with a squirrel, sometimes one of the pileated woodpeckers, but really, beyond Kwim, Gonzo was generally solitary. He liked it that way, but now, when he needed help, that isolation made things more difficult. The ivory-bill stared down at the three shiny, white eggs beneath him. His rump was itching from sitting on them for so long, but that was the least of his problems.

The woodpecker came to a disturbing realization. He didn't hear it, the double rapping, the *ke-bam* that should've echoed through the woods. He didn't hear Kwim feeding. He didn't hear her calling. Gonzo tried to work it all out in his mind. If he lost Kwim and still protected the eggs, what would it all matter? He could never raise them alone. He'd have to leave them to feed and get food for the chicks, if they even hatched. And without Kwim, he couldn't produce more eggs. Without his mate, the present *and* the future would be barren. The sad truth was, in order to protect the eggs, he had to leave them.

Gonzo took a long look at the unhatched. He climbed up onto the rim of the nesting hole, stretched his lengthy wings, and rubbed his rump against the bark to soothe the itch beneath his tail feathers. Gonzo was stalling, procrastinating. He knew what he had to do. *There's a thing needs doin',* he thought to himself. The woodpecker burst into the air. He made two bold flaps and suddenly veered back to the base of the dead cypress. He spotted Cooter, his one squirrel friend who lived three trees over.

The ivory-bill latched on to the trunk, calling out, "Cooter! I have to search for Kwim. She's missing. Keep an eye on our eggs. Call if you need me." He popped back into flight, a flurry of black-and-white feathers. "I'll be back."

"Wait!" Cooter called, "I'm not sure—"

"Whatever you want—nuts, grubs, anything—it's yours," Gonzo promised as he soared into the swamp.

He searched all day with no sign of Kwim. No new trees had been fed upon. None of the older ones had any more bark chiseled off. No feathers in the spill piles. No sign of being taken by a predator. And no sign of the man-flock, which was one of the reasons Gonzo loved the swamp. All the water, the poison ivy, the bugs, the briars, the gators, the snakes, the bears—all these things kept the man-flock and other problems away. For a woodpecker, the swamp is ideal. But why couldn't Gonzo find Kwim? He ate quickly and then returned to the roost. What had happened? What would happen?

The ivory-bill landed on the hole and stepped inside. "Kwim?" he called into the nest. All he saw was Cooter stepping around the eggs.

"No Kwim?" Cooter asked, knowing the answer.

"No, nothing," Gonzo mumbled. "Thanks, Coot."

"I need to tell you something," Cooter said solemnly.

The woodpecker raised his red crest.

"I saw Kwim earlier. I tried to tell you when you flew off."

"What'd you see?"

"Nothing bad, it's just that I saw her."

"Where? What was she doing?"

"That's the thing. I mean, she's going out to feed after sitting on the eggs, right? There's this huge sweet gum. It's dead, and it's laced with crawlers. I even called to her, but she flew right past it. Maybe it's not her favorite tree."

"Yeah, but she eats the grubs, not the tree," Gonzo said. "Where was she flying?"

Cooter shuffled. He bounced his back foot and twitched his tail. "That's the other thing. She was up above the canopy, heading south. Seemed strange, not like she was feeding but like she was going somewhere."

Gonzo felt sick to his stomach. It was something he felt might happen to him one day. Not that it would, just that perhaps it could. One of those funny feelings you get sometimes, the kind you try to push away and ignore. But it never completely disappears, like that one cricket singing a little off key that somehow manages to be heard above the cacophony of the nighttime swamp, one out-of-tune idea that won't completely disappear no matter how much else is in tune. Kwim had left him.

The squirrel scratched behind his ear, shook his head slowly, and said softly, "There's more."

Defenseless and crushed, Gonzo replied, "I know."

"You know? Then why'd you ask me to—"

"Just because you know something doesn't mean you have to admit it to yourself. I guess I'm real good at that."

"Kwim must've known too," the squirrel surmised.

"I'm sure she did."

Cooter rubbed his tail against the bark and climbed silently out of the hole.

The roost was infected with mites. The thin bed of frasse that lined the crevice, the constant itch, and the minute crack in one of the eggs all led to the inescapable fact. While the adults could flee the nest, bathe, or eat, the eggs couldn't be moved. It would be easier for Gonzo and Kwim to defend the nest against a raccoon, an owl, a hawk, or a snake than it would be to defend their home against the infestation of something so small. The mites had taken the eggs and driven off Kwim.

Gonzo perched on a branch. He decided that he, too, would go. He'd met his mate when he traveled south one winter to the lowest woods of the continent he called home. Nomadic and restless, Kwim had flown north from her home, a mountain forest on the southeastern slopes of the first large island below the massive continent. When they met, they were overjoyed. Gonzo thought he'd see gators fly before he'd see another ivory-bill, let alone one that was suitable for mating.

They'd both believed it was meant to be. But that, Gonzo had to admit, was likely the problem. Their union was decided by their circumstances, their needs, not by their feelings, their love. And even though Gonzo loved Kwim deeply, he could tell she didn't love him. Ivory-bills mate for life, but in the end, it seemed they'd chosen the wrong life. They mated for the life of their flock, not for *their* lives. The woodpecker wondered if maybe it wasn't "meant to be," if maybe the ivory-bills weren't "meant to be."

He decided to leave the swamp. He wouldn't search for Kwim. He wouldn't head south. Gonzo decided to fly north. Normally, he'd never consider leaving the hot South, but even a mole could see that the planet was warming. Why not widen his horizons? It was time to go in a direction he'd never gone before. The chance of meeting other ivory-bills was remote, but that would be the case no matter where he flew. Besides, he'd been told by a passing swift that there was a tract of woods to the northeast dominated by pines, fringed with oaks, some spots even a little swampy, that had just been hit by a hurricane. That meant wind and lightning strikes. There would be plenty of larvae-riddled deadwood. And even though pines tended to sap up his bill, Gonzo kind of liked the flavor.

However, one problem that tugged at his feathers was the fact that this barren forest of pines was surrounded by one of the thickest infestations of the man-flock on the coast. But Gonzo was feeling just a bit reckless right now and decided that it might be interesting to try hiding in plain sight. He gathered some nuts, left them for Cooter, and then set off on a much-needed adventure where he hoped there'd be plenty of easy peckings.

When he had heard that I-BIRD, the International Bird Intervention and Reintroduction Directive, was holding its annual conference at Monmouth University in New Jersey, where he was the senior faculty member in the biology department, he knew he had to attend, especially when he saw that the keynote speaker would be the world-renowned Vicente El Real, arguably the world's leading figure in the fight to protect endangered avian species. And really, the sole reason one might say *arguably* is because El Real was so young. Not yet forty, he'd risen to the apex of his field and showed no signs that his ascent wouldn't continue.

So, when Tony MacDonald, Director of Monmouth's Urban Coast Institute, invited the youthful savior to approach the stage of Pollak Auditorium, the standing-room-only crowd of birding's international luminaries included not only Professor Donald Dorfman, but Dr. Helen Campbell from Queensland, Australia and, of course, the young Kemar. While the three friends were all really "fish people," they held a deep respect for the efforts of I-BIRD, which was involved in preserving countless species of marine avians, and they hoped one day soon to form a sister organization for the ichthyology community—I-FISH perhaps. Kemar had read about El Real and marveled at his accomplishments. Secretly, the teenager hoped that one day he might play a similar role in the preservation of marine life.

Prior to the keynote address, there were seminars, presentations, workshops, and poster sessions discussing I-BIRD's fieldwork and findings. Kemar's seventeen-year-old brain was spinning with all the information. To sit in a room with so many professors and international figures was, at first, quite intimidating for the teenager. But when one survives the Khmer Rouge in Cambodia, a refugee trawler, and being abandoned at sea—all before the age of fifteen—a hall full of professors isn't quite so daunting after all. Besides, the boy had Dr. Campbell with him. He was in good hands.

Moments before the evening began, four people slipped into the seats on Kemar's right side. Dave Lackland of SeaTopia, a friend of Dorfman's, had brought three colleagues with him from the Marine Science Center on Florida's east coast: Rachelle LeBlanc, Rich Coles—both avian rehabilitators—and the only other teenager in the auditorium, a girl almost Kemar's own age, Samantha, who just happened to sit right next to him. The two teens hung on every word as Vicente El Real was introduced and stepped to the podium.

Applause filled the huge room. There was whistling and even the occasional bird call. The speaker smiled brightly and gestured for everyone, his peeps, to be seated. "Thank you, my friends, thank you. This has been a great migration for many of us. We have spent the last two days taking satisfaction, as we should, in our successes. And they are many. We have also taken grim inventory of the many challenges we still face, looking solemnly to issues we have yet to fully understand.

"Allow me to tell you a brief story. I was talking to my friend, a priest, just the other day. And to tell you the truth, I must admit, I was silently hoping for his approval, his affirmation for all that I-BIRD has accomplished. After all, are we not stewards of Creation? So, I was somewhat stunned when he turned to me and asked, 'Vicente, my son, why do you use the gifts that God has given you to save birds when so many of your brothers and sisters are in need? Shouldn't you care for *your* family, the family of man, first?'

"Rather than the approval I sought, there was contempt faintly clouded behind the question. Again, I was so stunned, I couldn't comfortably reply. I said, 'Father, I save the birds because I believe it is my calling.' I could see my friend did not understand that that could be one's calling.

"When I got to my car, I sat down without putting the key into the ignition. There was too much on my mind, too much I wanted to say to my friend. I believe this is what I, a scientist, a man of faith—and yes, you can be both—should have told him, the priest. 'I save the birds for several reasons. I save the birds because God saved the birds. Not only are they his creation just as we are, he chose to invite them onto the ark. He chose to save them. And we should not forget, it was, in fact, a bird that showed Noah the flood was over, that there was hope. If birds are this important to God, why shouldn't they be as important to man? Have you not heard of your own St. Francis? God apparently has decided that birds should inhabit the planet. *He* has woven them into the fabric of life. *We* have removed them. It's difficult to imagine a greater arrogance. If you worship the Creator, how can you not worship the Creation?'

"And now I preach to you, the choir, if you will. An extinction that occurs from a massive meteor strike is one thing, but extinctions that occur from reckless deforestation, habitat depletion, an unnatural rise in CO_2 levels, pesticides run amok, oil spills—all happening at the pace of man and not the pace of the planet—do not allow for adaptation, evolution, or anything remotely akin to *natural* selection. In fact, it's quite unnatural.

"Change that outpaces adaptation equals death. Roads that prevent migration create virtual islands on land and lead to death. Chemicals that prevent reproduction and cause disease and mutation lead to death. And death upon death upon death upon death leads to extinction. Any time a species disappears, we are one step closer to being alone. Eventually, it will be *our* turn, and likely not our choice. Would a world without birds be a better place? And wouldn't a world without birds also mean a world without count-less other creatures, perhaps even us? It is a web. We are connect-ed.

"On another visit, that same friend told me that he was at a regional church conference and came away quite frustrated be-cause they spent so much time discussing the fate of the spot-ted owl. He wondered why one species of owl would be important enough to spend so much conference time on when God's chil-dren had so many needs. 'Surely,' he said, 'if that one species dis-appeared, would we really know the difference? Most of the peo-ple in the room wouldn't know a spotted owl if one landed on them.'

"This time, I answered him. I said, 'It's not always so simple, so direct. Often, it's that the owl eats a nut that it distributes after digestion that germinates and becomes a tree where a moth's grub develops in the bark that eventually a spider eats, whose eggs might contain a chemical that is vital to Alzheimer's patients. And so, by saving the owl that begat the tree that begat the moth that begat the spider that created the eggs, you saved the person suffering from Alzheimer's. It's all Creation. It's all connected. And this is just the selfish view. It's corrupt because it's all about what nature can do for us—otherwise, nature's not worth paying attention to. Ah, but what people who think like that often overlook is that what doesn't seem connected to us today might actually be the thing that saves us tomorrow . . . Unless, of course, it's no longer here.

"If you want to look at the world and ask, 'What would the planet be without that owl? Who'd really miss it?' Why not take it a step further and ask, 'What would this world be without peo-ple? Who'd miss us?' What strand of the web do we provide? What wouldn't be here if we weren't here? And really, sadly, the answer seems to be, at this point in time, everything else would likely do just fine. It all works pretty well without us and did for eons.

"Our great environmental successes often seem to be built upon the 'catch-and-release' principle. Cause the problem, do something about it, and it's all OK. We emphasize the *release* and ignore the *catch*. Just because you put that fish back in the lake or the sea and it looks like the problem is solved, is it really? Was that creature injured? Will the injury cause its demise later in the day? Tomorrow? Is the animal so exhausted after it fought for its life on your line that it can't defend itself or flee from the predator it was hiding from before your bait lured it from safety? But you released it. Problem solved. Check, please.

"Was that habitat impacted? What garbage was left behind? Will that discarded fishing line continue to injure or kill after it is removed from the pole? Will it tangle, will it strangle, will it cut? Will it eventually decompose into plastic dust that our children's children will breathe? There are a thousand ways I might be hurting this creature—this environment—but as long as I let it go, as long as I didn't *actually* kill it, it's all fine. And so, by extension, as long as I reintroduce that condor, that kestrel, that salmon, that wolf, I'm off the hook—when, in fact, we are the hook.

"But what of all those endangered species that fall over the edge? The ones we fail to save. Look at the world—its life—as a symphony, each species a note. When one disappears, the symphony loses a note—a sharp, a flat, and sometimes an instrument. What would become of Mozart, Bach, if every fourth or fifth note disappeared? What would that symphony sound like? What if a note—indeed, several of them—were no longer available to the listener or the composer? What if woodwinds were no longer part of the orchestra? What would that do to music? What if a string was removed from a guitar? What if an artist lost a color every time a species disappeared?

"No more blue. No more green. What would we be left with? That's what's happening now. The greatest symphony imaginable is losing its notes. The greatest painting in Creation is having its colors washed away. This is what we're leaving our children. We're leaving them less, not more. And we're doing it because too many of us just don't care, because it's inconvenient to care.

"Like you, I have heard many sublime quartets. You can form them quite easily from an orchestra. But you cannot create an orchestra from a quartet. And that's where we're heading, reducing the orchestra into a quartet, reducing the grand painting—the landscape—into a silhouette.

"When I'm eighty and my granddaughter asks me, 'What did you do with your life, Grandpa?' how will I answer her? Will I tell her that I had a nice time filling the ocean with plastic, that I lived my good life destroying beauty that she and her children, my great grandchildren, will never know? She will never hear that owl hoot in the night. She will never see it chased by crows at dusk . . . because I didn't care. It didn't matter to me. Will I tell her that? Is that to be her inheritance?

"The day of reckoning comes when you have to answer your grandchild's questions. And, I'm told by those who have already faced their grandchildren's questions, the day comes faster than any of us could imagine. On that day, at that moment, I hope to tell that beautiful little child that her grandfather spent his life trying to protect and preserve Creation, that I tried to use all the abilities I was blessed with to be a steward—a good shepherd— to those creatures, great and small, who, although they almost certainly had the desire, they did not have the ability to protect themselves.

"When you devote yourself to an ideal, your reason for existence grows. You become more. Now I'm playing a role in something so much larger than me. All of us at I-BIRD are, and so we actually become part of that great thing ourselves.

"In closing, let me say, I received a note from my friend the priest about a month ago. I had sent him a draft of this speech with my comments about my reply to him. In his note, my friend said that he had given our exchange a lot of thought. He had prayed about it. He has since joined not only I-BIRD but Oceana, World Wildlife Fund, Nature Conservancy, Ocean Conservancy, NRDC, and other important environmental groups.

"Now I'm pleased to say there's no better environmentalist than a convert. And to borrow a phrase from my friend's faith, 'Go, and sin no more.' Let's save the planet one bird, one nest, one egg, one tree at a time. Thank you for your good work—your *great* work—for attending this conference, and for listening to my thoughts."

MacDonald returned to the stage with his student assistant, Layla. They shook hands with El Real, and escorted the keynote speaker to Wilson Hall for a reception in his honor.

The pigeon and the robin knew every feeder in the area, and there were many. That was particularly important to the pigeon who would peck some 160,000 times a day. The two birds were inseparable. In fact, the pigeon had hatched the robin and raised her. And while the robin preferred worms and insects to seeds, she'd learned early on from her pigeon parent to be an opportunistic feeder. The robin learned other useful things from the pigeon as well. She'd become an outstanding flier, developing chest and back muscles more in keeping with a pigeon than a thrush, which is essentially what a robin is.

She also learned to use an ability that all pigeons possess but relatively few other birds perfect. Squab had been taught to use the GPS system pulsing inside her beak, a trait that, when understood, allowed her to fly anywhere on Earth and know exactly where she was. Receptors in her beak pick up on the magnetic signature of her location.

Pigeons also know how to use the sun as a point of reference, innately sensing where the orb should be at any time of day. At night, they read the stars. The pigeon's brain, roughly the size of the tip of a human thumb, is packed with unique abilities and talents enabling the birds to cross-reference all this information. Zomis, the proud pigeon parent, had seen to it that all these gifts were developed in the orphaned egg that hatched into Squab.

Squab had also given a lot to Zomis. At the time Zomis gathered the lone egg and decided to raise it, the bird was confused. It was unsure whether it was rodent or bird, male or female, or maybe something in between, but sure in its mind that neither question mattered all that much anyway. Zomis had ultimately decided it would live life as a rat rather than a pigeon. It ate like a rat, spoke like a rat, shuffled like rat. It never flew, pecked, or remotely considered any of the blessings it was bequeathed as a pigeon. But somehow, the little blue egg—and, to be fair, a petrel named Lupé—had caused the pigeon to embrace who it really was, the last living passenger pigeon. In teaching Squab, Zomis retaught itself, regaining all that made it a bird, a pigeon. The robin and the pigeon had saved each other, which is often the case among children and their parents.

At the moment, the two were faced with a problem. The best feeder in the area belonged to a nice man-flock family whose young offspring filled it diligently. It had just been topped off with a delicious mix of seeds and soft, puffy cubes that were quite tasty. The youngsters were small, two-thirds the size of the adults, so the parents had hung the feeders at a level that the little ones could master. While this worked well for the children, it didn't serve some of the birds, who, truth be told, liked to feed a bit higher off the ground, and still others who often preferred to feed on the ground. The latter, however, was out of the question, even though the little ones always managed to spill a tempting portion of seed under the feeder.

The real problem had four paws, claws, teeth, and plenty of *cat*titude. Domino, the family cat, was well fed. In fact, he was huge. The feline had long, grey hair, a white patch that ran from his nose up between his eyes, massive paws, a mean streak, and was as silent as a shadow. Recently, however, a blue jay named Kip had found a round, shiny object. It made a high-pitched jingle when it moved. That clever bird took the object and dropped it in a sand pile where the young ones often played. And as soon as they spotted it, the little ones listened to it, bounced it, rolled it, and before you could say *nuthatch*, that round noisemaker was hanging from the cat's neck. It was the smartest thing that Kip ever did.

And while that jingle slowed Domino's roll, it didn't stop him. Clearly not the sharpest claw on the paw, the cat had an annoying habit. He would park himself directly under the feeder and wait for birds to fly in to eat. Once they landed on the feeder, Domino would hold his chin down over the jingle and launch himself so that he was face-to-face with the feeding birds. Then he'd swipe at them, trying to knock one to the ground. If he succeeded, the bird was done for.

Zomis and Squab waited with several other birds on branches beyond the cat's view. Zomis was especially frustrated. Even though the bird had returned to its pigeon heritage, one rodent quality that Zomis couldn't quite shake was his impatience when he was hungry. Zomis wanted to eat, and he wanted to eat now. The longer that lazy, well-fed feline made the bird wait, the more infuriated the pigeon became. Just a hop from full-blown seed rage, Zomis glared at Squab.

"What?" the robin inquired.

Zomis smiled.

"What?" Squab repeated.

The pigeon cocked its head to one side. "I'm hatching a plan. Let me fill you in. Remember that bell? Well, I have an idea."

By the time Zomis was done whispering to Squab, several other birds had shuffled in to listen. They had a plan—well, sort of. A plan that bet on brains over brawn. The birds had the brains—all of them—and Domino had the brawn. It would be an interesting wager.

Usually, the birds would wait until the cat tired or something else, a butterfly perhaps, caught his interest. Then he'd amble off, allowing the bird feeder to fulfill its function, offering seeds to birds rather than birds to cats. Today, however, Domino was in full pain-in-the-tail-feathers mode. As fate would fly, he'd fallen asleep under the feeder.

Zomis couldn't take it anymore. On cue, the pigeon spotted another visitor to the yard, whom the birds were betting the dozing Domino was oblivious to. It was time to act.

"Wait here," Zomis told Squab. "Whatever happens, stay here."

The pigeon launched itself onto the feeder and chowed like a champ, debris raining down upon the beast below. The comatose cat, decorated with an assortment of seeds, purred on. *How can he sleep through that?* the pigeon wondered. The one time the bird wanted to be noticed by the cat, *Dumbino*—as many of the local birds called him—slept on. Zomis felt a sharp stab in the belly as pigeons sometimes do, especially when some seeds are less fresh than others. Instantly, Zomis answered nature's call. And, as fate would dictate, that answer landed right on the white patch between Domino's eyes.

The warm splat woke the cat, startling him, and he immediately flung himself, jingling skyward, right at the offending pigeon. The large cat's quick move from deep sleep to flat out attack caught Zomis and his cramping stomach by surprise, causing yet another boisterous reply to nature's call. This time, the stimulus was horrified panic rather than rancid seeds, yet the result was the same.

Domino flashed a sinister smirk, pigeon poop plastered to his brow. Undeterred by the facial feces, claws extended from his broad paws, the cat swept the slicers across Zomis's side, knocking the wind from the pigeon's lungs. Zomis had never been so close to a feline before. The bird felt itself plummet to the ground, a shower of seeds escorting it down.

While Domino had certainly terrified the pigeon, his swat had drawn a pawful of feathers and little more. A faint drop or two of blood added just the right touch, leading the cat to deduce that he'd done more damage than he actually had.

The moment Zomis hit the ground, the pigeon began jumping, running, and flapping in a frenzy of fear. There was, however, method to its madness. Zomis zigzagged along the soil, feathers, dust, leaves, grass, and seeds whirling everywhere. Domino pounced and pounced and pounced but always seemed to be just a flap behind the bird, which further enraged the furious feline. The little jingle on his neck chimed along in tribute to his ineptitude. Adding insult to injury, crows, jays, sparrows, cardinals, doves, and other birds—not to mention squirrels, several chipmunks, and mice—all took deep delight in *Dumbino*'s frustration, rooting for his demise.

Domino, however, clung to one fact the others seemed to lose sight of. One slip, one mistake from the pigeon, one well-placed swat from the feline, and it would be over for the bird. The cat didn't have nearly as much on the line as the pigeon. If he could just slip a little nip on a wing tip, deadly bacteria could work its way into the victim's bloodstream. That's all it would take. Who'd be laughing then? That's when they'd see for whom the little bell tolls, the cat mused. Domino was determined.

So was Zomis, even though it didn't look like it.

The crows—smart birds—noticed first. "Hedges!" they screamed. "Hedges! Look out!"

The cat was herding Zomis, working the pigeon into a thick line of shrubbery where the yard ended. As long as Zomis couldn't fly, the cat would drive his prey into the thicket and pin the bird against the brush. After every pigeonless pounce, Zomis was forced to retreat closer to the bushes. Soon, the pigeon disappeared into the tangle of branches. There was no way it could fly, no way it could duck and run. The cat had his bird. Domino knew it. All those watching, cheering, grew as silent as if a hawk had entered the yard.

In a display of bravado meant for all the chirping, cackling onlookers, the cat stood tall, flexed his heavy muscles, and licked his front paws, confident that the doomed bird would be waiting, trembling. It was a moment to be savored. The inevitable was imminent. The cat lowered himself, paying tribute to his distant leopard lineage, took two quick steps, and launched himself into the bramble. A collective gasp filled the yard. To the onlookers, it was all their worst fears realized.

The branches were still . . . then they stirred . . . then still again.

Zomis popped out from under the bushes. Breathless, the pigeon looked quickly at all the slack-beaked witnesses and flew up to Squab. The robin was about to speak when Zomis raised one wing to silence the youngster, saying, "Wait for it . . ."

All anyone heard was a calm, clear *ffussszztt.*

"Rrrrreeewwwwww! Rrrrreeewwwwww!" The cat screeched at the top of its lungs. Branches bustled, leaves stirred, and out ran Domino. He bolted through the yard, jingling, until he threw himself into the strange den that the man-flock provided as his home. Deep inside, you could see his yellow eyes peering out in horror.

When the smell wafted up to the trees, everyone understood. And as the little skunk emerged from the thicket, there were no doubts. Zomis, it seemed, had actually been the one maneuvering Domino.

Squab looked admiringly at her parent and remarked, "Who said you can't herd cats?"

Later in the day, after Zomis and Squab had eaten their fill from beneath the feeder, the two perched on a choice bough. The appendage grew from the very tree that had brought the two birds together, a huge, mature oak located a flap from another sprawling man-flock nest. When Squab was just an egg in her own nest, a vicious wind blew a branch from that tree through a window in the adjacent structure, depositing the nest inside.

At that time, the pigeon dwelled inside the human nest, living the life of a rodent. The man-flock had filled the place with animals, mostly rare birds that, for whatever reason, weren't permitted to leave. One of them, Lupé, a Guadalupé Island petrel, had become Zomis's best, albeit only, bird friend. The ratbird had actually helped the petrel escape when the branch broke through the window during a fierce storm. That's when Zomis spotted the abandoned egg in the nest that wound up on the floor.

The robin's birth parents flew off even though they hadn't yet hatched the egg, never thinking the fragile embryo would survive the crash. So, Zomis rolled the egg away, incubated it, and raised Squab as its own, ultimately changing the course of both of their lives.

The two enjoyed sitting on the fateful oak. Often, they would look inside through the repaired window, feeling sorry for the birds who were contained in what they understood to be hard, shiny webs. Other than Lupé, and Zomis to some degree, they weren't aware of any birds who had escaped the massive structure or even the small webs that held them. The pigeon and the robin dreamt that one day they'd help all these birds return to the wind, to the wild.

Suddenly, a human entered the structure, rousing the two birds from their dreams. It carried a large cube that likely contained another bird. A moment later, it passed by the window, laid the cube down, and removed the covering. Then, Zomis saw him. The pigeon flew to the window, much closer to the structure than good judgment would allow.

Zomis was stunned. It felt as though something had squeezed its lungs. The pigeon couldn't believe what it was looking at. There, right in front of Zomis's beak, sat a petrel. It was Lupé. The man-flock had captured him *again*. Even though Zomis and Squab had just fantasized about releasing all the birds in that huge nest, Zomis now knew one thing for sure: the two of them would at least get Lupé out of there.

They watched, seeing precisely where the petrel was held. The bird looked thin, exhausted, and beaten, yet Zomis knew he'd hang on. It was time for another plan, a bigger plan than embarrassing a cat. Zomis knew this man-flock structure well. The pigeon had lived in it for years, out of sight and beneath the notice of its inhabitants. The thought of reentering the prison made the bird shudder, but for Lupé, Zomis would risk anything.

Squab, however, didn't know the bird, didn't like the risks, and didn't see the need to rush in there, beaks blazing, to break the unfortunate petrel out. "Let's wait, watch, plan, and *then* act," she reasoned. "What's a few days? It might make things easier in the end."

"Uh huh," Zomis mumbled.

"So, we slow down, we glide for a day or two?"

"That's my friend. A real friend. He doesn't look good, either. Every feather on my body tells me that we have to get him out of there—now."

"Now?" the robin repeated.

"Don't worry," Zomis said with a smile. "We'll have help."

The pigeon's plan would call for a break-in *and* a break-out. It sounded a little crazy to Squab, but Zomis assured her it wouldn't be difficult if they could just count on some help from some old acquaintances.

The two birds flew to the rear of the man-flock nest. Behind it, there stood an immense green container that the occupants continuously tossed food into. Zomis's former pack was never too far from the container. At night, the rats climbed into it and gorged themselves. Over time, they worked their way into the nest, believing there'd be more food inside, where the man-flock and their captive birds spent almost all their time. The rodents found out-of-the-way tunnels and discreet passageways, which the rat pack used to travel from outside to inside, from inside to outside.

Eventually, the massive nest became the pack's home. The tunnels were still used as needed, but now, even when the rats weren't feeding, the pack remained inside the structure, expanding the passageways. They connected dens that housed families, protected from the elements in a massive *rata*comb. Zomis had spent years with the rats, living among them, and knew the tunnels then like the bird knew the trees now. Zomis hoped the pack would remember the ratbird with fondness and decide to help. But one could never be completely sure of the rodents. They were unpredictable.

Zomis and Squab flew to the dark corners at the rear of the structure. The pigeon parent instructed, "I know you want to come with me, but you can't."

Squab feigned a look of disappointment, but truthfully, she was quite relieved. Anything to do with the rats made her uneasy.

Zomis continued, "I know the rats, they know me. Still, it's probably not safe. I don't want you near them."

"So, what should I do? If you think this is really worth it—and I'm not so sure it is—how can I help? We really don't have to do this right now."

The pigeon nodded. "You're right. *We* don't have to do this, but *I* do. If it weren't for that bird, I wouldn't be here, not like this. And when the wind dropped your egg in there," Zomis said, pointing to the man-flock structure, "I wouldn't have had the courage to make us a family."

"So," the robin added, "to chirp it another way, no Lupé, no us."

"*Eggs*actly. I'm going to get him out."

"OK, but I hope *no us* doesn't end up coming true. What do you want me to do?"

"Right now, just find a perch out of harm's way where you can see and hear everything that happens out here. If it looks like I'm in real trouble, try to warn me somehow. No unnecessary risks, though."

Squab nodded. "If you hear my song, get out of there." Then she looked her parent in the eye and repeated, "No risks, nothing stupid, either of us," thinking in the back of her mind that this entire endeavor was risky and stupid.

The two rubbed against each other briefly. Then Squab flew off into a tall tree.

Dense clouds and a low sun made it seem like dusk had come early. The rats were beginning to stir. Zomis knew the drill all too well. The first thing the ravenous rodents would do was visit the fresh piles of food the man-flock deposited in the hard, green container every evening, a veritable smorgasbord that sustained the pack. This was *their* feeder.

Zomis would wait and watch them eat, looking to see if any individuals from the old pack had shown up, giving them ample time to gorge themselves. Well-fed rats tend to be more open-minded than hungry ones. Besides, even though the pigeon was in a rush, Zomis figured they had the entire night, more or less, to get the petrel out. But it needed to be done before the man-flock returned in the morning.

It wasn't long before the first rat appeared. And that's exactly what she did. She just appeared out of the darkness, then another and another and another—two or three at a time. It was impossible to tell where they came from. They seemed to seep from the structure, oozing and dripping from cracks and holes. One after another, they emerged and scurried to the green container, joyous as they chewed and chewed. For a moment, Zomis relived the time when the ratbird scurried among them. The bird considered rejoining them but quickly laughed off the notion after realizing what would be left behind. Zomis was a pigeon, after all, and a parent.

The time had come. The large female who began the feeding had stopped. She shuffled into the shadows and watched the ravenous grey pack. Zomis recognized her. She was the one. If she approved, Lupé would go free. Zomis flew to her, landing a safe distance away.

The pigeon spoke to the shadow, "Vhateen, you look well. Do you remember me?"

The rat stretched her head out of the shadow and studied the bird, sniffing. She stepped closer, testing to see if the pigeon would

allow her. She laid her whiskery nose against its flank and smelled the feathers. The rat grinned, her yellow teeth catching a thin beam of light. She brushed against the pigeon with her considerable bulk and sniffed some more.

"Zomis, what brings you back?" Vhateen's mouth twisted into a tight grin, her hairless tail twitching behind her.

"I need a fav—"

"Of course you do. Why else would you be here?"

"There's a bird in there, a friend of mine."

"That's nice," the rodent mumbled. "You used to have other friends here, friends without feathers."

"Don't I still?" Zomis asked.

"Perhaps . . . You want me to deliver a message to this friend, this bird?" The rat looked away.

"Not exactly. I want you to deliver me."

Vhateen's eyes widened from their almost constant squint. "Clearing the dirt from your feathers did nothing to clear your mind. You are still as crazy, as confused, as ever."

"Well, I won't argue with that, but there is one thing I'm clear on. I need to get my friend out of there."

"Ah, the web becomes more tangled. This is not a visit, it's an escape."

Zomis nodded.

"Yes, your transformation is complete," the rat said. "You truly are a bird brain. Any of us in the pack would be thrilled to live in that man-flock den. Warm, fed, dry, without predators . . . and yet your friend has precisely that, and you want to help him by taking it all away. A bird brain, indeed."

"Well?"

Looking back at the other rats, Vhateen said, "I have no great love for the man-flock. They would kill us all if they could." The matriarch grinned at a scurrying youngster and continued, "They do try."

The pigeon nodded. It knew.

"But I also have no love for a pigeon who is accepted by the rats—this pack, in fact—as one of their own and then leaves to become a pigeon again."

"I was afraid of that."

"You were right to be. One of the few things you've been right about."

"Vhateen," Zomis pleaded, "it was nothing *ratsonal*. Part of me will always be rodent, but deep down, it's hard to deny that I'm a pigeon. I just needed to be who I was."

"I understand," Vhateen said as she shuffled back into the dark. "Then be who you are, and let the pigeons solve your problem." The rat returned to the structure.

Zomis wasn't surprised. The pigeon had apparently burned a branch with the rats and would have to find another way. Then, it seemed, another way found him.

A rat emerged from another part of the structure. Like Vhateen, he shuffled and sniffed his way closer. He had tattered ears, half a tail, and a little hitch in his step. "Hello," he hissed. "I couldn't help overhearing. Looks like you have a dilemma on your wings."

"That's *eggsactly* what I have," Zomis agreed, taking a healthy step back from the unfamiliar rodent.

"Allow me to introduce myself," the rat said, stepping closer. "I'm what you might call an independent contractor."

The pigeon and the rodent began to whisper. When they were through, they had a deal.

Zomis perched on the branch next to Squab.

"Well?" the robin inquired.

"Well, the big rat said no chance . . ."

"I figured."

". . . but that little rat, Jurm, said OK."

"Really? Can he deliver?"

"I think so, but first, we need to deliver."

"It's never simple," the robin observed.

"We can do this. As a matter of fact, it was Vhateen, the first rat, who figured this out for me. She said, 'Let the pigeons solve your problem.' And that's just what I'm going to do."

"So, what's the plan?"

"Actually, I need you to deliver a message . . . right now."

"Without you?"

"I'll get Lupé out," the pigeon said. "You need to tell his family what happened."

"Do you remember where this bird comes from? Do you even know if he has a family or where they might be?"

"None of that matters," Zomis declared. "He has a monarch."

"A *monarch*?" Squab asked, looking up to the heavens when she said it. "So, he has a monarch, and yet he winds up here? That's a little strange."

"The butterfly doesn't necessarily protect you from everything, but it did help him escape the first time."

"So, where is his butterfly now? Why doesn't it save him again?"

"There's no time for this. Just find another monarch—any monarch—and give it the message I'm going to give you. The news will get to his friends and family way before either of us could get it there. While you do that, I'll gather a flock, and we'll meet at the feeder."

"The feeder? You're not—"

"Find the butterfly. Only a monarch can do this. Give it the message and meet me at the feeder. Lupé's family needs to know where he is and what we're going to do. Go!"

Inside the large man-flock nest, Vicente El Real was fascinated with a very special bird—not the interesting petrel, but a pale-blue macaw, one of the most unique birds he'd ever seen.

"What do the papers say?" he questioned.

His assistant director handed him the sheets. "It's listed as a hyacinth macaw."

El Real smiled. "That's good."

"But clearly, it's not a blue macaw."

El Real raised his index finger. "A Spix is blue, and it's a macaw, just not the type they have in mind."

"So, you know what it is," the young lady who assisted him at the center observed.

"I think we both do."

"Then why won't you list it accurately in the report?"

"Because I love this bird, and I know how special it is." The ornithologist stroked the parrot as if he held the Holy Grail in his hands. In a sense, he did. "If it becomes apparent that this bird is here, there's no telling what will happen. It could wind up anywhere, in anyone's hands. Not everyone feels like we do. Not everyone knows how to care for a bird like this. It has to stay here . . . with us.

"If it's a *hyacinth* macaw," Vicente continued, "no one will care. No one will know. Then we can make sure this irreplaceable jewel is looked after by those who should rightfully be entrusted with such a treasure."

"I don't know, Vicente."

"Leave it listed as a *blue*. I will personally make sure the bird is taken care of. This is our best chance to save it. Who knows? We might save an entire species."

"For that to happen, we would need another." The young lady shook her head, clearly uncomfortable.

"There are others. You just have to know where to look."

The trees that surrounded the bird feeder were cooing. Here and there a thin branch swayed under the weight of the pigeons. The leaves rustled. The flock had been briefed. They were happy to help

Zomis. After all, their friend was assuming all the risk. They would get the meal while Zomis might become one.

Squab landed next to her parent.

"Done?" the pigeon asked.

"If you can find milkweed, you can find monarchs. The butterflies know. They will deliver the message."

"Good. By tomorrow or the next day, Lupé's flock—or friends, whatever he has—will know where he is and where to meet us. Good."

"What now?" Squab whispered.

"Now the fun begins. You fly interference. If he gets too close, chase him away, but don't be reckless."

"Chase who?"

"The cat."

"*Dumbino*? Didn't we just do this?"

"Sure, but that proved it. If he's dumb enough to follow me into the bush once, he'll do it again. I know it. That's a stupid cat."

"Maybe he wasn't *dumb* enough to follow you. Maybe he was hungry enough or bloodthirsty enough. I'm sure he'll be much more cautious after that whole skunk incident."

"Whatever gets him to chase me works."

"Where is he now?" Squab asked.

Zomis nodded toward the man-flock nest, the one whose occupants regularly filled the feeder, the ones who, for some strange reason, also seemed to provide for Domino's wellbeing. It amazed Zomis and Squab how easy it was for birds—cats and dogs, even—to train some humans to provide for them.

By day, the cat was most often found lounging lazily next to a large, shiny, nest-sized thing that happened to be filled with tasty little bites for the feline. These treats came in a variety of shapes and colors and apparently were quite appetizing, especially if you were a cat. Domino knew that by lying splayed out on his side next to his food, squirrels, birds, and others who had a hankering for the morsels would stay away from his stash.

While the birds appreciated the benefits of a well-fed cat, they also craved the kibble. And really, whenever the food disappeared, one of the man-flock would just fill it up again anyway. Yet *Dumbino* still refused to share. Although he didn't know it, Zomis was about to clean him out. The pigeon had good reason, for there was another who also coveted the colorful shapes.

The rodent whom Zomis had struck a deal with had a taste for the treats. Indeed, he'd heard about them through local lore, but alas, had never actually tried any. So, he agreed that if the pigeon could bring him half his own weight in cat food, he'd take the bird to Lupé.

Zomis was not very good at being subtle. The bird wore its emotions on its wing, tending to be simple, direct. The pigeon liked being that way, finding that it usually saved time and helped keep discussions honest. As a result, nuance was not a specialty. The bird concluded that the best way to anger the cat would be the direct approach, to pull its tail. So, that's what Zomis would do.

While Domino lounged, freshly bathed and floral scented after his run-in with the little skunk, the pigeon swooped in and landed behind the cat. It perched down on the fuzzy grey tail and bit hard. Shocked, the feline vaulted into the air, screaming, "*Mrreeooowww!*"

It was on.

Domino touched down on all fours, ready for a fight. When he spotted Zomis smiling at him just a whisker beyond a pounce, he was ready for an execution. Calling on eons of feline stalking strategy, Domino lowered himself, flattened his spine, stretched his claws, and then retracted them—for the moment, at least. He stepped slowly toward the bird, who, for some strange reason, perched in place, seemingly mesmerized by the movements of the predator. The cat stared into the bird's eyes, holding the creature in place with its gaze. Was it oblivious to the approaching doom?

The pigeon's beak was moving, taunting. Was this a warning to the enormous cat from the bird? Then Domino saw what was happening. The bird was eating something . . . one of his colorful shapes! This pigeon was eating its last meal. Today, it would die.

While Zomis chewed, Domino shaved off that whisker beyond the lunge that separated them. The bird was within the cat's pounce perimeter.

"*Rraaarrr!*" Domino was airborne, claws extended, teeth bared. He crashed satisfyingly down where Zomis stood and felt the warm liquid on his face, on his paws, on his chest. It told him he'd won. He would taste the blood of the bird. It defined him.

"*Mreeoww!* I am cat!" he declared to himself and any who doubted. Domino raised his paw triumphantly and tasted the wet warmth. It wasn't blood. There were no feathers, no bones. He tasted the paw again. The liquid was thick and white. He had pounced on a turd, a fresh bird bowel movement that Zomis had left, perhaps involuntarily, just for him. Then Domino realized the ugly truth. Not only had Zomis eaten his food and caused him to pounce on poop—the cat had, in full view of all the backyard creatures, licked the bird's scat . . . twice.

Once again, the naked truth eluded the feline. For surely, if Zomis had left the calling card by its own volition, then the pigeon had cleverly outsmarted the cat. If, however, the bird had defecated out of fear, the cat had no one to blame but himself, because had he not terrified the bird, he wouldn't have tumbled onto the turd. One thing was for sure. No matter how you sliced it, Domino was draped in dung again, which seemed to be developing into a *repurring* theme. It was more than he could bear.

But it wasn't over. Zomis was off in the distance, crawling clumsily through the grass, clearly looking for cover, trying not to be noticed.

I knew it didn't get away clean, Domino thought as he dashed after the damaged pigeon who zigged and zagged, flapped and fell, hopped and dropped, drawing the cat farther away from his sacred pile of food.

They descended in a wave, more like locusts than pigeons. The birds burst onto the abandoned food, one after another, after another, after another, after another. Each would land for an instant, swallow a few pieces of kibble for itself, and then fly off with a beakful. Tiny tastes were being airlifted away. The pigeons deposited the food in a container the rat had dragged out of the other man-flock structure nearby. Soon, the rodent had half his weight in colorful kibble. Next, it would be his turn to keep up his end of the deal.

When the moon had risen well into the night sky, Zomis returned to the *ratacombs*. Jurm was waiting for him. "Are you ready?" the pigeon asked the rat.

"I'll take you to the petrel. The rest is up to you."

"That's the agreement," the bird concurred.

Next, Zomis did something the pigeon swore it would never do again. The bird entered the stone nest. Memories alighted in its mind. Generally, Zomis didn't like to look back. What was the point in looking back to moments that had already happened? The past was two-dimensional. It couldn't be relived. It couldn't be changed.

The memories of what was likely the last passenger pigeon weren't worth recalling, Zomis felt. They were sad. But as much as the bird tried to bury its painful past, to live in the moment, being back in the stone nest, with its smells, the prisoner birds, and, of course, the rats, forced the pigeon to return to a time not so long ago that it lived among the rodents, having decided that the life of a rat—or any life, for that matter—would have to be happier than the one Zomis had been living. Eventually, however, the pigeon had come to see its place in the world differently, and Lupé was the main reason the epiphany had occurred. Now it was payback time. The pigeon would rescue the petrel.

Jurm knew his way. The pair scurried through dark passages, quickly, quietly, until they were deep within the structure. *How did I live like this?* Zomis wondered, pleased that it found the rodent lifestyle claustrophobic and revolting. It reaffirmed the pigeon's decision to leave the pack.

"Good luck," Jurm said as he turned to walk away.

"What? What do you mean, good luck?"

"Good luck," the rat whispered from the shadows.

Zomis smelled a rat—literally. "You did not take me to Lupé. Where am I? Where have you taken me? This was not our agreement."

"Do you not recognize the place you lived? Do you not recall the passageways you used to trek? Have you totally forgotten your home? Us?" Jurm said, disappearing into the dark.

Zomis understood. The rat had lived up to the bargain. This was the place Zomis had met Lupé, the place where it had scavenged scraps from the containers of the kept. The pigeon's eyes adjusted to the dark. For the moment, Zomis allowed the rodent consciousness to return, and the ratbird scurried from container to container, looking for the petrel. Zomis had helped Lupé escape once, and it could be done again.

The containers that held the captive birds were covered with man-flock weavings, so it wasn't easy to identify the inhabitants. Zomis moved from one to another, sniffing, the bird's wings clinched tightly to its sides. Head lowered, the pigeon hissed and drooled as it passed birds it had never seen before, smelled foods it had never tasted before. The pigeon discovered a cracked clam, one of its former favorites, and stuffed its feathery face into the wet shell. The slime, the salt, dripped down the down on its neck. Clams again. The pigeon slurped. It had been so long. *Why would anyone eat seeds when they could have clams?* Zomis mused.

Seeds? *Seeds?* The word rocked the ratbird. The feeder . . . Squab . . . The pigeon was forgetting itself . . . or was it actually remembering itself? This had to stop. Pigeon or rat, it was time to find Lupé. One last swallow of clam—OK, maybe two—and Zomis was back on track.

There it was. The container was exactly where it had been the last time. Zomis ran to it. "Petrel," the rescuer hissed. "Petrel."

A low, muffled *yes* followed.

Zomis grabbed the weaving that covered the hard, square nest and tugged at it until it slid off. The petrel withdrew to a corner. Lupé was thinner, huddled, looking weary and whipped, silent.

"Lupé, it's me! It's Zomis. Don't you remember?"

The petrel didn't respond.

"I know I look different, more like a pigeon than a rat, even if I still smell like clams, but it's me, your friend. I'm going to get you out of here. I've sent word through the butterflies. Your family, your friends will know where you are and that I'm helping you."

"My family?"

"I mean, if you have one. Let's get going. Come here, I need your help."

The petrel took a step out of the shadows. A beam of moonlight slipped across its face, and Zomis could not believe it. This petrel was not Lupé.

A petrel stood before the pigeon—a Guadalupé petrel, in fact—but it wasn't one Zomis had ever seen before. This was a female. Apparently, Lupé was not, as he'd believed, the last survivor of his flock. The female stepped back into the dark corner of the web-like container.

Even though it wasn't Lupé, Zomis didn't hesitate. "I think I can get you out of here. Would you like me to try?"

"Why would you do that for me?" the petrel probed.

Zomis looked around the room. The pigeon was getting nervous and began to wonder if it should just get out of there, but Zomis decided that as long as it was there, it would do one thing first. From outside the hard nest, it was easy to see that one twig-like piece had to be lifted and moved in order for the front wall of the container to swing open.

Zomis perched on top of the locked nest and lifted, sliding the silver twig. The container opened, and the pigeon stepped in. Zomis heard a throaty hiss, then a stream of hot, sticky oil landed at its feet. This was a warning. The petrel didn't trust the pigeon. *It would be so much easier if this were Lupé*, Zomis thought.

"I came to save my friend, a Gwatta petrel, just like you. Risked my life to do it. And now that I'm here and my friend isn't, I'd like to save you."

"Everyone wants to save me," the petrel responded. "That's why I'm here, it seems. What makes you think there are others like me?"

"There is one. And if my guess is right, he's on his way. We must leave now, while we can."

"Petrels don't trust rats. You smell of rat. There's something very rodent about you. I heard you with one."

"Look, I used to live with them. I used to think I was a rat, but a petrel helped me understand that I'm a bird, a pigeon. We can talk about this later, out there. But let's get—"

The door opened. The light came on, and a human stood in front of them. He seemed surprised, confused.

"Follow me, *NOW!*" Zomis screamed. The pigeon flew from the container and landed on a cabinet above the rathole it had used to enter the room. But Zomis was alone. The petrel hadn't followed.

The human removed a covering from himself. It was as if he took off his feathers or his fur, possibly a layer of skin. It slid right off his arms and back. He held it out, extended it, and stepped toward the petrel, who was now standing halfway out of the den. Zomis guessed that the man-flock wanted to drape the covering over the container or the bird, forcing it back inside.

The petrified petrel retreated into the shadows inside the den, disappearing. Confident that she was contained and hadn't slipped away, the human lowered his face to the petrel's prison and peered into the darkness. "Are you in there? Are you—*ahhhh!*"

The enormous two-legged creature dropped the covering, grasped his face, and leaned forward, banging his head on a hard structure, a small plateau, a protrusion. As he jerked back up to straighten himself, he slipped backward on a bit of the oil that had missed Zomis moments before.

A flurry of feathers flew from the container and landed next to the pigeon. A trickle of oil dripped from two holes on top of the petrel's beak. "I blasted him," was all she said.

"Let's go."

"What about him?" The petrel pointed to a sullen pale-blue macaw who quietly observed events from inside his own locked nest. But in the same instant, the human cleared the oily projection from his eyes, rose, and stepped toward the two birds.

"I'd love to let them all go, but there's no time," the pigeon replied, nudging the other bird closer to the waiting rathole.

"I'm *not* going in *there!*" the petrel declared, flying to a higher perch.

Zomis followed. "Then you'll never get out of here." The pigeon lunged to the hole.

From the corner of its eye, Zomis saw the petrel fly out of the room into the large passageway the man-flock used. For a moment, the human, who had picked up a short branch with a soft, flowing mesh attached to the end of it, didn't know which way to go, which bird to follow. As he turned to chase the petrel, Zomis decided to do the same. They both approached the doorway at the same time. Zomis was flying eye-to-eye with the human when the large creature thought he would seize the moment and the pigeon, as well. He raised the branch with the mesh, reared back, and . . . disappeared.

Zomis glanced back to find the pursuer supine and motionless. At his feet were several large, hard nuts. In the container above the toppled human, the pale-blue parrot smiled at Zomis. The birds nodded at each other, the human stirred, and Zomis was back on the wing, soaring through the long passageways inside the man-flock nest.

Not seeing the petrel, the pigeon flew through several openings until it arrived at an enormous den. The space was contained by the man-flock's hard, clear substance that seemed like ice but wasn't cold. It looked like nothing was there, yet rain didn't fall through it and cold didn't penetrate it. You could see the sky above, the trees beyond, but the pigeon was still contained in the large space attached to the stone nest. And there was the petrel. Zomis spotted her nestled among some strange, morbid gathering.

Along the perimeter of the space, sixteen, maybe twenty birds shoebirds, several small flocks, were all gathered on a faux beach—sterile sand, lifeless water, dead flocks. Feathers without flight were arranged in seaside poses along the sides of the clear den. It was bizarre, surreal, but Zomis could see the petrel hiding between a pair of what looked like nesting pelicans. The pigeon approached.

"What are you doing?"

"I'm not going in any ratholes," she declared.

"Well, it doesn't really matter now. That bird's flown."

"Do you feel it?" the petrel asked. "Can you smell it?"

"What?"

"The breeze. It's coming in from over there. If that ice stuff melts or moves, if it opens up, we can get out of here. Look, there are man-flock footprints coming and going from that spot. I think that's where they come in and out of here."

The petrel seemed to be right. And she seemed to be smart. Zomis nodded. They waited.

Earlier in the day, Vicente had typed a simple note: "Greetings, fellow bird lovers. The eagle has landed." Then he sent the message.

Later, back at his home, Vicente poured over documents that discussed everything from condor relief efforts in California to spotted owl sightings in the Northwest to piping plover nesting sites in New Jersey. He knew all the figures, all the endangered birds, all the conservationists, all the facts, all the rumors—he knew them all. He had to. Vicente was going places.

Gonzo was a strong flier, as large and as powerful a woodpecker as the planet could produce—although for the last century, the planet wasn't producing very many. It wasn't Gonzo's nature to wander great distances. His kind preferred settling down in a wooded swamp to enjoy life. All they wanted were trees with grubs and to be left alone. And alone they were.

The ivory-bill flew north by northeast in search of adventure. He wanted the new and unpredictable, felt he needed that to take his mind off Kwim and the crushing despair that his vision of a nest, young, and certainly a flock was slipping away from him. He decided that perhaps if he turned everything he was supposed to do inside out, he might just find his way. And while he could wind up doing the wrong thing, at least he was doing something, the woodpecker reasoned.

Flying at night seemed to be the best choice. The man-flock would never notice him. Hawks were roosting. His only real fear were owls, with just two types concerning him, horned and barred. Either one could have a taste for woodpecker, either one was very capable of taking him down. Although a target he might be, Gonzo wasn't the most inviting quarry. He was large and strong, with a beak that demanded respect, and predators often avoided prey that could injure them. If there was something easier to eat, the woodpecker hoped any owls would turn their attention from him and opt for the meal of least resistance and risk.

It was a long journey, a bit of a migration, but the time passed quickly. Gonzo settled into a mindless rhythm of pumping his wings and breathing deeply. He flew and flew and flew. He was amazed at the lights below him, so many, so bright. How could the man-flock command personal stars, personal fires, personal lightning? They were seemingly flying higher than any creature had ever done, yet the woodpeckers, the turtles, the gators, the frogs, the opossums, the salamanders—so many others had been around so much longer. Gonzo couldn't decide what, if anything, it all meant.

Still, it was staggering to consider the power this incredible man-flock wielded. Were they really so omnipotent that they bowed to no other? Could they really disregard consequences? Gonzo always considered whether he ate too many larvae of a certain insect, whether he stripped too much bark from too many trees. Even from dead trees, the balance could be upset. There was a sacred, perfect equilibrium that he and all those who shared the swamp tried never to lose sight of. It was the one underlying truth that couldn't be ignored or abused, not withoutdaring dire consequences. He knew it, the squirrels knew it, even the gators knew it: all things in moderation.

It was a balance, after all. It could be tipped quite easily in one direction or another, leading to irreparable harm. It wasn't unyielding, not set in stone. But for some reason, the man-flock didn't feel bound by this truth, or they didn't know it.

The latter was hard for Gonzo to accept. Kwim had always argued that the man-flock was as stupid as stone, but Gonzo couldn't agree with her. "Look at what they can do. Look at their numbers, their nests. They dominate the sky, the land, the sea. How could they possibly be stupid?" He remembered Kwim looking at him, her head cocked to one side, puzzled with her mate, surprised that he didn't see it.

"One does not reflect the other," she said. "The biggest eater, the biggest flier, the biggest builder, is not necessarily the best woodpecker. Often, the opposite is true. The best answer is not always *more*."

Kwim grinned, because this was a not-so-veiled peck at her mate, whom she frequently laughed at for eating mass quantities of bad food and for hollowing out gigantic roosting holes that were drafty and cold and ended up being too big to serve as good shelter. Her larger point was made, that ability and understanding were two very different things. And in Kwim's mind at least, the man-flock had a perilous abundance of the former and an alarming lack of the latter.

Gonzo, however, couldn't decide. He was battling a little stomachache and couldn't think very clearly. The woodpecker hoped Kwim was wrong about the man-flock, even if she was right about him.

The weather was clear. The breeze rustled his rump, nudging him onward. It was a good omen. Gonzo had arrived at a substantial dark patch just inland from the coast. He'd never been this far north. It was warm, tranquil, and relatively quiet. Yet even in his home swamp, the rolling nests of the man-flock whizzed past roosting and feeding sites, thankfully never stopping or slowing as they continued constantly on to wherever it was they went. This patch of woods also had several long, hard paths traveled by the rolling nests. The woodpecker knew that if he could steer clear of them, he might avoid winding up like so many deer, raccoons, and opossums that he'd seen feeding vultures and crows on the sides of the human trails.

Gonzo landed on an expired pine. He heard them immediately, burrowing beneath the bark. Even though it was long dead, the tree was full of life. Grubs, larvae, beetles, and other tasty morsels infested the deadwood. Another good omen. It was time to rest. In the morning, the weary woodpecker would eat. Afterward, he would search for a nice roosting hole and get the lay of the land.

He'd entered a new wood—a new world—yet it wasn't completely unfamiliar. He was perched above a northern hardwood swamp that joined an immense stand of pines. He could see cedar and white cedar, oak, sassafras, a walnut tree here and there. Below, pink orchids, curly grass ferns, yellow fringeless orchids, bog asphodel, and swamp pink all spread along the almost boggy forest floor.

Then he heard it, something from the old world, a sound he knew all too well. A far cry from the inviting bustle of bugs in bark, this was a wild wail that came in the night. It was to be feared. *Hoo, hoo-hoo hoo-hoooo, to-hoo-ah,* drifted across and through the trees.

Gonzo listened. There was no reply. *Hoo, hoo-hoo hoo-hoooo, to-hoo-ah.* A solitary owl was on the prowl. The woodpecker knew the call, knew the caller. It was the barred. As far as omens went, this one wasn't the best.

When morning broke, Gonzo waited until the sun had cleared the eastern horizon. The brighter it became, the less chance he had of flitting into the owl. Exhausted and half-starved would not be the best conditions if he were called upon to fight for his life. Unable to ignore the tantalizing taps of taste just below him, the woodpecker decided to begin feeding on the dead pine. He listened carefully to the vertical buffet, shuffled to the perfect perch, cocked his head, and unleashed the massive ivory bill that his kind was named for.

Nothing in these woods had ever seen or heard anything like it before. It's one thing for a red-bellied or a downy woodpecker, even a large pileated, to drill holes into a tree, but for Gonzo, it was a demolition. Massive sections of bark leapt from the tree as if trying to escape the beak's barrage. The woodpecker scooped up whatever morsels he spotted. Debris, deadwood, bark, and chips whirled around him. *Ka-black! Ka-black! Ka-black!* The sound ricocheted through the air in hyper staccato times a thousand. The forest fell into stunned silence except for the famished ivory-bill. *Ka-black! Ka-black! Ka-black!* Slowly, carefully, others made their way to the curious commotion.

Gonzo was feeding, and that was that. He wasn't very concerned with who noticed or how he was being received. This was a *bugffet*, and he was getting his feed on. Below, where the bark gathered at the trunk of the tree, birds flew in and pecked at the pieces that seemed abandoned by the massive woodpecker. Long strips of bark that contained a multitude of morsels overlooked by Gonzo continuously rained down on the pile, feeding those beneath, a gift from the woodpecker above.

Hearing a high-pitched, insect-like mumble behind his head, Gonzo continued to feed. The mumble, however, was persistent and flitted from one side of the woodpecker's head to the other. Barely audible under the cacophony of chiseled pine, the sound grew annoying. Gonzo wondered if perhaps he'd torn open the hole of a large carpenter bee.

The woodpecker glanced over his back and spotted a large green locust or possibly a chubby dragonfly from the corner of his eye hovering near his head. He swung his beak at the bug, swatting rather than swallowing since the tree already presented no shortage of his favorites, and locust could be bitter. But the beak never touched the mumbling bug. Gonzo swung again and whiffed. Having ceased his own incessant racket, he could now hear the monotonous mumble more clearly.

"Hey,what'syourproblem? Whatareyoudoing?"

Gonzo focused on the flier. It was a bird, not a bug. The avian speck, a hummingbird, hovered near the woodpecker's face.

"Youwantsomeofthis?" the little bird asked, clearly agitated that Gonzo had swung at him. And before the ivory-bill could utter a sound, the hummingbird flew in and pecked him in the face several times, removing the remnants of a grub that hung from the woodpecker's beak before Gonzo could swallow it.

"Floatlikeabutterfly,stinglikeabee.Youcan'tstopwhatyoucan't see. Icandothistoyouallday." The hummingbird spoke as fast as he flew. He flashed in and pecked Gonzo several more times, driving his pointed beak beneath the woodpecker's feathers, stabbing at the bird's head on the way out just to accentuate his point.

"Owww!" Gonzo whined.

"Ohlook,alittlenoogiefromthehummer. Speedkills,chickie,-speedkills!" The hummingbird began another sortie. A blur, he swept in, pecked Gonzo on the cheek, rolled under the woodpecker's outstretched wing, tangled his beak in a feather, continued down just beneath the belly and ripped the down from Gonzo's sensitive nether regions. All this happened in the time it takes to peep.

The diminutive bird's wings normally beat eighty times per second, but in the heat of the current battle, its wings were fluttering at a blazing two hundred beats per second. The only bird that can fly upside down and backward, the little speck can even reach sixty miles per hour on a dive. Then the ruby-throat made a cardinal mistake. He underestimated his opponent, assuming because the ivory-bill was so enormous, everything about him would be slow.

However, from the neck up, the woodpecker was as quick as anything in the woods. When he put his mind to it, Gonzo could thrust and parry with the best of them, and he was swinging a long sword, not a safety pin. As the grinning hummingbird flew into Gonzo's grill with woodpecker down plastered to his face, he was plucked from the air and held gently but firmly in the beak of the ivory-bill.

"Shurop rit! Cran shroo zhust shrehax?" Gonzo tried to say with the tiny green bird struggling in his beak. "Rhom zhust shrying shroo reat zhere."

The struggling speck paused. "Okay,Icanstopit,butIcan'trelax.I'mahummingbird. Wedon'trelax. JustletmegoandI'lltakeiteasyonyou."

The infuriated little bird wasn't lying. With a heart rate of anywhere from 250 to 1,200 beats per minute, Trice could take 250 breaths in as much time, and at the moment, he was on the upper end of the spectrum. But the price of this high-octane existence was that he needed to eat constantly to avoid starving, since his constitution burned calories almost as fast as he could take them in.

Gonzo squeezed his massive beak a little tighter until he heard the hummingbird grunt. Then, when he felt he'd made his point, he released his grip, and the little bird flew out. Still, Gonzo was a bit anxious. Hummers could be smart, tricky. Taking body size into account, they actually had more brain volume than the man-flock, and Gonzo knew how dangerous humans could be.

"Firstyoutryandswatmewiththatmutantbeak,thenyou'resqu eezingmeanddroolingalloverme. What'syourproblem?"

"I think we got off on a bad breeze here."

"That'ssafetosay."

"No, I mean, I didn't realize you were a bird," Gonzo said apologetically. "When I swatted at you, I thought you were a bug."

But the hummingbird didn't take it that way, flying a short feather from the woodpecker's face, saying, "Carefulwiththatbugstuff. Youdon'twantmeallinyourfeathersagain."

"No, no . . . didn't mean to disrespect you. Hummingbirds are awesome."

"Yougotthatright."

"So, we're good?" Gonzo asked.

"Yeah,we'regood."

"I couldn't really hear you when I was eating. What were you saying?"

"Justintroducingmyself,sssup?"

Below the two birds, an assortment of feathery feeders had gathered at the trunk to eat Gonzo's leftovers. Growing restless, they began to bellow, "Don't stop!" "Yeah, keep it coming!" "Come on!" "Hungry down here!"

Several woodpecker types, a pair of robins, a nuthatch, several tufted titmouses and blue jays, a cardinal, some crows, two pairs of doves, and others foraged in and around the pile of bark. A toad and a slippery salamander approached as well. Gonzo was making an impression.

"Sowhatareyoudoing,justpassingthrough?" the hummingbird inquired.

"Don't know. Just got here."

"Well,Iknowyou'reawoodpecker. Kindaimpossibletohidethat." The hummer pointed to the gleaming ivory bill, then nodded to the stripped-down pine. "Butcan'tsayI'veeverseenonelikeyoubefore. I'dsurerememberthat."

Gonzo nodded as well. He couldn't hide his disappointment, though. He'd hoped that maybe in this new forest with these new birds, maybe, one of them might say, "I know (or even knew) a woodpecker just like you." But that wasn't a phrase Gonzo had ever heard.

"Gotaname?"

The ivory-bill smiled. "You talk so fast."

"Idoeverythingfast. It'smynature. OtherbirdsthinkI'mimpatient,butactually,I'mnot. It'sjustthattherestofyouare s o o o s s l l o o o w w w w . Iguessit'sallamatterofperspective."

"Most things are. Do you do anything slow?"

"NotwhileI'mawake."

But when the hummingbird went to sleep, he'd switch from one extreme to the other, turning off his frenetic pace and replacing it with one of the deepest slumbers one could imagine, an almost self-induced coma that the birds referred to as torpor. The little bird virtually hibernated through the night and through long stretches of bad weather when he couldn't feed normally. He'd drop his heart rate from well over 200 down to 50 beats per minute and lower his body temperature from 107 down to 70 degrees. In torpor, the hummingbird's breathing became almost imperceptible. But when he woke in the morning, it was off to the races again.

"Howaboutthatname? Gotone?"

"Gonzo."

"Don'tlikeit," the hummer replied bluntly.

"What?"

"Don'tlikeit. SoundslikeGoner,likethere'snohopeforyou. Itravelquiteabit. Fromwhereweflynowabovetheequator,I'llwinterthatsamedistanceagainbelowtheequator."

"Wow! That's migration."

"Youbetyourbeakitis. Relativetomysize,nootherbirdmigrate-sasfar. SoI'veseenalot,butneverseenanotherlikeyou. You'reintrouble,aren'tya?"

"A little bit," Gonzo admitted, although he was a little put off by how *bird*sonal the hummer was getting.

"That'swhyIdon'tlikethename,toobleak. Mayhavetorenamey-ou. I'mthinkingZo."

"Well," Gonzo interrupted, hoping to glide the topic in a different direction, "what do you answer to?"

"I'mTrice."

"That's a solid name."

"Yes, it is." Trice pointed to the base of the tree. "Thenative-saregettingrestless. Andyou'reprobablystillhungry."

The woodpecker shrugged in agreement.

"Me,I'machingforsomenectar. Gottakeepitflowingwhenyou-haveametabolismlikemine. Thisheart'spumpinglikeanor'easterri-ghtnow,soI'mofftosucksomeflowers. Later,Zo." And Trice was gone. He was so fast, it was as if he had disappeared.

Then, strangely, everything seemed to slow down. Being around that hummingbird warped time, Gonzo thought. On the one wing, everything seemed to speed up. But on the other wing, because you were going so fast, you packed more of your attention and thoughts into each moment, and in that way, time seemed to slow down at the same instant it was speeding up. Trice was a trip. Zo wondered if there were more creatures like him in these woods.

Back to Nature

For better or worse, Kemar had a knack for meeting people. His visit to the I-BIRD conference was no exception. There, he'd chatted for several minutes with keynote speaker, Vicente El Real, who invited him to visit I-BIRD's research facility in New York, not far from where the conference took place at Monmouth University on the New Jersey Shore. When Kemar explained to Dr. Dorfman and Dr. Campbell that they, too, were invited and handed them El Real's business card, they seized the opportunity and scheduled the visit.

The trio arrived a little early, just as the center was opening. They entered quietly and found themselves in a longish foyer, an atrium of sorts that featured taxidermic displays of birds placed in what appeared to be natural settings and postures. The visitors were asked to wait in this lobby for a few moments while El Real and the others prepared to receive them.

Dr. Campbell picked up a brochure with the director's photo on the back cover and flipped through it. Dr. Dorfman, a bit more hands-on and about as inhibited as an otter, leaned over a railing and removed a displayed horseshoe crab. He waved Kemar over, and class was in session.

"*Limulus polyphemus.* The only horseshoe crab not living in Asian waters. Essentially unchanged for hundreds of millions of years. A living fossil that's actually more closely related to spiders than crabs. Quiz time, how many eyes do you think this common horseshoe crab has?"

"There are none," Kemar replied.

"I mean, if he were alive, how many eyes?" the good doctor pressed.

"None."

"So, you think that the common horseshoe crab is blind? Interesting. But really, most blind crabs would likely be found in the extreme depths of the ocean or deep in an isolated cave, and thi—"

"I'm not saying that," Kemar interrupted.

"So, if it were alive, you would agree that it's a sighted crab?"

"Yes, no doubt."

"Then how can you maintain that it has no eyes?"

Kemar smiled. Now he was the professor, and Dr. Dorfman was the student. "*H-O-R-S-E-S-H-O-E C-R-A-B*. No *I*s in horseshoe crab. Spell it yourself."

"Cute," the professor conceded.

Dr. Campbell giggled from behind a pamphlet.

"Now, let me tell you something worth knowing," Dr. Dorfman continued. "This crab has two lateral compound eyes, not *I*s." He pointed to them at the crest of its shell. "But there are also five additional eyes on the shell." Dorfman pointed them out, then flipped the crab over. "On the underside, there are two more eyes," he said, pointing to them near the animal's mouth. "Lastly—"

"Yes, there are sensors on its tail that aren't actually eyes but allow the crab to perceive light and dark, to help it judge day and night," Kemar recited.

"I must have told you this before," Dorfman declared to the boy.

"Actually, she did." Kemar pointed to Dr. Campbell, who gave her colleague a little wave.

Dorfman, not one to quickly concede defeat, countered, "Well, you haven't answered my initial question. Quickly, how many eyes?"

"That's easy, none. *H-O-R-S—*"

"You're hopeless," Dorfman grunted with an amused smirk. He handed the boy the stiff crab and walked away.

Kemar could see a faint imprint in the sand where the crab was displayed. He wanted to return the specimen to its exact spot but couldn't reach over the railing as far as the adult scientist did, so he carefully stepped into the display and leaned down to replace the prop. When he did, he heard a rustle followed by a faint coo, and the boy thought he saw movement from the corner of his eye. Kemar rose slowly and studied the exhibit. All these creatures were dressed for display. They were lifeless. The crabs were dead. The gulls were dead. The plovers, the storks, the oyster catchers, the pelicans, the least terns—all were props in an exhibit. Kemar turned back to his friends.

At that moment, Vicente El Real himself strode into the room. He seemed a bit flustered, perhaps a bit taken by surprise at their early arrival. The director clearly had other things on his mind. Ever the politician, Real did his best to mask his distress. "So nice to see you, Dr. Campbell, Dr. Dorfman. So glad you could find the time to visit the cen—" He spotted Kemar standing in the exhibit. "Young man, what are you doing? This is a fragile display, not a schoolyard playground. Please get out of there."

"I told him to stay behind the railing," Dorfman added, throwing his young friend further under the bus. Dorfman smiled at the nervous lad as Kemar caught his foot on the railing, slipped backward, kicked sand into the hallway, and landed butt first onto the very same horseshoe crab he'd so carefully returned a moment before, obliterating the lifeless husk into a thousand pieces.

Everyone stood there in shock, mouths open wide, agape in disbelief. The three adults were speechless except for Dr. Dorfman, who casually observed, "You'd be sitting funny for a month if that crab's tail had been pointed up." As was often the case, Dorfman was the only one who laughed. Apologizing, Kemar crawled around the floor, sweeping sand back toward the display, wiping up the imprint of his body, and trying fruitlessly to piece the crab back together as if it were some type of jigsaw puzzle.

El Real gathered himself and said, "Please stop. You're making it worse."

Panicked, Kemar continued.

"Stop, please. I'll have someone take care of this. Just please, be more careful around the living birds." El Real took a deep breath and escorted his guests into the research facility. As she passed by, Dr. Campbell could be heard saying, "I'm sooo sorry. He's really a very good boy, quite bright, I assure you."

Dorfman, however, turned back to Kemar, pointed at the devastated crab, and smugly asked, "How many Is in buffoon?" chuckling as he walked away.

Just before he entered the center proper, Kemar glanced back at the display and thought he saw something strange. A white substance dripped from the edge of a large rock onto the sand below, followed by a tiny grey feather floating down beside it. Dead birds defecating and molting didn't make sense. The whole display was starting to creep Kemar out.

After a few minutes, El Real excused himself, passing his visitors off to an assistant for the rest of the tour. Later, when he noticed the group being led into the room that housed the petrel and the parrot, the very same room where Zomis had hatched his escape plot, the director rushed back in and took over the tour, ushering them out of there as quickly as possible. Not only would it be embarrassing for colleagues to know what had happened in there the night before, it might also be dangerous.

There was still one cage in the room that had a blanket draped over it even though it was midday. In other rooms, birds who were being rehabilitated or calmed were set up with coverings over their cages, so this wasn't out of the ordinary. But under that blanket, Azul wondered and waited. He wondered what had happened to those two strange birds who were involved with the daring escape. He wondered if he would escape. Would a rat and a pigeon appear to set him free? Azul waited in the roost without an opening, hoping for a chance, for a little luck, a little help. He was quiet, still, but not tranquil. Azul could never feel tranquil here.

When the tour was complete, the director sat down in his large office with the two professors and Kemar. There were framed photos of Vicente with a variety of birds—presumably endangered ones—at rehab centers all over the world along with snapshots of Vicente posing with many of the world's most recognizable politicians and celebrities. There were plaques, awards, medals, trophies, and diplomas. It was a mini museum—a shrine, almost—to his incredible career, the lifetime that Vicente had devoted to protecting the diversity of birds on the planet. It was inspiring. El Real was good at inspiring people.

He answered questions, poured delicious, rainforest-certified, fair-trade coffee, and discussed collaborative opportunities with his guests. Kemar, left somewhat out of the conversation, excused himself. As he turned a corner toward the men's room, he walked straight into a large, solid young man who seemed to be of college age and sported a long ponytail. He had the air of a brainy surfer.

"Whoa," the young man said, raising his arms to slow Kemar.

Kemar apologized, "Forgive me." He noticed the name tag that read, "John—Intern."

"Don't worry, it's just as much my bad. I'm rushing too. Some boob actually fell into the shore display and onto the horseshoe crab, crushed the crap out of it. I think we have another one in the basement, so I'm off to get it."

"Looks like we're both in a rush," Kemar agreed, not wishing to discuss the identity of the boob. He had a good feeling about the pleasant intern.

"Yeah, basement for me." John looked back around the corner and added, "Men's room for you, hence the rush?"

Kemar nodded and flashed a wry smile.

"You better get going," John urged, pointing to the bathroom. "I got enough to clean up already. It's been a crazy day."

The two laughed, and even though nature bellowed, Kemar asked, "Why so crazy around here? Just because I . . . ahh, just because someone *accidentally* fell into the display?"

John laughed again. "No, it's not crazy because *someone* fell into the exhibit. A bird got out last night."

"Did they find it?"

"Nope."

"What type of bird was it?"

John paused. "A petrel. Might've been one of a kind, too. Everyone's on pins and needles around here today. And then *someone* takes out the shorebird exhibit. Crazy day." John opened a door and yelled, "See ya!" as he disappeared down the stairwell in search of a replacement crab.

After the men's room, Kemar took a little detour himself. The boy returned to the shorebird display—the scene of his crime—and with no one around, carefully stepped over the rail, back beyond where he'd fallen. He dipped his finger into the white goo on the large rock. It was moist, not dry and chalky. He picked up the mysterious grey feather and studied it.

There was a rustle in the shadows near the pelicans. Just behind the large stones at the rear of the exhibit, three of the atrium panes were propped open just an inch or two. A slight breeze found its way through the window screens, which were still lowered, and rolled the sand at Kemar's feet. He tiptoed out of the display, lest he be caught on the wrong side of the rail a second time.

When he returned to the director's office, it was clear that he hadn't missed anything. The instant Kemar sat down, El Real raised his index finger and glanced at the phone on his desk. A tiny light flashed.

"Forgive me. I must answer this." He took the phone, turned away, mumbled something to the caller, and hung up abruptly.

Dr. Campbell picked up on the interruption and tried to make it easy for the gracious director, who was evidently too busy to be entertaining guests. There was work to be done.

"Thank you so much for sharing your time," she said. "We've kept you from your important work for much too long. I know I'm dizzy with thoughts regarding all the work you and I-BIRD are doing."

They all got to their feet and shook hands. The assistant escorted them to the lobby where Dr. Campbell, Dr. Dorfman, and Kemar made their way out of the building. As he left, Kemar noticed that a fresh horseshoe crab was added to the display. He made an effort not to fall on it.

The trio strode across the parking lot and approached Dorfman's white pickup truck. Just before he climbed into the cab, Kemar said, "Oh no, my glasses aren't in my pocket."

Technically, the glasses weren't Kemar's, nor did they really improve his sight. They were his father's, and he carried them everywhere. It was his connection, a way to hold on to his father who was taken from him too early by the Khmer Rouge.

Dr. Campbell knew all about the youngster's life in Cambodia. She asked, "When did you have them last? Are you sure you brought them here?"

"I bring them everywhere. I think maybe they might've fallen out of my pocket in the bathroom."

"Maybe you lost them when you did a cannonball into the shorebird display?" Dorfman suggested. "Go get them. We can wait."

Kemar leapt from the professor's truck and raced back to the research center, but when he got to the entrance, he dashed behind the building and crept along the brick exterior until he came to the small windows that ventilated the atrium. A black Mercedes was parked in front of them, leaving only a few inches between its front bumper and the glass wall. Kemar squeezed clumsily into the tight space, worried that he might slip onto the hood and set off the car alarm. He wanted to push the window frame open farther, but it wouldn't be possible unless he could first slide the exterior screen up. It, however, was latched from the inside.

The boy glanced over both shoulders. He seemed alone. He reached into his pocket, moved his father's glasses to one side, and removed the small pocket knife he also always carried. Kemar hated to do it, but he saw no other way. He made two small incisions in both lower corners of the screen's frame. He neatly pried the screen out, separating it from the frame, reached a finger inside, and slid the latches, enabling him to raise the screen. It squeaked as he pulled up. He pushed the screen corners back into place. Then, to make sure the screen and the window would stay open, he selected two sticks from underneath the car, and propped them beneath the frame. Sure, some bugs might enter the center, but Kemar hoped a special bird might exit.

He whispered into the crack, "This is the best I can do. Good luck."

Kemar liked El Real, but he didn't like birds in cages. He pulled the glasses from his pocket. His father wouldn't have wanted him to lie to his friends, but he would've wanted his son to help the petrel. He knew his father would have understood.

Kemar returned to the truck, smiling and waving the glasses for his friends to see. Everyone was relieved that he'd gone back to retrieve them, especially the petrel and the pigeon.

There was an opening.

Although it was done in whispers, by now, Zomis and Soaria knew each other fairly well. The two birds felt the fresh breeze calling them, no mesh standing in their way, keeping them in the stale room with the lifeless creatures. "Let's go right now," Zomis said.

Soaria shook her head, no.

"Are you kidding? You don't like ratholes, *and* you don't like openings?" Zomis pointed to the window. "Why do you always pause when opportunity pecks? Lupé was not like this. He didn't hesitate. We must go now!"

"Not in the light. In the dark. Petrels prefer the dark. I don't know what's out there."

"Really? Well, pigeons prefer *out there* rather than *in here*, whether it's daytime or nighttime. You really think daylight out there is more dangerous than any time in here?"

"Then you should go. I'll come soon, but not now."

Zomis looked at the window. "That stick—the twig that's holding it open—could fall out or snap at any time. You do get that?"

"The sun will be down soon enough."

Azul would've been thrilled to fly through the window—any window—day or night, but for him, it wasn't an option. Contained in the covered nest, he had a lot of time to think. The parrot reflected on his situation. He probably should've seen it as the end, as if he were the last—which he very well might've been—and there would be no others. This was where the Spix's macaw would end. But Azul didn't see it that way. For him, there was a fine line between endings and beginnings.

While a flock might end with one bird, it could also begin with one bird. Why couldn't he be that bird? Well, probably because he was sealed up in some kind of hard, silver web. But if he wasn't locked up, *then* why couldn't he be a bird that fathered a flock? Ah, but a single bird can't father a flock, he reasoned. It would always take at least two, including the mother, a role he was unequipped to play. Still, for some reason, as bleak as things seemed, something told him this wasn't the end. It would get better.

As the director of I-BIRD, Vicente El Real came into contact with many different people involved in a variety of aspects of bird culture. Not all these people or these involvements were directly related to conservation, even if some of them purported to be. In his travels as an advocate for avian species, El Real had met heads of state, world famous environmentalists, rock stars, movie stars, superstar athletes, and Nobel Prize winners, among others. He'd also met collectors, breeders, smugglers, and poachers. It came with the territory. In order to save species, you had to know not only those who helped, but those who hurt, as well.

The director first became involved with breeders and collectors when he needed captive birds to breed with each other in an effort to reintroduce offspring into the wild to bolster endangered populations. Many breeders and collectors were actually quite willing to help. After all, they, too, loved birds. Several of them also loved money, and it often wasn't easy to know which one they prized more, the birds or the money.

Some of these people leveraged under-the-table deals with El Real, their price for cooperation with breeding. To ensure their help, El Real might have to surreptitiously supply an egg or a chick from another species being rehabbed. In return, these people might be able to supply birds from private collections or access to those who owned some so that I-BIRD could create more diverse gene pools. Vicente rationalized that there was a greater good here. While the bird he removed an egg or hatchling from might recover a touch more slowly, getting access to these black-market birds might allow other species to avoid extinction. Looking at it through that lens, the deals made sense to the director. He saw it as a greater good that demanded a lesser impiety.

As is often the case with ethical grey areas, slopes become slippery. And when slopes become slippery, people tend to fall. I-BIRD was an expensive not-for-profit organization to run. There was no shortage of bills to pay, but shortages of donations were not uncommon. In those lean times, El Real might lose track of an egg or a chick, and a large donation would show up in its place. Geese were laying golden eggs. At times, the director would use the windfall to purchase tracts of vital habitat or to hire poachers to protect birds they might otherwise threaten. It had all begun quite innocently, as these things often do, but innocent was not how it ended up.

Eventually, El Real began to divert some of the illegal funds into his own accounts. In order to have access to the kind of people who can afford philanthropy on this level, Vicente concluded, he'd have to be able to move in similar circles—dine, vacation, shop, live in their world. It was necessary. He needed access. It would allow him to gather more support. But it also allowed him to get rich. El Real had become his own version of Faust. And now, as he hung up the phone, having said goodbye to Campbell, Dorfman, and the troublesome youngster, El Real was about to commit an act that surpassed a modest impiety. He was going sell the last wild Spix's macaw.

He bid the staff good night and sent them on their way. John, the intern, was the last one out the door. He asked the director if he'd consider writing him a letter of recommendation for graduate school. John was hoping to get a PhD in ornithology from Cornell University. Proud to play mentor, El Real assured the young man that not only would he write a letter on his behalf, but he'd make a few phone calls to friends on the faculty as well. Christmas had apparently come early for John.

Finally alone in the building, El Real made one last call. "I'm on my way," was all he said. Vicente took the cage that housed Azul. He left the blanket over it and walked to his parked car. The cage rattled, and the parrot squawked. "*Shhh,* you're going to have a wonderful home. No trees or open flight, but mates, friends, a family perhaps, and safety—opportunities you wouldn't get in Brazil." El Real spoke more to himself than to the macaw.

He was steps from his new Mercedes when he saw the woman approaching. What was she doing here now? She walked directly toward him. It was getting dark.

"We're not supposed to do this here," El Real whispered emphatically.

"That's why I want to," the untrusting woman replied calmly.

"I'm not happy with this."

"You will be." She smiled. Her teeth were a little too white. They flashed as she held out a small zipped portfolio. "It's all there. Is this the bird?"

"We're gonna do this now?" Vicente asked, clearly upset. "Here?"

"Right now, right here. It's harder to arrest or rip off someone who is doing something unexpected. Come on, this is as good a place as any." The woman handed the portfolio to Vicente. As the director reached down to pick up the macaw, another person stepped around the building. Alarmed, Vicente leapt in front of the cage and lowered the portfolio to his side.

"Hey. Glad you're still here, Dr. El Real. I'm such a boob. I left my notebook inside, and I have to have it for class tomorrow. Actually, I also need to study from it tonight. Can I borrow your key? It'll only take a minute. I know exactly where I left it." It was John the intern.

Vicente breathed a sigh of relief. For a moment, he wondered if this deal was worth all the stress. Then he felt the leather portfolio in his hand. There was $300,000 cash in the case. That's what the last wild Spix's macaw was worth to the woman who would receive it and to the man who was supposed to save it.

"Your notebook?" Vicente asked.

"I need it to study tonight," John said apologetically. "I'm sure you remember those all-nighters."

"Of course. Tried to avoid them myself, but I wasn't completely successful."

The woman looked away and said nothing.

"Oh, I don't know anyone more successful than you," John said, trying not to get his nose too brown in the process.

The director smiled, produced a spare key from his pocket, and tossed it to the young man. "Lock up. Take the key with you and put it in my mailbox tomorrow."

John nodded his head. "OK," he agreed, glancing at the leather portfolio in the director's hand. Vicente grew suspicious.

The woman began to back away. She had neither the bird nor the money.

"One other thing," John remembered.

"What now?" El Real replied. This was getting tiresome. He had a transaction to complete.

The faux college intern opened his jacket. A badge hung from a chain. "FBI. You're under arrest for trafficking endangered species." The agent produced a weapon. Several other agents appeared from around the building. Three cars and a van pulled into the parking lot.

The woman walked off quietly, trying not to be noticed. When John motioned for two of his fellow agents to arrest her, El Real did the only thing he could think of. He snatched the blanket off the cage and pulled out the long, thin rod that held it closed. One side of the cage swung open. In the soft dark of the early evening, the parrot, being a very intelligent bird, didn't hesitate to take flight. He left the cage, while El Real was about to enter one.

As the intern snapped the handcuffs around the wrists of his former boss, Vicente said smugly, "There goes your evidence."

"Oh, we have plenty of evidence," John said. A colleague deposited a stray blue feather and some droppings from the bottom of the cage into a ziplock bag. The former intern added, "Can I still get that letter of reference? I really would like to go to Cornell."

A moment later, a pigeon and a petrel also glided across the parking lot.

Zomis and Soaria landed on a limb shrouded by leaves and other branches. A bright moon rose and cast soft shadows through opaque clouds, but it was otherwise dark. The two were relieved to be outside at last. Squab landed next to her parent. "Well, you sure took your time," the robin said. "Is everyone OK?"

"We would have been here sooner," Zomis replied, "but petrels prefer to fly at night." The pigeon cast a sour look toward its fellow escapee.

"No one said you had to wait for me."

"So, that's how your flock says thank you?"

"No one said you had to rescue me."

"Hey," Squab interrupted, "I thought you and Lupé were birds of a feather."

"We are."

"You wouldn't know it to listen to you two. And I thought Lupé was a male?"

"This isn't Lupé," the pigeon pointed out.

Squab looked even more perplexed than she normally did. "What?"

"I'm a petrel—a Gwatta petrel, in fact—but I'm not your legendary Lupé."

"But I just told a monarch that you were rescuing Lupé. Once you tell those butterflies to send a message, it's sent. For all we know, Lupé's about to get a message that we're rescuing him. And you think *I'm* confused?"

"Didn't turn out quite the way you expected, did it?" Soaria pointed out sarcastically. "If you two don't mind, I'll be on my way. Thanks for everything."

"On your way?" Zomis asked. "After all I just risked for you? All the effort we just put in, and all you have to say is, 'I'm on my way'? Really? What kind of bird are you?"

"Exactly. What kind of bird am I? *You* don't know because you've only seen one before. *I* don't know because I don't see too many myself."

Zomis countered, "I know a bird like you, but he's not like you at all, at least as far as his character goes."

"Lemme guess—Lupé. You're right. I'm not like him."

"No, you're not. You're, like, the anti-Lupé."

"That's exactly what I am. And, as I was saying, goodbye."

"Whoa, wait a flap!" Squab yelled as a silent butterfly flitted onto the branch. He nestled next to the robin who bore the same black and orange that the monarch carried so regally. The two stared at each other for a moment. Squab whispered, "There's a petrel—a Gwatta—who will be on the way soon. The butterflies are directing him to the Barrens. He'll meet us there. That's what I'm getting from this one."

"Actually, *you* will meet him there," Soaria said. "Be sure to say hello to Lupé for me." She launched herself off the branch, but she didn't go anywhere. The petrel spread her wings and threw herself forward, but again, she didn't go anywhere. Soaria turned to Zomis and Squab, "What are you two doing? What's the deal?"

Both birds shrugged, amused.

The petrel tried a third time to propel herself off the limb . . . and failed.

The little butterfly popped into the air and floated around the petrel. It was so easy for the insect to take wing. She seemed to smile at the bird.

Squab nodded. The robin looked at the petrel and said, "OK, give this a try. Instead of launching yourself toward the ocean, try south by southwest."

The petrel stared blankly, clearly frustrated with the robin.

"Indulge my child," Zomis appealed.

Soaria repositioned herself and halfheartedly flapped her wings. She rose softly and climbed higher. She stroked the breeze impressively and headed south by southwest but abruptly banked and tried to come about to east by southeast. Her body spun in that direction for an instant and continued to spin until it went full circle back to south by southwest. She landed on another branch, her webbed feet spread wide.

"Looks like the choice is not mine," the petrel concluded. She turned to the other birds and asked, "How are you doing this?"

Squab shook her head. "It's not me."

Zomis added, "When the monarchs say you'll be waiting in the Barrens, you *will* be waiting in the Barrens. It's a *flight* accompli. Very powerful little creatures, the butterflies."

The three headed off for the Barrens. Not too far behind, the single monarch followed at its own pace. The birds generally referred to their destination as the Barrens because it was a large tract of forest that was comparatively unpopulated by the man-flock, a vast forest of scrubby pines in sandy soil. Large sections also supported a variety of oaks, elm, mountain laurel, and a staggering array of other vegetation. Although it was called the Barrens, to the birds, the insects, and countless others—and, to be fair, even a few of the man-flock—it was really an oasis.

Azul was also on the wing, and he was going to get as far away from his captors as possible. He checked the stars. He felt the magnetic field of the planet. The macaw was far from home, but he was on his way. The parrot plotted his course while he soared through the night sky. He decided to follow the coast south, but he was concerned, because he was certainly not a seabird. He also knew that the man-flock often migrated to the shore in massive numbers. It would be difficult to avoid them. *Such a strange land,* he thought. *This is no place for a parrot.*

The macaw veered inland to follow a large river where he thought he might be better suited to survive. He kept looking for rivers that flowed south by southeast, as he guessed he could follow rivers and streams to the end of the land. Then he'd have to be prepared to cross open ocean—a dangerous prospect for the parrot—but Azul would peel that nut when he got to it. His focus now was to fly south and somehow get stronger and better nourished in the process. This was a difficult equation. It was almost impossible for him to store energy when he was constantly using it, especially during an unplanned migration that he was unprepared for.

Azul was also concerned about danger. At home in the Caatinga, he knew how to avoid the man-flock—at least he thought he did—and he had tricks, strategies to avoid other predators. He assumed that the same perils were present in this land, but was there anything else that could threaten him? Were there predators he'd never encountered? There had to be.

It was one of those moments when you peck yourself for even thinking about danger because just when you do, you know something bad will happen. Azul was being tracked. He could feel it in his feathers right down to their quills. It was night, not the best time for him. The evening was calm, clear, cool. And although it was dark, evenings in this place were brighter than in the Caatinga.

Yet Azul could feel faint shadows pass over him, thrown from the moon and the stars. Shadows in the night. There were several. Azul glided. He could hear feathers rustling in flight. There were birds on either side of him, another above, perhaps even another below. If these were owls, it would be over quickly. But if they were owls, he'd never have heard them. Their feathers would be silent.

No, not owls. Were they hawks? Two maybe, but not at night, not four or five individuals. Neither the hawks nor the owls would hunt like this, at least not the ones he'd known. Who would track him like this? Crows? They might try to drive him out of their territory, but not track him. They wouldn't stay on him and stalk him.

This was something he'd never encountered. They seemed smaller—not small, but smaller than him. This could be good *and* bad. They'd likely be more agile, quicker. But Azul would probably wield more powerful blows and bites. However, by increasing the number of assailants to five or six, both agility and power would rise for the shadows that surrounded him. Were others coming?

There was one quality that Azul possessed that few other birds—indeed, few other creatures—could match: intelligence. He could likely out-think his enemy. There weren't many birds with brains like parrots, so he put his macaw mind to work.

Azul quickly came to the conclusion that it would be almost impossible to escape the flanking flock. To turn and fight would also not be in his best interest. He decided that he needed to isolate one of the birds—engage it and get a sense of what he was faced with and maybe what these birds wanted from him.

The macaw was struck by the lights—not the ones in the sky, but the ones on the ground, the dead lights of the man-flock. The transition from the intense light to the relative pitch of night could temporarily blind someone if it happened too quickly. He could use this, he thought. The parrot spotted a very large, flat field where man-flock were bringing in their rolling nests and taking them out again, one after another. Lights from the many nests were popping on and off while other massive lights perched atop high, false trees, bathing the field in illumination. If he could hide himself behind one of the brightest, tallest lights and disappear, the birds that pursued him might get confused and turn away.

If they continued to search for him, he might be able to isolate one. Bird-to-bird, Azul believed he could probably handle any one of them. In the process, he might be able to discern what he was up against, what they wanted. With a little luck, he might also send them a message regarding what *they* were up against by making an example of one of their own.

The parrot climbed high in the sky. Then he tucked his wings to his sides and plummeted into the bright field below. His feathers fell flat against his face as he approached a speed he'd never reached before. The man-flock, their rolling nests, and the hard ground below made him nervous, but it had to be done. Azul fell even faster. He opened a wing, spread a tail feather, leaned one way, then the other, flying randomly, unpredictably. He dove dangerously close to a massive rolling nest, swung around behind it, and followed it for a flap.

Were the others keeping up? He couldn't tell. To turn and look would impede his momentum. He continued through the dark, just under a long bright beam and then did the procedure again and again, finally rising quickly and settling atop one of the tallest, limbless, leafless, false trees. The parrot crouched behind the lifeless ray of light that buzzed like a swarm of locusts. The perch was warm, hard. Azul scanned the sky and the ground below.

He saw it. At first, he couldn't believe it. He had to squint, refocus, and look again. It was a nest directly above his head. It was massive. The nest hugged the silver tree next to the single branch that had six gigantic buds growing out of it. The enormous blossoms were like flowers, each with a single star inside. They hummed and emitted the star's light. Azul watched, stunned.

The roost above resembled a parrot nest—certainly not anything his flock would use, but he'd seen something like this before.

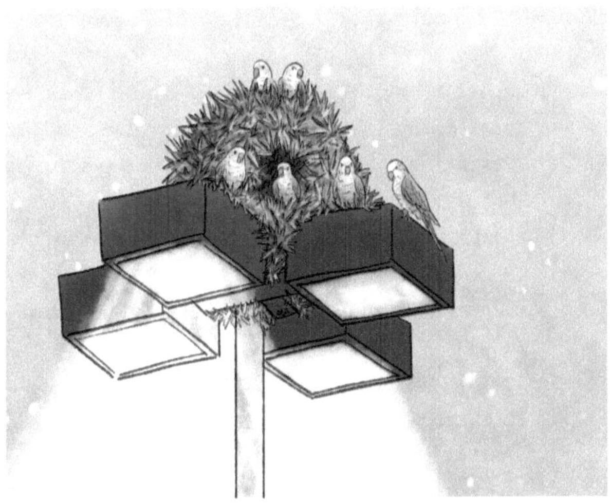

This one was large enough to house a dozen parrots his size quite comfortably. But that was impossible, since there were no parrots this far north of the equator. What species of bird constructed nests like these other than parrots?

"You're blue," he heard. The voice came from behind the beam of light, a feather from where Azul perched.

Out from the shadow stepped a smaller green parrot. Then another emerged, followed by several more. They were all around him. Two more peered out from the mass of twigs and sticks above him.

Azul studied the birds. They didn't appear threatening. They were smaller than him, about the size of a bulked-up pigeon. Predominately green, the individuals sported tufts of grey on their foreheads, cheeks, and throats. The grey extended down to the chest, where it was tipped with white. But the feathers that Azul found most attractive on these birds were those that formed a hint of blue dusting their tail and flight feathers. They reminded him of Nipiklee. These, however, were a different flock.

He would've enjoyed showing them to Nipiklee. No red on any of them, yet they were as striking as any parrot you could conceive.

"Wattah yoo lookin' aht?" one of them asked in a strange accent.

Azul couldn't determine whether the sound was pleasing, friendly, or threatening.

The smaller parrot asked again, "Yeah, yoo. Big Blue. Wattah yoo lookin' aht? Yoo neva seen ah parruht befaw?"

A second parrot landed next to Azul and said, "Come on, let's get yoo outta hea. It'll be bettuh if yuh not seen." The bird nodded toward the bulbous nest. One after another—Azul included—they crawled inside.

The blue parrot was amazed at the design of the nest. Inside, there was a collection of compartments that families roosted in. The parrots were quite proud of their home, evident by the grand tour they gave their guest. And while it was a little cramped for a bird the size of Azul, the macaw marveled at the skill, the crafts-*bird*ship involved with the construction. His hosts explained that they'd established colonies like this all over the area, which had spread sporadically down much of the coast. They called the nest a brownwood.

"So, there *are* parrots this far above the equator?" Azul asked in amazement.

"Well, dare were, a little sout of here, den dare weren't, an now dare is again," one of the birds explained.

Azul entered a larger, open chamber where several parrots waited for him. One of them directed him to perch.

Azul said, "I can't believe all this. I have so many questions. How did you get here? What type of parrots are you? Why were you chasing me? When—"

The green perched across from Azul raised a wing, interrupting the flood of questions. "First we eat. Den we tawk." He nodded, and another parrot dragged in a large piece of . . . pizza?

Without thinking, Azul muttered, "Man-flock food?"

The green tilted his head and said plainly, "Food."

Another parrot—an older female—waddled up into Azul's beak and challenged, "Whut? Yoo have some problem wid our food? Yoo don ligke it? It's nod good-anuff fuh yoo?"

Even before the green grandma pointed it out, the blue had realized that he hadn't received their hospitality with grace. Not only was that rude, it could be dangerous. The macaw quickly, sincerely apologized and asked if the offer to dine was still available. The grandmother green stepped back suspiciously and watched him eat.

After several bites, Azul looked up and said, "This . . . this . . ."

"Da man-flock call id *piizzzaahh*," a youngster said slowly with almost perfect diction.

Azul nodded politely. "Well, it's tasty. It's not like anything I've ever eaten before. Very good."

"Of cawse id is," the grandmother announced. "I gatha dis myself. I add berries an buds as toppins. Dulicious? Am I rihdt?"

Azul nodded, choosing not to interrupt his chewing, which Grandma noticed with satisfaction.

"Don *eggs*pect odda pizza to taste dis good. Nawnee's is da best."

"Nawnee?" Azul repeated.

"Everyone calls me Nawnee. You do da same." Then, pointing to the food, she asked, "Delicious? Am I righd?"

"No need to convince me. As a matter of fact..." Azul paused, determined to make up for his initial faux pas. "I hate to ask, but if it's not too much trouble . . . really, this is wonderful . . . could I have . . . a little more?"

"Cud I hava liddle more? He wans more," the grandmother announced as she puffed with pride. She turned to the others, who sat somewhat nervously, reached out her wing, and laid it on the macaw's flank. "Of cawse yoo can!" Nawnee smiled broadly, and the others followed suit. "Yaw hungry, an yoo know good food, of cawse yoo can have more. As mugch as yoo ligke!" The old female turned to the flock and proclaimed, "Looga him. A parrot his size must hava abbatite ligka dog." Now that Nawnee was happy and no one was offended, it was safe for everyone to laugh and join in the meal.

Azul had done the right thing. By asking for more, he'd honored the grandmother and his hosts. Suddenly, he was accepted. He was a parrot, just like them.

In the course of dining, the parrots continually brought in an incredible variety of food—much of it scavenged from the man-flock—then perfected with a twist of their own. While some of the fare didn't really appeal to the macaw's palette, he was fond of the array of nuts his hosts were able to provide. There were some nice-tasting buds and berries as well. Azul did his best to devour the buffet, and it didn't take too much effort.

The parrots spoke as they ate. The blue learned that his green friends weren't originally from this place. They'd arrived many summers before. The grandmother and one or two others were old enough to remember their home, which, ironically, wasn't far from where Azul was hatched. They referred to their flock as the Kwakes and explained to the macaw that their original members were taken from their natural home by the man-flock, who seemed to have a desire to possess parrots as well as other creatures, a fact Azul knew all too well.

The Kwakes, whom the man-flock might call monk or Quaker parrots, couldn't understand this need. They saw it in no other creature. To catch something in a predator-prey relationship or as a way to protect the flock or family made sense, but to catch another creature merely to hold on to it was beyond their understanding. In their minds, there was no discernible benefit for either creature. Regardless, the Kwakes were taken from their ancestral home and transported en masse to where they now lived.

It all began when an enormous nest—several of them, actually—constructed by the man-flock as a temporary prison somehow broke open, and a small flock managed to escape. Most of the poached birds weren't in any shape to fly halfway around the globe to go home. They reasoned that even if they did make it back, the man-flock might just take them all over again anyway. While the elders considered the group's options, one event changed everything.

A young green named Merc ate pizza. He brought some back to his roost. Once the others tried it, there was no going back—literally, no going back to their home. They became the parrots who ate pizza. Over time, they were certainly able to forage for more traditional sustenance—berries and fruit found in the limited shrubs and trees, buds and blooms in season. And strangely, there were those from the man-flock who actually left food out for the parrots. The Kwakes couldn't wrap their wings around why one group of humans seemed dedicated to imprisoning them while another group seemed to almost love them, putting out nuts and fruit for them. Perhaps this was just another way to keep them captive, Azul thought skeptically to himself. Through all this, though, the Kwakes couldn't shake their taste for pizza.

Over time, every now and then, another parrot would join the flock. Many were hatched, but others just meandered in, not unlike Azul. These parrots usually either escaped from the man-flock or were sometimes actually released, often as a *reward* for bad behavior. Some would fly on. Some wouldn't survive the winter. Others stayed. The parrots' presence grew, and it was still growing. There were many, many large nests housing flocks and families in this area, they maintained.

The macaw relaxed with the Kwakes. They'd eaten quite a bit, talking the entire time.

"We neva hada sky parrut stay hea before," one of them said.

Another added, "I don tink any of us ave agtually seen one-a yoo before."

"Not surprising," Azul agreed. "A bit disappointing, but not surprising."

"Not fuh nuttin, bud yoo know ya can't stay here," a middle-aged parrot said.

Taken aback, Azul replied, "I'm not sure I want to, but why do you say that?"

"Once dey see ya, dey'll come for ya." It was the grandmother. Nawnee was more than the flock's culinary maestro, she was their leader.

The others nodded solemnly. One spoke up, "Dey come fuh us now. Da man-flogck dustroy our nezts and try ta move us away."

"Some of em do," a youngster said.

"Yes, some of em, son. Some of em . . ."

The matriarch continued, "Dey bring us here, bud dey have no use for us, no appreciation for whad we are unless we'a imprisoned in dare nests. Den it's OK ta be here."

"Bud we are here, and we're stayin'," a parrot cawed out.

"Fuggetabowdit, we discussed dis many times," Nawnee reminded them. "Da point is, nod only are our homes dustroyet, some even come ta recapture us. Can ya believe dat?"

"So, for that reason, I'm not welcome to stay?" Azul asked.

"No, da Kwakes will always welcome yoo," an older male said.

"Bud ya must undastan," grandma warned him, "yoo, who has been tagen yaself, yoo who has seen so many tagen, yoo who has *egg*scaped . . . once da man-flogck sees a sky parrut among us, dey will come fa yoo. One of dem will havta have ya. Anyting diffrent, dey must possess. Nod-for-nuttin, but yoo, my friend, yoo are diffrent wid a capidol *diff*."

Azul understood.

"Ta us, yoo are family. Ta dem, your'a prize."

"Bud even if ya leave—an ya should—we can still help ya," the young male added.

"How can you do that?" the macaw inquired.

"We know tings. We know birds. Our flogk flies well beyon here. We have friends, lotsa dem. Dey will help. Maybe dey owe us a favah."

The next morning, Azul took one last look at that exotic pizza. The more he ate it, the more he seemed to like it. It was addictive. He would miss it. He knew, no matter where he flew, he'd never see pizza like that again.

"Kinda grows on ya, doesn id?" the grandmother cooed.

"It's even better today than it was last night."

"Ahhh, dat's duh ting. Good pizza always tasdtes betta duh negxt day." Nawnee winked at Azul. "Now yoo know."

Gonzo had eaten his fill. Pretty much every bird in the forest knew the ivory-bill had arrived. It was ironic that a bird who stripped bark from trees, a creature so large, so loud, and so conspicuous, could still be so invisible, especially to the man-flock.

The large woodpecker was happy with his decision to fly north. At the moment, it looked like food was fairly abundant, roosting holes were plentiful, and the locals seemed cordial. There were other issues that Gonzo probably needed to think about, but he didn't want to. Adventure could be a wonderful way to forget, to escape. Adventure had a quality that made the ivory-bill feel more alive. When everything was new and fresh, life became unpredict-able. All the senses were occupied in the moment, and he was forced to look forward. There was no time to look back.

It was time, however, to get the lay of the land. Gonzo woke in the hollowed-out roost of a freshly dead pine, compliments of a recent lightning strike. It was still a little sticky, a little sappy, but for a night or two, it would do. The gooey sap also had a way of trapping pesky mites that liked to slip under feathers, so while a couple of his plumes might wind up sticking together, at least the woodpecker wouldn't be itchy.

Gonzo pecked at the wood around the entrance. It was a trick he'd learned long ago from his parents. He'd lightly open the wood around the entrance, allowing sap to flow, which, for some strange reason, seemed to prevent snakes from crawling into the hole. It was a good way to protect eggs, young, and himself. The ivory-bill liked to use the techniques that his parents taught him. It made it seem like they were nearby.

Gonzo flew to a broad oak and clung to its side, shielded by a thick branch. He shuffled around the tree and surveyed the woods. Several small streams fed half a dozen large ponds that drained into each other, two of them created by beavers. A little farther away, the whole wet tangle flowed into a small river. It wasn't actually a swamp, but it was wet enough for Gonzo. The river continued until it reached the ocean, which wasn't very far away. The sea didn't really interest the ivory-bill. After all, he was a woodpecker, not a sandpecker.

There were two things that prevented Gonzo from actually *liking* this habitat. First, the man-flock was still a little too close for his taste. And just beyond the woods, the man-flock became much more than a flock. There were so many of them, it was more like a plague or an infestation. Secondly, while these northern woods were wet, it wasn't a proper southern swamp. That meant no gators, which could be good, but it was also bad, since the cantankerous reptiles served as a useful man-flock repellant.

The swamp, with its poison ivy, bugs, gators, snakes, and leeches, often ensured that other creatures could enjoy the privacy they needed. These woods, although complete with bugs, ivy, ticks, snakes, and other deterrents, weren't quite as imposing as the swamp. But this was part of the adventure. And any real adventure entails risks. Gonzo smiled to himself. He'd just shuffled a step further out on a thin, bouncy bough of life. It felt good.

There were woodpeckers in these woods. He could hear them, see them. Of course, none seemed to be ivory-billed, but the woods clearly contained downy, hairy, sapsucker, red-bellied, and a few pileated. Gonzo enjoyed watching and listening to them. It made him think that if these birds, so similar to himself, could succeed, then maybe there was hope for him.

He listened to the high-pitched *wuk, wuk, wuk, wukakakakuk, wuk, wuk, wuk, wukakakakuk* as it rose and fell in pitch and volume, a manic laugh of a call, the signature of the pileated. The call was answered by another. A pair was marking their territory. Were they marking it for him? Their presence, their pairing was a good sign for the ivory-bill, since they were one of the closest living relatives to Gonzo's flock. A flap or two smaller, an extra white stripe under their beaks and across their necks, no white on their backs or wings, and, of course, a beak one-third the size of the ivory-bill's, yet they were essentially cousins.

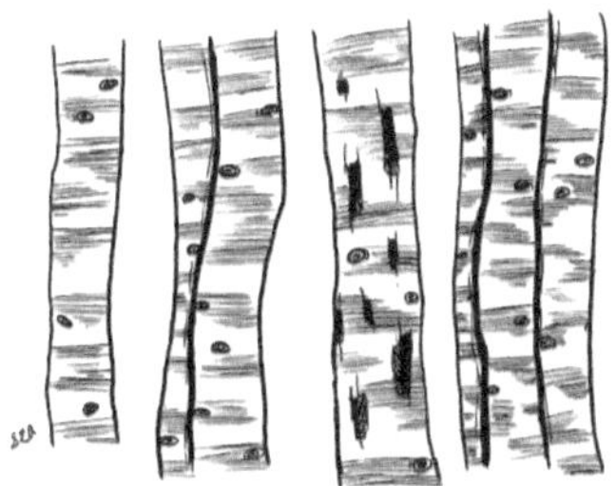

Looking across the woods, Gonzo spied a cluster of thick, white birch. The largest of them was pocked with intrusive rectangular holes that a pileated had chiseled in search of carpenter ants. Strips of bark were peeled off to expose the meal—not exactly Gonzo's favorite, but if he was hungry enough, he'd happily eat ants.

They were close. The pair was drumming on a tree. They were either feeding or they were reminding someone that this was their corner of the forest. Then Gonzo heard that unmistakable hum.

Trice appeared.

"Hey, Zo. Gotsomethingyoumightbeinterestedin."

"What's that?"

"Followme." And Trice was on his way.

He took it easy so the woodpecker could keep up. Trice was drawn to the large woodpecker, but he wasn't completely sure why. He wondered if it might be because of the large red crest Gonzo displayed. Red was the ruby-throat's favorite color. It signaled flowers with tubular blooms that supplied nectar, and Gonzo's red-pointed noggin made Trice think of those delectable flowers.

A few moments later, the hummingbird hovered next to a massive dead oak. Gonzo landed on one of the bare branches and smiled. The woodpecker was also enamored with the hummingbird's plumage. It was a bit of an illusion. While Trice seemed iridescent, like thin bolts of lightning skipping through wild flowers, his feathers actually had no real pigment at all. What made the plumage explode was the way the light refracted off of it. The hummingbird's feathers would appear dull at one angle and then ignite at another, flushed with color when kissed by sunlight. It was impulsive, magnificent, bold, and it made Gonzo smile.

"Isthisamealorwhat?" Trice asked.

"Looks good," Gonzo agreed. He popped onto the tree and took hold. The ivory-bill eyed the dry bark like a bobcat eyes its prey. He cocked his head, angled his beak, and tore into the trunk.

Trice grinned. "Ilovewatchingthis."

Debris rained on the forest floor. The hammering could be heard for miles. After a moment, Gonzo paused and turned to Trice. His ivory chisel was covered with black ants. He sucked a few in and wiped the rest from his beak.

"What?" Trice queried.

"Ants."

"Yeah,amillionofthem."

"Really appreciate this, but not exactly my favorite."

"Otherwoodpeckerslovethem."

"I'm not other woodpeckers," Gonzo said, half to himself. He looked back at his diminutive pal and inquired, "What other woodpeckers?"

"Well,themforexample," the hummingbird pointed to a pair of pileateds watching from an adjacent ash. "Theyloveants."

The two pileateds glided onto the branch Gonzo had originally landed on. They all just kind of stared at each other for a moment until one of the pileateds said, "So, you found our tree."

"Your tree? Oh, sorry, I—"

"It'snottheirtree," Trice interrupted. "Youmightaswellsay-it'stheants'tree."

"Well, we didn't mean that we own it," the other bird ex-plained. "What we meant is that we've been feeding here for a few days. If you look on the other side of the trunk, you'll see our holes. But, of course, there's plenty for everyone."

"Maybe not when *he's* done," the other pileated joked.

"Oh, I don't eat that much," Gonzo said with a defensive laugh.

"Well, you sure make a mess."

"Trice eats more than any of us," the ivory-bill continued. "Not in actual quantity, but compared to his body weight, Trice blows us away. Isn't that right?"

The hummingbird smiled broadly and wiped his brownish wingtip across his green forehead. "Really,Ihatetobrag," he said, "butZo'sright. Ifyouconsidernectarandinsects,Ieathalfmybody-weighteveryday."

"Yes, yes, very impressive, but I've seen him eat half his body weight in one meal," the female said, pointing to her mate.

The male pileated shrugged. "It may not have stayed with me long, but I ate it."

"Speaking of nectar," the female continued, "why don't we welcome . . . is it Zo?"

The ivory-bill nodded. "Trice calls me Zo, but my name's Gon-zo."

"Well, let's welcome Gonzo, then . . . with a celebratory splash?"

"What are you proposing?" her mate asked.

"I'm thinking a little fly-by to the berry patch."

"Yes, a soaring idea," the male agreed. He turned to the ivory-bill. "Are you up for a little adventure, big bird?"

Gonzo grinned. "That's why I'm here."

"Yathinkweshould?" Trice wondered.

"Sure, a little drink, a little juice, why not?" the female coaxed.

Off they flew, two pileateds leading the way, an ivory-bill and a hummingbird in tow.

They arrived at a large pond ringed with the sandy, acidic soil that pines seemed to do so well in. There were turtles, frogs, dragonflies. Bass jumped, beavers chewed, and a kingfisher fed. It was a nice spot. The pileated pair glanced back to make sure the other two were still there. Irises and tiger lilies were in bloom, so Trice buried himself in their petals, declaring them "*Iris*istable!"

The three woodpeckers landed on a toppled tree.

"Nice spot, but we came all this way to drink from a pond?" Gonzo questioned.

"Not exactly." One of the pileateds pointed to a bush across the way. "Try one of those." He nodded to the dark-blue, almost purple fruit. Little round berries from green bushes that ringed the pond were scattered among the dry, fallen pine needles that covered the ground. They were the size of large pebbles and looked even less appetizing.

The ivory-bill was perplexed. "Rotten fruit and ants? There's got to be better food around here. I know there is."

"Indulge us," the female said while the male tossed a plump berry at Gonzo's feet. "Go ahead, trust us. It's good."

The ivory-bill paused. He looked for Trice for reassurance, but the hummingbird had given way to his own gluttony and was out of sight. In the interest of adventure, Gonzo picked up the overripe berry, squeezed it gently until a little juice dripped into his mouth, and then swallowed it. He hopped off the log and into the pine needles, where he took another, then another, and another. They didn't exactly taste good, but they warmed his belly and his throat. There was also a gentle fizz that the ivory-bill found enchanting.

The two pileateds beamed. "Fizzberries," they said in unison.

After he ate a dozen or so, Gonzo began to laugh. He didn't know why, but he began to chuckle. It all seemed so funny. The pileateds laughed as well, although it was unclear whether they laughed with him or at him. Either way, it was all quite amusing as they became berry-merry.

The ivory-bill handed a bursting, overripe berry to one of the other woodpeckers and said, "Put that in your peak and boke it."

The pileateds erupted in laughter. "Peak and boke it! Ha!"

"He means beak and poke it. That's one fizzed woodpecker!"

"He doesn't know what he means," the other laughed.

Gonzo sucked down some more berries. He was having fun—actually having fun. He smiled, took a step forward, and fell flat on his face. A large white mushroom exploded under the weight of his head. The ivory-bill giggled. Without bothering to rise to his feet—not that he could if he tried—Gonzo stretched out his neck and grasped a lone berry. He swallowed the fermented orb, rolled onto his back—a bit dizzy—and watched the clouds blow across the sky. The woodpecker was fizzed, no doubt about it.

The two pileateds were standing at his sides. Gonzo's ivory beak was covered with a fruity, purplish-blue residue. As tasty as the fizzberries were, his newfound friends didn't seem to be enjoying nearly as many. Gonzo opened his wings to make it easier for the pair to help him up. He tried to raise himself.

Then, suddenly, he was pinned to the ground, pushed back onto the pointy pine needles. One of the woodpeckers opened its beak and grasped his throat. The other climbed on top of his chest and reared back, preparing to drive its spike-like mandible into the ivory-bill's heart.

Is this really happening? Are the berries playing tricks on me? Gonzo wondered for an instant. Then the beak came crashing down. Gonzo slouched to one side, and the female screeched, "Hold him!"

"He's fizzed," her mate replied as he tightened his grip on the bird's neck. "His neck is thick, and I'm having trouble seeing him."

Gonzo was gagging, choking.

"You can't see him? He's huge. How many berries did you eat?"

"Hardly any. I can see everything else, I just can't see him clearly."

"Yes, he seems fuzzy, out of focus."

"I know!"

"Just try to hold him!" The female jumped into the air, closed her beak tightly, and plummeted with her prow again pointed at the ivory-bill's heart. Gonzo tried to free himself, but he was blacking out.

The male woodpecker released his grip on the ivory-bill's throat to catch his own breath, and Gonzo batted the female attacker with his massive wing. It was enough to deflect her second assault. But where had the male pileated gone?

Trice had arrived. What he lacked in size, he made up for in heart—literally. Proportionately speaking, the hummingbird's heart is larger than any other warm-blooded species on the planet. Trice was all over the male pileated in a blink, so Gonzo prepared to square off against the female. When he stood, however, he was enveloped by several other pileateds. They seemed to come from every direction, pecking and tearing at him. The female joined them.

Why are these birds—these woodpeckers—trying to kill me? Gonzo couldn't help thinking. He meant them no harm. He was one bird in the forest. One bird!

It became quiet. The pileateds stopped attacking. They all froze for a moment—Trice too. The woodpeckers flew off urgently. The squirrels climbed into their nests quickly. The frogs slipped underwater. The chipmunks raced into their holes. It was as if suddenly, out of nowhere, a terrible tempest was upon them. The woods became silent except for one sound. *Hoo-hoo-to-hoo, hoo-hoo-to-hooooo . . . hoo-hoo-to-hoo, hoo-hoo-to-hooooo.* Rabbits took cover. Turtles trembled.

Trice appeared next to Gonzo. "Youknowwhatthatmeans? Canyoufly? Weshouldprobablygetoutofhere."

"I can fly."

"Good. Let'sget—oh,turds. We'resittingducks."

"What?"

"Don'tmove. He'srighthere."

The terrified woodpecker asked, "Wh-wh-who? Who?"

"*Eggsactly,*" Trice replied.

The owl had landed a belly feather from Gonzo. Although he was thick and large, he'd evolved to fly silently and did it quite skillfully. Behaving more like an ostrich than a woodpecker, Gonzo was afraid to turn around. Trice was in a better situation. He was so small, so quick, he wasn't worth the owl's attention. But the ivory-bill was another story. A skilled predator wouldn't allow the opportunity of an injured meal—easy peckings—to pass unnoticed.

The owl lowered his head. He turned to the two trembling birds and asked, "Was not that nobly done? Aye, and wisely too."

"ABardowl," Trice whispered.

Shaking his head in disgust, the owl continued, "One draught above heat makes him a fool, the second mads him, and a third drowns him . . . That which hath made them drunk hath made me bold." The barred slowly swiveled his head almost 270 degrees until his concave facial feathers locked on to the sound of the flying pileateds and funneled the rumble to his ears, which were located at two different heights on the sides of his face. If the sound reached the lower ear first, the owl instantly knew it came from below, but if it graced the upper ear first, the Barred would know the prey—or the threat—came from above.

Gonzo was petrified. First the berries, then the brawl, and now the Bard—it just kept getting stranger and more dangerous from one moment to the next.

"That we would do, we should do when we would," the owl said. "Cowards die many times before their deaths."

"Yes, yes, exactly, absolutely," Gonzo agreed. He turned to Trice and quietly mumbled, "How do you answer something like that? I have no idea what he's saying. I don't want to say the wrong thing. Do you know what a barred owl is capable of?"

"Noneedtowhisper,pal," Trice said. "Hecanhearyourheartbeat. Actually,rightnow,Icantoo. Don'tworry,ifhewantedyoudead,you'dbeinpiecesrightnow."

"Comforting."

"WelcometothePines."

"Rest, rest, perturbed spirit," the great owl soothed. "Be not afraid of shadows." He turned to Trice and said, "The poor wren, the most diminutive of birds, will fight, her young ones in her nest, against the owl."

"Actually," Gonzo nervously interrupted, "this is a *male hummingbird*, not a mother wren, and I'm sure I speak for my male hummingbird friend here when I say, none of us would *ever* fight against *any* owl."

"Letitgo," Trice advised. "L e t . . .i t . . . g o o o." It was the slowest he'd ever spoken, but Trice really wanted to be understood.

"Of course, right . . ." Gonzo stammered. "Ah . . . female wren . . . precisely." Gonzo grinned uncomfortably at the hummingbird.

"Boldness, be my friend," the owl enthused. "So shaken are we, so wan with care?" The Bard smiled knowingly. "Extreme fear can neither fight nor fly."

"Yes, I am nervous to say the least," Gonzo groveled.

"Presume not that I am the thing I was . . . The case is altered."

"So, you're saying that I shouldn't fear you?"

The owl looked coldly into Gonzo's eyes and said, "He's mad that trusts the tameness of a wolf." But his expression softened as he continued. "I have suffered with those that I saw suffer."

"You mean us?" the woodpecker suggested. "You suffered with us?"

"So,you'vehadproblemswiththosewhomwe'vehadproblems with?" Trice added. "Thepileateds?"

The owl cocked its head toward the hummingbird and nodded.

"Theenemyofmyenemyismyfriend?" the ruby-throat suggested.

The owl nodded again. "Peace here—grace and good company . . . Fear me not . . . I am alone myself."

"As am I," Gonzo quipped.

"A-hem," the hummingbird grunted. "Alone?I'mnothere?"

"Well, Trice is my friend—my very good friend—but other than him, I'm about as alone as a bird can get."

"What is your substance?" the Bard inquired. "Whereof are you made?"

"I have come here from the South, the swamps. I needed to see something else, and I wound up here in your pines. And until a little while ago, I was really quite taken with these woods."

"Tis new to thee."

"Forgiveme,barredowl,butit'splaintoseewhywehavecometo dislikethepileateds."

"Yes, but why would *you* scare them away?" Gonzo continued. "Why would you help us?"

The owl looked off into the woods where the pileateds disappeared. He turned his head 180 degrees, back to Trice and Gonzo, and said simply, "Green-eyed jealousy."

The two friends glanced at each other but didn't press the owl, who warned, "Beware . . . of jealousy! It is the green-eyed monster, which doth mock the meat it feeds on." The Bard rotated his head back to the woods. "The croaking raven doth bellow for revenge . . . Seek to know no more."

The owl nodded to the sky, inviting his two new friends. "To fly, to swim, to dive into the fire, to ride on the curled clouds," he said as he stretched his thick, broad wings and pumped his bulk into the mist. The sheer power of the bird in contrast with the silence of its flight bewitched Gonzo and Trice—something so big, yet so quiet. Seeing that the woodpecker and the hummingbird were still frozen in a mix of fear, admiration, and confusion, the owl called to them, "Be swift like lightening in the execution!"

Gonzo turned to Trice and asked softly, "What do you think?" The word *execution* lingered in his mind.

"Itcan'tbeagoodthingtogethimallturdedoffatus."

"Do you trust him?"

"Wekindofhavetotrusthim,don'tyouthink?"

"If we can trust the owl, what a friend to have."

"Absolutely,buthe'sascrazyasanuthatch."

"No doubt." Though by then, the two birds were on the wing in tepid pursuit of the bizarre barred, who seemed eccentric but not unwise.

While they flew, Trice whispered, "Youknow,Zo,I'veheardaboutthisowl. AtleastIthinkit'sthisone. Hisname'sBardus. You everknownabarredowl?"

"Where I come from, we stay away from owls his size. This is the closest I've ever been to one. Do they all talk like him?"

"I'veknownscreechowlsthatcangetprettyloud,butI'venever spokentoabarred,either."

"Where do you think he's taking us?"

"Idon'tknow,butitlookslikewe'rehere."

Bardus landed on a high, thick limb. He motioned for Gonzo and Trice to join him. The little hummingbird looked like an insect next to the owl.

"Well, here we are," Gonzo said nervously.

"Yup,hereweare," Trice echoed.

The birds were at the edge of the forest, looking out at a noisy, crowded, smoky field of hard, black, flat ground made of a type of stone. The black pasture was artificially lit as honks, growls, roars, rings, beeps, and a sea of other sounds rose from the mass of manflock below.

The owl swiveled his head to what seemed like a painfully unnatural position. Looking behind him, he stared at his companions for a moment and said, returning his gaze to the confusion below them, "Something wicked this way comes."

The birds noticed that Bardus's neck functioned as a stabilizer to keep his head level and his eyes balanced as the breeze bounced the limb. Looking more closely, they could see that the owl could individually dilate his own pupils to focus more clearly on whatever he watched. This bird had abilities other fowl didn't possess.

"Iknowthisplace," Trice said solemnly. "Actually,Iknewthisplace."

"O ruined piece of nature, this great world shall so wear out to naught."

Thehummingbirdcontinued,"Thereweremountainlaurels here,orchids,iris,lilac . . . Iwouldcomeherefornectar. Itwasaniceplace."

"All that, here?" the woodpecker wondered aloud.

"Praising what is lost makes the remembrance dear," Bardus whispered.

The birds turned to the owl.

"Where is the life that I led?" the Bard asked the wind. Then the owl said sadly, "He's truly valiant that can wisely suffer the worst that man can breathe . . . Is man no more than this? . . . Oh, pardon me, thou bleeding piece of earth that I am meek and gentle with these butchers . . . This is a sorry sight." Smoke and smell wafted from the leveled forest.

Gonzo looked the owl in the eyes and said, beak-to-beak, "This was your home. This was your roost."

"Clear wells spring not, sweet birds sing not, green plants bring not forth their dye . . . Shall I be plain? I wish the bastards dead . . . Man delights not me."

"I have felt the same," Gonzo agreed. "They just keep taking."

Trice, who was by nature a very merry bird, seemed a bit uncomfortable with the darkness of the mood. "Don'tletthischangeyou. Ilostthisground,too,butIwillnotletitchangemyheart."

"The weight of this sad time we must obey, speak what we feel, not what we ought to say," the owl said to the hummingbird. "In time, we hate that which we often fear."

"Iwillnothate," Trice said and then repeated it slowly, more to himself than the others. "I   w i l l   n o t   h a t e ."

Bardus mumbled quietly, smugly, "Thou doth protest too much."

The woodpecker joined in. "They're everywhere. I've seen it even in the swamps, the last place you'd expect to find the man-flock, and yet there they are. Even at my last roost, as deep in the swamp as you could imagine, even there, flaps from my roost, their long hard path, elevated and dry so they could ride their dead beasts that growl and smoke night and day . . . even there."

"There is no darkness but ignorance . . . I find the people strangely fantasied; possessed with rumours, full of idle dreams, not knowing what they fear, but full of fear . . . O, what men dare do! What men may do! What men daily do, not knowing what they do!"

"Yes, Bardus . . ."

The owl cocked his head.

"It is Bardus?" the ivory-bill asked.

The owl nodded. "I am that merry wanderer of the night."

"Well, I'm Gonzo. That's Trice."

The owl nodded again.

"You're right, though," Gonzo continued. "They are afraid. You can smell the fear. I think it might be the reason for all this, all this destruction."

"Butwhataretheyafraidof?"

Gonzo shrugged. "I think they're actually afraid of themselves. Everything they do seems to be about them and their fear."

"Great men tremble when the lion roars." The owl shook his head slowly, painfully. "Oh, wicked, wicked world . . . This world to me is a lasting storm . . . Blow, blow thou winter wind. Thou art not so unkind as man's ingratitude."

"Come on," the woodpecker suggested. "I can't take any more of this."

The three birds flew from the fringe of the Barrens where the man-flock encroached, deep into the 650-thousand-acre sanctuary, where 17 trillion gallons of water lurked just below the surface of dwarf plains and dwarf trees, until they were miles from any road. The ironic reality was that while most humans would define the term *barren* as sterile, without life, without vegetation, for the creatures who lived in the Barrens, nothing could be further from the truth. This was a lush source of life, an oasis. The only thing barren about the habitat was the number of people.

The irony, if one considered it, was that the man-flock often defined *barren* as any environment *they* didn't inhabit. Without their presence, an environment was instantly deemed barren, when, in fact, it could actually be quite fertile and often was.

A deeper irony was revealed when one considered the man-flock definition of *development*, which they took to mean to make fuller, bigger, better. To the creatures of the Barrens, however, development in the human form meant quite the opposite. It meant death, destruction, displacement, and extinction, something much more fitting to the label *barren*. Too often, the man-flock and the birds had opposite definitions for the very same words. To many creatures of the forest, the Barrens would be their best hope, their last stand.

Eventually, the three birds found themselves perched near a stand of shrubs that resembled the berries the pileateds had led Trice and Gonzo to earlier. The pair looked at Bardus and asked, "Fizzberries?"

The owl grinned and nodded. These, however, were smaller, gentler, less potent berries. They were a bit more Trice's size and speed.

"Not me," Gonzo moaned. "For some reason, my head feels as heavy and dense as a stump."

"Funnyhowfizzberriesmakeyourheadfeellightasafeather-whenyoustarteatingthem . . .butlateronit'slikethewoodpeck-ersaredrillingonyournoggin."

"I have very poor and unhappy brains for drinking. I could well wish courtesy would invent some other custom of entertainment." The owl winked at his friends. "It provokes the desire, but it takes away the performance."

"You think he's trying to tell us something?"

"I'mneverquitesurewhathe'stryingtotellus,Zo."

Bardus ate a single berry and flew off.

Zomis, Squab, and the petrel flew away from the glow of the man-flock nests and the false stars that lit the night wherever the humans lived. The three birds pursued a vast dark patch. To Soaria, it looked like a small unlit ocean, but there was no water beneath them. They were in search of trees, soil, fresh water, and dirt. This wasn't the habitat of the grey, web-footed Gwatta petrel. And while the monarchs seemed to think she belonged there, Soaria wasn't so sure.

She settled on the bank of a slow-moving river, preferring unknown water to unknown trees and dirt. Squab and Zomis, however, preferred the forest to the river, an environment they were better suited for. The trio had left the man-flock behind, but none of them were completely comfortable with the untested woods where Zomis had chosen to hide the petrel.

The moon emerged from a thick cloud. Bright beams bounced on lumbering water. Soaria grinned to herself and lunged into the air. She looked down at the pigeon and the robin and said, "Where there's water—even fresh water—there are usually fish. Time to eat."

Since both of them typically fed during daylight, they were skeptical that this saltwater bird could find fish in a river at night. Although they, too, were hungry, they settled down to watch the show. Even Zomis, a pigeon, one of the greatest fliers in the sky, admired the petrel's ability. She was a bird among birds. They marveled as Soaria seemingly hovered just above the rolling water. It looked as though she were stepping across the soft swells, actually walking on water.

But while her talent on the wing was indisputable, success at feeding herself didn't follow. Her beak remained as empty as her belly. She persisted, but the fish in this water didn't school up like shoals in saltwater. The little fish here preferred to hide under rocks, logs, and lily pads. When the novelty of watching her dance and dive without success wore off, Zomis and Squab began hunting through leaves and lichen for something to satisfy their hunger.

The petrel continued to pound the water. The harder she worked, the hungrier she got, yet she just kept fishing as if the mere act of diving in and out of the water over and over would somehow nourish her. Perhaps it did. A single word kept slipping into her mind: *seek*. Over and over, *seek*. She didn't know where it came from or what it meant. The word came quietly, soothingly, yet persistently. *Seek*.

The moon faded from the night. The sun erased the dark blue. The water became clear. Soaria rested, thinking she'd try her luck when the sun was a little higher in the sky, lighting up what lurked under the surface. She wasn't quite sure whether she should fish more like the pecking herons she'd seen before or the plunging pelicans. Perhaps the most effective technique for her would be something in between—maybe the skimmers' method would work. She studied a kingfisher off in the distance whose method made sense to her.

Zomis and Squab continued to forage not far from where Soaria stood. The petrel tucked one leg underneath her body, faced into the breeze, relaxed her eyes, and began to pray. The breeze caused her to sway as if she were in flight, but the single extended leg anchored her to the earth. The rising sun warmed her windblown feathers while the gentle rush of the river sang its own unique song. The petrels believed that when all their senses were engaged by the planet in this way, their thoughts would be shared directly with God's, the one they referred to as Pettr. She began to silently recite her *bird*tra.

More accomplished petrels knew all four of their unique words to the verse. Soaria was somewhat of a hatchling in her spiritual journey with only one of the words—*soar*—revealed to her thus far, but this didn't keep her prayers from reaching Pettr. She could hear them all.

Soaria decided to add the word that wouldn't leave her while she was fishing—*seek*. In her mind, she repeated, *soar, seek, soar, seek,* over and over.

After a few moments, Soaria heard it buried in the breeze. "I can help . . ." Then she heard another word. "Here. I can help." There were several other words that she couldn't make out, so the message wasn't completely clear, but she definitely heard, "I can help . . . here."

Soaria concentrated harder. Was this Pettr? Was it some voice from the woods, the river? Pettr had only directly given her one word before this—*soar*—and Soaria had only just added seek, so she wasn't completely clear whether this was Pettr's voice or not. It was, however, a good time for Pettr to get involved, she thought. Often the Creator was involved without anyone's knowledge or notice. Pettr didn't always reveal herself. Did the butterflies bring the petrel to these woods, or was it really Pettr? It could be difficult to tell, but surely something brought her here.

Soaria heard another sound: wings flapping, large wings. She opened her eyes wider and glimpsed an enormous dark shadow flying off into the woods. It resembled a great heron, but it was a bit shorter, stouter, darker, perhaps a night heron. Was it a bird she'd never seen before?

The petrel looked over to Zomis and Squab. The robin was wrestling with a long, plump worm, and the pigeon had its head buried in a clump of moss. "Did you see that?"

"See what?" Squab replied, the worm wriggling around her face. She shook her beak and twisted her head, but she couldn't get near the worm as it tightened its grip on the feathers of Squab's neck.

Zomis looked up, glanced at the petrel, and then studied the robin for a moment before declaring, "That's a snake, Squab! That's a SNAKE!"

Squab began to thrash and jump, screeching and shaking. Zomis flew over and tackled her, pecking and pulling at the young viper until it released Squab's neck and slithered back into the undergrowth.

"You can't tell the difference between a worm and a snake?" Zomis scolded.

Squab explained, "I was hungry."

"So was the snake." Zomis turned to the petrel. "Did you just ask us something?"

"Never mind." Soaria returned to her meditation. She faced the wind and tucked her leg back underneath her abdomen. She focused on the frogs. The incessant peeping was something she'd never really heard before. It reminded her of the peeping of chicks in a rookery. She let the sound spawn dreams of ocean islands covered with colonies of petrels. Deep down, Soaria knew they were only visions, but deeper still, she believed they could be more. And then she heard *seek* once more. *I'll have to keep adding that word to soar when I pray,* she thought.

Something struck her on the head. It almost knocked her out. Everything went blank for an instant, and when Soaria regained herself, she wasn't exactly sure whether a moment or a migration had passed. It took a few blinks before the petrel could gather her senses. The object that struck her on the head was at her feet, a big hunk of man-flock food: stale bread.

"This should help." It was that same voice! It was God, Pettr was speaking to her. But this time, the Creator sounded like a male. *It could be either,* she thought. *It matters not.*

"Yes, Lord, but how can this help?" the petrel replied.

Zomis turned to Squab. The two birds had only heard Soaria's side of the conversation. "*Lord?*" the pigeon cooed. "That bread must have really rattled her skull."

Squab giggled. "It would have to be *really* stale to crack *her* skull, but if it fell from heaven, I guess it might dent her thick head."

While the two birds laughed, suggesting that their skulls were even thicker than hers, Soaria listened to the voice from above. "You are hungry. This will help."

"Thank you, Pettr," Soaria proclaimed to the clouds. "I don't want to seem ungrateful, but bread is not actually what I eat. But really, thank you, Lord. And if you want me to eat it, I wi—"

"It's not for you to eat. And my name's not Pettr."

Soaria opened her eyes wider and lowered her gaze until she saw one of the strangest birds she'd ever seen clinging to a tree just a hop from where she stood.

"Lord God, what a bird!" the petrel said without thinking.

"I get that a lot, but I'm not God. Name's Gonzo, and, as I said, I think I can help you."

At this point, Squab and Zomis were shrieking so hard they were flapping, rising, and launching themselves into shrubs and stumps because they couldn't control their convulsions. "She thinks the woodpecker's . . . *God!*" Squab whooped. "He is big, but *God?* She thinks he's *GOD!*"

"Stop it!" Zomis screamed. "You're killing me! It's toooo funny! First, a piece of bread knocks her out, now this! *'I'll eat it if you want me to, Lord.'* Cooohooohooo!"

The petrel ignored the other two, saying to the woodpecker, "Really? If you think a hunk of stale bread is what a petrel needs for nourishment, I don't think you can help."

The hummingbird whizzed in and hovered next to Soaria's head. He whispered, "Hedoesn'tthinkthat. Andhe'sprettysmart,soifyou'dliketoeat,whydon'tyoulistenmoreandspeakless?"

The petrel tried to shoo Trice as if he were some kind of bug, but like most flies, he was much too quick for her waving wing.

Gonzo climbed down from the tree. He smiled smugly at the petrel and bowed to her companions. "Learned this from a clever egret named Galstep." The woodpecker ripped a generous chunk off the piece of bread. He stepped onto an algae-covered log along the bank of the river and perched majestically. "I'm going to turn this bread into fish," he said seriously.

Zomis called to him, "My friend, the only way a woodpecker is going to produce fish is if they're swimming with beetles under the bark of a tree. And I can't imagine that's gonna happen." Squab and Soaria giggled.

"Ye three of little faith," the woodpecker replied.

"Andlittlebrains," Trice added.

"I *will* turn this bread into fish," the woodpecker declared. Gonzo walked out onto the tip of the log, where it reached beyond the bank and hung over the water. He placed the bread at his feet, tore two pieces from it, and dropped them into the lazy flow so that the water pushed them into the log, rather than on the other side, where they'd be carried away downstream. Gonzo lowered his head. He leaned over until his long beak was almost in the water. The woodpecker slipped but gathered himself when he dug his nails deeper into the smooth rotting wood.

"Don't fall in," Soaria teased. "You don't look like much of a swimmer."

"Or a fisherbird for that matter," Squab added. More giggling ensued.

Gonzo slipped again. He disappeared behind the log, and there was a violent splash. His huge wings flapped frantically. A single, massive wing reached over the wood as Gonzo struggled to regain his perch on the lubricious log. The wobbly woodpecker took a single step, stumbled for several more, and fell forward, landing at the petrel's webbed feet. When his head struck the ground, two small fish flopped from his beak. The petrel stared at the fish and then at the woodpecker. By the time she fully appreciated his feat and Gonzo had also gathered himself, the two little fish, called pumpkinseeds, had flailed and flopped their way back into the water.

Trice flew in and spoke to Soaria. "Hemightnotbemuchofa fisherbird,butyouan'tevencatchfishwhenthey'redroppedatyour webbedfeet."

Zomis and Squab loved that.

The petrel brushed some leaves from Gonzo's tail feathers and asked, "How'd you do that? Tell me the magic."

"No real magic here. Like I said, saw an egret do it. He flew by and picked up a piece of bread the man-flock abandoned, and rather than eat it, the bird dropped little pieces in a pond and waited. After a little while, the fish that were hunkered down under cover rose to the surface to eat the bread. And when they did, Galstep snatched them up."

"That's brilliant. What was the name?"

Puffed with pride, the woodpecker announced, "Gonzo. The name's—"

"No, not you. The smart one, the egret. What was his name?"

"Galstep," the woodpecker mumbled. He continued, "Yeah, with a beak like mine, I thought it might work."

Soaria smiled. "So, that's how you turn bread into fish."

"Yeah, if you can't get the beak to the fish, why not bring the fish to the beak?"

The petrel grabbed the bread and proceeded to feed herself. It wasn't quite the same as dining on the open ocean, but the fact that she was feeding rather than being fed nourished her in a way she hadn't felt for quite some time. While she ate, the others introduced themselves until Soaria dropped a fat fish next to Gonzo and said, "For you. Thanks." Then she returned to feeding.

After she left, the ivory-bill slipped the fish back into the river, muttering, "Vile things, fish. Absolutely disgusting. A lovely gesture, but I'll take a grub every time."

The early equatorial sun baked the rocks and the iguana efficiently. Stithl hugged the stone to absorb as much heat as possible to erase the night's lingering chill. When he was nice and warm, the lizard slid off the black lava boulders where he regularly sunned himself and began his trek to the crisp saltwater of Galahope. Along the way, he passed lazy lizards licking flies from slumbering seals. Lightfoot crabs removed vermin from the mammals' infested hides. Other iguanas randomly sneezed salty snot, expelling sodium ingested while feeding in the sea.

Stithl nodded to an enormous tortoise called El Solitario Jorge. The iguana could never understand how a creature as large as Jorge could go for months without eating or even drinking, if need be. Back in the brush beyond the shoreline, the ancient tortoise rose up on all fours, looking ridiculous yet relaxed, as finches—several at a time—plucked parasites from his skin.

Low tide offered the safest, easiest time for the iguanas to feed, but Stithl would have to share the algae beds that were closer to shore with thinner individuals who were too afraid to venture into the colder, deeper water, not far from where the arctic current wells up year round. In order to dine in the choicest fields, Stithl would have to swim. He'd also have to brave the Cromwell

Current and the constant surge of the surf, something he'd done many times before.

The iguana entered the surf, swam past the shallow beds without a nibble, and worked his way into the deeper, more productive water. Penguins and a lone seal passed alongside and underneath him. Great flightless cormorants fished next to him. While many on the island referred to the cormorants and penguins as flightless, Stithl thought that was a mistake, for surely in this water that was as clear as the sunlit sky, these birds were flying and feeding with all the grace a swallow chasing a dragonfly might display above the surface of the sea.

Stithl continued on, using his long, vertically flattened tail that had evolved to help the planet's sole seagoing lizard to swim with snake-like undulations. A little farther out, a thousand blue-footed boobies dove into the shallows, synchronized to pilfer a school of fish that wandered in from the deep blue.

To Stithl, the boobies were a nuisance not only in the sea but on land as well. They weren't the best neighbors—loud, numerous, constantly courting and displaying, and always staining the beautiful dark-grey lava rock white with poop. An eagle ray passed beneath Stithl as the water became deeper. Gasses from hot magma bubbled up between rocks and coral below.

Suddenly, the iguana was shoved aside. He knew instantly what was happening. It could be dangerous, even lethal, but Stithl recognized the sea lion, Vecin, and figured this would be more of an inconvenience—a major inconvenience, but probably manageable because this pesky mammal's bark was sometimes worse than his bite.

Vecin nipped at Stithl's waving tail as if it were a toy. He pursued the lizard effortlessly, nudging him off course with his nose. Then Vecin smiled, grabbed Stithl almost gently in his mouth, and tossed him tumbling over a coral outcrop. Before Stithl could straighten himself, the sea lion bumped him with his head, bouncing him on the end of his nose.

The iguana only had so much time in the water before he'd have to return to land. This wasn't helping. And then, as quickly as it began, it was over. Vecin moved on. Stithl decided that the next time he ate flies off the snoozing Vecin, he just might slip and nip the sea lion once or twice in one of his more sensitive areas—payback.

Once Stithl reached the lush algae garden, hooked his claws into the crags and crevices in the hardened lava, and buried his lumpy face into the soft green vegetation, he had no doubt that the journey, with all its effort, all its risk, was worthwhile. The lizard clipped the algae as low as his teeth would allow, eating voraciously at his own underwater farm. The iguana even employed his own form of crop rotation. He'd gorge himself in one area over several large rocks, then the next day, he'd move to another patch, and the following day, he'd move on again. By the time he returned to the first set of rocks in the rotation, they would once again be covered with fresh algae, red and green. Of course, if some wayward damselfish wandered into his fields, they would often indulge in the bounty, but there wasn't much Stithl could do about that, and there always seemed to be enough for everyone.

The iguana had grown large, a good thing because it helped protect him from one of his most lethal enemies while grazing in the underwater meadows: cold. The added body mass insulated the reptile and allowed him to stay in numbing water that would kill most other cold-blooded creatures. But if he stayed too long, he would slow down so much that he wouldn't be able to swim effectively, and Stithl would die. This was a very real risk.

Nature, however, had been good to Stithl. His kind had been blessed with the ability to move blood away from the surface of the skin, letting it flow deeper within the body, where it stayed warmer longer. He and his fellow iguanas also had the ability to drastically diminish their heart rate, allowing them to stay in the water for up to two hours.

Stithl loved this way of feeding. He reveled in the underwater meadows—the sounds, the sights, the sun slicing through the sea, beams bending with the undulations of clear water. It was an awe-inspiring environment to find sustenance. With his heart rate muted and his blood retreated, Stithl slipped into an altered state of consciousness, a kind of lizard zen.

The iguana lowered his head and mowed the meadow until the algae was short and his belly was full. When the tip of his tail became numb, Stithl knew it was time to head home. To overeat was tempting but reckless. So, he released his grip on the rock and allowed the surge to sweep him up. The first few strokes were always the hardest, but as his limbs loosened, he slid through the water with steady purpose.

Stithl felt the swell against his side before he saw the solitary fish. It flitted among rocks and boulders strewn across the iguana's path. It circled him in flashes. Stithl's chilled body and blood-deprived mind made him curious, more than perhaps he should have been. The fish seemed too small to be dangerous, yet it was clearly pursuing him. Size wasn't always proportionate to danger, the lizard had learned.

The fish paused in a single sunbeam, and Stithl could see its features. Fairly small, mostly yellow, it had black bands, a thick black bar running through its eye, and a distinctive white stripe directly behind it. The fish that circled him was called Wankane by those on Galahope. To the man-flock, it was known as a raccoon butterflyfish. It was rare among the lizard's rocks, but he'd seen them before.

The fish sidled up to the iguana's head and said, "A message for you, I have. From my cousins who fly in the sky, it comes to me, and now to you."

Stithl was concerned that he'd spent too long underwater and might be suffering brain freeze. He had never chatted with a butterflyfish before. The lizard decided that if this wasn't a hallucination, he didn't know what was. He continued paddling toward shore, thinking any further delay would be unwise. But the apparition persisted. It seemed to know his name.

"Stithl, you are. Friend of Lupé, I'm told." The butterflyfish slipped underneath him and popped up on the other side of his head.

A second butterfly replaced the first so that the iguana had a fish on either side of his dark-green face. The newer arrival said, "Tell his friends, family, you must."

The other echoed, "Tell them, you will."

Then Stithl did something that worried him. He spoke to the fantasy, treating it as if it were real. "Whut? Whut-da-ya wandt me ta dell 'im?"

"Not us who want. Zomis, it is. The pigeon told the robin. The robin told the butterfly of the sky. Cousins we are. Now butterflies of the sea tell you."

Against his better judgment, Stithl latched on to a boulder. "So, whut exagdly are ya dtrying ta dell me?"

"A petrel, your friend Lupé, it is," one of the butterflies whispered.

"Izee in drouble? Where?"

"In the place, the place where he and Zomis lived," the other fish said.

"Saved him, the pigeon has done. Taken him back from the man-flock, it has."

"Flown to the woods, they have," the other fish added. "Flown to the Barrens."

Stithl could feel the undertow. A wave was coming. He pressed his nails hard against the boulder, but the surge ripped him from the rock, smashed him into another, and pushed him to the shore. The butterflyfish were gone. Dazed and confused, Stithl crawled out of the sea like his ancestors had done epochs earlier. Normally, he'd climb onto a rocky outcrop. It would take most of the afternoon in the high sun to warm his body to the point where he could properly digest his meal. Then he'd return to the surf and do it all again. But today was different.

Dragging himself across the rocks, Stithl reasoned that either the fish and their story were real or they weren't. But which was it? Real fish likely wouldn't lie to him. They knew names, places, specifics they had no way of knowing. Still, the butterflies had to be lying, or at least mistaken. The lizard knew for a fact that Lupé was on Galahope, not in some woods called the Barrens.

The more he warmed, the more he digested, the faster he moved. Walking steadily, he spotted Glyde alone on a ridge. At first, the lizard thought it was Lupé, a mistake he often made. But this bird, while incredibly similar, was younger, leaner, fitter, yet less worldly than his father. Stithl called to the petrel. While Glyde generally didn't relate well to other birds—or perhaps they didn't relate well to him—he genuinely enjoyed the company of the iguana, whom he viewed as an uncle, more or less.

The petrel floated down from his perch to greet the out-of-breath lizard. "Where's yah fadtter?" Stithl demanded.

"Don't know. What's with you? You look like you did the time the sea lions played toss-the-lizard with you. Don't tell me they did it again and I missed it."

"Nah, dey didn't, bud I feel kindta like dey did. Agtually, I needt ta tell ya dadt sometin dadt mighd be impotant."

"What?"

Stithl paused and faced the beaky youngster. "Dit I juss say I needt ta tell *ya* sometin or I needt ta tell yah *dadt* someting?"

"What's the difference?"

The lizard just resumed his walk, lumbering toward the hole that Lupé and Sirka called home, while keeping an eye out for hawks.

Glyde landed on the iguana's back with a youthful lack of inhibition. "Ya really don'dt weigh much, bud id's kindta hardt ta be indcandtspicuous ta da hawgs when dere's a pil'a feadtters mounded ta ya spine."

"You know, if you told me *why* you need to find my dad, I'd be more likely to leave. Heck, I might even find him for you."

"So, findt him. Yah don'dt needt ta know our business ta do dhat, if ya really wandt ta help."

"Interesting proposition. I would really want to help if I knew what you wanted to talk to him about. So, let me help. Make it easy. I could fly to him. He could fly to you. No more dragging yourself over rocks and sand. Wouldn't that be nice? So, what's going on?"

Stithl kept walking.

"Oh, I get it," Glyde declared. "Are you two planning some kind of surprise for me?"

The iguana looked back over his shoulder, up to where Glyde perched on his dorsal spines, and said, "Ya tink? Ya've gohdtta be kiddnt."

Glyde nodded, his expression soured. "I get it. It's a surprise, all right, but it's not for me. It's for my sister. I should have expected that. You know, we have the same hatchday." The youngster stepped off the lizard's back.

At that moment, the lumpy lizard felt bad for his feathery friend. He'd seen it. He knew. The Darums—the flock that Lupé joined when he took Sirka as his mate, the flock that she belonged to but wasn't really his own—all seemed to accept Keusha without reservation, but they always kept Glyde at wing's length. Keusha was deeply woven into the nest of Darum life, while Glyde always seemed to remain on the periphery of the flock. To be fair, his sister was accepted in part because she tried to be. Glyde never put much effort into it. But Stithl knew his petrel nephew didn't make the effort because he believed acceptance was a hatchright, not a social game. He refused to play.

It was easier for Keusha. She was pretty. She looked like her mother, like a Darum. Glyde looked like his father, a Gwatta.

Taking all this into consideration as his brain warmed in the sun, the empathetic iguana gave in and told the petrel about his encounter with the illusory butterflyfish. Glyde found the story fascinating. Other than his father, he'd never seen a full-blooded Gwatta petrel, and apparently, now there was another. When the two arrived at the family nesting hole beneath the rocks, they rushed in to tell Lupé.

They were both there, Lupé and Sirka, tending to an egg. The old silent butterfly who followed Lupé to Galahope when the petrel first arrived was also there, sitting in a corner of the den, smiling as if he knew what Stithl was going to say. Glyde spoke up quickly, announcing that Stithl had a very important message. The lizard explained in great detail what had happened as he returned to shore from grazing. When he was done, Lupé spoke.

"Sounds like Zomis has returned to being a pigeon." Lupé seemed amused at the thought of his old friend embracing its inner bird. "The petrel that Zomis has freed is certainly not me, so it would seem no one has to worry about *my* rescue, since I'm already here."

"So, what do we do about this bird, this petrel?" Glyde asked. "Shouldn't we go get it?"

Sirka said nothing but was visibly concerned.

Lupé looked around the den. He saw his son, Sirka, the egg. He noticed the sunlight beyond the entrance to his home and walked into the warm glow.

Glyde stood next to his father and asked quietly, "What do you want to do?"

The older petrel breathed the sweet, salty air of Galahope and answered, "Nothing."

"Nothing?" the young petrel repeated, a hint of disappointment and confusion in his voice.

"Nothing," Lupé said, nodding. "Galahope is home. This is where we've made our stand. This is where we live or die." Lupé walked back into his den. He faced the old monarch and said, "Can you ask the butterflies to tell the petrel where we are . . . that we are?"

The insect flitted off into the light beyond the entrance.

Glyde approached his father once more and probed, "That's it? Another petrel from our flock—a Gwatta—and you don't go get it? Really?"

"It just has to know where we are. The rest is up to it and Pettr." Lupé motioned to Sirka, to the egg, to Glyde, and said, "The risk isn't worth the reward. Maybe it'll come to us."

The youngster considered his father's conclusion.

"So, ya nodt goint anywhere?" the iguana interjected. "Goodt—I mean, I mighdt nod even have da story righdt. Tink aboudt idt. I'm half frozen, fulla algae, bouncin aroun da surf. I wouhdn't truhss me. I remembuh one dime, my cousin, Prow, wass in da same sidg-suation, an he came across a blue-foodted booby fishin undawa-ta. Now I saw diss wid my own eyes, mindt ya. My cousin wass so whagked out andt ogxygen duprivedt dadt he triedt ta madte wid da birt. Imagine, rebdile madtin widt a birt?"

Lupé took a healthy step back and said, "I'm starting to worry about you, Stithl. Don't get any ideas."

Glyde also cocked his head and took a step back from the iguana.

"Idt's my cousin!" the indignant iguana demanded. "I'm *all* rebdile, I assure ya!"

"Right, your *cousin*," Lupé teased. "You don't think I've seen the way you look at me?"

"Dahd's disgustin! I come here, adt my own peril I mighdt addt, ta dell ya an impodendt message an diss iss whadt I'm subjegtedt ta? Pedtrel pavershuns?"

"You're the one who brought it up," Glyde peeped.

"Andt now I gohdda hear idt from a hadgling!" Stithl protest-ed as he stormed out of the den.

Into the Woods

Azul left the Kwake parrots and flew south. He planned to follow the shoreline as far as it would take him, stopping along the way to feed and roost. The northern parrots told him that he might be joined by other parrots from flocks just like theirs who'd established colonies down the coast. Apparently, parrots were returning to this part of the world in a whole new way. There were now more once-captive-now-wild parrots than anyone had imagined. His friends from the north assured Azul that their friends to the south would know that he was coming and be on the lookout for the pale-blue macaw, ready to help him if they could.

Azul hadn't gotten far before he felt a tug, a pull into some woods just to the west of the shore. He spotted small, short pines growing in dry, sandy soil and became distracted. The unexpected expanse reminded him somewhat of the Caatinga, and he became curious, flying into the Barrens.

Azul hoped to have a nice rest, an overnight roost where he could savor the sounds of the woods, gather himself a bit, and press on the next day. If he could find an edible nut, maybe berries or fruit, he'd be thrilled. Azul smiled, thinking he'd settle for that strange pizza the monk parrots gave him, although it didn't seem likely in this setting.

The dwarf pines gave way to a deeper, more varied forest. Azul pressed on in search of food. Along his way, he saw squirrels, chipmunks, and deer—animals who also appreciated a good nut. There was no shortage of acorns from a variety of oaks dispersed among the pines. Azul wondered if any of those would be tasty and nourishing.

He landed on the branch of a chestnut oak, a tall tree with a thick trunk growing near a shy pond. Azul waited and watched, weighing whether the time was right to take a drink. The water looked clean. It had a leafy tint that the macaw wanted to taste. The large tree had acorns hanging here and there. Little groups of them clustered on the forest floor. The parrot felt he could make this work.

While he waited, Azul shuffled along the limb to a clump of acorns and plucked one. He held it up to his beak, stripped away the cap, and tore into the seed. It was soft and manageable, but as it spread across his tongue, the parrot cringed at its bitterness. His cheeks hurt as they constricted involuntarily. Azul spit the chewy mush onto the forest floor.

That's when he heard it. On its own little plain, separate from the many sounds of the woods, he heard it—the peeping, the giggling. He could see where it was coming from. The little tree frog was hugging the branch with his sticky toes to keep from falling off because he was laughing so hard. It was a high-pitched yet muffled laugh, a snicker that sounded like he was trying not to explode but still had to let it out anyway.

The frog's back legs kicked at the branch, an attempt to release some of the amphibian's pent-up hysteria. But the little peeper was losing the battle. Water began to drip from the creature's eyes. The bubble beneath his throat expanded as the frog giggled louder and louder.

Finally, Azul said, "It wasn't *that* funny."

The tree frog stopped snorting, lifted up his tiny green face, raised one long, bulbous finger, and calmly countered, "I think it was." And then he was swept away in a river of laughter that could no longer be contained.

"Clearly, peeehee, peeehee . . . Clearly, peeehee, peeeheep, peeeheep, peeeheep . . . Clearly, you can't tell an acorn from your a—"

"That's enough," Azul interrupted. "You must be starved for entertainment in these woods."

"OK . . . Gotta breathe . . . Lemme breathe . . . OK, no, it's not that. It's just, I watched you grab that chestnut acorn and couldn't believe you were going to eat it. And then you did! And that whole squinty-face spitty thing you did, well, you don't see that every day." The frog hopped down to the forest floor, landing comfortably in a patch of lichen. Azul followed.

"So, you knew I wouldn't like that acorn and you let me eat it anyway?"

"I didn't *know* you wouldn't like it until you didn't like it. And by then, well, it was too late to do anything."

"Other than laugh," the parrot pointed out.

"*Peep*cisely," the frog agreed.

"So, my friend—you don't mind if I call you friend?" Azul asked.

The peeper smiled. The sun bounced off his green skin, illuminating the striking black stripe that emerged from his nose, ran through his eyes, and continued down his sides. "If this is not a bonding moment, I don't know what is."

Azul continued, "Since you seem to know so much about acorns, do you eat them?"

"Never. Strictly insects." Then, as if on cue, the frog bent over and sucked up two ants carrying what looked like an appendage from a beetle. He ate that, too.

"Well, since you *somehow* know so much about acorns, would you be so kind as to direct me to a source of more palatable fare?"

The frog pondered for a peep and then advised, "Actually, just behind you a hop, there's a little pile of dark beauties."

Azul looked over his shoulder, spotted what the frog referred to, and took a step toward them. "These don't look like nuts to me."

The frog's eyes widened ever so slightly. "Ah . . . that's because they're not."

The parrot touched one gingerly with his toe. It slid from the half-scattered pile. It was soft, a touch squishy. Azul picked it up. "Fruit?"

The frog nodded and was about to explain, but Azul interrupted him. "Don't tell me! Berry? Ummm, grape? Am I right? No, no, don't tell me. There's only one way to know for sure."

Again, the frog acquiesced. "True, only one way to know *for sure.*"

The parrot stuffed one dark beauty, then three more into his beak and chewed, rubbing his tongue over the moist, fleshy morsels that gushed from the corners of his beak. Abruptly, he gagged—choked, in fact—and spit the morsels onto the ground. Azul wheeled around to the frog and shouted, "That's not fruit! You did it to me again! You said they were dark beauties! It's disgusting. It's rotten. It's rancid! What did I just put in my beak?"

"OK," the frog responded, "first, I said *they* were dark beauties." The elfin amphibian pointed over Azul's other shoulder.

Azul looked quickly and saw a small spread of purple berries under a green bush.

"We call *those* Huckleberries," the frog explained.

"But you knew I had picked the wrong fruit and you didn't say anything . . . again."

"Au contraire, I told you that they weren't nuts. *And,* as I tried to tell you what they actually were, you said, I believe the phrase was, '*Don't tell me.*' Then you repeated the phrase. So, I did as I was instructed. I didn't tell you."

"You said they were fruit. And they are not like any fruit I have ever eaten!"

"In point of fact, I never *said* they were fruit. While I might have appeared to agree with your assertion, through body language and facial expression, that they were fruit, I was about to explain precisely what they were when you instructed me *twice* not to and consumed several before I could intervene. You can't imagine my disappointment at not being able to restrain you." The tree frog flashed a wide *amphibigrin.*

Seeing he wasn't going to get anywhere with the amphibian, Azul simply asked, "What did I eat? Was it rotten fruit?"

The frog smiled. "In a manner of croaking, we in the Barrens refer to them as *fruit of the deer.*" The frog's smile broadened, and his rear leg began to twitch involuntarily.

Azul thought about it for a moment and closed his eyes slowly. Realizing what the small pile of black balls called *fruit of the deer* actually was, the parrot frowned. Then he hopped over to the pond and calmly, yet vigorously, swished his beak in the leaf-stained water. "I know I shouldn't ask. I should have learned my lesson, but are you going to help me find any edible food? Preferably something some other creature hasn't already eaten?"

"I'd be happy to," the frog peeped with pride. "There are several trees—oaks, in fact—on the north bank of this pond. They, however, are white oaks, and their acorns, I'm told by a well-fed whitetail buck, are quite delectable."

"Thank you."

"Now, keep in mind, the chestnut acorns are pretty uncommon around here. The whites have a long nut, just like the chestnuts, but they're thinner and the cap is smaller. Got it?"

"Got it, friend."

"Bremal. The name's Bremal."

"I'm Azul."

The frog nodded.

"By the way, Bremal, any reason I shouldn't roost here for the night?"

The tree frog slowly waved his head from side to side, incorporating a subtle, rhythmic dip every time it changed direction, signifying neither yes nor no. "Been getting lots of visitors lately. Strange weather patterns seem to be bringing unexpected pilgrims to the Barrens—and other places too, I'd guess."

"The Barrens?"

"That's where you are, Azul. The Barrens."

"But this place looks pretty lush. Why do you call it barren? Oh, wait. I get it. It's one of those opposite things, like if I called you Stretch."

"What do you mean?" The analogy was completely lost on Bremal, who was actually quite long for a tree frog.

"Well, you're not much bigger than an acorn," the parrot pointed out. "Why would anyone call you Stretch? It's like a reverse nickname."

However, sometimes, when one doesn't get the joke, it's much better not to explain the humor, to just let it go. That, unfortunately, was something Azul failed to grasp.

The parrot had apparently struck a nerve. "Oh, sure. Compared to you, I seem like a pipsqueak, but let me tell you, among tree frogs, I'm a mountain, a beast. My peeps don't get bigger than *me*. And as a matter of fact, a lot of my friends—and I have a lot of friends—they actually call me Stretch!"

"Hey, I'm sorry, Bremal. I'm new to these woods. I'm from very far away. Don't listen to me. I don't know anything. I just ate deer poop, what do I know?" Trying to make up for the faux pas, Azul continued, "You know, now that you mention it, it must've been the light or something, because back where I come from, there are tree frogs as well, and now that I think about it, compared to them, you're like enormous. I mean, you're pumped. They'd faint at the sight of you. You really are a specimen."

Bremal shrugged. "Yeah, I get that a lot. I do a lot of hopping, I eat right, I take care of myself, you know."

The parrot felt better, and more importantly, Bremal did too.

"Now," the frog said, "when you get to that north bank, the white acorns—the long, thin ones—will have a whiter meat, not yellow like those chestnut acorns you just . . . peeeheep . . . sorry, Azul. I couldn't help myself. But I think you'll like those better."

"Thanks, I'll give them a try." The parrot looked at the frog for a moment. "They're going to taste *better?* You're not setting me up?"

Bremal flashed his huge, mouthy *amphibi*grin and shrugged off the suggestion as absurd. "If you roost back over here tonight, maybe I'll climb up and hang with you a bit?"

"OK," Azul replied. "I'll make sure I find a thick enough branch to support two big bucks like us."

"Good thinking," the imposing tree frog agreed. And for an instant, it seemed to the parrot that Bremal was flexing.

Not far from the north end of the pond, Gonzo settled into an abandoned raccoon hole in a dead pine tree. He'd roosted there for the past several nights and found it quite comfortable. Still not sure how long he'd stay in the woods, Gonzo was generally enjoying himself. He was faced with so many new things, his mind was active and his skills were sharp.

He nestled into the softened pine. Gonzo closed his eyes, relaxed his muscles, and let his thoughts drift wherever the evening breeze took them. At times, his thoughts would give way to fantasy. Then the fantasy would bloom into dreams. On rare occasions, the dreams would spawn visions.

The woodpecker considered the woods around him. They weren't home. It wasn't the southern swamp, and yet part of him felt it could be home. Should he do it? Should he leave the trees that his kind had always lived in and try some new place—these Barrens, perhaps? On the one wing, it felt kind of right. On the other wing, the Lord God Bird had always been a creature of the swamp, the cypress, a denizen of the Deep South. But really, how well had that world served his kind? At the moment, and perhaps beyond, he was a flock of one. There was nothing in the swamp that suggested the ivory-bills would flourish, save for Kwim, who was no longer in the swamp. His flock was withering on the vine.

And so, what of these woods? Were they the answer? Gonzo certainly hadn't seen any of his kind here, but with the climate so confused, maybe the South was moving north. Was this an opportunity? Was the planet telling him something? Or was this a more ominous development? It was a lot for a woodpecker to think about. Only the Great One would really know. The more

Gonzo thought about it, the more he concluded that the decision to stay couldn't be settled by reason alone. It was equally a matter of heart. He would have to feel the answer. Gonzo wished he had another to talk about this with, an elder.

The woodpecker considered Zomis. As a passenger pigeon, it seemed his new friend was also in a flock of one, but as nice as Zomis appeared, the bird seemed a bit lost. It was a pigeon, a rat, a robin. Zomis certainly seemed confused at times. Granted, the most seemingly befuddled birds were often capable of incredible insight, of hatching profound truths. They were originals. They saw the word differently, not like everyone else. There could be value in that. Perhaps, Gonzo thought, he would consult the puzzled pigeon.

Then he considered the petrel. Soaria was almost a flock of one herself. Was she looking for something similar to what the ivory-bill searched for? He would chat with her, too. A moment later, the woodpecker was asleep.

Emersssso didn't mind working for her meals. In fact, she kind of enjoyed it. She wasn't lazy. As a result, she was large, thick, well fed, strong, alert. She was a good listener, quiet, stealthy. She was opportunistic, yet she understood that you often make your own opportunities. Those who were smarter, stronger, more patient, better prepared often found themselves with greater opportunities. So, ironically, the harder she worked, the easier life became. Sometimes, fortune even found her.

Emersssso had seen the bark flying off the tree the previous afternoon. She'd watched the long strips, many still filled with grubs and insects, crash to the ground and form a lovely loose pile. She'd also seen the most enormous woodpecker hugging the tree trunk, chiseling away. *Delicious*, she thought. But it was neither the bird nor the insects that really interested Emersssso. It was the pile of bark. This was an opportunity knocking, like the savory woodpecker knocking on the tree. She would answer its call.

The robust kingsnake slithered up to the tree beneath the cover of leaves, sheltered through shrubs and shade. She worked her way deep into the pile of debris, pleased when even more rained down upon her as the large woodpecker continued to feed. It was just a matter of time. Eventually, something would notice the pile and poke through it in search of a meal. In the woods, there was often just a pine needle between finding a meal and being one. Emersssso waited, tasting the air around her with her astute tongue. She rubbed it over the roof of her mouth to process what she'd found.

It didn't take long. The snake, however, was mildly surprised by what turned up first. It wasn't the mouse, squirrel, chipmunk, rabbit, or robin she expected. Rather, another snake—a pine rattler—slithered toward the pile. The venomous viper coiled up a short distance from the mound, not seeming to notice the kingsnake's presence.

Its poor eyesight caused the snake to rely on movement to judge the distance and size of potential prey. Emersssso was perfectly still. As a pit viper, the rattler, maybe a scale out of its element in this section of the Barrens, could also detect the body heat of those around it, in some sense allowing it to see in the dark. Emersssso knew all this. Sitting still in cool leaves out of the sun lowered her heat signature enough that she remained unnoticed.

Then the ants showed up. They seized a loose grub, enveloped it, and carried it away. They found another and did the same. A fat salamander appeared from under a leaf and picked off straggling ants. Emersssso smiled. Next, a tree frog hopped into the mix, snatching ants with its tongue, perhaps considering the salamander as well, but for the moment content with the insects. Emersssso could feel the rattler stir. It seemed hungry, impatient. The muscular tree frog was certainly food, but for the kingsnake, it wasn't a *meal*. She wasn't here for a snack, even if the rattler was.

While many animals, much larger beasts, seemed terrified of the pine rattler—and rightfully so—Emersssso wasn't. She knew them well. She understood that they were basically docile snakes who preferred to use their venom for hunting rather than defense.

Not to underestimate the rattler's ability to kill, the kingsnake was well aware that they carried limited quantities of the toxin and required a long time to replenish their supply, so use of the lethal liquid was generally a last resort.

Emersssso could taste the frog. And if she could, so could the rattler, who appeared confident that it was approaching the pile, which by now had a pair of short-tailed shrews and a robin stealthily picking through the debris. The buffet was growing. Still, Emersssso waited.

Not often seen during the day, the brown long-tailed weasel was slender and silent, almost a mammalian version of a snake. He would prey on virtually anything and no doubt had his sights set on whatever he could ambush in the bark. He crawled closer and closer, hugging the ground, masked somewhat by the continued rapping of the woodpecker and the commotion of the robin and others feeding below. Emersssso could spot the weasel without even seeing or hearing him. She could taste him.

The reptile thrust her split tongue, like a feeler, into the air and pulled it back into her mouth, capturing scent particles that emanated from the weasel. She rubbed it against receptors on the roof of her mouth and tasted him. The mammal couldn't hide from the snake. But Emersssso took it a step further. She could tell which

of the two tines on her tongue, the left or the right, had more of the scent on it. The one with the extra scent indicated the distance and location of the prey. Emersssso processed all this information instantly.

Behind his tan face, the weasel exposed his needle-sharp teeth. Tensing his muscles, he snapped into action, singling out the plump, voracious robin—who just happened to be Squab. The weasel charged the bird, slamming her into the tree, pinning her to the ground. He thrust his face deep into Squab's chest, trying to get under her feathers, to reach the flesh. Squab felt a tooth slice into her flank. She pecked wildly at the weasel's neck.

The weasel instantly stopped attacking. He lay on top of Squab like a rock, almost as if he'd fallen asleep. Squab wondered if she'd struck a fatal blow with her frenzied defense. Then the robin understood.

The weasel's head began to disappear down the throat of a large rattlesnake. Squab's beak had done nothing to stop the attack. It was the hemotoxin from the rattler's bite that quickly killed red blood cells and disrupted the blood's ability to clot. The robin had been doing what robins do. The weasel had done what weasels do. And the rattlesnake did what rattlesnakes do. The scales of the ophidian rubbed against Squab's feathers while it ingested the meal. The robin backed away, felt a sudden stab of pain where the weasel had wounded her, and was unsure if she could fly.

Realizing what was happening below, Gonzo stopped feeding and climbed down the trunk of the tree to help Squab if he could—if it wasn't too late.

But before Squab could fly, before Gonzo could help, the kingsnake seized the opportunity she'd been waiting for. Emersssso appeared out of the leaves and shadows. She crashed into Squab, bursting past the robin as if she weren't even there.

Squab gathered herself again, happily accepted her good fortune and dashed to the other side of the tree trunk. The roughed-up robin flew to a high branch to watch from a safe distance, realizing that when properly motivated, she could fly in spite of the injury.

With the weasel halfway down the rattler's throat, his hind end still protruding from its unhinged jaws, Emersssso grabbed them both. In an instant, she wrapped her long, muscular body around them and began to squeeze. With its mouth full, the rattler was unable to bite the kingsnake. Even if it did, the kingsnake had the ability to resist the venom that worked so well on others, and since some was already used on the weasel, Emersssso gambled that the rattler would be unable to muster another lethal dose so quickly—certainly not one that could stop her.

A moment earlier, Gonzo reached the base of the tree. He shuffled to the back so the trunk separated him from the snakes. He stretched his neck and peered out from behind the wood. The last thing the woodpecker saw was Emersssso leaping at Squab—or so he thought. He was determined to protect the robin.

The king, the rattler, and the weasel rolled closer to the tree. The woodpecker launched himself into the air, spread his wings wide, and landed on the coil. He went for the constrictor's head, digging his claws into the viper's face.

Not quite talons, a set of dagger-sharp claws armed the ivory-bill's toes. His feet were surprisingly strong, enabling the large bird to grasp on to branches and bark while climbing up and down trees throughout the day. Gonzo grasped Emersssso's face and held on like he was in a tornado, which, in a sense, he was.

As the foursome rolled through the pile of bark and leaves, Gonzo called to the robin, who he assumed was part of the tussling tangle, "Hang on Squab! I can get you out of this!"

The struggle continued until one of the woodpecker's nails slipped into Emersssso's eye socket. Losing an eye is never worth a meal, so before any real damage could be done, the constrictor released her grip on the rattlesnake and slithered off into the shadows, confused as to why the enormous woodpecker would prevent her from feeding, enraged that she'd been interfered with.

With the kingsnake gone, the rattler dragged its kill under a rotting oak, trying to clear its throat and catch its breath.

That left Gonzo alone on the forest floor. *Is Squab gone?* he wondered. *Is the robin in the kingsnake's belly?* The woodpecker shook his head, assuming he was too late to help the bird. He looked up to the sky, contemplating the loss. There, on a branch not very far away, Squab waved at him and smiled.

Having eaten his fill of the strange, white acorns, Azul had to agree with Bremal, who'd declared them a far superior seed. The well-rested parrot found his evening's roost to be quite comfortable. He took a drink of the cool, leaf-stained water and savored its unique flavor. A few more acorns and Azul was ready to fly. The macaw was a little disappointed that he was unable to bid adieu to the buff tree frog, but he was glad to have met Bremal.

After heading south above the inviting Barrens, Azul veered east just a feather or two so that he'd connect with the coast as the woods waned. The parrot liked the Barrens. It was a restful stop. He looked at the clouds and thanked the Great One that such a place had managed to survive while pondering how many birds depended on these woods to launch their migrations, to continue or complete their migrations, or, sadly, to attempt a final stand. Azul would remember the Barrens fondly, but he pressed on.

The sky parrot had been given markers to look for to find other newly wild parrot colonies. He'd been assured that he'd be well received by any parrot throughout his trek home. They were an intelligent species. They'd understand the importance of Azul's flight. The thought warmed him, but Azul couldn't help but wonder if all would go well. Whether or not he ever got there, the sky parrot was going home.

By the end of the day, Squab and Gonzo had told the others about the fracas with the snakes. Squab proudly displayed the red slices across her flank and attempted to explain how she saved Gonzo, but no one believed her, not even for a flap. When the band of birds retired to their roosts, regaled by the tale of danger and rescue, they were aflutter with anticipation at what dreams the adventure would inspire.

Emersssso didn't like to lose. And on the very rare occasion when she did, she subscribed to the adage, "Lose the battle, win the war." However, she also didn't believe in revenge. There was no time for that, no place for the added risk when one was trying to survive in the Barrens. Revenge increased uncertainty and invited its return. Its pursuit was a distraction, so Emersssso generally paid it no mind. Still, every now and then, fate would present an opportunity, a chance to eat where the execution of the hunt might also settle a score. This was one of those times.

It was a simple fact. One hunted to eat. Doing so and not eating was one of the worst feelings the kingsnake knew. It was an ache, a fresh emptiness in her mind and her belly. Imagine being hungry, working flawlessly for your sustenance, having not only one but two meals in your grasp, enough to keep you nourished for over a month, and another creature, who's not even trying to eat, attacks you and ruins your work.

The pileateds understood. This was, in fact, how they explained it to Emersssso. They saw the opportunity. They encouraged the kingsnake to right the wrong, and Emersssso agreed. Not only would she eat, which she needed to do, she'd taste vengeance at the same time without going out of her way to get it. This was a flavor that didn't come with most prey. This meal, this woodpecker, would taste a little sweeter than the others.

As luck would have it, the pileateds were able to tell the viper exactly where the woodpecker nested. Their directions were impeckable. And when Emersssso had finally dispatched the ivory-bill, the pileateds promised to tell her where the robin nested and perhaps others as well. Emersssso liked the pileateds. They understood right from wrong. They had honor.

The snake slid across the forest floor, stealthily, carefully, yet confidently. She came to a patch of lichen. Two small feathers rested on a leaf, one black, the other red. Emersssso tasted the breeze and grinned. She wrapped her long, strong length around the dead tree in front of her and climbed silently. The slight pitch of the trunk simplified the task. A knot here, a bit of bark there, a patch of fungus protruding, a shard of branch jutting. It wasn't difficult to scale the pillar.

She approached the hole, larger than most, more square than round, just as the pileateds described it. She could see the stars sparkling through a small opening at the top of the roost. This might be a problem. It would be better if the bird was completely sealed into the tree. If it broke free, it could fly out and away. The kingsnake didn't come all this way to be left hungry once more. Emersssso wondered whether she should attack from above, surprising the bird and forcing it to flee through the main hole in the trunk while she covered its instinctive escape. The snake slithered upward. She looked down into the roost through the crack. Gonzo slumbered beneath her.

Emersssso extended her tongue, captured the scent inside the hole, and rubbed it in her mouth. Tasting the sleeping bird, tasting vengeance, she lowered herself into the roost. The kingsnake laid her head next to Gonzo's, close enough so she could feel his breath against her cheek. She coiled herself underneath his body, weaving her head under and around him, careful not to nick a feather until the moment was right. One more coil would suffice. Emersssso slid around the woodpecker's impressive ivory bill so she could hold it shut. But before she could complete the move, she felt pain—deep, sharp, stabbing, crushing pain in her tail. She was being lifted out of the tree.

The kingsnake quickly tightened her hold around Gonzo, who was also lifted through the entrance of the dead tree into the cool night air. The woodpecker awoke unable to breathe, scared, confused, in flight but not flying. Neither the snake nor the woodpecker could see what grabbed them. Whatever it was, they were losing altitude. This was a lot of weight for anything to fly with.

The creature that latched on to Emersssso had very serious talons that pierced her scales with ease. Since she'd been lifted from the tail, the snake could neither strike nor coil around her abductor. She turned her attention to her fellow abductee, tightening her grip. As long as she held on to him, it seemed she could accomplish her main objective and the intruder would be forced to either drop them both or land, either of which suited Emersssso just fine.

The nails on Gonzo's feet were useless. They paled in comparison to what had split the scales of the snake's tail. To be useful, the woodpecker would have to get to the snake's head, just as he'd done earlier, but at the moment, Gonzo couldn't move. Every time he exhaled, the constrictor felt it and squeezed a little tighter so that the woodpecker couldn't fully inhale. He was slowly suffocating.

The threesome flew across a field, slipping closer to the ground. Emersssso smiled. Other than a sharp pain in the butt, things didn't seem quite so bad to her. If she could dispatch the woodpecker once they hit the ground, whatever was on her tail would be in for a fight. In another moment or two, she'd have her chance. Afterward, she would gather up the fresh woodpecker carcass and dine. With luck, she might dine on her abductor as well.

But before she could blink, a crushing impact to her head eclipsed the pain in her tail. Her skull felt like it was caving in. In a final attempt to free himself, Gonzo used the sliver of oxygen that remained in his lungs to fuel a desperate assault, unleashing the full force of his massive beak on the cranium of the viper.

The snake loosened her grip on Gonzo, hoping to swing herself free. The pounding stabs to her head intensified. Then, in a last-ditch effort to save his own life, the woodpecker shifted into over*peck*, banging on her brow in an endless staccato of brutal blows. A succession that would pulverize the sturdiest oak forced the kingsnake to reluctantly release the ivory-bill, who glided, gagging, to the ground.

Once the weight of the woodpecker was gone, the snake hung motionless as it was carried higher and higher into the night, leveling off just above the canopy, the feathered abductor now handling its scaly cargo almost effortlessly. He lowered his grip to the tender tip of the tail and spoke to Emersssso. "My brain, more busy than the laboring spider, weaves tedious snares to trap mine enemies . . . The game is up."

Defiantly, Emersssso hissed, "I am a kingsssssnake, not a sssspider."

"Away," Bardus demanded, "you are an ass, you are an ass . . . When he fawns, he bites; and when he bites, his venom tooth will rankle to the death."

"No venom here," the snake appealed. "I am purely a consssstrictor. No venom at all."

"Bloody, bawdy villain! Remorseless, lecherous, kindless villain! . . . A deed without a name!"

"Owl, where are you taking me? What will happen to me?"

"Measure for measure must be answered . . . What's to come is still unsure . . . Thou flea, thou nit, thou winter-cricket thou!"

"I owed that woodpecker! You can't deny me that!"

"A deed of death on the innocent? . . . I have a touch of your condition . . . Blood will have blood." The owl climbed a little higher into the sky.

"Put me—"

"No tongue! . . . All eyes, be silent . . . Unquiet meals make ill digestions . . . I do begin to have bloody thoughts."

"Put me down, great owl, pleasssse," Emersssso pleaded, willing to say anything at this point. "I am ssssorry. I should not have ssssought revenge. I will not ssssseek it again. Sssspare me."

"Happy are they that hear their detractions and can put them to mending," Bardus hooted. As he lowered himself, the snake's hopes rose. Bardus lowered himself a little more and allowed the upper branches of the canopy to crack against Emersssso's fractured skull. The Bard grinned and said, "This most excellent canopy . . . this brave o'erhanging firmament, this majestical roof."

The snake's cranium took another bow.

"Th' offender's sorrow lends but weak relief to him that bears the strong offence's loss . . . Things past redress are now with me past care . . . What's done cannot be undone."

"I can undo thissss! I can undo thissss!" the snake pleaded. "I should not have lisssstened to the pileatedsss. They sssset me to thissss, to kill their coussssin. I ssssee it now. They sssset me to it. I should not have lisssstened. I can undo thissss. I, too, will protect the grand woodpecker. I will make it up to him, and you as well. Give me a chansssse."

The owl smirked. "Full of newfound oaths? . . . Do you smell a fault? . . . Oftentimes excusing a fault doth make the fault the worse by th' excuse . . . You spotted snake with double tongue."

"I am not sssspotted. I am banded—barred, actually . . . like you!" she wailed. "I have no double tongue. It issss all one tongue! I will make it right! Owww!" Her head struck a sassafras branch. "Releasssse me!"

"All things are ready if our minds be so," Bardus tested.

"Oh, my mind issss ready. Really, I am sssso ready."

"How shall thou hope for mercy, rendering none?" Now the owl was getting to the point.

"I have learned. I have learned. Pleassse, no more. You're killing me."

"We have scorched the snake, not killed it . . . I never did repent for doing good, nor shall not now." Believing he'd made his point—actually, several of them—Bardus rose once again, high above the Barrens. Bathed in the honest glow of the moon's reflected light, the owl grinned and opened his talons wide, releasing his grip on the battered snake.

As he watched Emersssso plummet to the forest below, he saw her connect with several branches, snapping one, slipping off another, until the vanquished viper was able to grasp a bow and wrap herself around it, ending her fall.

Bardus swooped down over the tree, landed next to her, and whispered, "There the grown serpent lies; the worm that's fled hath

nature that in time will venom breed, no teeth for the present . . . I know what you are." The owl paused and looked her over carefully. The snake would survive, but it would surely remember. "To the elements be free, and fare thou well."

With that done, Bardus returned to Gonzo, who he assumed would be delighted with the owl's intervention. The woodpecker, however, seemed despondent.

"How is it that the clouds still hang on you?" Bardus inquired.

Moments later, Zomis, Squab, and Trice appeared. They, too, came to check on the ivory-bill. Something was bothering the woodpecker.

"Are you OK?" Squab asked.

"Yes, I'm fine, thanks to Bardus." Gonzo nodded to the owl.

"So, why are we not celebrating?" Zomis wondered.

Always ready to celebrate, Squab agreed, "Why not, indeed?"

"Becausewe'renotallhere," Trice pointed out.

The group took a collective breath, followed by an instant of silence.

"Where is she?" Zomis asked.

"I believe she's gone," Gonzo said.

"She'sgone. Youcouldseeitinhereyes. Alittlefood,alittlerest . . ."

"And she's on her way," the pigeon added.

"On her way where?" the robin asked Zomis and the others urgently.

"You'd have to ask her," Gonzo replied.

"Our remedies oft in ourselves do lie," the owl observed.

"But she can't be gone," Zomis thought aloud. "We've sent for Lupé. I'm sure he's on his way, and she's not here? Quickly, we must catch her!"

"She's a petrel. Have you ever seen a petrel fly? Have you seen *her* fly?" Gonzo shook his head as if there was no hope of catching up to Soaria.

Zomis spun around, panicked, and faced the woodpecker. "I'm a pigeon. Have you ever seen a pigeon fly?"

"Didn't mean to ruffle your rump. No offense intended, my friend. Let me put it to you this way. You fly over the ocean much?"

"Not much."

"Not *ever*," Squab added.

"Granted, you're a beast of a flier over land, but petrels are the pigeons of the ocean. And my guess is she's over the ocean right now. You really think there's a good chance of catching her? And once you do—if you do—what then?"

"She's gone," the hummingbird stated flatly.

"At least the petrel's where she belongs," Squab said in one of those strange moments when she unexpectedly pointed out what everyone else seemed to be missing, a role she wasn't exactly used to.

"But how could she leave when the butterflies made her fly here?" Zomis asked. "Why would they suddenly let her go?"

"Ask a butterfly," Gonzo answered. "We're all a bit confusing. Why should they be any different?" After a moment of stunned silence, the woodpecker continued, "Maybe the monarchs used Soaria to bring you and Squab here. Maybe that's what they wanted."

"But why?" Zomis pressed.

Gonzo shrugged. "We have the questions but not the answers."

Bardus was abnormally silent. The owl hoped that the petrel's absence was, in fact, due to her flight to freedom and nothing else.

The owl knew that Soaria wasn't with them, but he didn't know if she'd left. Creatures had a tendency to disappear in the Barrens, especially when they weren't familiar with the woods or its ways.

Soaria wasn't the only bird to disappear from the forest early that morning. A sky-blue parrot also departed, making his way to the coast, heading south. He hugged the shoreline, blending subtly against the pale-blue horizon and the wispy white clouds. Azul pumped his wings with purpose. He refused to indulge distractions, dedicated to making progress on his migration. Well rested and fueled by white acorns, the macaw made surprising headway.

Azul enjoyed looking down at the sea. The water was mesmerizing. The flying, the cool, salty air, the moisture on his beak . . . it was invigorating. *Could anything be freer than a bird flying home?* he thought. But he wondered what he'd find when he got there. Aura was already taken away. Would the last few caraiba trees still line the hidden stream that supported him? Would his green-feathered friend Nipiklee be waiting for him? Would he just be removed again by the man-flock like so many others before?

For a moment, Azul wondered why. Why was he even doing this? Would he find peace back in the Caatinga, or had he been better off the night before in the Barrens? Or the night before that with the monk parrots? Or, dare he say, the night before that with the man-flock? He didn't know. He couldn't answer. But beyond knowing, he felt. He *felt* he needed to return to the stream. He was drawn to it. Live or die, the sky parrot would make his stand there.

Azul couldn't help himself. He couldn't be a parrot and not be a thinker, so he continued to grapple with the paradox of migrating home. Was home actually home if it changed, if it became a place that no longer looked like home? Was there a point when home would cease to be home? Azul reasoned that it would no longer be home if it couldn't support any sky parrots. But what if it could support only one or two? Shouldn't home be able to support a flock? Is home a personal concept or a collective one? Azul was further frustrated by the sad fact that he had no one, no others like himself, no elders—or even juniors for that matter—to talk with about any of this. Would home still be home if you didn't know anyone there, if they didn't know you or any of your family or friends?

He was reminded of a popular parrot phrase about raising chicks that he'd heard many times before: "It takes a flock." But what if there was no flock? Would that mean you couldn't hope to raise young, because there would be no flock to assist?

The parrot looked back down at the sea, spotted a huge shoal of fish he couldn't identify, and pretended he was among them. He pretended that he was one of many rather than a flock of one and followed the great school swimming as one.

The day gave way to evening perhaps a bit sooner than expected. Azul needed to rest, needed to eat. In a typical migration, a bird can easily lose one-third of its body weight. Once the fat is burned off, muscle is consumed. Truth be told, Azul wasn't nearly ready to embark on such a migration. It wasn't something his kind generally did, as evidenced by the fact that the macaw found himself a bit farther out to sea than he should've been.

Rising thermals won't typically form over water, which made it harder for him to fly. Azul became concerned with the thought of what would result if he was forced to the sea below. There was no webbing between his toes, and his feathers weren't oiled, not like those of the seabirds. If he became waterlogged, he wouldn't be able to fly. If he couldn't fly and was over the open ocean, he'd drown. Why did he allow the school of fish to distract him? What was he thinking, flying over the sea without having the shore in sight? Then Azul understood something else. Air pressure was falling rapidly. The early onset of dusk wasn't the result of day giving way to evening sooner than expected. The day was giving way to an approaching storm.

The parrot shifted course, flying southwest so that he might, with a little luck, reach the coast before the squall reached him.

That was when Azul made yet another realization. While the approaching storm was definitely a problem, it wasn't his main problem. Azul had made a fairly foolish miscalculation, the kind of error a fledgling might make. Elated to be in flight, intoxicated with freedom, the macaw had flown and flown and flown, figuring he'd rest when he was tired.

Now he was tired. And now the wind was changing, as well as the light, the precipitation, the temperature, and the sea below. Still quite a distance from shore, Azul had pushed himself to the limit so that he was rapidly approaching exhaustion, and there was nowhere to rest—no island, no tree, no beach to land on. Lift and thrust were about to have a great battle with gravity and drag.

The storm overtook the bird. Azul couldn't lift himself above the tempest. The wind was stronger than his wings. The parrot thought, just maybe, he could sneak beneath the gale and glide above the sea. This worked for a few flaps, but soon, Azul was slapped by the rising swells. He became soaked from the mist that churned in the air. Water was falling from above and rising from below. The parrot's feathers became heavy—saturated—and flight became even more laborious. The bird tried to search the surroundings for something, anything to land on, some man-flock structure, some man-flock waste. *They leave debris everywhere,* Azul thought. *Why, the one time I need some, can I not find any?*

The parrot was swatted into something solid. *How can water hit so hard?* the dizzy parrot wondered as he slipped into the sea. Convinced he'd drown, Azul used all the strength he had left, along with some that he didn't have, to lift himself into the wet air. Even so, he was flying just on top of the water, inches above the ocean. The parrot could scarcely make it out, but it looked like there was a structure on the water. Jet black with white bones, it swayed on the waves. Maybe it wasn't even there, his ringing head and what was left of his reason suggested. Was that what he'd flown into? A floating island of the man-flock rolled with the swells. There was no choice. Flapping like a hysterical hummingbird, Azul willed himself into the air and thrust his drenched feathers over the rail. He slid into a dark corner of the deck and collapsed.

It was a nice time of year for Teach. The Japanese whaling fleet was in dry dock after failing miserably in their latest effort to "study" the cetaceans in Antarctica. Had they actually been studying the whales to understand, protect, and propagate the creatures, Teach would've been very happy to assist them. But the "researchers" defined *study* as the brutal execution of thousands of whales with the real goal of processing and packaging their remains for human consumption and personal profit. That type of study, Captain Teach and his fellow stewards would not allow.

Since the International Whaling Commission was willing to create laws but had little interest in enforcing them, the Ocean Stewards decided to take matters into their own hands. The group of humans who gathered together from all over the planet were, in a sense, stewards of the sea, with whales, tuna, baby harp seals, and other imperiled marine creatures serving as their flocks. They viewed those who illegally, abusively, and unsustainably preyed on these defenseless animals as beasts attacking their flock, and they were committed to driving the threat away.

But this was a quiet time of year for the Ocean Stewards, if there really was such a thing. Ships were being repaired and improved, crew members were being signed on or reassigned, strategies were being formulated, and, of course, money was being raised. This is what brought Teach and his ship, the *Roger Caras*—often referred to as the Jolly Roger—into the Atlantic.

The vessel was on the way back from a fundraising effort that took the crew from Halifax, Nova Scotia down the Atlantic coast, meeting, greeting, and hopefully engaging sympathetic supporters along the way. The Ocean Stewards weren't just battling poachers, they were combating industries, corporations, governments, cultures, and ideologies. In order for them to do that, they needed to raise money.

Having spent decades sailing in Antarctica, Captain Edward Teach could sleep through a cyclone if he wanted to, so the tepid tempest of the previous evening did nothing to stir his sublime slumber, which, when he wasn't defending whales, could border on hibernation.

Surprisingly, Azul's slumber was equally deep. The bird was out cold. When the sun peered through an opening beneath the rail, the parrot awoke to a knot on his head and a pit in his stomach, not to mention some uncomfortable sneezing, along with pain that seemed to radiate from every quill on his body. Hearing footsteps, Azul curled deeper into the shadows, into a puddle of foamy saltwater that kept him uncomfortably wet and cold.

Jack was performing a post-storm inspection of the helipad when he noticed the blue feathers. He picked them up and studied the plumage. The soaking feathers made the crew's lone aviator curious. He took them inside and laid them on a work bench. *Blue feathers, out at sea, on our deck?* he wondered. *Totally drenched . . . A seabird? Not likely. Alive? Not a chance.*

Having awoken from his deep sleep and feeling restless, Teach wanted the Roger back in the fight, and that's precisely where the ship was headed. He had one stop to make in the Bahamas, where a wealthy supporter had a gift for the stewards. A dry dock had been quietly reserved so the Roger's hull could be retrofitted with better ice-breaking capability. While they were there, the copter would also be equipped with airborne radar, and the crew was going to add a pair of drones, greatly extending the small fleet's ability to track illegal whaling vessels. All this would be paid for by their Bahamanian benefactor. It was well worth the stop.

Not far from the wet corner where he was huddled, Azul spotted another crevice that appeared dry and, for the moment, was situated directly in the sun. That was where he needed to be. The macaw scanned the deck. It was quiet. The tiny, tinny island bounced on the sea. The man-flock was nowhere in sight.

Azul had two options. One was to crawl along the outer wall, which was generally in the shade, and take the longer path to the dry crevice. The other option was to make a straight dash to the spot and risk being seen, but minimize the amount of time he'd be exposed. Azul scanned the deck a second time.

Seeing no humans, he decided to sprint for the crevice. Running as fast as his two wet legs could carry him, he burst from the dark and streaked through the light. He hopped over what appeared to be a long, thick vine, ran a bit more, and hopped over another vine. Just as he approached the crevice, tucking his wings tightly against his flank, everything suddenly went black. Azul felt his legs give out from under him. His beak slid along the hard surface beneath him. Then there was nothing—no sound, no smell, just black.

Azul was in Brazil, back in the Caatinga, standing on a high branch in a caraiba tree. He didn't know how he got there, but since it was where he wanted to be, the parrot accepted the situation. He scanned the sky for hawks, watched the ground for man-flock and mongoose, then shuffled to the tip of the branch and plucked a dry brown pod. The fruit tasted nutty as it mushed over his tongue. Azul closed his eyes in satisfaction. The fruit was as nourishing as cold water or clean air. To chew, to taste, to swallow was pure joy. In fact, just standing on the branch feeling the warm wind work its way through his feathers down to his bare skin while the limb bobbed in the breeze allowed Azul to relax in a way he hadn't felt since he was taken from his home.

The macaw chewed more of the dry fruit. Above his head, another sky parrot—his mate—reached down and preened his feathers. Azul said a quick, quiet prayer to give thanks for being home. But when he opened his eyes, the sky parrot knew instantly that he was nowhere near his Brazilian home. The branch that he perched on was, in fact, the extended arm of a human. The caraiba nuts that he savored were really peanuts pulled from the fingers at the end of the arm. And the gentle preening that Azul thought came from Aura came, in reality, from the human's other hand. Indeed, Azul was a long way from his beloved caraiba tree.

The parrot dropped the peanut and tried to size up the situation. As scared as he was, Azul sensed no danger. The human was gentle. They sat together in the open air. Nothing prevented the parrot from flying off. He stretched his wings, and a sharp pain raced up the back of his neck. Azul closed his wings to his sides, and the pain subsided.

The human picked up the peanut, and, for some reason, showed his white teeth to the parrot. In most mammals, this is a sign of aggression, but it didn't seem to be so with this one. When Azul made no movement toward the nut, the human cracked the shell and ate it himself. He lowered the arm the parrot was perched on, yet rather than jump to another location, Azul climbed up the arm to the human's shoulder. He felt safe with this man-flock but couldn't explain why.

This one had thick white hair on top of his head. It reminded Azul of a cockatoo's crest he'd seen when he was captive. He decided to call the human White Feathers. As long as Azul wasn't contained or clipped, as long as the large human was gentle and cared for him, Azul thought that he might stay with this one, until, of course, he was ready and able to fly off on his own.

That was fine with Captain Teach. As someone who commanded a ship, a small fleet—an international organization, in fact—he'd always felt connected to the buccaneers of seafaring lore, yet the Ocean Stewards were certainly more steward than privateer. The idea that they answered to no individual nation or flag and adhered to a code rather than a corporation fueled their image as pirate-protectors on the high seas.

As such, the fact that a beat-up, water-logged parrot would somehow find its way to Teach's shoulder, where it literally leaned on him for support, seemed to make ironic sense not only to the macaw but to the captain of the Jolly Roger as well.

While Teach and Azul toured the deck of the *Roger Caras*, the parrot couldn't understand why all the man-flock they encountered seemed to show their teeth to him. At first, it was unsettling to see so many teeth, as if each human was saying, "I can eat you with these." After a while, however, it seemed to the parrot that the display might be some sort of greeting.

When one human would flash their teeth, White Feathers, who carried Azul, would do the same thing. Some even displayed a raised hand, which would normally suggest being struck. They all seemed to be friends, so the teeth-flashing and the waving hands had to be a type of salutation. For a moment, Azul wished he had some teeth to flash at the man-flock. Perhaps they wouldn't hurt him if he could do that.

After a grand tour of the floating island, the human prepared to enter one of its many dens, but the parrot wasn't ready for this. Even though it hurt, he stretched his wings and glided away from White Feathers, refusing to go anywhere that separated him from the open sky.

Teach swung the door wide and held it open, inviting Azul into the room, but the parrot held his ground, clinging to a rail, inviting White Feathers to stay outside with him. The human nodded to the bird and closed the door behind him. Alone on the rail, feeling fairly safe, Azul noted that the floating island was drifting southward at a steady pace and decided to take the ride.

Adhering to the practice of most petrels on the wing for prolonged periods of time, Soaria used the opportunity to reflect. She was different from her counterpart, Lupé, who felt that being so gravely endangered was a *bird*date requiring him to place his flock's needs above his right to live his own life, never fully understanding that the two might actually be more or less the same. Soaria felt that since she was essentially on her own, she had no responsibility to solve anything. If living this way happened to save her flock, if she found a mate and added to their numbers, that would be wonderful, but it wasn't her mission or her purpose by any stretch.

Rather than be *birdened*, this attitude freed her to blow in and out of life's twists and turns like the wind itself. For Soaria, life was lived in the moment, not in the past or the future. The petrel had no grand plan or vision for herself. She did only what she pleased, always, because she had no one to satisfy but herself, and that suited her just fine. Like the parrot, she was headed south, at least for the present, but unlike the parrot, she couldn't have been more at home on the open sea. Soaria flew without haste, happy in the day, happy to be free, happy to have saltwater beneath her.

"She's back!" Squab announced to Zomis, who was busy foraging with a pair of mourning doves the pigeon had *bird*friended.

Since they were so similar, Zomis found their company refreshing. And for the doves, the passenger pigeon was a strangely exotic, eccentric acquaintance. Zomis ignored the robin and continued to peck at the ground with the other two birds.

Squab landed next to her parent and repeated, loudly, "She's ba—" until she spotted a stout worm wriggling under a leaf. Jettisoning her previous thought, the robin thrust her face into the leaves and pursued the morsel. She hopped and popped around the leaves until she accidentally bumped beaks with Zomis.

The pigeon raised its head, took notice of Squab, and asked, "Did you just say something?"

"There it is!" the robin proclaimed. She plowed her face deep into a pile of leaves, knocking over one of the doves in the process.

"My word!" protested the indignant bird, who was accustomed to dining with much more panache. When food was in play, however, the robin could be single-minded. Zomis repeated, "Did you say something?"

Squab vaingloriously withdrew her head from under the leaves, displaying a long, slender catch within her beak. She paused a second so the others could revel in her acumen, although none of them did, and then she swallowed the soft, supple . . . twig. "*Kuhaa . . . kuhaahahaa . . . kuh . . .* Choking! *Kuhaahaa . . .*"

The doves were aghast that the young robin might asphyxiate herself, but Zomis reassured them, "Wait for it . . . wait for it . . . here we go."

"*Kuhoowa . . . ku, ku, ku, HOOWAHHH!*" Squab hucked up the wet twig along with a couple other tummy tidbits none of the others could identify.

"Ohhh, eeewww," the disgusted doves groaned, looking like they, too, might spew.

"Don't worry, she'll be fine . . . does this all the time. This is nothing. You wouldn't believe what this bird's eaten." Zomis seemed strangely proud of its offspring's misstep. The pigeon gently held Squab's head down while she returned the rest of her stomach contents to the forest floor. "Almost looks like she's feeding hatchlings, doesn't it?" the proud parent asked affectionately.

"Ewww . . . absolutely foul," one of the doves complained.

"Weren't you going to tell me something?" Zomis reminded her.

Squab straightened up and rubbed her wing across her face. "Yes, that's right. Look, there's a grub on the bark right there!"

"Focus, focus," Zomis redirected.

Squab looked back at her parent. "Yes," she said, still looking past the pigeon, back at the grub. "Yes, she's back."

"Who's back?"

"The petrel. I saw her near the river. The spot where she was pulling shiners from the water, she's doing it again."

"Really?"

"Yup. Looks like she's gained a little weight. Must be getting good at it. Probably bulking up for a migration. But she hasn't left yet."

Zomis popped into the air and swung by Gonzo's roost on the way to the river, shouting the news to the woodpecker.

Trice was already at the river's edge when they arrived. "It's another," he told them.

"What?" Zomis asked.

"It'sanother. It'sapetrel,butit'sanother," he hummed.

Zomis paused, studied the bird, and declared, "Trice is right. It's not her. It's Lupé!"

And then Zomis flew over to embrace an old friend. As the pigeon approached the petrel, rather than return the greeting, the bird stepped back, lowered his head, spread his wings, and warned Zomis off.

The pigeon turned back to its friends. "This is not Lupé."

"And it's definitely not Soaria," Gonzo added.

The unidentified petrel relaxed his posture, raised his head, and said, "You must be Zomis. I've heard quite a bit about you from my father."

"Your father," the pigeon repeated. "Your *father . . .*"

"But you don't really look the way he described you to me."

"A lot has changed since your father and I were companions." Zomis smiled at the youth and nodded. "A lot has changed." Turning to the ragtag flock of friends, the pigeon announced, "This is apparently Lupé's son," and waited for the petrel to introduce himself.

Young and inexperienced in social situations, the reclusive bird merely smiled and nodded until the pigeon prompted, "Your name?"

Ruffled by his miscue, he straightened up and responded, "Seamore. My name is Seamore."

Without thinking, "Uhh, haha hoo," slipped from Squab's beak, who instantly raised an apologetic wing.

"It's OK, I know. There's a whole thing about why my parents felt I needed to be named Seamore. But most of my friends, I don't actually have so many, but most of them call me Glyde."

"Yes," Zomis agreed while thinking that Lupé could've named his son Zomis as the petrel had promised to do when he and the pigeon parted ways migrations earlier. "Yes, Glyde is good." *Although Zomis would have been better*, the pigeon thought.

"Nicetomeetyou," Trice added.

The others followed suit, introducing themselves. Then, from deeper in the woods, a low, unseen voice wafted in. "Welcome hither, as is the spring to the earth. To thee no star be dark!"

Glyde looked nervously to the others.

Squab assured him, "No worries. That's Bardus, our barred owl, a very good friend to have, although sometimes a little tough to understand."

"I am a father for each wind that blows," the owl hooted. "We few, we happy few, we band of brothers."

Glyde leaned over to the robin and whispered, "What?"

Squab shrugged, peeping faintly to the petrel, "Band of *bros?* I'm a *sister*. Like I said, he can be difficult to—"

"I see thou wilt not trust the air with secrets," the owl interrupted.

Squab shook her head, "Turds, that owl hears everything."

"So, where is your father?" Zomis asked. "I can't wait to see him again."

"Well, to tell you the truth, ah, well actually, my father's back on Galahope."

"Why didn't he come with you? When will he get here?"

"Ah, funny thing, he's probably not coming. And, ah, well, he doesn't really know that I'm here . . . but by now, he's probably guessed."

The woodpecker spoke up, "You mean you came here alone? All this way, and you didn't tell your parents?"

Glyde nodded.

"So, the butterflies didn't give Lupé the message?"

"Kind of. It wound up with butterflyfish, who told an iguana, who told me and then told my father."

"So, he does know," Zomis concluded. "When can we expect him?"

"I don't think he's coming."

"Why not?"

"Well, he seems to think that he's made his stand on Galahope."

"Really? Galahop?"

"Galahope, actually. Yeah, there's me, him, my mother and sister. There's an egg . . . and there's a flock of petrels, the Darums, that are almost identical to the Gwattas. My mom's a Darum. My dad wants the petrel to come to Galahope, but he's not leaving there to bring her. So, I figured I'd come and get her."

Zomis looked at the other birds, shuffled his feet for a second, and said, "Well, I've got good news and bad news."

Glyde stared blankly.

"The good news is I'm thrilled to meet you. You're the pecking image of your father. Really, it's wonderful to see you."

"And the bad news?"

"Yes, ummm, the female, Soaria . . . Well, she's gone."

"She's what?"

"Gone," Trice quipped. "Thepigeonsaidgoneasinleft,departed,went . . . nothere."

"OK, as in *got it*," Glyde said to the hummingbird.

"Sorry,justtryingtohelp."

"Where'd she go?"

"East, to the ocean is the best guess, but after that, none of us are sure."

"You're a Gwatta petrel," Gonzo said. "Where would *you* go?"

"Not sure. Ocean, definitely. Then south, I guess. Maybe west as the water warms. But that's taking me back to where I came from. Don't know where she might be from. I never had to think about something like this before."

"What are you going to do?" Squab asked.

Glyde shook his head. "Not sure. I need to eat, rest a little bit. I flew like a tern in a tornado to get here. Not quite sure what comes next."

Squab looked at Gonzo and asked, "Can I show him that fishing thing you taught Soaria?"

The woodpecker nodded. Squab seemed elated, overjoyed to be able to teach someone something.

"I know how to fish," Glyde mumbled.

"Yes, of course you do, better than any of us, no doubt." The robin could see how arrogant her comment might've seemed. "It's just that this river in the woods is not the ocean. This is a local trick that might actually be fun."

"Fun and food? OK." Glyde grinned. "That sounds pretty good. Let's see your trick."

Pleased to have someone her own age as company, Squab cackled as they flew off. "Wait till you see the bump I have from when a weasel ran me over and the bruises from when the snake squeezed me. They're soaring!"

"So, you got run over by a weasel and squeezed by a snake, and I'm going off to feed with you?"

"No worries, Glyde. You should see what happened to them." Squab boasted as though the demise of the snake and the weasel had anything to do with her.

The petrel looked back to the others, a bit ruffled until Zomis pointed to the owl and shrugged. Glyde understood.

The two birds seemed rather happy to share each other's company. While Glyde liked to project the image that he was no fledgling and didn't need company, the birds could see that he was lonely and a bit nervous. Zomis wondered what his life on Galahope was like. Moments later, there was splashing and giggling from the riverbank.

Gonzo, Zomis, and Trice perched on a pine and let the sun warm their feathers. The woodpecker wondered aloud, "A petrel left, a petrel arrived, so now what's next for you and Squab?"

"*Bird*sonally," the pigeon answered, "I'm thinking these pines are pretty nice. You two are good company. I like the mourning doves. I'm feeling a little connection to them. The pines aren't bad."

"AndSquabseemstobeenjoyingherself."

"As long as nothing eats her," Gonzo added with a chuckle.

"Yes, and to have an owl like Bardus watching our tail feathers," Zomis added. "That's a blessing."

The trio sat quietly for a moment and watched a cloud shaped like a turtle float across the big sky.

"It will get colder soon," Gonzo pointed out.

"Soon enough," the pigeon agreed and then turned the conversation to the great woodpecker, asking, "How about you, Gonzo? What are you thinking?"

"Lots of things. Yeah, these pines are welcoming, but I'm not so sure about a winter up here. I might be able to do it. The weather's changing, getting warmer up this way, but it also seems a lot more unpredictable, extreme . . ."

The pigeon and hummingbird nodded.

"Love the swamp. It's home. But I haven't been able to accomplish much there. I think I need change, just not sure how much or if this is it."

"Do you know what you want?" Zomis asked.

"What do you mean?"

"Well, when it's all said and done, when there's no more wind under your wings, what do you want?"

"More wind."

"No, really."

"What do I want out of life?"

"That'swhatZomisisasking."

"I guess, in the end, I don't want it to be the end. For the ivory-bills, I mean. I don't want to be the last."

"I know that feeling," the passenger pigeon said, "but there's a difference between you and me."

"What's that?"

"I'm pretty sure I am the last. I've never seen another passenger pigeon except for my parents, and I don't believe I ever will."

"You haven't actually been trying," Gonzo offered hopefully.

"It may not look like it, but to be honest—and that's something I'm trying to be with myself lately—to be honest, I'm *always* looking. No matter what's going on, there's a piece of me, a corner of my mind, that's always searching. But there's another piece of me, deep beneath my feathers, that tells me I'm the last."

"Doyouhavethatfeeling?" Trice asked the woodpecker.

"I don't know . . . maybe sometimes." Turning to Zomis, he said, "You have Squab."

The pigeon grinned reflexively. "Yes. Squab has saved me. It was Squab who transformed me back into a pigeon. Squab and Lupé. I was lost before then. Yet Squab is a robin. I can't ignore that. She might save me, but she's not going to save my flock."

"Youneverknow. Anddon'tforget,yousavedheraswell."

"I have always raised Squab first as a bird, second as a robin, and occasionally as a pigeon. From the time I spent with the rats, I know as well as anyone what it's like to deny who you are. I would never lead Squab down that path."

"You can't deny who you are unless you know who you are," Gonzo said mindlessly.

"So,Gonzo,sometimesyoufeellikethelast,butsometimesyoudon't."

"That's because I'm not the last. I know that. I know there are others, somewhere. I had a mate. We had eggs."

"EGGS?!" Zomis repeated.

"We had a nest with three eggs."

"Younevertoldustherewereeggs!"

"That was the happiest I've ever been. Kwim too. Never were there better protected, better cared-for eggs. Never was there a better nest. Never was there a pair more thrilled to become parents . . . but all that wasn't enough. It wasn't meant to be."

"It was meant to be," Zomis argued. "It happened. You found a mate. You had a nest, and you had eggs. You had that, so it was meant to be."

"But they never hatched. Kwim never stayed."

"Theydidn'thatch?" Trice echoed.

Silently, Bardus appeared above them and perched on a long bough, rocking it with his bulk.

"No snake, no hawk, no crow ever got close to our nest. One of us was always awake, guarding the roost. It's amazing how little rest you need when you have a purpose, when you have eggs."

"So, how could they not have hatched?" Zomis whispered.

"We didn't know. We didn't know," Gonzo repeated. "We couldn't have known."

No one pressed the woodpecker to explain. They let the cool breeze clear their minds. After a little while, the ivory-bill continued, "At first, it was difficult. As soon as we realized, we bathed and preened constantly. We blamed ourselves, then we blamed each other, but really, I think we always blamed ourselves."

"What happened?"

"There was frass at the bottom of the nest."

"Of course there was," Zomis said soothingly. "Every nest has wood dust at the bottom of it."

"That's what we thought, but then we began to itch. Something was biting us. The wood dust particles were not frass. They were mites. They attacked both of us. We did everything we could. We were in and out of the nest so much, so often, taking baths, then sitting on the eggs. We weren't even sure they would hatch." A grin slipped across Gonzo's beak, and it disappeared with his next word. "Those miracle chicks were set upon by a colony of mites. There were so many, and they were so tiny, we couldn't pick them off, not with these huge beaks. And we couldn't relocate the eggs. The nest, all of us were infested. Their lives were over before they even began, and it wasn't the first time that it happened. Like I said, it wasn't meant to be."

"No," Zomis countered quietly, "you found a mate, and you laid eggs. I'm telling you, it was, it *is* meant to be. You have a real chance. That's more than I have."

"I don't have a mate anymore. And I certainly don't have eggs."

"You will," Zomis said. "As strongly as I know it won't happen for me, I can feel that it will happen for you. Don't give up."

"Thanks, Zomis . . . No, never give up," the woodpecker said, matter-of-factly.

"As small a drop of pity as a wren's eye . . . Fight till the last gasp." Then the owl leaned down and whispered, "We know what we are, but know not what we may be."

Morgan, who was on board the *Roger Caras* as first mate, was intrigued by the stowaway parrot who'd endeared himself to Teach and the crew. The weather had been calm for the past few days. Azul resided comfortably on the open deck, taking meals from Teach when they were offered, his being the only shoulder the macaw would perch upon.

Many pictures had been taken of the "pirate" captain with his parrot sidekick, who by now had been dubbed Flint after the famous parrot that sidled up to Long John Silver in Robert Louis Stevenson's classic *Treasure Island*. Azul was bright enough to realize that the sound *Flint* was the man-flock's way of referring to him, just as his cackling *White Feathers* was the parrot's way of referring to his new friend, Teach.

Morgan searched through a collection of books on endangered and threatened species to see if he could find more info about the sky-blue macaw, reasoning that the more they knew about the bird, the better the stewards could care for it. It took a little longer than the first mate anticipated, since most of the books were focused on marine creatures, but when he finally came across a volume on imperiled avian species, there was the pale-blue macaw. Morgan marked the section and made his way to the captain's quarters.

"Glad you're here," Teach greeted his first mate. "We're basically done with this tour, but before we retrofit the hull for better ice-breaking, I want to discuss our efforts with the bluefin tuna and the grouper. They're on the brink. I want to do something now, something substantial."

Morgan nodded solemnly.

"What if we held off on the upgrades and used those funds, combined with what we just raised, to put another vessel in the water? Is it worth it, or are we robbing Peter to pay Paul?"

The two sailors discussed their options into the early morning. After they'd come to some useful conclusions, Teach noticed the file under Morgan's arm and asked him about it.

"Yes, that's really why I'm here. I have to tell you—"

"What's the problem?"

"It's not really a problem," Morgan replied, "at least I don't think it is."

The captain waved a hand, signaling that it would be best if the first mate would just get to the point. The dawn air was crisp but soothing, so Morgan opened the porthole to his captain's quarters. A moment later, Azul took the opportunity to perch on the porthole's frame so he could be closer to his friend without relinquishing his ability to fly away.

"The parrot . . . Flint is not an ordinary parrot. As a matter of fact, it could be the most—if what I found here is right—it might be the most special parrot on the planet." Morgan handed the book to Teach. Besides information pertaining to the Spix's macaw and its highly endangered status, Morgan had remembered and found a *New York Times* article about the arrest of Vicente El Real and the escape of two endangered birds from the I-BIRD facility. Morgan pointed to the silver band on the parrot's ankle.

Teach smiled, "Perhaps he's a bit of a pirate himself. Many a buccaneer donned a silver bracelet . . . or a broken shackle. Flint is my kinda bird."

"Well, now that we kind of know who he is, what do we do with him?"

Teach stared at the bird for a long moment, looked back to his first mate, and said, "No need to tell anyone else about what you've found."

Morgan nodded.

"Keep researching. Let's learn all we can about Flint. Make some calls, but don't tell anyone why you're interested."

"I'm helping my niece with her science project."

"Exactly."

"It looks to me, maybe, like he's trying to fly home, back to Brazil," Morgan said. "I mean, if he's here now and he started out from New York."

Teach continued to observe the macaw. "Flint's a smart bird. He's not a seabird—definitely not pelagic—and he knows it. He also knows we're heading south. And he believes he's safe. I don't want to violate that trust."

"It's almost as if he's landed on the Jolly Roger to declare asylum," Morgan suggested.

"That's exactly what he's done. I'm thinking that we fatten our friend up as best we can. We keep this whole thing quiet, and we bring him home."

"Sail to Brazil and turn him over?"

"Sail to Brazil and let Flint decide. Like any other crew member, Flint comes or goes as he chooses."

The first mate and the captain shook hands. Operation: Flint's Freedom was underway. The stewards were about to protect yet another species. It seemed Azul had put his eggs in the right basket after all.

Where the Heart Is

Glyde had eaten, slept, eaten again, and left—much to Squab's chagrin. The petrel explained to the robin that he hadn't flown all this way to frolic in the pines, as interesting as they and the company were. He needed to find Soaria. For the first time in his life, he had something of a purpose, and he was going to see it through. The young petrel hit the sky with resolve, flying steadily, forcefully. A sympathetic wind helped him wing his way out to sea and then south in search of warmer water, where he gambled the female would be headed.

Among seabirds, petrels aren't especially large, and among petrels, Glyde was particularly long and lean, a typical awkward adolescent. Yet when on the wing, he was strangely graceful and energetic. He was an unfinished product, an unrealized vision. It remained to be seen how he would emerge into adulthood, but for the moment, the lanky, slender flier ripped through the sky with ease.

Due to their rather remote environment, petrels often go unnoticed by other creatures. They can, however, live in colonies of great numbers, depending on the species and the suitability of the habitat. And while Glyde's flock didn't live in a large colony, all petrels, regardless of their numbers, fly with remarkable strength and skill. They're master navigators and as agile as anything with feathers. They can go for long periods without ever touching soil.

Glyde generally enjoyed being anonymous. He felt it gave him freedom. It un*bird*ened him, allowing him to go where he wanted, when he wanted, without the imperative to impress or amuse anyone else or to maintain some façade or image of himself to please others. In that regard, at least, he was not unlike Soaria. The petrel, somewhat tongue-in-beak, wondered if anyone had even noticed his absence from Galahope, although clearly, his parents would've noticed. He wasn't looking forward to facing them when he returned.

His sister, however, was another story. Keusha had woven herself so tightly into the nests of the Darums that she never had a moment to herself. She was constantly flapping around someone, something, and seemed totally lost when she wasn't. It exhausted Glyde just watching her flit from one involvement to the next with no end in sight. To him, it made no sense. But to be honest, his sister was loved—even adored—while he was barely a raindrop on their rumps.

"Ha," Glyde chuckled. "Adored is sooo *plover*rated."

The petrel flew and flew and flew. He skimmed out morsels here and there as the opportunity presented itself. He flew below the breeze, just above the water. Eventually, Glyde became lost in his thoughts, meditating and praying. He didn't notice three tiny birds behind him until they were almost sitting on his tail feathers. Then he understood. They were drafting. This tweaked Glyde. It was a pet peeve with him—no thought to personal space, no etiquette whatsoever. These three just invited themselves to claim the literal windfall of Glyde's flight.

Reacting—or perhaps over-reacting, as many young fliers do—Glyde decided to flip them the human, which, in this case, meant he would raise several tail feathers straight up over his rump. Had he eaten a few more anchovies, he would've added sound effects, but for now, merely flipping the human would suffice. Glyde decided to slow down, let them pull up nice and close to his rump, then he would snap those tail feathers to attention, increase his thrust, and burst away from the impolite interlopers.

The petrel slowed. The three behind his behind came closer. Now! Glyde flipped his tail feathers up in a show of blatant disregard, bordering on rump rage. He pumped his wings and lunged forward furiously. But with his tail feathers erect, the petrel encountered a sudden wall of resistance. The feathers caught the air, pushing his rump down, pulling his head up, flipping Glyde beak-over-butt backward, drenching the petrel as he tumbled upside down into the rolling swells. Glyde couldn't have looked like a bigger squid if he'd tried. He gathered himself, bobbing on the surface for a moment, allowing the water to slide off his oily feathers, and hauled himself back into the air.

After a few flaps, the three small birds had returned, although this time, they flew alongside the petrel. The smallest of them peeped, "What's with flipping us the human? You don't even know how to do it, you turd."

Glyde was about to blast the little itch with some hot oil, thinking to himself, *Really . . . so you want to play?*

But before Glyde's annoyance took control of his actions, one of the other birds, apparently the mother, said, "Wilbird, that's enough. What have I told you about cursing at strangers?"

"I know *I* shouldn't curse at strangers." The bird's monotone recital of the phrase suggested this wasn't the first time the issue took flight. Wilbird turned to the one who seemed to be his father and completed his mea culpa by piping, "Dad'll do it." He returned his attention to his mother and explained, "This bird flipped us the human."

"You were riding my rump!" Glyde argued.

"Sorry about that," the father said. "We didn't realize it would upset you."

"It's a big ocean. How about a little *bird*sonal space? You really need to draft my butt?"

"Believe me," Wilbird added, tucking his beak under his wing, "it was no picnic for us. *Peeewwww!*"

"Wilbird! Didn't I just tell you that's enough?" The father swooped in and pecked the tiny plover on the head.

"Did you see that? Did you see that, Mom? He pecked me! He pecked me!"

"*Suuunnnnny,*" the female cooed.

"Ah, come on, Piper, he was begging for it," the father implored.

"Sure was," Glyde quipped.

"Mind your feathers, petrel!" Sunny swung by and pecked Glyde on the head just as he'd done to his own son.

"Great, now I'm flying with the dysfunctional plovers. I, ah, really don't want to listen to this, whatever it is, for an entire migration, so why don't I just flap my way and you flap yours, OK?"

"Well," Sunny said, "what if your way is also our way?"

"Oh, it's not. I'm sure it's not."

"Well, where are you going?"

Glyde paused. "Where are *you* going?"

"We asked first!" Wilbird said. "We asked first!"

"I'm going to find a friend."

"Good luck with that," Wilbird mumbled. "Like he has a friend."

The little plover's father chuckled. "Good one, son." Then he said, "Finding a friend? That's a why, not a where. I asked *where* you're going."

Suddenly, Glyde knew where Wilbird got his peevish personality from. He was reminded of the old adage, "The egg doesn't roll far from the nest."

"Perhaps if we traveled together we could help each other." Piper suggested.

"How are *you* going to help *me*?" Glyde asked, not realizing or caring what it might sound like to the plovers.

"So, we're useless because we're small, really? You're not so big yourself," Sunny declared. "I'm done. Who needs this bird? I'm done."

Little Wilbird threw his wings into the air, mimicking his father as he proclaimed, "Me too. I'm done with this turd."

"This what?" Wilbird's mother interrupted.

"This, ah . . . *bird*. I said bird." Wilbird looked to his father for support.

Sunny glanced at Glyde, looked back to his family, and piped, "Yeah, *bird*. That's what I heard junior say." Then he turned to the petrel and challenged, "What do you think he'd say?"

Piper quietly worked her way in between the bickering birds and spoke to Glyde. "I can see you're a petrel, but you're not from this water. Am I right?"

"Yes, that's true."

"We are. We nest several days north of here to hatch our young on a beach called Seprespa. Once they fledge, we fly farther north to feed for the rest of the summer until we begin our migration south, which is what we're doing now. Seems like you're doing something similar."

"Perhaps . . ."

"If we flew together," the young mother suggested, "we could draft off each other, although that might not do much for you. We could, however, lead you to very fertile feeding grounds. We know them all. We might even be able to show you a shortcut or two along the way."

"I don't really plan to do this trip very often."

"You know, since I haven't seen your kind before," Piper continued, "could your flock be as scarce as we piping plovers are? A few more eyes might help keep us all safe."

"Your flock is scarce?"

"Yes. Not as bad as some, but far fewer than we could be, than we should be."

This was the one appeal that resonated with Glyde. He understood the prospect of extinction all too well. The petrel considered Piper's offer to travel together. "Can you keep those two man-brains quiet?" he asked her.

"No guarantees, but I'll do what I can."

"So, if you're endangered, I guess little prince Wilbird is pretty important to your flock."

"He sure is," the fledgling's mother replied. "He sure is."

"Wow, you birds really are in pretty bad shape if you're depending on *him*," Glyde replied just loud enough for Wilbird and Sunny to hear.

For the first time since meeting Piper, Glyde noticed her smile and giggle.

As they flew into the day, Glyde and Piper discussed their lives. The plover explained that Seprespa was in an area the birds called Long Branch. The beach was surrounded by the enormous nests of the man-flock, and often, the sand teemed with humans.

"Why would you choose to nest in the midst of them?"

"It does seem strange, doesn't it?" the plover agreed.

"So, why do it?"

"It's not as much of a choice as you think. There really aren't many ideal nesting spots for plovers. Seprespa has a good location for birthing and migrating, the right food on shore, and our flock nested there long before any man-flock had ever seen the beach."

"There still have to be better choices."

"I guess," Piper conceded, "but I'll let you in on a secret. As annoying and as dangerous as they can be in large numbers, there can also be benefits to nesting around the man-flock."

"That's funny," the petrel said. "My father told me that even though the man-flock almost ended his life, one of them also saved him."

"Some have helped us, too."

"How?" Glyde asked, unconvinced yet curious.

"Let me guess, you're a ground nester?" the plover said.

Glyde nodded. "Not a lot of trees at sea."

"So, you know how dangerous it can be for a bird who nests on the ground. We lay our speckled eggs on the open sand in a small scrape above the high tide line. I know it sounds crazy, but at least when our young fall, it's not out of a tree, and we're right there to pick them up."

"But you choose open sand? A scrape? Petrels don't even do that. We burrow." *Brave birds, these plovers,* Glyde thought.

"Yes, we're out there, we certainly are. We have to deal with foxes, raccoons, crows, hawks, dogs, cats, the list is long. But on Seprespa, the man-flock—a group of them, at least—actually help us. They will construct a large hard web over our scrape so that we can get in and out but most of those larger predators can't reach us."

"Really? The man-flock will do that for you?"

"And more. They'll make noises that scare the carnivores, especially crows. They'll even chase their own kind away. And I've seen them do one thing that I have trouble believing, but I've seen it."

"What's that, Piper?"

"When we hatch young, like my little Wilbird . . ."

Glyde looked over at the offensive offspring and rolled his eyes.

". . . we don't actually feed them."

"Plover parents don't feed their hatchlings? That's cold."

"From the time they can walk, our little ones carry themselves to the shoreline and forage on their own."

"Before they can fly?"

"An entire moon before."

"Wow!" Glyde spouted. "That's dangerous. It's amazing your young survive at all."

"It's a miracle," Piper agreed, "but it's our way. The man-flock, some of them, seem to understand this. On our beach, our Long Branch, they will walk with the chicks to the shore and protect them while they eat. When the little ones are done eating, the man-flock will escort them back to the scrape, making sure no harm comes to them. I have witnessed this many times."

"They are a strange flock, the humans." Then Glyde told Piper about his journey, his search for Soaria, and what life on Galahope was like. After a few days, they arrived at one of the winter homes of the plovers, a very nice stretch of beach where the water and the weather would be perfect until it was time to return to Seprespa.

The piping plovers' winter beach ran north-south along the ocean, curved into the southern shore of an inlet, and then continued again on the other side of the little inlet for many miles. On the north shore of the inlet, a tall man-flock construction rose from behind the dunes. It was made from the ubiquitous flat, dull, red man-flock stone. It rose straight up, as tall as three or four large oaks stacked one on top of the other. At the tip, a bright light shone all night long. It was as if a small piece of a star were trapped inside and flew around in a circle every night, searching for a way to return to the heavens. The birds called the inlet and the beach Piece, for "Piece of a Star."

As the foursome landed on the south shore of Piece, Glyde could see pelicans, crested terns, least terns, willits, sandpipers, ruddy turnstones, skimmers, a pair of osprey distracted by a mullet run, and a variety of gulls, all sharing the sand, the sea, and the sky. Although petrels are open ocean birds and tend to shy away from beaches, Piece looked like a nice inlet. Still, Glyde reminded himself that he wouldn't stay for long. There were, however, plenty of birds here who he could ask about the female petrel. Whether he got any leads or not, he figured he'd wind up well fed and on his way quickly.

Suddenly, Glyde was shoved aside when Wilbird plowed through him as he chased a sand flea. The profane plover peeped, "Turd," just loud enough for Glyde to hear, then smiled and ran off, his orange legs tearing across the shoreline. The hungry youngster dove into a clump of seaweed, plucked what looked like a tiny marine worm, and sucked it down.

Immediately after the petrel rose and brushed the sand off his feathers, he was knocked down again, this time by Sunny, who quickly helped him up and apologized. "Sorry, bird. My bad."

Glyde nodded graciously. At least the father had some manners. But as the petrel brushed the sand off his feathers a second time, he thought he heard Sunny mumble, "Turd," when the plover sprinted to the shoreline, where he pecked at tiny crustaceans rolling in the surf. Wilbird landed next to him, a chip off the old rock, and said, "Nice one, Dad." The two plovers snickered while they tore into the feast.

Glyde turned to Piper, who calmly pecked at a miniscule snail. The mother plover displayed a contented smile and said, "Birds of a feather. They're definitely birds of a feather."

"I've got another name for it," Glyde muttered.

By the end of the day, Glyde had slipped to the back of the beach, away from the breaking surf. He struck the pose that his father had taught him, a posture that carried the shorebirds' prayers more directly to God, whom his flock referred to as Pettr. There were also words involved, a *birdtra*. Lupé knew the words but couldn't share them with his son. They were only effective if each bird found the words in their own time, in their own way. Also, the same words didn't always work for the same birds.

At this point in his young life, Glyde knew only one word, *sand*. Usually, there would be four words in the *birdtra*. Somehow, some way, if he were truly flying the good flight, the right words would be revealed to him. At that point, he might not only send thoughts to Pettr, he might have actual conversations with the Creator, and he would be called Savn by the flock. That wasn't Glyde's goal, although it was for many. The petrel merely needed help, and so he asked for it.

Glyde stood facing into the wind, raised one leg tight against his body, and closed his eyes—an act of faith, since closing one's eyes in the wild could be a dangerous thing to do. Balanced on a single leg, swaying in the breeze, bolstered by the chorus of the creatures on the beach, with the calm inlet water lapping at the shore, Glyde was transformed, transported.

He was able to talk to himself—not the way a daffy duck might, but within his own mind. The petrel could reach places within himself that held answers he normally couldn't find. It was a focus, a concentration, a meditation, a prayer. He probed whether he'd done the right thing leaving Galahope, whether he was on the right track. He began to get answers. The answers came, he was sure, from within, but the petrel wasn't sure they truly came from him.

Was his father speaking to him? Lupé was a Savn. It wasn't beyond him to do such a thing. Glyde could hear the voice. It was speaking to him, but he couldn't understand it. Perhaps he needed more words in his *birdtra* to clear up the message. The petrel repeated *sand* over and over. "Sand, sand, sand, sand . . ."

The voice sounded like a bird was calling to him. It was shouting into the wind, so the words were carried away rather than delivered to him. The full, clear tones never reached him. Instead, he heard a murmur, a rumble. It sounded like it might be his proper name—*Seamore, Seamore*—but it was little more than a droning moan. It could be anything. Frustrated, Glyde opened his eyes and shook off the sand that had blown onto his face. The sun setting behind the dunes brought him back to Piece.

At that moment, Wilbird was racing along the beach, a bit out of control as young plovers often are, passing right in front of Glyde. The sight of the petrel teetering on one leg was just too much for the petulant piper. When he streaked past Glyde, Wilbird extended his left wing ever so slightly, just enough to graze Glyde's rump, spinning and dumping the dizzy petrel back in the sand. Wilbird looked back with a hint of a smile on his stubby orange beak.

Before he could say anything, Glyde quipped, "Yeah, I know. Turd."

Wilbird widened his grin into a full-on smile and ran off, protesting, "What? It was just a graze, a total accident. No blood, no fowl."

Again, the petrel dusted himself off. He stretched his wings for a moment and tucked them back at his sides, having decided to resume his meditation. Then he heard, "Over here. In here." The voice came from within a long dark hole in the side of a dune.

The holes weren't uncommon along the beach. These were the homes of gopher tortoises. The creatures were substantially smaller than the grander tortoises of Galahope, but they were tortoises nonetheless. Back home, Glyde always had good relations with the extraordinary reptiles. In fact, one named El Solitario Jorge was a good friend, but this was a different beach on a different ocean, and he wasn't quite sure what to expect. He approached the burrow but didn't enter.

"In here. I shouldn't be seen telling you this, but I know what you're after . . . and I know where she is."

"What makes you think I'm after anything?" Glyde bluffed.

"Ah, we're all after something, someone . . . I saw her two days ago, the only other bird I've ever seen who looks so much like you.

And you're the only bird I've ever seen who looks so much like her. And you both show up so close to each other on the same beach? Stands to reason, doesn't it, that you might be looking for her?"

Tortoises are smart, no doubt about that, and apparently observant, too. But this one wasn't especially neat. Its burrow had a musky, dank odor that Glyde didn't appreciate.

"Like I said, I'm not really looking for anyone, but it is interesting that you think you saw a bird from my flock."

"I saw one, all right. Sadly, *you'll* probably never see her."

"What's that supposed to mean?"

"It means that she's probably dead. I can't imagine any bird surviving that . . ."

Two days earlier, Soaria drifted onto Piece Beach as a brief stop on her meandering migration. She perched on a wooden rail overlooking the water and searched for food. It was quiet, she was alone, and life was good. In a few days, she'd fly home. Then all would be as it had been.

A stiff gust flared across a dune, and the petrel spread her wings to keep from being blown off her perch. She stabilized herself, but the gust shifted, and Soaria spun. Her wingtip caught the wood, and she suddenly crashed to the ground. Pain ripped at her flank, across her ribs. Something sharp had pierced her. She struggled, dragging herself out onto the sand. The petrel's vision blurred.

She couldn't fly. She couldn't run. Her right side became numb. Soaria was bleeding into the sand.

A stick with a single sharp tooth on one end and what looked, ironically, to be feathers on the other end had entered her side beneath the skin above the ribs and protruded near her shoulder. She could feel the middle section of the stick still inside her, the weight of it holding her down.

Another stick ricocheted off a large clam shell jutting from the sand next to Soaria, cracking it. The petrel was under some type of attack, and it wasn't over. Frantically, she dragged herself, using her good wing and her legs, into the surf. A third stick struck her, bouncing off her back without impaling her. Soaria threw herself into the water and let the current carry her out. Ignoring the pain, she closed her wings tightly to her sides, trying to keep the stick from moving within her. Every time it did, sharp, ripping pain burned throughout her body. She floated away from the shore on the outgoing tide, continually leaning one way or the other to keep from being pulled under.

Soaria could see him running along the beach, picking up the pointed sticks except for the one that was now part of her. A small human, obviously excited, stood on the shore and waved his featherless wing at her. He turned and walked away, launching sticks as he disappeared behind the dunes, leaving Soaria to fight for her life.

The stick against her ribs slipped slightly lower. The petrel hoped it might work its way out. If it continued to weigh her small body down, she'd certainly die. Feathers on the lower end provided drag against the water. The stick slid farther and farther down until all that remained above her shoulder was a small section with the sharp tooth on the end.

As that little shaft of wood also worked its way down, the tooth began to back into the hole it had made in her shoulder. That's when it became clear to Soaria that the stick wasn't going anywhere. It was attached to her. The tooth was pointed at its tip but wider at its base, where it hung on to the wound and tore at it. The petrel worried that if the tooth managed to reenter the wound, the damage it would do would be unimaginable, unbearable. It's one thing to tear at flesh. It's quite another to rip at what's beneath.

Then another problem presented itself—actually, two of them. Just beyond the pair of rocky jetties that protected the inlet—one to the north, another to the south—Soaria floated out to sea. She was bleeding from two rather large wounds, and a small bird like her only contained so much blood. If the bleeding continued, it would be over soon. The second problem was that she was bleeding into the water. And this location on the coast was one of the most shark-infested areas on the continent.

Soaria had always believed that there was a plan, that Pettr had a purpose for her. She had no real vision of what her life would entail, where she would fly, how the journey would end. She was pretty sure it wasn't supposed to end this way, yet here she was. There could be no escape from this. The only remaining mystery was how she'd die in the next few moments. Would she bleed out, be eaten by a predator, or drown in the sea? Maybe one of the ospreys would carry her away to its nest. The answer came quickly.

Even though the tiger shark patrolling just offshore had sharp eyesight and keen hearing, the often docile fish could not ignore its other senses. Electroreceptors more sensitive than any in the animal kingdom began to fire as they picked up the movements, the thrashing. Simultaneously, its nostrils just under its snout—nostrils used exclusively to smell, able to pick up trace amounts of blood from kilometers away—noticed Soaria immediately. The two-thousand-pound, twenty-foot-long predator had to investigate. The petrel was easy to find.

Blinding pain raged through Soaria as she was violently dragged underwater. Having eaten earlier but not quite enough, the shark grabbed on to the bloodied stick dangling beneath the bird and yanked them both underwater. The petrel began to drown, and she welcomed it. The shark gave the stick and Soaria a bone-jarring shake. Even underwater, half unconscious, the petrel heard the *snap*, thinking her body—her spine—had just succumbed.

Floating to the surface, it became clear that it was the stick that had snapped, not her spine. With the shorter, toothed portion of the shaft still in her, the almost lifeless bird waited for the shark to return and complete the assault. Bloody and broken, Soaria waited, almost hopeful, but the tiger didn't return. Perhaps it also waited. Perhaps it was gone. It wasn't, however, the only shark in the sea.

The petrel prepared herself to meet Pettr. It was time, yet part of the bird refused to believe that her time had come. She couldn't think clearly anymore. She couldn't maintain focus. So, she let go. Soaria was heading to a place where there were many Gwatta petrels, where the currents always carried food, where the winds always delivered you home, and where the man-flock didn't propel sticks into birds' bodies.

Soaria felt herself rise, weightless, out of the ocean into the sky . . . the sky. The sun warmed her wet feathers as the water dripped back into the sea. The salt on the side of her mouth tasted like home. The wind welcomed her. It was over.

Rich Cole wasn't originally from Florida, which was probably one of the main reasons he loved the lifestyle so much. After spending the bulk of his life in the mid-Hudson Valley of New York, much of it in an office staring at a screen as a computer security compliance officer, with *feet* of snow on the ground, he savored every second of his retired life in warm, sunny Ponce Inlet, thrilled that he'd followed his daughter south when she moved to Florida. He surrounded himself with the fascinating flora and fauna of Atlantic coastal Florida, whether he was navigating the backwaters or the back roads.

This was a playground for Rich. He experienced it, studied it, and explained it as a master naturalist at the Ponce Inlet Marine Science Center. There, Rich and his colleagues not only participated in constant public outreach and education, they also took things a huge step further, rescuing, treating, and releasing thousands of turtles and hundreds of injured birds. In fact, when Rich was on site lecturing to interested visitors, he could almost always be found with a diminutive screech owl named Otus perched on his shoulder or forearm, an injured rescue who couldn't be released.

But at the moment, Rich wasn't working, and Otus was back at the Marine Science Center, so the owl's human friend was on his own, exploring. Even though he was solidly into retirement, Rich explored with all the wonder, all the enthusiasm of a Cub Scout on his first camping trip. He spent the morning on his boat in the backwater floating with manatees munching turtle grass, following dolphins chasing bunker, observing ibises feeding at low tide. Rich decided to swing through the inlet in his fifteen-foot Palmer Critchfield—a great place to find dolphins and a variety of birds—and motor out to beachside to see what was running through the surf. He checked with his crew—granddaughters Ashley and Michelle—and then set course.

After he passed the lighthouse and cleared the jetties, he was just about to open up the forty Merc that powered his boat when he saw a dorsal fin slicing through the swells. Pointier than the spotted dolphins' rounded dorsal, cutting a flat, even line through the water rather than the upward-downward swipe of the marine mammals, Rich knew immediately that he was looking at a large solitary shark. He dropped the motor into neutral, allowed the outgoing tide to carry his skiff closer to the impressive fish, and nodded as it thrashed at an ambushed meal. Rich understood that everything needed to eat, and the titanic tiger shark was no exception. The current carried him closer, and its dorsal fin slipped from view. Just as he glimpsed the stripes on the side of the tiger, it vanished beneath his boat.

As curious as their grandfather, Michelle and Ashley peered over the port bow with him to see if any clues lingered in the water regarding what the shark was dining on. The foam was tinted red and pink. A dark-grey spot floated lifelessly within the bubbly slick.

Rich pulled up beside the carnage, wondering why the tiger would leave a meal. Perhaps his boat scared the fish off, or maybe this was just debris. Sharks were notorious for attacking buckets, floating flip flops, boogie boards—almost anything, if it was presented right and the mood hit them. As Rich drew nearer, he could see feathers on the water. Seagull? Pelican, perhaps? There wasn't much left of it, if it was. The naturalist leaned over the rail. What he found wasn't a piece of a bird. It was the whole thing, more or less.

It was a petrel—what type, he couldn't say. The bird was mangled, to say the least. Rich spotted the arrow in its flank, and for an instant had to fight back his rage. Had someone really done this? This was exactly what Rich hated about human behavior. It was a crime, an actual crime. Hoping that maybe, just maybe, there might be clues, Rich picked up a net and scooped the dead bird impaled by the arrow out of the sea.

He laid what was left of Soaria on his deck and studied her injuries. He'd seen this before. An ibis had been pierced by an arrow and had flown around for days with the projectile protruding from its body. The bird was tracked on and off for more than a week until it disappeared. No one knew what happened, but most assumed the worst—which appeared to be the case for this poor creature, as well.

Rich held the little petrel in his hands. It genuinely bothered him, deeply, when any living thing died senselessly. But even as his boat swayed on the swells, he could feel it. There was a rhythm to it. Inside the petrel, its heart was beating, barely. He examined the arrow wounds. There was a trickle—no, it was less than a trickle. It was an ooze—an ooze of blood from the punctures. This petrel was alive, somewhat, and likely wouldn't be in the next minute or two, but right now, there was still life inside the bird.

One of his granddaughters asked quietly, afraid of the answer, "Can we help it?"

Rich laid Soaria onto a towel and gently draped a corner over the bird's eyes. Then he jumped behind the wheel and turned his boat around. The Marine Science Center was located literally in the shadow of the Ponce Lighthouse, and Rich could almost reach out and touch the pillar from where he floated. The boat roared to life, and Rich raced to shore. There was a chance.

The voice from the tortoise burrow ceased. By now, following the sound, Glyde had wandered deep into the den. "So, the man-flock has her? And she's just a few flaps from where we are?"

"You could say that, but there's something else you should know," the helpful voice whispered.

"Tell me everything . . . everything."

"Do you think you can handle the truth?"

"Just tell me, tortoise. I can handle it."

"OK. Are you ready?"

Glyde nodded. He could almost see the reptile. "Hurry, time may matter."

"No, it won't matter, because you're out of time. And I'm not a tortoise."

With that, the source of the voice sprang forward, snapping at Glyde, who retreated instantly toward the light at the other end of the long tunnel.

The petrel had been speaking to a fox, a creature he'd never encountered on Galahope.

The animal ripped feathers from the bird's rump, laughing. "Oh, if only your friend hadn't made it to the water, she would have filled my belly before dying for nothing with the man-flock. But you will do."

Glyde ran. He couldn't fully extend his wings in the tunnel. And because he'd just lost a mouthful of tail feathers, he wasn't sure how well he'd fly if he did get beyond the opening. All the petrel could do at this point was flee. The fox was close enough for Glyde to feel its breath on his back. There was also that pungent, musky odor that Glyde had smelled earlier. It should've warned him, but having never encountered a fox, he didn't know where the scent came from or what it meant.

From this moment on, if there would be any moments beyond this for the petrel, that smell would remain seared into his memory. Suddenly, a word, a single word began to echo in his mind. He couldn't silence it. *Sand, sand, sand.* Over and over, it reverberated, welling up from his subconscious. He recognized the word. It was *his* word. Yes, it made sense.

The fox seized one of Gyde's partially extended wings, clamped down on the tip, and dragged the petrel closer.

Sand, Glyde thought. *Sand*. It was an act of desperation. The bird turned to one side, spread his webbed feet, and launched two piles of loose sand into the fox's face.

Blinded by the irritating grains, the fox released Glyde, who burst through the opening of the tunnel. But as he tried to fly to freedom, his pinched wing and missing tail feathers kept the petrel grounded.

The predator hadn't given up the pursuit. He shook his head, rubbed his eyes, and returned to the chase. "Nice try," he growled as he pounced at the petrel.

When Glyde heard the fox, he couldn't believe it. *Will this be the last word I ever hear?* he wondered. It just couldn't be. And then he heard another word.

"Turd!" It was Wilbird, no doubt coming to gloat at Glyde's demise.

Unbelievable, he thought. *What a time for this. What a way to die, mocked by an annoying plover while whatever this thing is rips me apart.*

"Turd!" There it was again. But the cry wasn't mockery. It was a war cry that Wilbird delivered right into the petrel's ear, so Glyde ducked abruptly, and the fox stumbled over him. The canine quickly regained his footing and returned to ravage his prey.

Then the predator froze as if he were somehow suddenly afraid of the bird. The petrel raced off into the dunes, but the fox didn't follow. When Glyde looked back to the beach after hiding under a small shrub, it all made sense.

For some reason, the man-flock often made companions of animals. It was a strange practice that no wild animal fully understood. Nonetheless, the practice continued. Having dealt with humans and dogs on the beach quite often in Long Branch, the plovers were masters of the situation, as Sunny and Wilbird demonstrated.

Apparently, the plovers located a rather large dog, a young Australian shepherd named Max, out for a vigorous jaunt on the sand. Sunny began to display, just as he would if his eggs were being jeopardized and he needed to distract the threat. The classic faux broken wing, combined with Sunny's special mambo, instantly caught the hairy mongrel's attention. The bird strutted across the sand, flapping and piping for all he was worth. Sunny definitely had moves. The display entranced the curious canine, who followed the plover right up to the hole that contained Glyde and the fox. Unlike the petrel, Max knew what occupied the den well before he got there. He could smell it a mile away.

When the petrel and his pursuer emerged from the burrow, as Sunny hoped they would, the distracted dog forgot all about the piping plover. The fox presented a much tastier challenge. His sharp scent made the Aussie's nostrils flare. Max, a rescue from a rough shelter, loved his family, tolerated other people, and *hat-*

ed any dog that crossed his path. Another canine on *his* beach, and it was *growling?* Was it growling at *him?* This had to be dealt with severely.

Max handled these moments in two stages. He began with the nice way. He'd bark a deep, foreboding challenge. If the offender didn't withdraw instantly, Max moved to stage two, the not so nice way. In this particular instance, Max decided to forego stage one, preferring to go directly to the aforementioned not so nice way. It was on.

Apparently, the fox was so absorbed with Glyde, it had somehow failed to take note of the drooling dog. While this disrespect upset Max—he did tend to take these things *dogsonally*—it didn't displease him. Somewhere deep inside his DNA (his doggone nasty attitude) the sixty-five-pound Aussie, who was bred for protecting livestock and didn't have a lick of fat on him, had determined that the little bird was livestock and the fox was a very real threat. It was time for him to do what he'd been put on the Earth to do: eliminate the threat. The monstrous mongrel struck a pose—hackles up, teeth bared—took one more good whiff of the fox, and lit after it like a greyhound chasing a rabbit.

When the two plovers landed next to Glyde under the bush in the dunes, Wilbird pointed to the fleeing fox and announced, "Now there's a real turd."

Glyde took solace in the idea that in Wilbird's eyes, there actually existed a greater turd than himself. The petrel had apparently attained the status of a *lesser turd*.

Later in the day, toward dusk, the petrel went with the plovers to feed at the shoreline. Since flight was still difficult, Glyde scavenged with his little friends. Although this worked well for the plovers, the petrel suspected that feeding like this wouldn't sustain or heal him.

Just then, a tall egret strode over to the trio and graciously dropped a pair of greenish, silvery white mullets at Glyde's feet.

The petrel looked up, and the egret nodded. Glyde snapped up one of the morsels.

The egret took a long single step and angled its head down the beach, looking away from the inlet. He grinned but seemed unsure whether he should speak. The egret nodded down the beach a second time and said, "No tricks. No foxes. I don't fly that way, OK?"

"OK," Glyde replied tentatively, not sure what he just agreed to.

"My name's Galstep. And that's the one."

The petrel looked confused.

"The man-flock, the one who took your friend out of the sea . . ."

Glyde stared deep into the egret's eyes.

"That's the human. I saw the whole thing. I even checked with the crows. Nobody remembers faces better than the crows. I asked several. It comes to this shore often, sometimes on a floating island, sometimes rolling on a small roaring nest, sometimes with two little ones. It likes this beach, and none of us have ever seen it harm anything here. Well, it's taken a fish or two." Galstep grinned and shrugged. "But who hasn't done that, right?"

"Of course," the petrel replied to the towering egret. He swallowed the remaining mullet and added, "Case in point."

Galstep nodded.

"That's the one the fox was talking about?" Glyde asked, pointing to the human.

The egret nodded. "Not sure what it means to you, but I thought you'd like to know." The lanky male paused, speared another tiny mullet, and dropped it at Glyde's feet before he turned to walk away. The great egret took a few steps, stopped, and turned, raising and flaring the plumes on his back. He said, "Take care, Seamore." And then he shook his head as if he'd wasted the thought.

Glyde swallowed the fish. *Seamore?* he wondered. *How could the egret know that?* But if the petrel pursued Galstep to find out how he knew his name, he'd lose the opportunity to hatch his plan for the human, a plan that absolutely flew in the face of the egret's advice for him to take care.

Glyde looked at the human who was walking toward him.

Pecking at a clump of seaweed, Piper raised her head and asked, "What are you gonna do?"

"I'm gonna do something really stupid," Glyde replied. And then he did it.

Azul was enjoying his stay with the Ocean Stewards, and that's precisely what was bothering him. The parrots had told him about living with humans, how kind they might be one day, how unpredictable they might be the next. While the macaw didn't think it was likely that he'd encounter some of the horrors he'd heard about, he was still concerned, particularly with how comfortable he was with White Feathers and his friends. But as long as there was always open sky above him and nothing holding him down, Azul decided that he'd accept the man-flock's hospitality, at least for the time being.

Eating on the floating island out at sea was an interesting experience for the parrot. There were no trees where Azul could perch to pluck nuts and fruit. It was almost as if the man-flock understood this. They devised wondrous ways for the macaw to feed. Morgan and Jack would team up every day with the Roger's chief cook, Mary, to devise culinary contraptions to challenge Flint. Toilet paper rolls, small cardboard boxes, empty food containers, and paper cups were used as vessels to contain the parrot's meals. The trio devised ways to layer the contents so that the bird would be faced with a veritable Rubik's Cube, a multitiered puzzle with delectable delights stashed throughout, provided you had the chops to reach them—and Flint didn't disappoint.

During downtime on calm seas, one of the crew would climb the mast or some other structure and hang that day's dining dilemma for Flint to discover and decipher. The parrot's persistence, his focus, his intellect, his dexterity, his creativity captivated the crew who gathered to watch the show. Wagers that usually involved chores or some embarrassing settlement rather than cash were often made regarding the macaw's success or failure. You bet against Flint at your own peril. The lone parrot could absolutely handle the best efforts of the humans. And Azul—or Flint if you were talking to the crew—really enjoyed the challenge, the sport. It wasn't just eating. It was an activity. It was living rather than existing.

This daily exercise helped Azul mentally and physically. The Ocean Stewards recognized and valued that their shipmate Flint had a great mind, one that required stimulation and therapy, just as a recovering human would need. In fairly short order, Azul was healed.

By that time, the *Roger Caras* was in port in the Bahamas, done with the public information junket and preparing for the next campaign to defend life in the sea. Everyone was getting their game face on. Radar was being installed in the helicopter, and the ship was being fitted with several surprises for any poaching fleets they might encounter. Similar work was being done on the rest of the Ocean Stewards' fleet in a variety of ports. The crew had less time for Flint, and the parrot began to wonder if the warning of the Kwake parrots about humans not taking friendship as seriously as parrots do was coming true.

Still, whenever White Feathers appeared, Azul would land on his shoulder. It happened so often that it became habit for both of them, neither feeling quite comfortable without the other. When White Feathers went inside the floating island or stepped on land, Azul would fly to another perch and wait. For the first time, in a strange, unexplainable way, the whole parrot-person dynamic began to hold some appeal to Azul. That was when the macaw made up his mind to leave.

From their port in the Bahamas, the parrot knew that with a little luck, he could probably island-hop most of the way home. Although his flock had different names for the locations, his plan was to fly south through the West Indies into the Lesser Antilles, from Grenada to Trinidad and Tobago, across the northeast coast of South America until he was home in the Caatinga. It would be an incredible journey but no greater than the migrations of many other birds. What Azul didn't know was that Captain Teach and First

Mate Morgan planned to sail the macaw to the shores of his home, returning him to the place man had taken him from. But even if the parrot had understood, there was still a good chance Azul would've done it his way.

It was time to go. Azul knew where he was. He knew where he had to go. He was healthy, rested, and renewed. Now was the time. Well, almost.

The macaw waited until morning. He and White Feathers had a routine of starting their day appreciating the rising sun, savoring the sounds of the sea. Azul wanted to make sure White Feathers was the last man-flock he saw before he left. It was important to the bird that his friend understood why he was leaving. Azul didn't want White Feathers to think that he'd tired of the human's friendship. He was leaving because he had to, not because he wanted to. If anyone would understand, Teach would.

Perched on the captain's shoulder, Flint climbed down his arm and settled on the rail that faced him. They stared at each other for a long moment, both comforted by the strained squeak of the mooring lines, yet at the same time, both restless to drop the lines and sail off.

As many times as he'd seen the sky parrot, Teach continued to marvel at the majestic macaw. Such an incredible creature, and it chose to be with the Ocean Stewards on the Jolly Roger, chose to perch on his shoulder. Teach smiled. He handed his friend a grape. No goofy contraptions, just a grape. The parrot rubbed his thick beak against the back of White Feathers's hand, leaving the grape where the human held it.

Flint popped into the air and climbed high above the mast. Ignoring his breakfast hanging from a string, he flew on. Flint was gone. There was only Azul. Teach knew exactly what had happened as he swallowed the grape, still smiling.

Azul's first day of flight was long, perhaps overly ambitious, yet even though he wound up tired and hungry, the parrot hardly noticed. It felt good to be back in the sky. With luck, Azul would soon arrive in Cuba, although the macaws didn't call the island by that name. In fact, the birds to the south referred to the entire string of islands in and around the West Indies as the Seeds.

They viewed the little spits of land scattered above their home range as metaphorical *seeds* that had been spilled onto the sea. And like seeds, they were fertile, growing unique flora and fauna. The sky parrots understood all this and, in their infrequent journeys, would use the Seeds as roosts to rest, to replenish, or to avoid heavy weather. Azul would recess in the largest island of the Seeds, the most northerly, often referred to as the Pod, which was known to the man-flock as Cuba.

There were several reasons Azul believed the Pod would be a good place to rest. The northeastern end of the island was wild and unsettled. The location was perfect to continue his migration along the Seeds to the southeast. Azul also expected to find food without too much effort. The area supported an indigenous flock of parrots that his friends to the north had told him about. The birds called them Pod parrots, robust green birds that lived on the Pod and several surrounding Seeds. As he arrived, Azul hoped that he'd be welcome.

The macaw knew that large islands like this one were usually home to creatures that one might not normally see in their own environment. The parrot enjoyed this aspect of travel. It could be dangerous and unpredictable, but it was also exciting to see Creation move in unexpected directions, to see what cast of characters filled the same niches that existed from one habitat to the next. For example, Azul had already noticed from his perch that this forest had a hummingbird so small, it was pollinating plants just like a bee. The same forest had a larger hummingbird as well, but because it was so much bigger, there was no real competition between the two birds who drew sustenance in different ways. This harmony, this balance fascinated the parrot. It was one small cipher in the incredible equation of nature, of life.

The palms, the fruits, the nuts, the lizards, the green parrots— they reminded Azul that even though he had a long way to go, he was getting closer. He was going home.

Resting, Azul continued to observe the story that was the forest in the Pod. He noticed a rodent he'd never seen before. This one, a nutria, was out on a limb—literally. As an omnivore, it tended to prefer flora rather than fauna, yet it was currently pursuing a lizard. It stalked a petite brown anole that seemed to be stalking a small beetle. The curious parrot scrutinized its claws, five on each foot, strong enough to grasp the bark, like the squirrels he'd seen when he began his journey from the north.

Slowly, almost imperceptibly, the nutria stepped closer to the lizard, who either didn't see the rodent approach or was convinced that its camouflage rendered him invisible. Overconfidence can often be a very perilous state of mind. The nutria took another small step. It had to be within striking distance, Azul observed. The rodent hitched back on its haunches and prepared to strike the anole, which had stranded its prey, the beetle, on the tip of a long branch that reached just above a swampy lake.

The nutria struck, lunging forward, but before it could lay its teeth on the little reptile, a not-so-little reptile rose from the water and snapped its own jaws at the rodent. Propelled by its powerful tail and an equally powerful hunger, a crocodile launched itself out of the swamp and into the branch, depositing the beetle, the lizard, and the rodent into the lake.

Azul was instantly reminded that while this remote forest jewel was undeniably beautiful, if he relaxed too much, especially in an exotic, unfamiliar setting, this could easily become a forest fatale.

"Makes you wonder, doesn't it?" a voice from above hissed squeakily down. "Sometimes I see something like that, and the hair on my neck stands up stiff. That ever happen to you?"

Azul could see the tip of a tail—a mammal's, no doubt—protruding from a clump of leaves above. His instinct screamed at him, *Fly!* But recalling a patrolling sparrow hawk, he stayed where he was.

The mammal continued, "Well, I don't mean the hairs on *your* neck, of course. In your case, we'd be talking about feathers, but you do comprehend my point? This can be a fairly hair-raising or feather-raising forest, as the case may be."

The macaw remained silent.

When the rest of the tail emerged from the rustling leaves, the parrot realized that it wasn't a tail at all. It was a nose, a pretty long one. The proboscis belonged to a female solenodon, a very rare mammal on the Pod. The venomous rodent was about as long as Azul was tall. It looked like something that would result if an opossum, a shrew, and an anteater had a baby. The creature was covered with light-brown hair, except for the long scaly tail and the naked snout.

"This is a nice place, but be careful," the animal warned.

"Good advice, I'm sure," Azul replied. "I'll be gone in the morning, so I'll do my best to stay out of trouble."

"Stay in the trees if you can. An abandoned roost would be even better. It can get crazy here at night if you don't know your way around."

"I will." Then the parrot stopped speaking. He cocked his head and leaned to one side, listening. Azul looked at the solenodon for an answer.

The mammal grinned and whispered, "Wait . . . Wait for it . . ."

The strange call began again. Azul was absorbed.

"There's more," the solenodon whispered, its tiny eyes shining.

The call seemed to cease, but really, it was beginning again. A loud staccato rapping followed. It sounded like the man-flock had invaded the woods, yet it wasn't them at all.

Azul couldn't contain himself. "What is it?"

"Carpintero," the solenodon explained. "Carpintero."

"Is this a bird?"

"A very special bird. A woodpecker, as large as you . . . some bigger. And rare. You've never seen one of them before? Ghost birds, they are phantoms."

"No, I've never seen one, but I'm pretty sure I have heard that strange call before. I know I've heard that unmistakable whapping."

"Where? Here, on the Pod?"

"No, north. Far north, recently."

"I've heard that they exist in great swamps to the north, but I wouldn't know. I know this forest but not much else. Solendons don't really fly or swim."

"This was well beyond the northern swamps. I didn't see it, but I heard it. I'm pretty sure I did, in a forest called the Barrens. I was only there for a night. Could I meet this carpintero?"

"If you're also *here* for one night, not likely. I've lived here my whole life and can count on one foot how many times I've actually seen them. And to *meet* one? I wouldn't know where to begin. But listen to that carpintero. Beautiful, is it not?"

"Yes. They have a song that should be sung, that should be heard."

"Don't we all?" the rodent responded rhetorically.

Azul had been watching a sizeable, somewhat square hole in a dead tree from a distance for some time. The solenodon had wandered away earlier, and the parrot was hoping to find a roost for the night. The danger of entering the hole in a strange tree almost made it not worth doing, but, balanced against the peril of roosting in the relative open, Azul deferred to the cover of the tree. He would, however, wait until he was fairly sure as to what, if anything, might be inside.

The sun was beneath the canopy. The shadows were dark and long. Soon, it would be night. Azul approached the roost. He shuffled quietly to the opening and heard nothing. He saw nothing, smelled nothing. The parrot peered into the tree. His biggest fear was a snake, a hawk, or some predator he'd never encountered before. His biggest hope was an uninhabited hole with a second exit. The parrot held his breath and climbed into the refuge. He glanced quickly over his wing to see if anything approached or made note of his entry.

The space inside the tree had definitely been used as a nest. Moss and leaves covered the base. Dark feathers were scattered about, a white feather here and there. The roost was warm, dry, comfortable. Azul looked out at the evening sky, troubled that the nest didn't seem abandoned. If it was active, if it had a current resident, that bird might return at any moment, unless it was nocturnal and had left to feed.

Thankfully, this didn't seem to be a predator's den. There were no pellets containing bones, no remnants of butchered meals. The feathers weren't alarming, not raptor-like at all. Still, in this unfamiliar forest, there was no telling what had laid claim to the roost. Even non-predators could be lethal when defending their homes. Azul would rest, but he likely wouldn't sleep. Rest would have to be enough.

But something else was happening. A shadow darkened the opening. A large bird—dark, with an impressive wingspan—landed on the rim of the roost hole. Azul backed away, and before he could size up the situation, the bird was gone.

After a restless, jittery sleep, the parrot waited for the dawn to disappear before he ventured beyond the tree, allowing the nocturnal predators to begin their daytime slumber and providing some time for the daytime hunters to hopefully relieve their hunger with an early meal. Once the forest was calm and bright, the macaw emerged to fuel up on nuts, fruit, and water. Then he would fly. This would be the routine for days to come.

Glyde was definitely not lying to Piper when he said he was going to do something really stupid.

As was often the case, several man-flock were scattered along the beach. Some of them had long branches stuck into the sand with almost invisible strings—like something a spider would produce, but not woven into a web—emerging from the tips and running out into the water. The man-flock would attach small fish, pieces of larger fish, worms, sand fleas, or some other temptation to pull fish from the sea. Generally, this behavior was between the man-flock and the fish. Occasionally, a human's temptations, or an attractive catch, would become the property of a lucky bird.

But the birds weren't always lucky. The smart ones were the ospreys, the fish hawks, who caught their meals themselves. Many pelicans, egrets, herons, skimmers, and others would do the same. But the birds who relied too heavily upon the litter of the man-flock often paid a steep price. Besides disease, dependence, and a diminished ability to fend for themselves, it wasn't uncommon for birds who existed on man-flock waste to wind up physically injured. And that was exactly what Glyde had in mind.

It was a huge risk, one that could easily cost him his life. The petrel would have to time it perfectly. And he would have to be precise so that, hopefully, he could appear more injured than he actually was, which wouldn't be hard to do, since he was already a bit beaten up by the fox.

As the human who'd skimmed Soaria out of the sea approached, Glyde launched himself into the air. He picked up speed, stayed about man-flock height above the ground, and flew directly into the line that reached from the tall, thin branch into the inlet. Glyde hoped to get tangled, become noticed by the one who seemed to rescue Soaria, and then be taken wherever she was.

The first part of the plan worked perfectly—maybe a little too perfectly. Glyde easily tangled himself in the almost invisible line, but never having done anything like this before, he didn't have a clue as to its tensile strength. Not only did it cling to and tangle the petrel, but as Glyde struggled—at first for dramatic effect, later out of sheer horror—the fine line cut into his body, easily slicing through feathers and flesh.

To make matters worse, as the human who found Soaria passed the pole, he looked out to the inlet, admiring the osprey plucking a fish from the water, and never noticed Glyde's predicament. He walked on aimlessly while the petrel strained to free himself from the grasp of the line. Glyde quickly realized that the more he flailed, the more entangled he became. After a few frantic moments, he stopped struggling and hung motionless above the sand, a trickle of blood dripping onto the dry, white clam shells beneath him. Glyde watched the human grow smaller as he strode steadily into the horizon. Then he was gone, and so was Soaria.

With his life on the line, quite literally, Glyde considered his options. He had none. Suspended above the beach, swaying softly in the breeze, the petrel couldn't believe what he'd done.

Wilbird and Sunny stood below him looking up, shaking their heads in unison. "Bird, what are you doing?" Sunny asked.

"I thought that that man-flock would take me to Soaria. The egret said he was the one who saved her. I figured he'd save me and take me to her."

"So, you did this to get to the female?" Sunny asked, somewhat stunned.

Glyde closed his eyes and nodded painfully.

Wilbird looked at the other two and said one word. "Chicks."

Now it was Sunny's turn to nod with disgust. "You know," the plover continued, "you could have just followed him. You know how to fly. He might have returned to the place."

"Guess I didn't think of that," Glyde admitted.

"Yeah, this whole bird flying thing isn't very obvious," Wilbird added sarcastically. "You know what I'm gonna say?"

This time Glyde, in complete surrender, calmly said, "Yup, *chicks*. Or is it *turd*?"

"Let's go for both," Wilbird decided.

"Lesson learned," Sunny concluded. Then he asked, "You hurt?"

Wilbird pointed to the blood-stained shells.

"I don't know what we can do," Sunny wondered aloud.

The two plovers looked thoughtfully at the tangled mess of line and feathers, trying to come up with a solution.

"Can you just hold still?" Sunny asked impatiently.

Glyde was bouncing up and down, making it difficult to assess the severity of the situation. The petrel bobbed up and down again.

"Really," Wilbird added, "it's not helping. Stay still."

"It's not me," Glyde countered.

The long, thin branch flexed forward and then shook back and forth. Then it happened again. Confused, the plover pair looked at each other, then back up at the petrel. An instant later, the branch bent violently forward. Glyde cawed in pain as the line tightened around his torso and the blood dripped a little faster, pooling in an upturned clam shell beneath the bird.

The branch rose slowly, twitched, and jerked back down to the water. Sunny and Wilbird scattered. One of the man-flock pounded the sand, racing toward the pole, but froze in his tracks when he saw the petrel tangled in his line.

Another human, a female, sprinted to his side, screaming, "You got something big! Reel it in. Don't lose it! Reel!"

The male pointed to the bird tangled in his tackle.

"Get him out!" The female reached for Glyde, grasped him firmly, and tugged. "Just pull him out. You want that fish, don't you?"

The male nodded and grasped the line that extended beyond the tangle. "I'll keep this line taught so we don't lose the fish. You pull that bird out, but be quick."

Glyde had never felt so much pain. The human's grip pushed the air from his lungs while the line sliced off feathers, opened new wounds, and cut deeper into existing ones.

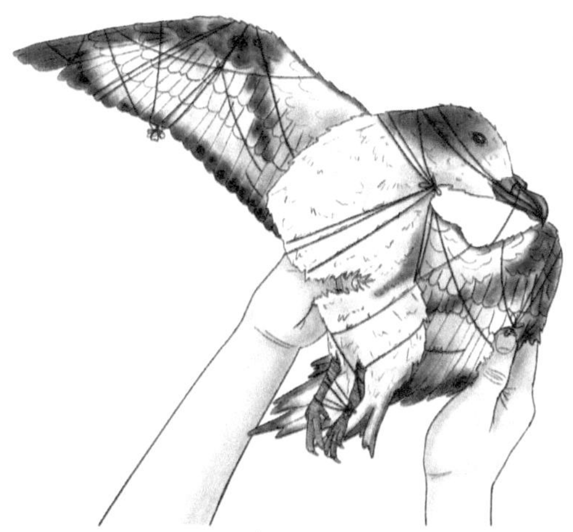

What had happened? How could so much go so wrong so quickly? He'd lose his life over this. And while he never really valued his life all that much, it suddenly meant a great deal to him. Ironically, it wasn't until these final moments that Glyde realized how precious life—his life—actually was, what a blessing it should've been, yet the more he reflected, the less he felt. Glyde became detached from the horror of the moment. He became detached from life, or perhaps life was becoming detached from him.

On this unfamiliar beach with a human pulling his life from him, in a quest to find a female he didn't know, had never even seen, he was, instead, getting to know himself and surprisingly would've given anything to be back at Galahope, just for a moment. But, of course, Glyde was out of moments. It was time to go.

The large human, the one Glyde wanted to encounter when he flew into the fishing line unnoticed, was now coming back down the beach. A bit of a fisherman himself, he was attracted to the activity at the shoreline. Expecting to see a fellow angler land a nice catch, he instead encountered a woman tugging at a battered bird encased in a tangle of monofilament in what fishermen referred to, in a bit of dark irony, as a *bird's nest*.

The woman shook grey feathers drizzled with blood from her hand and declared, "Disgusting!"

Disgust, however, had nothing to do with the bird and everything to do with the two humans.

Rich Cole couldn't believe what he saw. Actually, he did believe it. He just couldn't accept it.

The female dropped the bird on the sand as if discarding an empty can and turned her attention to the remaining tangle in her husband's line.

Rich went immediately to the devastated bird. He was stunned when he finally saw it up close. It was a petrel, another one. Up until two days ago, he'd never seen one on the beach. And now, in a seventy-two-hour span, he'd seen two, both on the brink of death and both belonging to a species he couldn't identify. *This is more than coincidence,* he thought. But this wasn't a time for thoughts. It was a time for deeds.

The naturalist carefully picked the petrel up and placed him in his cap. He held the hat against his chest, hoping the dark would calm the bird, holding him snugly. Rich had two options. He could hurry back to his Harley Nightster and race to the recovery center, which would take twenty to thirty minutes at best, or, if he got lucky, he might be able to get someone to run him across the inlet in their boat, and he would get the petrel medical attention in five minutes.

Scanning the inlet, the only boater within earshot was a young man paddling a kayak along the shoreline. Rich couldn't wait. He ran waist deep into the water and called to the fellow. The kayak approached cautiously, unenthusiastically, yet curiously. The young man kept a safe distance and asked, "You OK?"

Rich had lucked out. The young man was Ben Smith, a vacationer from his home in Raleigh, North Carolina. Ben was a student at UNC Charlotte, an Eagle Scout, a young man of faith. He walked the walk. One look at Glyde, and Ben would do the right thing.

Ben laid the bird in his lap and wrapped a blue towel loosely around the baseball cap. The petrel didn't move. He paddled the package to the opposite shore, pulling Rich, who borrowed a youngster's boogie board for the three-minute ride. In three more minutes, a dying petrel and its soggy savior would be in the medical unit of the Marine Science Center. Its chief avian rehabilitator, Rachelle LaBlanc, would do whatever she could for Glyde. The first time the petrel had ever been in human hands was moments before. This time, he was in good hands.

Rachelle unwrapped the towel, spread open the cap, and gently, gently removed Glyde. The petrel looked into her large eyes. He browsed the room. Hollows with shining square webs lined the walls. Most of them had something like the soft skin the man had spread over him hanging over the front, but even in this condition, Glyde knew there were birds in those hollows. He wondered if Soaria was in one of them. He could feel that she was. Glyde looked back at the two humans. He was not afraid.

Gonzo had eaten his fill. He'd become comfortable with the pines, preferring the northern reaches with the greater variety of large trees, many of them deciduous, to the more easterly, southern tracts that were isolated but dominated by smaller, scrubby vegetation with many more conifers. Grubs were easy to come by almost anywhere in these woods. There were fewer snakes and foxes, no alligators at all. And while the Barrens were surrounded by vast swarms of man-flock, many parts of the forest generally remained ignored by the humans.

Although he couldn't count the pileateds or the kingsnake among them, Gonzo had made good friends. The woodpecker had begun to appreciate these woods. By living in them and becoming part of them, even if only for a short while, he felt he'd been welcomed by the spirit of the forest, which made Gonzo confident and calm. He came to know his place, appreciating just where and how he fit in.

The ivory-bill had woven himself into the rhythm of existence in the Barrens. Maybe he did belong. Still, while all this had happened and in spite of his quiet success and good companions, the pines didn't really feel like *home*. Perhaps it was an unfair expectation, given how briefly Gonzo had been in the forest.

The cold was coming, creeping forward. It would be a little while before the leaves settled on the sandy soil, but the inevitable was imminent. Even though he hailed from the South, Gonzo wasn't a stranger to cold. He'd seen snow. He'd perched on boughs that broke from the burden of ice clinging to bark. To Gonzo, even though he was told that the winter season in the Barrens was becoming somewhat shorter than it had been, starting later, ending earlier, the reality of its approach was more an inconvenient truth than a deal breaker. He believed he could weather it.

As climates warmed, which they seemed to be doing, his range might increase or possibly shift. But if they warmed too much, the wise woodpecker wondered, could the shift be so extreme that rather than expand his range, the ecosystem might disappear altogether? The prospect chilled him more deeply than any cold winter wind ever could.

Then, another thought took flight in Gonzo's mind. If, at least in the relatively short term, the range of ivory-billed woodpeckers did expand as the result of climate change, that might not be a good thing. With a population that probably numbered fewer than the feathers on his face, an increased range might disperse any remaining woodpeckers so much that they'd never find each other and perish without reproducing.

The pair of pileateds appeared, climbing down the trunk of a robust pine directly across from Gonzo. The ivory-bill looked toward them, making eye contact but saying nothing. He looked at the other trees and the sky as well to see if anything was afoot. One of the pileateds, whom he came to recognize as Runk, said calmly, "The way we see this—"

"We?" Gonzo interrupted.

"Our flock, our friends," Runk replied.

"And there are many," Moss, the other bird, added.

"As I was saying, the way we see this, there's nothing that having you in these woods does for us. All you are is competition, unneeded competition for food, nesting sites—"

"And when you feed the way you feed," the female interrupted, "bark, insects—trees, even—disappear five, maybe ten times faster than when we feed, and that's if there's only one of you."

"Moss is right. What happens when there's a hundred? Then where do *we* go?"

"A hundred? I can't find *one*." Gonzo turned to the other woodpecker, "Look, Mess—"

"It's Moss."

"Sorry. Moss. I've lived in swamps and woods in the South, where there are many more pileateds than there are up here. Ivory-bills and pileateds have never had a problem, no issues at all."

"Well, we're not in the South," Runk said. "Different place, different rules. And we were here first."

"All that means is that *you* came here before *me*. It doesn't mean that pileateds found these woods before ivory-bills, and it definitely doesn't mean that I can't be here now."

"We think it does mean that."

"But I don't . . . Look, if my presence stresses your feeding grounds or disturbs your nesting sites, just let me know and I'll move to another corner of the woods. I get it. If I can do any reasonable thing to make this work better for you, just let me know. I'll do it."

Runk nodded. "Then go back where you came from."

"That doesn't seem *reasonable*," Gonzo answered.

"It does to us."

"Well, reasonable suggests that we all—myself included—find it acceptable. What you're actually saying is 'My way or the fly way,' and that doesn't work for me."

Runk looked coldly at the large ivory-bill. "What we're saying is, our way *is* the fly way. The only way this works is if you leave."

Gonzo was becoming frustrated, but he thought he'd give it another try. "I know what it's like to worry about serious competition. I know better than most what it's like to worry about my existence. I understand, so if there are things we can do to make this OK, maybe even good, let's do it."

The pileateds exchanged a look. "What you need to do," Runk reiterated, "is leave these woods . . . while you can."

"So, your answer is to threaten me?"

Runk shrugged.

"Leave the Barrens now while you can or you'll never leave," Moss added.

"Yeah . . . Well, right now, I'm not going anywhere. If you ever want to look at this a little differently, I'm easy to find and open to suggestions."

"Yes," Runk agreed. "You are easy to find." Then, he and Moss flapped up into the canopy and were gone.

He didn't hear him coming. You couldn't hear him coming. But now that he was part of the pines, Gonzo could sense him, feel his presence. A blink later, Bardus was beside him. The Bard and the woodpecker sat together, hushed. The sun dipped just beneath the rise of the trees, not yet swallowed by the horizon. Shadows were long and deep. Insects caroled to the ripening stars. Peeping frogs called to entice mates.

A long line of turkeys—a mother leading six or seven youngsters—marched her chicks into the bush. She sensed the owl and signaled to her young, and they disappeared—literally disappeared into the leaves, sticks, plants, the soil. Gone. Unseen. Silent. When she felt it was safe, the hen signaled again, and one by one, the little turkeys reappeared, marching on behind their mother.

Dusk. It was that extraordinary time when the day retreats into night, and briefly, the two coexist, neither fully in charge.

A little later, a pair of crows landed on the ground beneath Bardus and Gonzo. They spaced themselves almost a body length apart, lowered their beaks into the thin layer of leaves that coated the forest floor, and began to fling their heads from side to side. As the leaves tumbled away, exposing what was underneath, the crows snatched up insects, one after another—a worm here, a beetle there, an ant, a cricket, a spider, a centipede, whatever crossed their beaks. It was a quick meal before nightfall. The crows worked as a team. What one missed, the other often grabbed.

They were much more successful together than alone, the woodpecker thought.

More successful together than alone. The words echoed in Gonzo's mind, like a snippet of a nightingale's song that repeats itself over and over, infecting the listener. Bardus nodded as if he could hear the woodpecker's thoughts. Gonzo grinned. The owl's hearing was good, but was it really so acute that Bardus could hear *thoughts*? Not likely, the ivory-bill concluded.

The crows continued mowing through the leaves. One stopped the other. They paused, froze for a moment, and flew away. Disappointed that the birds didn't reach him, disappointed that he didn't reach the birds, a bobcat stepped out from under a hedge of laurel where he was crouched, invisible, directly in the path of the crows' buffet until one of the birds noticed him.

More successful together than alone. Gonzo turned to the owl, who'd just taken a deep breath as if he were about to speak, or perhaps hoot.

"Light thickens, and the crow makes wing to the rooky wood . . . Night-owls shriek where mounting larks should sing . . . 'Tis my occupation to be plain. I have never seen better faces in my time than stands on any shoulder that I see before me at this instant."

Gonzo glared at Bardus, amazed as always by the owl's unique elocution. He wasn't quite sure, but he suspected that the Bard had given him a compliment as he bid the crows adieu.

"There's no art to find the mind's construction in the face . . . Why, what's the matter, that you have such a February face, so full of frost, of storm and cloudiness? . . . I fear your disposition."

"I don't think there's much you fear. Nothing about me, that's for sure," the woodpecker replied, avoiding the owl's larger point, the idea that he appeared solemn to his friend. "I'm just watching those two crows. They work well together."

"Truth has a quiet breast."

"You think I'm not being truthful? Weren't you sitting here with me while we both watched those crows?"

"A friend should bear his friend's infirmities . . . An honest tale speeds best being plainly told," Bardus observed, clearly not following his own advice with respect to the latter suggestion. The owl never said anything *plainly*.

"Well, to be honest, while I was watching the crows, it made me think a little bit about things . . . I think I could spend the winter here. I think I could make it, but I'm not sure I want to."

Bardus nodded. "Thoughts of great value, worthy cogitations."

"It was good for me to come here. Great to meet you, to become your friend, but no matter where I go, no matter what I do, I carry a *bird*en that most others can't imagine. And while you nobly want to bear your friend's infirmities, I'm the only one who can. Do you understand what I'm trying to say?"

"I hear you say not much but think the more."

"Funny, I spend most of my time trying to understand what you're saying, but now, the worm has turned."

Bardus paused. He seemed to be processing Gonzo's thoughts and his response. "What we have, we prize not to the worth. Whiles we enjoy it, but being lacked and lost, why then we rack the value, then we find the virtue that possession would not show us whiles it was ours."

"Yes," the woodpecker agreed, "I miss my home. I think I miss the swamp. You're right. I didn't realize that until I left it behind."

"Is not their climate foggy, raw, and dull?"

"For some, but for others, it's a paradise. I think I need to go from here, but I'm not sure where. I'm not sure when. I guess I'm just not sure."

"We would, and we would not . . . Nothing will come of nothing."

"I know . . . but what is nothing? Is staying here nothing? Is going home nothing? Is finding another forest nothing? I have to get this right, and I'm just not sure."

"To be or not to be, that is the question."

"Oh, I know the questions. It's the answers. And not merely for me. I need answers for my flock, real answers."

Bardus grinned. "His greatness weighed, his will is not his own. For he himself is subject to his birth."

"I do have obligations that are larger than me. I think when I came here, I wasn't flying *to* them—I was flying *from* them."

Again, the owl gazed at his friend, waiting before speaking. "I never knew so young a body with so old a head . . . I understand a fury in your words, but not the words . . . not a whit. We defy augury. There is special providence in the fall of a sparrow. If it be now, 'tis not to come. If it be not to come, it will be now. If it be not now, yet it will come. The readiness is all."

"Yes, words, words . . . but how does one, how do *I*, how does the *ivory-bill* ready itself? I don't believe we do that here, now, in the Barrens. So, if that's true, what's next? How will I ever be two crows working together for survival? To borrow a phrase from you, Bardus, *there's the rub.*"

"That deep torture may be called a hell, when more is felt than one hath power to tell."

"More words. No answers, my friend."

The owl turned to look back at the spot where the pair of crows fed together. He casually swiveled his face back to Gonzo and quietly said, "Journeys end in lovers meeting."

"What? What does that mean?"

As if he'd known all along, as if he was waiting for the woodpecker to say it for himself but had given up on the bird's ability to see what was as plain as the massive beak on his face, the owl repeated, weighed down by the fact that he had to say it not once but twice, "Journeys end in lovers meeting."

Having realized that the Bard could so easily see so deeply into his soul, there was a long silence that was awkward for Gonzo and deeply satisfying for the owl. Eventually, the woodpecker snipped, "So, it's all about the mate? That's what you think this is? Really?"

"The bird of wonder . . . the maiden phoenix . . ." Bardus smiled and cocked his head. "O beauty, till now, I never knew thee." Then—was it possible?—it seemed the owl giggled.

Gonzo flew off to a thick oak that had been struck by lightning several seasons earlier. He reared back and began chiseling bark from its lifeless trunk. The dry, hard wood echoed through the forest. This timber had timbre. Gonzo gorged himself on fat grubs and sweet larvae, his version of comfort food.

The woodpecker was overwhelmed and distressed by the epiphany that he might be moving on, that he could be so dependent on the memory of his life with Kwim. He didn't think it was fair. He wasn't really in a position to test the waters, to try life with another female. There were no others, not that he knew of. And at this point, there wasn't Kwim either.

There was an old adage among woodpeckers: "There are plenty of grubs in the tree." Gonzo swallowed down several more grubs while he reflected on the obsolete saying. It might've been true when his forbears said it, but not now. As far as Gonzo knew, he was a flock of one. Yet as frightening as that thought was, Gonzo's biggest fear was that he'd end up being a flock of none. And it took these pines that were barren of ivory-bills to help him see the equation.

The woodpecker noticed Zomis and Squab watching from a nearby limb. "You two looking for me?"

"Tell him," Squab whispered loudly to Zomis. "Go ahead, tell him."

Gonzo stopped hammering at the tree.

Zomis said nothing.

"*Yeeees?*" Gonzo prompted.

The pigeon shuffled farther out on the limb, closer to his friend in the next tree, with a gait that seemed more rodent than bird. "You've noticed it, haven't you?"

"I don't know, noticed what?" the woodpecker replied.

"The chill, you can feel it at night."

"It's coming," the robin added. "Only gonna get colder."

"Well," Gonzo quipped, "doesn't get as cold up here as it once did, I'm told."

"Maybe, maybe not," Squab said. "One never really knows. There are individual nights that get colder than ever."

Gonzo turned to Zomis, "So, what is it you're supposed to tell me?"

"No sense pecking around the pod, better just spit it out . . ." Zomis mumbled.

"Sounds good to me. Whenever you're ready . . ."

Zomis took a deep breath, stood up as tall as possible, nodded to Squab, and then said, "Looks like Squab and I will be heading south in the morning."

"Can't pull worms from frozen ground," Squab explained. "I'd need a beak like yours just to break the ice."

"Barren winter, with his wrathful nipping cold," Bardus agreed.

"Is Squab getting a case of weather feathers?" Gonzo teased.

"She's got it bad, but she's a robin, what can you do? They're notorious snow birds."

"So, you're leaving?" the woodpecker asked. "Tomorrow?"

"I could stay, but Squab's my daughter," Zomis said. "Gotta stick with her."

The ivory-bill smiled and shrugged as if to say, "Of course, you do." But deep down, what he was really saying was, *Lord, I wish I had a child—anyone, for that matter—who needed me the way Squab needs you.* You could read it in his eyes.

What escaped Gonzo was the fact that Zomis was in virtually the same situation as he was, and yet the lone passenger pigeon was needed . . . by a robin. There was no reason why Gonzo couldn't form familial relationships with other birds, but the woodpecker didn't see that, didn't want that.

Trice rose, hovered while sipping an iris, and then joined the conversation. "Whereareyouheaded? Anyidea?"

"Just south. We'll stop when we're comfortable, then head north as winter fades."

"Aslongaswe'reonthesubject," the hummingbird hummed, "I'mleavingtoo."

The others acknowledged Trice. They knew. Trice could never survive the winter, not even a mild one. He'd likely already stayed longer than he should have in the northern forest.

"You know," Gonzo commented, "if things keep warming, one day some of us might not have to leave at all."

"I hope that never happens," Squab squawked.

"Yeah, I get it. But when I'm in the swamps, I don't need to migrate. It's kind of nice being settled."

The other birds just stared back at Gonzo, imploring him to think about what he'd just said. The whole *imploring* thing, however, was lost on Bardus, who broke the silence by saying, "Now is the winter of our discontent. Now sits expectation in the air. Make use of time, let not advantage slip. Stir with the lark tomorrow."

"So, looks like we all head out tomorrow?" Gonzo asked. "That's the plan? Everyone flies south in their own way?"

The robin and the pigeon agreed, the hummingbird next. Then they realized . . . Bardus. The birds turned to the tree where he was perched to see what the owl would do. He was gone.

But Bardus wasn't as gone as they assumed. He'd merely withdrawn a few flaps deeper into the pines and disappeared. A little distance often increased his power of thought, and the barred owl definitely had some thinking to do. Would he stay in the forest of his birth? Would he go? Where? With whom? Since it seemed everyone else had decided to leave in the morning, he'd have to figure it out quickly.

Faster than spring-time showers comes thought on thought, Bardus reflected. And after considering the impact of what his friends were doing, the owl concluded, *Our thoughts are ours, their ends none of our own.*

"Your friend has overstayed his welcome." The voice carried clearly from behind the tree. From each side of the trunk emerged a pileated, crawling cautiously across the bark like only a woodpecker can do, not sure how the dangerous owl would receive them.

"Your friend may think he's found a home, but he hasn't," Runk began.

"We're not done with him yet," Moss warned.

Considering the situation, Bardus saw no immediate need for violence. After all, they'd been through this already. And with Gonzo leaving in the morning, it all seemed moot at this point. The pileateds, who the owl believed were misguided, wanted Gonzo gone.

At sunrise tomorrow, he would be. Problem solved. No need for any more nastiness. Bard faced the two birds and calmly quipped, "Flies the grasps of love with wings more momentary-swift than thought."

The pileateds looked at each other, confused. "What is he saying?" Moss asked.

"I don't speak Bard. Who knows?"

Bardus bellowed beneath a hefty hoot, "Tomorrow, and tomorrow, and tomorrow!"

Moss and Runk disappeared behind the trunk and put their heads together, almost literally. Runk whispered, "You thinking what I'm thinking? *Tomorrow? The grasps of love?*"

Moss stared blankly.

"That ivory-bill is leaving tomorrow to *grasp love*."

Moss bobbed her head up and down.

"You see?" Runk said.

Now Moss shook her head side to side.

"He's leaving all right, leaving to go get his mate . . . and bring her back here. It's the start of a flock. It's an invasion."

Moss opened her beak with the shocking realization Runk had laid before her. The two whispered for another moment and flew off.

Bardus was stunned. He could hear everything—whispers meant nothing to an owl. What had happened? He thought he was solving the problem, but feared he'd made it much worse. His talons dug deep into the bark of the branch as he lamented, "Speak less than thou knowest . . ."

He was home. He could feel it. He could smell it. He could taste it. Sadly, tragically, there was only one spot like this left on the planet because the rest of them had disappeared, almost unnoticed. Regardless, Azul was home. It seemed like a long absence, but the same stream still wound through the same fields, rumbling through a final stubborn stand of caraiba trees, the trees that sustained his flock for thousands of years until they were removed so cattle and goats could graze the land. Before any new trees could grow large enough to reforest, they were chewed up and swallowed by livestock, so soon there were almost no seeds being produced, and the caraiba virtually disappeared from the Caatinga, much like the Spix's macaw.

But something seemed different to Azul. Had he been gone that long? It looked like there were actually more caraiba trees—many more. They were small, not much beyond the sapling stage, but these hadn't been eaten. Then he saw why. The man-flock had erected a barrier all around the young trees that would prevent grazers from eating or trampling the caraibas.

Azul watched intently. One of the man-flock appeared to be watering the plants. Another was removing dead and diseased branches. It was both wonderful and frustrating. Why had they suddenly found value in the caraiba? Why had they not done so earlier? What was the reason for doing this now? It couldn't have been for him, since he hadn't really been part of this place for months.

The parrot perched and thought. If these trees weren't for him specifically, could they be for sky parrots in general? His flock? What flock? Could there be others? It was impossible. He would've known if other sky parrots were living in the Caatinga. He did know—there weren't any.

Nipiklee. Nipiklee would know what was happening. Azul began to fly, not worrying about hawks or dangers, just flying, searching for Nipiklee. Was she still here? Soon, all the creatures of the Caatinga would see that he was back. Poachers too. The parrot needed to be more careful, yet he couldn't control himself. After such a long incredible journey, he wanted to find his green friend and get answers. But before he could find her, she found him.

"*AZUL!*" the little green parrot exploded. She cawed his name as she flew alongside him, almost landing on his back. Azul didn't know how much he had missed her until he actually saw her. At that moment, he realized she was one of the main reasons he'd made the migration. Now that he was home, he could admit to himself how much Nipiklee meant to him. To do so sooner would've been too painful a *birden* to carry. It's easier to cope if you can pretend to yourself that you haven't lost so much in the first place. Now that he was home with his devoted friend, however, life would be better.

They flew down to a natural pond where the stream pooled. The two birds drank, splashed, and ate small chunks of mineral-rich soil from the bank. Azul recounted all that had happened to him since he was taken away. Finally, out of breath, he asked his friend, "So, why are the trees growing once again? What has changed?"

Nipiklee smiled a deep smile that had the faintest trace of grief feathered on its edges, so faint that it was totally lost on Azul. She shuffled closer to the blue, rubbed against him to reassure herself that he really had returned, and whispered, "Let me show you . . . tomorrow."

"Now," Azul cooed softly.

Nipiklee would always say yes to Azul, only yes, no matter what he asked. The green parrot looked deep into her friend's eyes and beyond them into his heart, resurrected her previous smile, and flew off, knowing Azul would follow.

After a brief flight, she landed on a tree not far from where the caraiba were fenced off. A flap later, Azul landed next to her. He looked at Nipiklee expectantly.

"Shhhh," Nipiklee said. "Listen. Just listen."

Azul cocked his head. He did hear something. Actually, he heard quite a bit. The macaw looked back to Nipiklee, shocked, perplexed. She smiled again, nodded, and pointed to a building that was shrouded by a grove of mature trees.

"In there?" he asked.

Again, Nipiklee nodded, then warned, "Be careful. I can't quite figure it out. It's incredible, unbelievable, but they're all held, and whenever the man-flock is involved, you never know for sure."

Azul understood, at least somewhat. "Yes, I'll be careful, but I have to see—"

"I know," the green agreed. "Listen to me, though. If I see danger, I'll let you know, and you get out of there right away, OK?"

"Yes . . ." Azul turned and flew. He drifted in, silently touching down on a thick bush next to the structure. There was a fairly large open area contained within a dense but pliable black mesh, a web of sorts. The sunlight and the breeze could pass through. The rain could even drip in. Insects could come and go. But others, larger fauna, would be on one side of the web or the other. Azul had seen the man-flock use this before as a barrier, similar to what surrounded the saplings near the stream. But it was what the immense web contained that blew the parrot's mind.

Inside, there were twenty, maybe thirty macaws, mostly young, exactly like him. It was an entire flock, a real flock—inexperienced, a little strange, but a real flock of sky parrots nonetheless. It was a loud, cawing, cackling, screeching, flapping flock.

Parrots with crafty beaks and resourceful, dexterous toes were busy climbing great limbs that had been hung in the enclosure. Macaws in captivity—those kept in isolation—don't generally fare well. This, however, was a little different. Azul closed his eyes for a moment and let it sink in. He wanted to store it away safely in his memory just in case he never heard it again. And when he opened his eyes, he half expected all of it to be gone, with him waking up alone in a small cold web on another side of the planet. But when he opened his eyes, he was still perched on the bush in the Caatinga, and the loud flock of sky parrots was still just a flap away.

Clearly, they weren't free, yet it looked like the man-flock was taking very good care of the birds, about as good care as one creature can take of another that is captive. Food, water, perches, roosts, almost everything save for open sky that any parrot would need to survive was provided.

Nests! There were nests, several . . . with *eggs!* This flock was growing, not shrinking. Again, Azul had to close his eyes for a moment, almost afraid to reopen them. When he did, his eyes were wet with tears. It was more than he'd ever dreamed. And it was only the beginning.

Off in a shaded corner of the enclosure, alone, sitting quietly, was a female. Older than the others, Azul knew her by name. It was Aura.

Azul screamed her name. Suddenly, there was silence. All the parrots froze as if a hawk had entered their roost. Aura, however, didn't freeze. She snapped to attention, answered her mate's call, and flew as close to him as she could get. The two birds gazed at each other. Azul climbed to the end of the branch, exposed, no longer covered by the bush, leaning mindlessly into the mesh that kept him from Aura. They couldn't touch, but they could feel each other's breath, identify each other's scent. A portion of the void within them was restored. The pair leaned closer, feathers catching in the twists of the web that pulled at their plumes, but there was no pain.

A voice called to him, yet it wasn't Aura. Azul turned away from his mate and heard Nipiklee screeching, "Fly! Get away! Fly, Azul!"

Without knowing why, he burst into the air and flew off a safe distance, where Nipiklee joined him.

A moment later, one of the man-flock came around and walked to the bush where Azul had perched. He looked at Aura, then examined the bush, bent over, and picked up a single blue feather. Had one of Aura's fallen through the screen? The human twirled it gently in his fingers. He called to another. They attached something to the top of the bush. It resembled a very large shell and was filled with beautiful caraiba nuts—an invitation or a trap? The two man-flock stared out into the brush and then walked back around the corner.

Azul turned to Nipiklee with his mouth wide open and said, "Aura! A flock!"

Nipiklee nodded.

Glyde came to in a small dark burrow inside one of the man-flock's enormous nests. He couldn't see much, couldn't feel much, but could tell there were others around—a couple man-flock and lots of birds. He could smell them. He could hear them. Glyde couldn't tell, however, if the one bird he'd done all this for was close by. Where was Soaria? He listened carefully and tried to identify another female, another petrel.

There was shuffling, then something pushing at the front of the burrow. A hide or skin, very soft with some strange short fur or hair was draped over the front of his enclosure. A hard mesh kept him from being able to grab it with his beak, although Glyde wasn't very mobile at this point anyway. Light shone in where the fuzzy hide had partially slipped off the burrow.

The petrel angled himself to peer out from the opening. It was a tough angle—he couldn't see much. It seemed there were many burrows stacked one on top of the other, most filled with individual birds who seemed to be in various stages of recovery from one injury or another. This sure seemed like the place where Soaria would've been taken. Still, Glyde couldn't locate her.

He heard the shuffling again. The light that poured through from the disheveled cover was interrupted by a broad, lumbering something with two huge eyes peering in on the petrel. Back on Galahope, a silhouette like this would cause an instant shudder. It was an owl, a type that Glyde didn't really know. The ones at home were deadly. This one seemed different, less threatening.

"How are you doing?" the top-heavy mound of feathers inquired.

The owl looked to be all head straight down to its feet. It was thick, large, dark, and resembled a waddling tree stump. Glyde had the feeling that the bird was harmless, yet he cautioned himself, inexplicably hearing his father's voice remind him that no matter how it looked or sounded, this was still an owl. It was the way Lupé would want his son to think.

In fact, this was a great horned owl, a rather robust one who'd been unlawfully removed from its nest at a few days old and was fed by its man-flock captor. By the time it reached the Marine Science Center, it was unable to hunt, find suitable habitat, or fend for itself, so the center adopted the owl. And in its own special way, Bubo managed to join the staff at the center. The humans actually referred to Bubo as a *species ambassador*. The owl, no doubt, would've been proud to know it was an ambassador, if he only knew what the term meant.

"CAN . . . YOU . . . HEAR . . . ME?" the owl asked loudly, slowly. "HOW . . . ARE . . . YOU . . . DOING?"

The bird's bulk interrupted the light, eclipsing it, casting darkness within the enclosure. When he noticed what he'd done, the owl giggled nervously. Remembering that most other birds couldn't see in the dark as well as he could, Bubo stepped aside, allowing the illumination to return. "I am so sorry," the owl apologized, contorting his body so he could peer into the man-flock burrow with one eye yet not obstruct the petrel's light. "That is better, right?"

Glyde stayed silent. He didn't explain that he, too, could see quite well at night.

The owl continued, "To be honest, you don't look so good." Then, thinking better of what he'd said, he added, "But you look *sooo* much better than when Reach brought you in."

"Reach," the petrel said without thinking.

"I do not know what it means, but that is what they seem to call him."

"The man-flock?"

The owl nodded several times. "I am Bubo. Oh, do not be nervous."

"I'm not nervous."

The owl opened his eye wider. "Your words say one thing, but your heartbeat says another. I can hear it."

Embarrassed, Glyde quickly tried to quiet his heart, but he realized he had no idea how to do that. Then, once he understood his limitation, he became aware that his heart was beating even louder.

"You do not like me." Bubo concluded plainly.

"No . . . no, it's not that."

"Are you in pain? Am I bothering you?"

"No. Well, yes, I feel like a whale is sitting on me. But no, you're not bothering me at all."

"Should I get out of your feathers?"

"No, that's not necessary—"

"So," the owl persisted, "why do I feel like you don't like me?"

"It's me. Where I come from, birds like you, they hunt birds like me . . . a lot."

"Oh, you do not have to worry about that," Bubo snickered. "I could not hunt you or hurt you even if I wanted to, and I definitely do not."

"Glad to hear that, but I have to tell you, you really could hurt me if you wanted to. I don't think I've ever seen an owl wider than you."

"No, I do not know how to do any of those things. I have no understanding of—"

Before the owl could complete his thought, the petrel fell asleep. Bubo waddled over to the next burrow and began another conversation, this time with a wobbly willet, something he would do for the better part of the day. He was an ambassador, after all.

Glyde woke up with the sun. At least that's what he thought was lighting things up. He still hurt all over, but he felt like the whale that was sitting on him the day before had rolled off and been replaced by a seal—progress. After daybreak, there was food, some handling, a few pokes, strange wraps on parts of his body, and when it was all said and done, there was . . . Bubo.

"I have a few questions for you, Bubo."

"Feel free," the owl replied. Then, thinking better of the phrase, he apologized, "Forgive me. Unfortunate choice of words."

"No, no problem at all. That's kind of what I want to ask. How come *you're* not in one of these burrows? How come you just walk around here like this place is your home?"

"Because it is."

Glyde tried to explain. "No, I mean not just this is where you live or where you're kept. I mean, like this is your *home*. My home is Galahope, an island in the Ocean of Peace. See what I mean?"

"Yes, I understood the first time. This is my home, like an island in the ocean is for you."

"No . . . Forgive me, Bubo, but you don't understand—"

The owl cocked his head as if the change in angle would somehow increase his ability to comprehend.

"Clearly, you're an owl. So, there's a place, an environment that's perfect for you. A place you were meant to be, a place where you fit into the web of all that happens. That place is not here—not that there's anything wrong with here, but it's not your *home*."

"No, it is here. This is my home, my place. This is where I fit in perfectly."

"It can't be," the perturbed petrel pressed. "This—everything around us—is the man-flock. And you're not the man-flock."

"So, for that reason, I do not really belong here?"

"*Eggsactly*," the petrel declared, triumphantly.

"But you are also here, and you are not the man-flock," Bubo continued.

"That's my point. I'm here, but this isn't my home. I'm a bird, one who has been created to exist in a special environment."

The owl considered the petrel's proposition. "You know, there are a lot of bugs all around here—spiders, ants, roaches, worms, mites . . . even mice, a rat or two . . . I know some of them by name, and they all seem to exist perfectly in this setting. I have seen countless pigeons and crows do quite well around here, not to mention seagulls and pelicans. Some have been released from here and still stay close by. Seabirds, even."

"All right, now you're getting *me* confused."

"Maybe it is not so simple. You say home is where you are designed to fit. But I believe home is just where you fit. And I fit here." Then Bubo giggled. "There is something you don't know."

"Apparently, there's quite a bit I don't know. Enlighten me."

Bubo cranked his head 180 degrees and looked behind him. He scanned the room carefully, then he pressed his face against the mesh in front of the burrow and whispered, "I am not really an owl."

Suddenly, the giggling made sense to Glyde. Bubo's nest was a few eggs short of a clutch.

The owl rotated his head completely away from the petrel. Then he rotated his body so that it came into alignment under his head, which was facing out into the collection of burrows stacked one above the other. Abruptly, the owl scurried away, stopping in front of another patient. He immediately pulled the covering away with his strong beak and began hooting wildly. *Hoo-hoo-hoooo hoooo.* The deep sound filled the burrows, causing some to rattle. *Hoo-hoo-hoooo hoooo hoooo.*

Glyde could feel the hooting reverberate on his sore ribs. The owl began the hooting again until one of the man-flock appeared. It stared at Bubo for a moment and then reached into the burrow where the owl stood. A young duck with a patch of its skull visible on the top of its head lay limp and didn't seem to be breathing. The man-flock carried it quietly, quickly away.

What am I doing here? the petrel thought. *Why did I do this? What's going on?* Glyde watched Bubo follow the man-flock and the duck until all three slipped from view.

Later, when Glyde awoke from an unplanned nap, the owl was chatting with a one-legged crested tern in another hollow nearby. Initially, Glyde forgot the owl's name and, frustrated, muttered, "Ah, what's his name?"

The owl swiveled his head, announced, "Bubo," and waddled over to the petrel.

"What happened with that duck? Were you hooting for help?"

"Yes, her heart stopped. She needed care."

"How'd you know her heart stopped?" Glyde asked skeptically. "She was covered."

"I hear things. Actually, I did not hear it."

"And you called the man-flock?"

Bubo nodded matter-of-factly. "They seem to like when I do that. I guess they do not hear as well as owls."

The petrel shook his head, wondering if the owl actually listened to the heartbeats of all the birds and could tell when one solitary beat ceased. It was hard to imagine. "Quite a hoot you got there. I could feel it, I mean really feel it in my ribs."

"It gets their attention," the owl said with a smile.

Glyde dragged himself to the front of his burrow. He was as close to the owl as he could get. "OK, you seem to have a good perch about what goes on here. I need to know something." The owl stepped closer. "I'm looking for a bird—a petrel like me, except this one's a female and she would have showed up a couple days ago. Seen her? Is she here?"

Bubo stared at Glyde for a moment, blinking several times. Then he turned and walked away.

A few moments later, Glyde heard it, twice and then no more. It began as a sharp, clear caw but seemed to run out of breath quickly. Still, it was the sound of a petrel, a Guadalupé petrel.

Bubo returned, looked Glyde in the eyes, and nodded yes.

He knew instantly. There weren't many caws like this one on the planet. It had to be Soaria.

"Her name's Soaria. You need to give her a message for me," Glyde implored.

Again, Bubo turned and walked away. This time, he didn't return.

Second Chances

Azul watched Aura from a safe distance. He knew exactly where she was, but he was spooked by the man-flock and the large enclosure. He didn't escape and fly all this way just to get captured again, even if his mate was inside. So, as hard as it was, he waited. Azul ignored the nuts the man-flock placed on the bush. He didn't want to provide proof of his presence. He'd get his own when he desired, which he enjoyed more anyway. But tonight, with a sliver of a moon and plenty of clouds, he'd return to Aura. Tonight, they would speak.

The man-flock had gone. The sky parrots were roosting. The wind woke. A light rain trickled down. Azul nodded to Nipiklee. Then he glided silently toward the enclosure. The parrot descended onto a branch across from an unoccupied perch within. He made a single soft whistle, and Aura settled on the perch. She shuffled to the end of it, just as Azul had done on the branch, but wasn't able to get close enough to him.

In the same instant, they both jumped to the hard web that kept the parrots apart, grasping it with their strong feet. They touched. For a moment, their feet held on to mesh and each other. They laid their beaks in an opening, pressed in, and touched again. Rain drops slid from Azul's head, down his beak and across Aura's, and dripped into her mouth. The pair stayed like this for a while before speaking.

Eventually, Azul asked, "Are you OK?"

Aura held his foot tighter and smiled. "I'm fine."

"What is this?"

"I don't know." She explained, "The man-flock took me far from here . . . to another male sky parrot, to mate."

Azul tilted his head. Feathers on the back of his neck began to rise. "To *WHAT?*"

"But I refused. They brought him another female. She was not from the Caatinga. Neither was he."

"Where were they from?"

"The man-flock. The pair had never lived outside an enclosure. None of these parrots have, except for Orsi, Norte, and Bahia."

"They're here?" Azul said excitedly. "My cousins?"

"Your cousins are here, but except for them, none of these parrots have ever taken a nut from a tree. None have ever prepared a hollow, let alone defended one. None have ever been stalked by a hawk."

"Then they're not sky parrots."

Aura nodded. "They are something in between. I think they can become sky parrots, and I think the man-flock knows this. It seems they're trying to help us."

"This is the first time I've seen them planting caraiba and chasing livestock away. Are they really doing it for us?"

"I think so. The flock is growing. When was the last time you heard that?"

Azul shook his head skeptically. "In *there*, the flock's growing. Out here, there's one sky parrot. How many of those birds would survive out here?"

"I know of four."

"How many others?"

"Maybe, with luck . . . three or four more."

"Out of thirty? With more on the way . . . But what's the point if the man-flock keeps you all in there?" Azul wondered aloud.

"What if they—and I really can't imagine it—but what if they don't? What if they release us all?"

"That won't work. We both know that."

Aura shrugged. "But maybe the man-flock doesn't. I can't make sense of this."

"We don't need to understand what the man-flock has in mind," Azul said. "They're underestimating *us*. I've met some northern parrots that have done incredible things. We can hatch our own plan."

"You got one?"

Her mate grinned. "Half a plan."

"Half? That's like having half an egg . . . one wing . . . half a beak . . ."

"I get it. Look, right now, their goal seems to be to produce as many parrots as possible, so as long as you refuse to mate, you're really no use to them."

"That's your plan? That's not even half a plan."

"It's working so far," Azul pointed out. "I mean, here we are."

"Very good. Yes, here we are. I'm in here, and you're out there. Perfect."

"We're parrots."

"Another breakthrough. You know, you've gotten much smarter since the last time I saw you, Azul."

"Stop. I mean, we're smart. Let's think it through. If they decide you're useless for their purposes, then you're useless. Why would they keep you here? You could disappear, and they wouldn't care."

"I have a better plan," Aura suggested. "What if I did show them that I was interested in mating?"

Azul cocked his head again as the feathers began to rise on his neck. "Really? That's your plan? Time to start mating?"

"Yes, time to start mating . . . with you."

"But I'm out here. I mean, I'm willing to try, but—"

"Of course, you are," she said, frustratingly amused at his willingness. Then she continued, "Are you kidding, Azul? Take your own advice. Think it through."

"Ah, I get it. You're thinking that if you'll only mate with me and they know I'm out here, they might let you out to do that?"

Aura smiled.

Azul nodded. He liked where this was going. But suddenly, he squinted his eyes and shifted his beak. The feathers rose on the top of his head as he said, "What if their solution is not to release *you?* What if they decide the answer is to capture *me?*"

Vicente El Real had made a deal. In exchange for a hefty fine and probation, the man who exploited the very creatures he was entrusted to protect was able to avoid prison. In his most wily way, he proffered a plan to use the very birds he wronged—the actual individuals—to save their species. The erstwhile president of I-BIRD had records of every bird, every chick, every egg that he'd sold. He also maintained coded records of all his clients, their contact information, and other individuals whom he may not have dealt with directly but was aware of nonetheless. It was an insurance policy, a bargaining chip, a treasure trove for the authorities.

In the case of the Spix's macaw, one of many breeds he'd transgressed, it was El Real who suggested to the legal community that he might be able to reveal which people owned which birds. He then suggested that if a government like Brazil could reclaim, or at least *encourage*, the loan of a substantial population of these parrots, they might actually be able to create a captive breeding program that could ultimately lead to a large breeding flock and the opportunity to reintroduce birds into the wild, not unlike the California condor or the Mauritius kestrel.

But all this, of course, would be based on Vicente El Real's ability to locate the records of birds and owners. And since it seemed that the freshly convicted felon was at least as interested in ensuring his own survival as ensuring the survival of the macaws, the program was launched.

Birds valued well into six figures on the black market began to appear. Amnesty was given to any "collector" who generously loaned their birds to the Brazilian government. Given the possessor's cooperation, Brazil refrained from exercising the country's legal claim to ownership of the macaws and right to seize them . . . for the time being.

El Real guided authorities to the whereabouts of other birds as well. Soon, ten, then twelve, then fifteen macaws were all gathered in one place. At first, two problems loomed large. Would the birds pair up and mate? Several already had. And if any others did, would the gene pool be varied enough to produce healthy young? The majority of these birds were directly related in one way or another.

Over time, another half dozen birds or more were loaned. The macaws would be grouped and regrouped to further grow the gene pool. Eggs would be laid and hatched. Young would fledge, new pairs would form, and the breeding population would expand slowly. It was a grand plan, hatched by Vicente.

Immediately, a preserve was established at the birds' ancestral home, the stream where Azul was born. Habitat was being developed and protected. The Nature Conservancy, World Wildlife Fund, and other top-tier environmental organizations got involved. Local people, including former poachers, were employed by the project. No one really knew whether this was too little too late or the answer to the parrots' prayers. Surely, other breeds had faced as much peril and pulled through, but then again, others had faced much less and gone extinct.

The sun had fallen beneath the mountain laurel. There was light, but it was dim, and it wouldn't last long.

Bardus had arrived at the hollow with the large, somewhat rectangular hole. He entered and prepared to explain his concerns to Gonzo, saying, "If you have tears, prepare to shed them now."

The woodpecker looked at the owl, confused.

"Company, villainous company, hath been the spoil of me . . . We are not the first who with best meaning have incurred the worst . . . There is strange things toward . . . Pray you, be careful."

Bardus disclosed what he'd told the pileateds and how he feared that they'd misinterpreted what he'd meant. He finished, saying, "I am sick of this false world . . . All is not well. I doubt some foul play with the night . . . Foul deeds will rise."

The woodpecker, however, was unconcerned, reasoning that he'd be on his way home at first light. There was little the pileateds could do about that, and since he didn't really plan on returning anytime soon, there was nothing to worry about. However, Gonzo was concerned about something else. He hoped that his friend Bardus might join him as he journeyed south.

Without saying yea or nay to the southern migration, Bardus pressed his friend not to underestimate the danger the pileateds presented. The owl warned, "These days are dangerous. Virtue is choked with foul ambition, and charity chased hence by rancour's hand . . . Be wary then. Best safety lies in fear . . . To fear the worst oft cures the worst."

Bardus reminded Gonzo of how slyly the woodpeckers got him to eat fermented berries knowing what the effect would be, and then, taking advantage of the situation, they tried to end his life. And even after that failure, they tried again, sending the snake, Emersssso. The owl saw no reason why the pileateds would suddenly stop targeting his friend. And now that the woodpeckers believed Gonzo was preparing to leave, they might act quickly, desperately.

Still, the ivory-bill denied the threat, maintaining that the pileateds were basically out of time. He'd be gone in the morning. But just when Bardus acknowledged Gonzo's point, he heard it.

The owl whipped his large head completely around, looking out the opening of the hollow. There was scraping on the tree's crust, like a woodpecker scuffling across bark. Bardus turned back to Gonzo. He, too, heard the sound. How many? How many woodpeckers were the pileateds able to recruit? Strategy raced through the minds of the two birds. They were restricted to the roost hole. They couldn't easily flee, but upon consideration, they concluded they might not want to. Let the pileateds enter one and two at a time. They might not fare so well once they were inside.

Bardus readied himself. He could be fierce when defending his territory, having driven off great horned owls as well as eagles. He looked at his friend, and said, "Tis true that we are in great danger; the greater therefore should our courage be."

Then, the first, and what turned out to be the only, woodpecker stepped through the opening. Gonzo and Bardus were stunned. The Bard saw the largest woodpecker he'd ever seen, save for Gonzo. It looked exactly like an ivory-bill—roughly the same size and dimensions, the same enormous beak, covered with black feathers, sporting a white patch on its back. The only real difference was this bird was a touch thinner, and its prominent crest was black, not scarlet red like Gonzo's. Whatever it was, this woodpecker was not a pileated. This was an ivory-bill.

All three birds froze. They stared at each other for a moment that felt more like a migration. Gonzo and the other bird stepped toward each other, passing Bardus in the cramped hollow as if he wasn't there. They preened until Gonzo said, "Kwim ... my Kwim."

The other bird just cried.

The dark crest, Bardus thought. *Of course, a female, his mate.* Suddenly, the owl felt like a third wing. He hopped to the roost hole and prepared to fly, but as he jumped through the opening, something sharp scraped viciously and wildly across his head. Bardus ducked back into the roost immediately. The accompanying *Caw!* left no doubt, a red-tailed hawk was outside, and in a moment, it would likely try to enter before anyone could escape.

The hawk might've been there just for the owl, who it would assume was direct competition that should be eliminated. But something told the birds in the hollow that the hawk was somehow connected to the pileateds. More likely, the hawk was sent to slay Gonzo before he left and might not know the owl and another ivory-bill were even inside.

Perhaps the hawk thought that Bardus was Gonzo trying to escape, especially given it was night, not the red-tail's favorite time to hunt. It was, however, Bardus's time, a nocturnal predator who, better than anyone, understood the phrase "the dead of night." No other bird of prey can hunt in extreme darkness like an owl. Not only could Bardus remember his surroundings, enabling him to avoid obstacles in flight, but his huge eyes occupied almost 70 percent of his skull, giving him almost flawless night vision.

Kwim was confused. She wasn't used to seeing ivory-bills with barred owls, but there was little time for that.

Gonzo was also confused, but more about how and why his mate had found him. But there was no time for that, either.

Bardus demanded the pair exit through the small hole in the back of the roost, telling them not to look back, to return, together, to their swamp in the South. While neither would hear of it initially, Bardus was resolute, saying softly to the pair, "From fairest creatures we desire increase, that thereby beauty's rose might never die . . . Die single, and thine image dies with thee." He smiled at Kwim, bowed regally, and said, "You are the cruelest she alive if you will lead those graces to the grave and leave the world no copy."

The owl would deal with the hawk, or perhaps the hawk would deal with the owl. Either way, the ivory-bills would escape. It had to be that way, a *flight* accompli. "When shall we three meet again?" Bardus asked. "In thunder, lightning, or in rain? . . . Though this be madness, yet there is method in't."

The trio hatched a quick plan. They were correct that the pileateds had sent the hawk. The ivory-bills were smart. They understood the situation, yet they were reluctant to leave Bardus to do battle alone. Still, there was no denying, a single ivory-bill was as rare as hen's teeth—a pair, even more so. They had to survive. There was no choice.

Bardus didn't want to battle the hawk on the wing. He wanted him in the hollow. At home in the dark, the stocky owl could play to his strengths and use the roost as an equalizer. "I must go and seek danger," he told the pair before they left, "or it will seek me in another place and find me worse provided."

Since hawks weren't usually quick to fight large owls. This one was probably under the impression he was taking on the solitary woodpecker, although like Bardus at times, the red-tail wouldn't back down from barred owls, great horned owls, or even eagles. Maybe that was the argument the pileateds had flown to persuade the raptor, that the ivory-bill was encroaching on the hawk's range just as they believed it encroached on theirs. Yet, with an instant of reflection, a nuthatch could see that the ivory-bill presented no competition for food or nesting sites. Red-tails, however, were never known for their powers of reflection or reason. Regardless, there was an incensed hawk about to climb into the hollow, and Bardus hoped he could crack open an egg full of kick-rump on this bird.

The owl motioned the pair to the small hole at the top rear of the hollow. He whispered, "Arm thy heart and fit thy thoughts to mount aloft." When the pair hesitated, Bardus coaxed with a half smile, "The course of true love never did run smooth."

Gonzo and Kwim grudgingly climbed up the wood, the way only a woodpecker could, and waited for the hawk to enter. Once it was inside the roost, Bardus would attack. That was the moment for the ivory-bills to fly.

The Bard readied himself, muttering, "A falcon, towering in her pride of place, was by a mousing owl hawked at and killed." Bardus turned to the pair and whispered once more, "Courage mounteth with occasion . . . Be bloody, bold, and resolute." Then, facing the hole in the hollow, he added, "Threaten the threat'ner."

At that moment, the hawk stepped confidently into the hollow, a dull expression on its face—no fear, no emotion. It was there to dispose of the woodpecker and whatever else got in its way, including Bardus.

The owl stood solidly between the hawk and the pair. He vowed a loyalty oath to the ivory-bills without taking his large eyes off the hawk. "Defer no time, delays have dangerous ends . . . I am your own for ever." Then, not waiting for the hawk to strike, Bardus stepped toward it, declaring, "Come not within the measure of my wrath . . . Now thou art come unto a feast of death . . . Bloody thou art: bloody will be thy end."

The owl could feel the pileateds' purpose here. It enraged him. Bardus launched himself at the intruding hawk. Not expecting to be greeted by the ferocious owl, the hawk paused for an instant. Bardus climbed into its feathers and knocked the raptor off its feet.

Gonzo nodded to Kwim. He hated to do it, but he climbed farther up the inside wall of the hollow and out the smaller second hole on the other side of the tree with Kwim behind him.

At the same time, however, the hawk's mate was climbing into the rear hole to make sure no one could escape. The hawks, who often hunted in pairs, planned to come at Gonzo from two directions while he was trapped in the tree. They failed to realize Bardus would be waiting, and they never dreamt the woodpecker would have a mate with him. Still, this was a pair of experienced, mature red-tailed hawks. They weren't overly concerned about taking on an owl and two woodpeckers.

But the hawks had made a mistake, a big one. When the female red-tail heard the melee and realized her mate was battling an enraged owl, she moved quickly, lest her partner get injured, which could interfere with feeding and their daily lives after they disposed of the troublesome trio. This was supposed to be quick and easy.

In her haste, she dove into the hole ready for battle, but she chose the wrong hole. There were two on the opposite side of the tree trunk, one above the other, one larger than the other. The hole the hawk entered was large and ragged, not the chiseled portal crafted by a woodpecker. Without realizing it, the hawk had burst into the hollow of an enormous raccoon.

Normally, Scaugie was an incredibly relaxed, docile beast, as sweet as he was large. He could afford to be that way because he was so immense that nothing in the pines—not the bobcats, not even the coyotes—cared to mess with him. It just wasn't worth the risk. So, Scaugie lived a charmed, mellow existence. He didn't bother anyone, and no one bothered him.

The raccoon had lost his mother as a pup. He wound up being raised by a human family who lived on the edge of the pines. They kept a large enclosure behind their home in the woods. It had logs to climb on, a nice little pond, and plenty of food inside. Twice a day, a helpful male human would enter the enclosure, fill Scaugie's pond with fresh water, and leave an assortment of wonderful food. The human was careful, however, not to reach into or near Scaugie's den. He knew that was sacred ground for any raccoon.

When he saw fit, Scaugie would crawl out of his den, climb across a long branch, and then step onto the human's back while he performed his daily chores for the raccoon. Scaugie marveled at how similar the human's hands were to his. The human marveled over the same thing. Scaugie liked to climb on his tall friend's back, play with his ear lobes, and sniff his hair. The human never neglected the raccoon.

At night, other creatures from the woods—other raccoons from the trees—would visit the enclosure, hoping to steal a scrap or meet the raccoon inside. Eventually, when Scaugie was full grown, the human left the enclosure open. The raccoon wandered out, exploring the lake, the trees, the trails.

He stayed near his human friends for a few winters, testing the limits as to how large a raccoon could get after finishing off leftover dog and cat food every evening. Over time, he worked his way deeper into the pines, until he found the perfect location. Recently, a strange woodpecker moved in below him. Scaugie didn't really know him well—they kept different hours—but he liked the bird because it was as large among woodpeckers as he was among raccoons.

There was really only one thing that upset Scaugie, and that was someone—anyone—invading his privacy, which happened to be just what the rushing raptor did. As she flew into the den, talons extended, crying a shrill attack call, she was met by a solid wall of muscle, teeth, and attitude. The riled raccoon charged the bird, stuffing her back through the opening before she knew what hit her. The hawk tumbled to the ground, dazed, while the pair of ivory-bills escaped over her head into the moonlight from the rear of Gonzo's hollow.

The hawk gathered herself for an instant and wondered whether to pursue the woodpeckers, but when she heard her mate battling Bardus, she quickly forgot about Gonzo and Kwim.

The owl and the hawk, both hefty in their own right, almost filled the den, so the female couldn't get in to help her mate. She didn't fit and was forced to peck and swipe at Bardus whenever he passed the opening, which was difficult, because it was awkward and dark, and the two inside were moving so much. For a moment, the owl's back was pressed against the entrance. The female slashed at him. A clump of short, thick owl feathers stuck to her talons. Warm red liquid clung to their quills. She smiled.

Inside the hollow, Bardus gave at least as much as he got. Both birds were pretty beat up, but the owl had more to fight for—more purpose—and it showed in his ferocity. The hawk had come looking for a quick, easy meal. The owl was fighting for his life, and more than that, for the lives of his friends. Bardus was a noble bird.

Both birds threw themselves at each other talons first. They gripped and ripped, they swung their beaks into the fray, biting, slicing, tearing.

Bardus declared, "By heaven, I'll make a ghost of him that lets me." Bardus sunk his talons into the thighs of the hawk. He dodged the biting beak, spread his wings just wide enough to make a single quick flap, and rolled the raptor on its side, using the leverage to deliver his own blows, mashing and slashing the attacker.

Eventually, the hawk concluded that this was too much peck for not enough meal. The pines were packed with much easier, less perilous fare. He began to wonder why he was even fighting this insane owl, failing to realize that in battle, doubt often leads to demise. As the hawk and the owl continued to tussle and tumble, the red-tail found himself near the roost's entrance. Bardus slammed him into the inner tree and stumbled backward a step after he delivered the blow, and the hawk slipped out the opening. The Bard quickly rose to face his adversary, but the hawk was gone.

"He which hath no stomach to this fight," the owl muttered, "let him depart."

The attacker emerged from the opening and painfully flapped to a nearby branch. Tree by tree, branch by branch, the embattled hawk worked his way back to his nest. Although he didn't dine on ivory-bill this night, he was developing a curious taste for pileated that he'd quench when he recovered.

The female hawk, Rend, was faced with a decision. Should she tend to her mate, ensuring his safe return to their nest, or should she settle the score with the owl? Considering each course of action and partially blaming herself for diving into the raccoon's hole instead of the woodpecker's, she flew to her mate's side, frustrated that she couldn't finish what he'd started.

Rend, however, had done more damage than he'd realized, more than Bardus would admit to himself in the heat of battle. Now that it was suddenly quiet and he was alone in Gonzo's hollow, the searing, sharp pain set in. The owl felt light-headed and dizzy as blood drained from his body. A deep slash delivered by the female left a gaping laceration in the bird's flank and across its abdomen. Bardus folded his wing over the wound and tried to press it closed. He sat calmly, muttering, "The bright day is done, and we are for the dark . . . Death, that dark spirit . . . Is this the promised end? . . . Rest, perturbed spirit . . . This all lies within the will of God."

The owl closed his eyes and sat down. In his mind's eye, he could see Gonzo and Kwim. He smiled. It was a good battle. He'd fought well. He had made a difference. Bardus opened his eyes. The vision of the two ivory-bills remained. He could see the pair just as if they were with him as he flew to the next life. His friend

Gonzo seemed sad. The woodpecker shook his head, whispering, "Bardus, oh Bardus." Gonzo wrapped his wings around the Bard and held him tightly. Then the owl realized that this wasn't just happening in his mind's eye. It was really happening. The ivory-bills had returned.

"We're too late, Bardus," Gonzo said. "We never should have left you to the hawks."

Kwim stood silently behind her mate.

The owl grinned and shook his head. "Be not disturbed with my infirmity."

Leaving the nest with Kwim made so much sense when things were happening quickly and Bardus sent Gonzo on his way, but now, looking at his friend, imagining what the owl was faced with, Gonzo couldn't believe he'd abandoned him. He held Bardus as tightly as he could.

"I met a fool in the forest, a motley fool."

Gonzo grinned and agreed. "I met one myself."

"Ill blows the wind that profits nobody."

"You flew into the ill wind to profit me, to profit the ivory-bills."

Bardus nodded. "He lives in fame that died in honor's cause."

"No dying here tonight, Bardus. No dying. We're here. Kwim and I will make sure all is right with you before we go anywhere."

Kwim stepped closer and stretched her wing across the owl's back.

Bardus whispered, "The long day's task is done, and we must sleep . . . My soul is in the sky. Tongue, lose thy light. Moon, take thy flight . . . All that lives must die, passing through nature to eternity."

"Stop that, Bardus. You'll be fine. You're the strongest bird I've ever seen."

"What's gone and what's past help should be past grief."

Kwim held the owl. She didn't know him, didn't know what to say, yet she was overcome with grief. He'd just offered his life, willingly, for them. As the owl declined, all Kwim could manage was a soft, soulful, "Bardus."

It's true that owls hear sounds others can't, but some of them hear sounds that aren't even made, and Bardus heard all Kwim's sorrow, all her sentiment in the expression of his name.

Now the Bard spoke to her. "My good will is great, though the gift is small."

Kwim shook her head no. She looked at the owl's blood on her feathers. For the first time, the female ivory-bill had red like Gonzo's plumage. "There is no greater gift," she whispered. "You gave all."

Bardus looked out the opening of the roost and replied softly, "The fields are fragrant, and the woods are green." The owl closed his eyes.

The ivory-bills waited, but the eyes didn't open again. The pair climbed out the rear hole of the hollow and flew off exactly the way Bardus wanted them to.

And only as they left the hollow did Bardus gaze on them, saying, "The vine shall grow, be we shall never see it."

Glyde didn't quite understand. He was healing quickly, fully, but that wasn't the issue. The man-flock confused the petrel. They were regular visitors to his strange den and handled him a bit more than he preferred, occasionally stinging or poking him. Glyde scratched it up to the idea that they probably thought they were helping. While the process didn't really make sense to him, he figured that it made sense to them, so if he actually did recover and somehow was put into contact with Soaria, it would all be worth it.

However, what really bewildered Glyde was Bubo. The owl was clearly avoiding him. The petrel wondered if he'd offended his well-disposed chum, but the owl was such a strange bird, Glyde couldn't begin to guess what might have been offensive to him. It had been days since they last spoke. Even when Bubo passed by and Glyde called to him, the bird just kept walking. How could an owl, one who'd heard a duck's heart stop beating, not hear the petrel's call? Something was going on, and Glyde was desperate to find out.

As he got stronger, Glyde was able to use another one of his abilities to get Bubo's attention. He didn't really want to do it—some might interpret the action as an insult, even an aggression—yet Glyde felt he was left with no choice. If Bubo didn't notice the petrel's call, he'd notice this.

One morning as the owl waddled past the hollows, Glyde cawed out to him loudly. When it seemed there would be no response from the owl, Glyde reared back and launched a warm, sticky liquid from two holes on top of his beak. It was basically a cross between snot and spit, sometimes referred to by petrels as *snit*. Glyde was well practiced in the hawking of snit. In fact, he was something of a marks*bird*.

The gushing discharge spewed like a small rivulet until it found its mark atop Bubo's wide head, saturating and dripping deep into the owl's short, thick feathers. Bubo stopped in his tracks, turned his head the way owls do, and faced the petrel without speaking.

Glyde waited as if to say, "It's your move, Bubo." The petrel wondered if perhaps this strange owl might possess some ability to return fire with some bodily function of his own. Bubo was large. There was no telling how much of *something* even a not-so-great horned owl could project Glyde's way. Had he started something he couldn't finish?

The owl shuffled closer, leaving a light slick of slobber behind him. "I suppose you think I deserved that?" Bubo asked.

Glyde grimaced, not sure where this was headed.

"Well, maybe I did," the owl said, answering his own question. He bent over to allow petrel drool to work its way out of his feathers while it puddled at his feet. "Then again, maybe I did not."

The petrel was expecting retaliation, but when it didn't come, Glyde explained, "I must've called you a hundred times over the past few days."

"I know . . . I know."

"So, why didn't you answer me? I need to talk to you. You're out there. You see stuff I don't see. I need to know how Soaria is and where she's being kept. Did you tell her I'm here? I don't know what's going on."

"I know."

"Well? What can you tell me?"

Bubo shook his drooping head, snit still dripping from his plumage. "I know I was avoiding you. I did not want to, but I just did not know what to do."

"Get to the point," the petrel pressed. "What happened? It's about Soaria, isn't it?"

Bubo nodded. "She is gone."

"What? Where'd she go? Was she released? Didn't you tell her I was here?"

"Yes, yes, I told her . . . and she heard what you did, what you did to find her."

"So, what did she say? Is she waiting for me? Should I meet her somewhere?"

Bubo shook his head. "I told you, she is gone. You cannot meet her."

"You don't know where she went? There's no message, no instructions for me? And I'm still stuck in here?"

This time, the owl nodded. "There is a message. I will be right back."

Bubo waddled off beyond where Glyde could see him. Several of the other birds noticed the bespattered owl and began to peep. One duck wise*quacked*, "Didn't *expect*orate the petrel could do that, did ya?"

But Bubo continued on his way while whistles, caws, and cackles rained down from the hollows.

In a moment, the owl returned to Glyde. He stretched out his broad wing, and a long, thin, grey feather fell to the floor. Clearly, it didn't come from Bubo. It wasn't an owl feather at all. Glyde stretched his neck and picked up the feather. He knew what it was immediately. It looked almost exactly like one of his.

"This is the message?" he asked.

"She wanted me to give it to you."

The petrel was perplexed.

"I told her you were here. I told her what you had done to get here and why you did it. I told her the whole story before she left."

"And she gave you—I mean me—one of her feathers? What's that supposed to mean?"

"Well, I—"

Glyde interrupted, "Didn't she tell you where she was going? How I could find her? Where we might meet?"

Bubo looked at the petrel strangely. This time, it was his turn to be confused. He said, "I told you she was gone."

"So, how am I supposed to find her now?"

"Ah." Bubo understood that his friend didn't understand. He said slowly, quietly, "No, she is gone."

Glyde looked suspiciously at the owl, "Gone as in not here, but still alive, right?"

Bubo shook his head. "She is gone."

The petrel released a long, deep breath and sat down, staring at the single feather. He said one word. "Gone."

"Yes."

Glyde continued to look at the feather. Without looking up, he said, "That's why you avoided me. You didn't know how to tell me."

The owl nodded. "And I did not believe the news would help you heal. You need to heal."

"How did she die?"

"She just did not get better. It happens sometimes. We try, but not everyone can be saved."

"When you say *we*, you mean you and the man-flock? They did try, didn't they?"

"Oh, yes. They always do here. And when it was over, they felt it as deeply as any of us."

Being a Guadalupé petrel mourning another Guadalupé petrel whom he'd flown several thousand miles to see, Glyde had difficulty believing anyone could feel the loss he felt. But having seen what he saw from the man-flock in this place, he knew what Bubo said was more or less true. These people cared.

The petrel laid his beak next to the grey feather and breathed in. "Why the feather? Why would she give this to me? She knew about me?"

"She knew you were here and assumed your father must have sent you in his place. Soaria wanted you to bring the feather back to her home, to leave it with her family and tell them what happened to her . . . I guess so she can rest."

"She wanted me to do that?" Glyde asked, adding, "So, there are others, a family."

"It was the only thing Soaria asked of anyone while she was here."

"Maybe she wanted her family to know about my father, our family . . . She didn't, by any chance, tell you where her home was or how I might find her family?"

"Yes and no."

The petrel stared at the owl, obviously waiting for some much-needed elaboration.

Bubo continued, "Yes, she told me where she was from. No, she did not specifically tell me how to locate her family."

"I guess I'll cross that sea when I get to it."

Bubo smiled a tiny smile. "So, you are going to deliver it?"

"I am." The petrel slipped the feather under his own, against his flesh. It disappeared into his grey plumage, almost becoming part of him.

The man-flock who ran the Brazilian preserve noticed Azul right away. The lone wild macaw who thought his stealthy sorties were inconspicuous actually drew quite a bit of attention. And just as he and Aura predicted, the man-flock began to see that the amour-less Aura was obviously worked up about the arrival of the wild macaw, who just happened to seem drawn to her.

It was decided that a private enclosure for the female would be constructed. This structure would have two areas: one that housed Aura and another somewhat open area that would allow the wild parrot to approach. If he did fly in, the second chamber could be closed, and the preserve would, presumably, have another mating pair and a wider gene pool. That was the upside, the version that most people felt was best for the birds.

There were a few, however, who wondered whether there was actually more value in having at least one wild parrot flying free. If they got to the point where captive macaws were going to be released, it might help to have a leader out there who knew the environment and could model how to survive in it. How much of the Spix's activity was derived from instinct versus learned behavior was unknown. Having a mature parrot who knew the Caatinga, its dangers, its nesting sites, its feeding cycles, its weather, its secrets, might prove invaluable.

But that rationale, balanced against the possibility of adding another unique set of genes into the breeding project, lost the day. Construction on Aura's roost began immediately. Every second the male parrot was left in the wild meant risk. There were too many ways the macaw could be lost. It was decided that he had to be captured.

Azul and Aura watched the construction. The cozy roost was an efficient size for a pair of parrots to begin a family, although the wide-open Caatinga was a better size. The structure was positioned well beyond the main edifice, yet several flaps from the bush line. While both parrots assumed this work was meant for them, they weren't exactly sure what the man-flock had in mind.

Free from any enclosures, Azul perched with Nipiklee. The green parrot was happy to have him back, but she knew one way or another, she would lose him to Aura. Nipiklee hoped that no matter how things turned out, she'd still at least have a friend. The two watched everything the man-flock did, studying, thinking, trying to understand. Late at night, Azul and Aura would discuss the situation while Nipiklee flew watch.

The structure was finished quickly. The man-flock wasted no time in bringing out Aura. When they approached her, Aura knew what was coming. She knew she was going to be relocated into the new roost, to be used as bait to attract Azul. The other sky parrots had also taken notice of the man-flock's activity. Just before they came for her, Orsi, her nephew, landed next to her.

"We know," he said.

"You know what?"

"We know that was built for you, for you and the wild one … Uncle Azul?"

Aura's eyes widened when Orsi mentioned her mate by name. It was something she didn't often hear.

"Why are they doing this?" he asked.

"They want us together. They want more parrots."

"Do you want to go to him?"

"What difference does it make? But yes, of course I do."

Orsi leaned closer to his aunt, more serious than she'd ever seen him. In fact, she'd never seen him serious, not ever. If there was a joke to be told, a parrot to be laughed at, a situation to be made fun of, you could always count on Orsi to find the humor and share it. He was never happier than when parrots were falling off their perches, feathers twitching in uncontrolled laughter. Yet at this moment, Orsi was a different bird. Aura caught herself glancing over her wing as she wondered if her nephew was actually setting her up for some prank before the man-flock took her away.

Aura reiterated, "What can you do? The man-flock will do whatever they want. They always do."

Orsi scanned the enclosure. Others were watching. They seemed to be encouraging him. The parrot said softly, "If you don't want to go—and I chirp for everyone—we will stop them."

Aura looked at the other birds. Many nodded, looking directly at her. Some of the older birds cackled and grunted. *They're serious*, she thought.

"Thank you," Aura said to Orsi.

At that moment, Aura, Orsi, and the rest of the sky parrots realized they weren't just parrots or pairs. They were a flock, an actual flock—even in captivity. They'd fight for Aura, perhaps die for Aura if she needed them to, if she wanted them to.

The older female asked curiously, "If you all have this fight in you, this defiance, why haven't you done anything until now?"

Orsi replied, "First, there probably isn't a parrot in here that isn't related to you somehow. In some measure, your blood is in all of us. That means something. But the reason we've never resisted . . . Why would we? Right now, there are more sky parrots and we're closer to home than almost any of us have ever been before. Every day another is born, we get a little stronger. We have each other. It looks like we're flying in a good direction. There seems to be a helpful wind beneath our wings. Why fight that now? What is there to gain?"

Aura understood.

"Never mind us," Orsi continued. "If you need us . . . the flock . . . If Uncle Azul needs us, anything . . . we're all in."

The macaw matriarch smiled. It wouldn't be necessary. Before she could say another word to Orsi, the man-flock entered. The parrots all looked at Aura. The human reached out its hand, and for the first time in her life, Aura flew to it willingly and perched on the creature's arm, surrendering to the fact that she'd be moved to the smaller roost near the bush, but praying that it would bring her closer to freedom with Azul rather than bring Azul into captivity with her.

As she assumed, she was carried to the roost and released inside. Aura could see the rest of the flock a short distance behind her, the bush line not too far in front of her. What appeared just a few flaps away was actually her home, the Caatinga, where she was born and raised, where she was taken. Almost all the other macaws behind her had never plucked their own caraiba, never drunk from the stream, never tasted the mud along its banks, never soared above the trees, never flown for miles carried by a warm breeze. Aura had done all those things many times and thought, *I will do them again.*

The new roost was only open on one side, the side that faced the Caatinga. The other three panels were more or less closed, with little portals that provided ventilation and light. The Caatinga side, however, while enclosed in the mesh woven by the man-flock, was otherwise completely open to the bush. Connected to the open-facing wall was another hollow. The top, sides, and bottom were all made out of the same woven mesh. But this hollow had no front panel at all. It was as if the man-flock hadn't finished constructing it. As it existed, any bird could easily fly in and out of that part of the structure.

Aura perched quietly, grooming while she watched the woods, waiting for dusk to hatch into night. Then, at some point, Azul would fly to her.

Azul had witnessed the entire move. He watched the man-flock construct the strange hollow. He watched Aura move into her roost. The male stood on a branch with Nipiklee, out of sight.

"So, what's your plan?" the green parrot asked her blue friend.

"Plan?" Azul replied. "First, I think we need to understand what's actually going on here."

"You mean you don't know?" Nipiklee asked.

"Do you know?" the macaw inquired hopefully. The green just shook her head.

"Well, I'm thinking that they're not done making whatever that thing is. And the way it looks now, I can still fly right up to Aura, right next to her."

Nipiklee nodded. "Through that open side in front?"

"Why not? Looks easy to do."

"How does that change anything? She'll still be in there, and you'll be out here. As close as you are, you might as well be forests apart."

"Except we're not forests apart," the macaw countered. "All I have to do is get her out of there. I was able to escape to get back here. I've seen others, a pigeon and a petrel, escape the man-flock. It can be done."

"So, how can it be done?"

"Details . . ." Azul replied sourly.

The two birds perched pensively as the moon joined the stars high in the sky. Scrutinizing the structure, they grew frustrated.

Azul squawked, "I need to get closer. I can't decide anything from here."

"You also can't get hurt from here," Nipiklee warned.

"Then I'm definitely too far away," the macaw declared defiantly, prepared to leap from the branch.

"Wait," the green whispered. "Wait . . . don't rush in there."

"The man-flock will probably finish this nest tomorrow. This might be my only chance to get Aura out of there before they close that opening off. I need to act now." Azul popped into the moonlit sky and glided silently onto the top of the unfinished hollow.

Aura called to him, "Be careful! I'm not sure what this is."

"Don't worry, I'll be careful."

Azul climbed onto Aura's side of the roost. He examined the closed sides. They were solid wood. There were no cracks, no openings other than the small holes that were covered with the hard, shiny web. He paced back and forth nervously. "Aura, follow where I go from the inside. Do you see any splits or separations? Are there thin spots we might be able to chew through?"

Convinced that the outer walls were sealed, Azul climbed under the mesh into the open front that led to Aura. He wanted to get close to her, to see if the mesh between them could be peeled back, stretched, cut, split, anything. But as he began to climb into the exposed opening, Aura cawed to him, "No, no! Stay on the outside! Don't climb in here!"

"I am on the outside. This hollow is not sealed. I need to reach you."

"No," Aura insisted. "I can examine the mesh. You stay out there."

"But there might be something on my side you can't see. Don't worry."

"Stay there! I am worried."

"By tomorrow, this could be all closed up. We need to get you out now." Azul gripped the mesh with his strong toes and lowered himself into the second hollow, the open hollow. As he dipped his head into the space, he was abruptly dislodged and knocked to the ground. Nipiklee swooped in beneath him and entered the hollow herself, landing on an inviting perch that hung in front of Aura's den. The moment Nipiklee set down on the perch, the birds heard a snap. An instant later, a tinny crash sealed the green parrot into the hollow when another webbed wall fell across the open front of the roost.

Azul popped to his feet and stared at Nipiklee and Aura. Both birds yelled in unison, "Fly!"

This time Azul didn't argue. He flapped quickly and disappeared into the bush. The green turned to the blue female and said calmly, "I'm Nipiklee."

"I thought as much," Aura replied. "I've heard a lot about you."

Nipiklee nodded, unable to speak as the reality of what she'd just done began to take hold.

A light came on in the man-flock nest, followed by another light. Soon, there were footsteps. A pair of humans approached. They came directly to Aura's roost, expecting to see Azul.

When the humans arrived and saw the green parrot caught in their trap, their disappointment quickly grew into laughter.

"What do you want to do with it?" a younger female asked her male companion.

"We're not breeding green parrots, are we?" he replied.

"Should we check with Randi?"

"I think she also knows we're breeding Spix's, not greens. And I think she likes her sleep."

"So, we let it go and reset the trap?"

"Yeah, I'll do it."

"You sure?" the young lady asked.

"Yes, no problem."

"OK, you're the expert." The tired associate turned and trudged back toward the lights.

The man opened the cage and spoke softly to Nipiklee. This was a good moment for Vicente El Real. After all the harm he'd done, after all the dishonor of his demise, to release a bird back into the wild helped restore him. He lifted the door to the cage and wired it open. Once Nipiklee was off the perch, he could reset the trigger mechanism. Vicente stood back and waited for the beautiful green parrot to fly off.

After he reset the trigger, Vicente gazed at Aura in the cage. The two stared at each other for a long moment, each contemplating the other in their own way. Both were frightened, but for different reasons. Vicente grimaced as he considered all the birds he'd taken from the wild in one way or another. How many had actually died before they ever arrived where they were being smuggled to? How many suffered along the way? How many reached their illicit destinations, only to endure life unhappy and confused? He had done this. It was his legacy just as much as his success stories were.

El Real looked back at the breeding facility. A half grin replaced the grimace. He could never undo what he'd done, but this project helped. As penance, if there could be such a thing, Vicente knew he'd spend the rest of his life helping, the sad irony being that it was what he should've been doing all along.

Vicente stared at Aura. He thought about the green parrot flying off into the bush and how good that felt. He looked out into the bush. From behind a tree, deep in the woods, Azul studied the human, not recognizing him. Vicente would've liked that. At this point in his life, that's exactly what he wanted to be, unrecognizable. Vicente El Real reached down to Aura's section of the cage, undid the latch, and opened the door. Then he walked back toward the lights. "A note returns to the symphony," he mumbled to himself. It was the second time he'd released a Spix's macaw. It felt better than selling them.

It took a moment for the reality of the situation to sink in. Aura watched the human stroll off, relieved. The strange mesh, the repetitive pattern that was constantly superimposed on her vision, was no longer there. A section of the enclosure suddenly seemed to be gone. Was this a trick? Was it done intentionally? Aura stopped asking questions. The only thing that mattered was the answer: there was an opening! She burst through it into the bush.

Before Aura could perch, Azul was flying beside her.

"Follow me!" he called.

Aura followed him deep into the Caatinga, away from the man-flock, away from the captive parrots, away from their favorite trees. Azul wanted to be alone with her, undisturbed, unafraid.

They settled deep into the top of a tree that was thick with foliage so that they couldn't be seen or heard. As soon as the pair touched down, understanding that they were finally reunited, Aura asked, "Where do we go now?"

Azul considered the question. He hadn't come all this way back to the Caatinga to then go somewhere else. He'd already seen enough of somewhere else. "I came here to be here," he concluded. But Azul also realized that deep down, in his heart of hearts, he didn't really expect that he'd wind up reunited with Aura. He assumed that he'd live out his days, perhaps with Nipiklee at his flank, as content as he could possibly be. Now, however, the equation had changed. Aura was here. There was something—someone—who made him feel alive, another worth living for, another impossible to live without. The parrot backed off his initial declaration, asking, "Where would we go?"

Aura shook her head side to side. Who knew? Could it be true that on the entire planet, there wasn't room enough, wasn't habitat enough in the wild for *one pair* of Spix's macaws? There had to be a place, but where? The monk parrots to the north had found an answer, but that didn't seem to be the solution for the sky parrots. If there was a place, why didn't Aura or Azul know about it? Why wasn't their kind found in other locations?

"You've seen much more of the world than I have," Aura said. "Have you not seen other woods that we could survive in?"

"I have seen those woods. There are places unlike here where we could try."

The pair noticed Nipiklee in an adjacent tree watching them. Aura waved her over. The three birds perched together, thinking.

"There's one thing," Aura finally said.

"What's that?" her mate replied.

"About leaving . . . about trying somewhere else. There's one thing that feels like mites under my feathers."

Nipiklee smiled. "I knew you two couldn't leave me."

"No, it's not that," Aura said matter-of-factly. As the green parrot winced, Aura added, "You could come with us. You should."

"What about the mites beneath your feathers?" Azul pecked.

"Well, I'm sitting here looking at what any of us would describe as our home, and what do I see? Actually, a more fitting question is, what don't I see?"

"Sky parrots?" Azul answered.

"Yes, that's true, but really, what I don't see now are goats, cattle, pigs."

"There's no shortage of any of those creatures in the Caatinga."

"But not *here*. They're gone. And why are they gone? They've been removed. The man-flock did it."

"That's who brought them here in the first place," Nipiklee reminded.

"True, but the bigger question is: Why did they take them away? From here, now?"

Azul listened carefully. He thought he saw where this was going but wanted to be sure about the conclusions being drawn.

Aura continued, "So, now that the destructive beasts have been taken away—"

"Sure, but either way, the man-flock is still here," Nipiklee interrupted.

"With the beasts gone, the trees return," Aura continued. "When the caraiba trees return, so does our world."

Azul understood.

Turning to Nipiklee, Aura explained, "Yes, the man-flock is still here, and they can certainly be destructive beasts, but I think this is a different flock. They're planting trees—our trees. They're constructing barriers to protect them. They seem to be doing a lot of things that are good for us."

"They also have a large, healthy flock enclosed behind one of their barriers just a few flaps from all this," the green protested.

"But for how long?" Aura asked with a small smile on her face.

The feathers on Azul's neck ruffled and rose. "You really think all this is for us? And you think they're going to let those parrots out of there to live freely? Really?"

"One let me go, didn't he?"

"Sure, but the others wanted to catch me."

"Those are the ones," Nipiklee peeped, "that we have to worry about, and they always seem to outnumber the gentle ones."

"If they wanted to hold us, keep us locked up, why would they remove the beasts and plant the trees? Why would they restore this our way if we're never going to be part of it? Why would they gather so many of us here?"

"Why would they ruin it in the first place?" the male mumbled. "Be careful, this is man-flock logic we're squawking about."

"I have a good feeling about this. I think all those parrots in there are a wild flock waiting to happen."

"Ya think?" Azul asked. "The man-flock is just going to let them go? Really? Besides, most of those birds wouldn't know a hawk if it bit them on the rump. I don't see it."

"I think that's where *we* come in."

"So, you think we're out here to . . . to show them how to be macaws?"

"I think so. To show them how to live here, how to survive as sky parrots."

Nipiklee whispered, "I know how to survive. I could help."

"We're counting on you, Nipiklee," Aura said.

Azul looked over the bush line at the stream flanked by cara-iba saplings. He tried to envision the landscape populated with a free flock of sky parrots. In his lifetime, he'd never actually seen that. He wondered what it would sound like. How a day would pass when he didn't have to fear being trapped and taken away. What it would be like to have friends . . . a family. He looked at Aura and nodded. It was worth the journey. It was worth coming home.

Flying from the cold, heading south by southwest, the pair of ivory-bills said almost nothing to each other for most of the trip. It wasn't anger. They just felt as though there was nothing to say until they reached their destination. Once they came upon familiar territory, they searched for a secure hollow to serve as a temporary shelter. When one was found, an abandoned roost that appeared to have plenty of life left in it, they widened the entrance to accommodate ivory-bill dimensions, then flew off to dine on local grubs and beetles.

Their hammering echoed for miles through the wet woods, announcing to all in the swamp that the great woodpeckers had returned. It was a sound that was too long absent, a sound that belonged. Without it, it was as if the rainbow were missing a color. With it, the woods were more complete. Squirrels, turkeys, salamanders, turtles, foxes, even the gators all listened to the woodpeckers' tooting and banging, realizing how much they'd actually missed the sounds when they were gone.

Fed and full, the pair returned to rest in their roost. They climbed into the hollow, drowsy, done. Finally, Gonzo said softly,

"I have to ask . . . How? How did you find me? And where? Where did you go?"

Kwim lowered her head onto his flank. "I wasn't really ever leaving you. I was finding me . . . At least I thought I was. But what I found instead was us."

Gonzo was clearly confused. He listened as Kwim continued.

"I flew south to the Pod, the big, hot island where there are still some others similar to us. I found them. But it didn't matter how many of them were there. None of them were you. And I learned again that it's you. It can only be you."

"It's us."

"Yes, it is." Kwim nuzzled deeper into her mate's feathers. "Whatever happens, it's us."

"Yes, but how did you find me? I could have been anywhere."

Kwim explained that she was in a tree stripping bark and eating tasty tropical bugs. Beneath her, on the ground, a solenodon was picking at scraps. They both seemed to get full at the same moment.

A little later, they found themselves at the same small brook, drinking. The two exchanged pleasantries. They started chatting. One thing led to another, and the solenodon told Kwim that he'd met a sky-blue parrot earlier in the day migrating south and that during their discussion, the parrot told him that he believed he'd glimpsed and heard an ivory-bill when he was in the early stages of his trek. Since the solenodon had never heard of anything like an ivory-bill from anywhere other than his island, he found the information interesting.

When Kwim told him that she, too, wasn't from the island originally, the solenodon claimed he could tell by the way she spoke, her accent. The mammal shared the rest of the parrot's story with her. "He was right. I was interested. What ivory-bill wouldn't be? But it's what I heard next that told me it had to be you."

"What did he say?"

"Well, it wasn't the solenodon. When I returned to my roost, the parrot was actually sleeping there. I talked to him myself. It's funny, the first thing he says to me is that my call has the same accent as an ivory-bill he heard up north. Do I really have such a thick accent?"

"Apparently."

"Well, the birds on the island sound a little different from us. Not nearly as dignified—the parrot's words, not mine—and he noticed that."

"Smart birds, parrots."

"Yes! So, I had him tell me exactly where he was when he heard . . . you. And then I came."

"Wow, what are the odds?"

"It's not about odds. *We're* supposed to be. That's all there is to it. It's meant to be. So, when I arrived in the pines and heard you drumming on a tree, I knew right away . . . but I waited a little bit."

"Preening?" Gonzo asked with a grin.

"Maybe . . . a little. Then I found you and Bardus."

At the mention of the owl, they both paused. Kwim wondered if Gonzo would somehow blame her for what had happened. She didn't know that Gonzo had planned to leave anyway, that Bardus would've demanded he go and her presence didn't really change anything. She waited to see how her mate would respond.

But Gonzo didn't like blame. Often, things just happened. There was an ego attached to blame that Gonzo disliked. Just as one might claim credit for success, claiming the blame for failure, at least to Gonzo, seemed to unnecessarily inflate one's importance. Success or failure, whatever happens, it's about *me.* Blame can oversimplify and sometimes get in the way of solving the real problem. The woodpecker knew that what happened to Bardus wasn't about Kwim. It was about him, Bardus, the pileateds, the hawks, and the Creator more than anything else. As with most things, the situation was too complicated to point a wing at one individual.

Gonzo had certainly experienced loss, and though he didn't always understand it, he was able to accept it. Yet if he'd lost Bardus and not reunited with Kwim, that might've been too much to handle. But he did have Kwim. She had come to him. They felt stronger about each other than ever before. The woodpecker wondered if that was what had been missing all along, the connection, the conviction. They had that now. Could it be the spark that would fuel a family? It was another question Gonzo couldn't answer.

While he was thinking things through, Kwim had risen and flown off a short distance to a thick dead cypress. There was a crack running down a high section of the tree. There were no branches around the thin crevice, making it uncomfortable for anything other than a woodpecker or a nuthatch to perch upon securely.

Kwim looked back at Gonzo, who'd traced her to the tree. She nodded at the notch. Then her mate did as ivory-bills have done for as long as there have been ivory-bills. He chiseled at the crack, widening it with a majesty only woodpeckers possessed. Before long, the pair was inside the tree, carving out a splendid roost. And while Gonzo knew how to excavate the cavity, it was Kwim who knew how to make it a nest. She wasted no time preparing the honest hollow.

Gonzo and Kwim entered the roost and huddled closely. Through half shut eyes, they gazed at the swamp, wondering if any place could be so beautiful. They listened to the creatures who'd missed the ivory-bill calls, and they were soothed by their sounds, in turn. Before the woodpeckers closed their eyes completely, before they fell asleep, they heard one more sound deep in the dark woods, carried like wind.

Hoo-hoo-hoooo-hoo-hoo . . . hoo-hoo-hoooo-hoo-hoo.

They fell asleep. Two birds with one dream.

Glyde had been among the man-flock longer than he'd anticipated, and now that Soaria was gone, the petrel's motivation had lost altitude. The idea of returning a feather to a flock he'd never met, located in a place he'd never been, without any real hint of where it might be, wasn't really something an injured bird could wrap his wings around.

There were other birds all around him. They came, they went. A few, like Bubo, stayed. It all seemed kind of surreal to the petrel. Glyde had little desire to return to Galahope, little desire to do much of anything. Of course, he missed his parents and Stithl, maybe even his sister to some degree, but beyond that, Galahope didn't really feel like home to him. The petrel had forgotten that just days before, he'd lamented ever leaving the islands. He was confused, thinking one thing one moment and something else the next.

Glyde reminisced, recalling that when he was a youngster, he considered flying to the island where the Gwattas originally hailed from, north of Galahope. But if the island actually led to the flock's demise, why bother, he reasoned. Later, he regretted not making that journey. It was perhaps one of the reasons he'd flown to find Soaria.

Glyde had been moved to a much larger enclosure that allowed him some limited flight, flaps and hops, a mindless chat here and there with one of the other residents, yet the petrel remained depressed. While he was nourished physically, he felt starved emotionally.

His food arrived lifeless, presented in some man-flock shell. It wasn't anything like feeding oneself on the open ocean. Had Glyde understood how carefully people like Rachelle and Rich prepared and enriched his food, he probably would've felt better. In fact, the humans wanted Glyde back on the wing over the ocean as much as he wanted it. Had he known how much the man-flock cared about him, specifically, he might've actually felt special.

But at the moment, he didn't understand, and his depression wouldn't allow him to understand. Fueled by the feeling that the one chance he had to be with another just like him—a female, something that never seemed possible on Galahope—was now gone, likely forever, Glyde tumbled deeper into the flames of hopelessness.

Regardless of how he felt mentally, the petrel was healing physically. Pain had been replaced with soreness. The ability to fly, to stretch his wings and work his muscles, had returned. His legs were again strong. Was he, however, strong enough to survive on his own *out there?* That remained to be seen, but it was getting to be time to find out.

In the larger enclosure outside the aviary, Glyde had the opportunity to challenge himself physically, although he rarely did. Still, every now and then, he'd flit from one side to the other, usually fueled by nerves. He could hear the surf. He could taste the salt in the air. He could hear the other birds. He could feel the warm wind and shafts of sun against his feathers. As much as he refused to admit it, it began to feel rather nice. Glyde fought the feeling, the pull of the sea, the allure of freedom, plunging instead into the abyss of self-pity.

At night, the petrel passed the time looking up at the stars. He knew them well. They told him things. Stars were light. And as long as so many lights shone so brightly, he believed there was hope—not necessarily for him, but for the Gwattas, perhaps.

Yet Glyde wasn't really sure what he believed. Hope was hope, not a belief. Yet he'd been taught to believe. He was expected to believe. But he'd seen so many things that told him not to believe. They sometimes clouded over the other things in his life that spoke of hope, that veered toward something beyond himself, beyond his own life.

The enclosure was covered in the ubiquitous man-flock web that held him within. Small, hard squares separated the petrel from the rest of the world. Glyde gazed through the squares, using them to frame groups of stars. It made no sense, yet he'd perch for entire evenings, tilting his head one way or another so that certain stars were centered inside the squares. It comforted him. There were oceans of stars to play with. They sparkled in the sky just like they did when their reflections bounced off the still sea.

The petrel was again framing stars, plotting them within the grid of the enclosure overhead, when there was a rattle and the stars in the squares disappeared. Gone. It was dark, pure night. Something eclipsed his view. The word *stars* echoed in his mind, blending with the rattle of the enclosure, harmonizing with his *bird*tra, *sand*. Then Glyde heard another word. It came from above, not from within himself like *star* and *sand*, but from right next to him. It was familiar. He heard the word again.

"Turd."

Glyde looked up. Just over his head, blocking out the stars he'd been studying, was Wilbird, the one and only.

The plover shook his tiny head in mock disgust and repeated, "Turd."

Then Glyde did something he hadn't done in a long time. He grinned. Wilbird just had that effect. He was amusing, kind of annoying in an entertaining way. Glyde was *almost* happy to see him.

"Yeah, I flew into a duck the other day, Dotty, who apparently took a *flight*eous conk to the old billholder."

"So, you two must've had a lot in common," the petrel mumbled.

Ignoring the quip, Wilbird continued, "After a bit of small-squak the daffy bird quacked that she was just released from this place. Said she'd seen a petrel almost die and then come back to life. So, I wondered if it was Turd."

Glyde bowed regally, acknowledging the moniker.

"Dotty duck also told me about the hen."

"The hen?"

"You know, the chick."

"The chick?"

"Yeah, the female."

"She has a name. I mean, she *had* a name. I mean, it's still her name . . ."

"I know. I know. The duck told me. Sorry about that. Thought I'd flap over and see how you were doing."

That was the thing about Wilbird. He'd peck at you relentlessly, and then, in all seriousness, he'd ask you how you were doing. He cared. So, as much as he could get under your short feathers, you couldn't just declare him a ruddy's rump, because deep down, Wilbird was OK. Still, sometimes, it was hard to admit, and Wilbird liked it that way. That was how he flew.

Before Glyde could fully appreciate the plover's gesture, Wilbird continued, "What's that over there?" pointing to the food in the enclosure. "Are those little shrimp? There's like four, five. Are you gonna finish them? Help a bird out. Pass a couple up here," the plover pleaded, casting doubt upon his true motivation for visiting the petrel in the first place.

Without commenting, Glyde passed several morsels up to the plover, who replied, "Thanks," chewed quickly, and then mumbled as he swallowed, "Turd."

The two birds sat quietly, Glyde passing morsels to his guest. They watched the stars and conferred about hope for the petrels, hope for the plovers. The sparkle in the night faded and disappeared as the dawn rinsed the stars from the sky. The birds wondered if their flocks also would be rinsed from the sky just like the stars. But if their kind were at all like the celestial gems, they'd return, just as the stars would when the sun set later at dusk.

There was a rustle just beyond the enclosure, and the human called Reach approached. Wilbird winked, plucked one last shrimp, and flew off. Another human followed, one called Roe-shell. Although the man-flock in general made him nervous, he didn't fear these two. In a moment, they were inside the aviary, standing next to Glyde.

Suddenly, it was dark. The petrel could feel human hands on him, firm, secure, but not angry. Roe-shell examined him, just as she'd done a thousand times before. Glyde had already completed a thorough conditioning period. The petrel knew the drill. She stretched his wings and bent his legs, shifting him from one side to the other, leaving no feather unturned. Roe-shell noted that Glyde's plumage was well oiled and clean. It was a good sign. The dawn light reclaimed the sky. The human stared into Glyde's eyes for a long time, taking a deep, thoughtful journey into the bird. The petrel looked back into her eyes.

Roe-shell moved her head up and down slowly. Her mouth widened, and her teeth appeared.

It really must be so strange to have a mouth with teeth, Glyde thought. *Why are they so proud of them, constantly displaying?* Reach also showed the petrel his teeth.

The pair gently placed the bird into a much smaller den, one they could pick up and carry, which is exactly what they did. The man-flock carried the petrel to the beach, lowering him onto a small floating island that rested partially on the sand, partially on the water. Glyde didn't know what was happening. He didn't really care.

The tiny island began to move. The two humans sat down. At first, the noise startled Glyde. The roar was unexpected. But Reach seemed to command the rumbling patch as it bumped across the water, carrying them away from the shore on a course out to sea, so the petrel stopped worrying.

Glyde didn't attempt to make sense of the situation. He rested quietly in the snug enclosure. This wasn't like flight. It was noisy. Everything bounced and rattled, groaned and growled. As the petrel tried to ignore the commotion, a rainbow that rose in the distance to the east caught his attention. Petrels believed that when they died, they would soar up to the sun. If they flew the good flight during their lives, they'd be permitted to pass through the orb, which they believed was the eye of God, Pettr, to join their lord on the other side.

The world they lived in, the world they were leaving, they thought, was actually inside God's body. The afterlife was on the other side, the beyond, a beautiful world they'd share with Pettr and others if, of course, they had flown the good flight. So, death for these aspiring birds-of-paradise was actually a birth, a fledging from this world into eternity. Those who hadn't flown the good flight would not be permitted eternity. If they'd chosen to ignore Pettr's voice, they would not suddenly hear it on their final flight.

Like most other creatures, the petrels assumed the essence of their religion was true for all—not just their flocks, not just birds, but true for all living things. This was one part of the man-flock's nature that confused them. With all that humans could do, all that they knew, the birds couldn't explain why the man-flock would do so much damage to the world. When they removed a forest, blackened an ocean, melted the ice, straightened a river, smoked the air, drained a pond, the petrels saw it as altering, almost attacking God, since for them, the planet was physically part of Pettr's body. They couldn't make sense of the behavior.

All these thoughts came back to Glyde because of the rainbow. When he was young, his father told him a roosting story before he slept about bluebirds who actually tried to fly over the rainbow and succeeded. The Gwattas believed that if one could fly over the rainbow, they might glimpse the other side beyond Pettr's eye.

Glyde studied the rainbow. It was vivid, thick—not at all wispy or fleeting as so many rainbows often appeared. This one seemed solid, like you could perch on it. Slowly, steadily, it grew larger as the floating island sailed closer. Red, orange, yellow, green, blue, indigo, and violet claimed the sky opposite the sun.

Suddenly, Glyde found himself not only moving closer to the rainbow, but looking down at the two humans riding on the sea. Perhaps it was the little purple seed Roe-shell had given him. It might've been the constant bouncing. Or maybe the strange fumes rising from the butt of the tiny spit that carried them rattled his mind. Whatever it was, the petrel was flying.

It was a strange flight. He'd flap his wings once or twice and cover an incredible distance, gliding, soaring on and on with a single stroke of his wings. He felt almost weightless. Then he was there, perched as he'd imagined on the crest of the rainbow. Behind him, beneath him, was the ocean. He could see the two humans, a speck on the sea, sailing toward him. In front of him was mist, cool, salty, blowing in thick and thin patches just beyond him.

Glyde began to think of his words, his *birdtra: sand, sand*. He tried adding *stars* and repeated the two words softly. The sun pierced the white haze, heating it, thinning it. Deeper into the cloudy dew, there seemed to be activity. An island? A shoreline?

Birds for sure, but Glyde couldn't quite decipher the image. He couldn't decide what was happening. He couldn't decide whether he should fly into the confusion or turn from it.

A bird emerged from the mist. It perched next to him and said, "It's not an easy choice, is it?"

Glyde could hear the bird, but the mist clung to it, hovering around it. He couldn't see the creature clearly.

"You could fly in there if you really wanted to."

Part of the petrel longed to enter.

"But you would not return," the one shrouded in mist continued. "From that point on, there would only be the other side."

"The other side," Glyde repeated. He knew. The bird didn't have to tell him.

"When I came here to the rainbow, I had no choice. Most don't. My last life was over. There was only the next for me."

"But that's not where *I* am?"

"No. Well, it would've been the same for you, but it seems that you might have a choice." A wing emerged from the vapor surrounding the speaker and pointed to the pair of humans, still a speck, a tiny sparkle on the sea.

When Glyde looked back to tell the bird that he was ready to leave the temporary, ready to begin forever on the other side of the rainbow, the petrel was gone. Yes, it was a petrel, he realized as it disappeared, a Gwatta like himself.

He heard the bird's voice again. It whispered, "Choices to make, Greatgrandson . . . choices to make." And then he heard no more.

Great-grandson? Really? Glyde wondered. Could that bird have been his great-grandmother, Pakeet?

The fog beyond the rainbow washed over him, wet and cool. It chilled him to the bone. The other side wasn't as inviting as Glyde anticipated. He hesitated, wondering whether the rainbow was an invitation or a warning. Was it there to lead him to the next life or keep him from it?

"Do you have the feather?" another voice asked. "Did you lose it?"

Without reflecting, Glyde slipped his beak under his wing, deep into his own feathers and produced the single plume that Bubo had given him. It was the closest he'd gotten to Soaria . . . until now.

Perched next to him on the crest of the rainbow, the female petrel grinned. "Beyond the mist is indescribable, but you shouldn't be in such a rush to get there. It will wait for you. It is forever."

Glyde said nothing. He knew it was her.

"Why did you do it?" she asked. "It makes no sense."

"I needed to meet you," he mumbled.

"I'll bet you didn't think we'd meet like this. Be careful what you fish for, right?"

"It's OK," Glyde said, accepting what might turn out to be his demise.

"No, it's not OK. I need you to do something . . . for me."

Glyde listened, unsure what he could do for anyone at this point.

"My feather, I need you to take it somewhere."

"Where? Why?"

"To my flock, my family."

"You have a flock?"

Soaria nodded. "I had one."

"Well, really, at this point does it even matter? I mean, for either of us?"

"It matters. Will you do it?"

"I don't know how. And I don't know if I'm capable. You do see where we are right now?"

"This is your choice. This is your chance. Take the feather and return it. Continue your life inside the world of Pettr or step off the rainbow and fly to the other side to begin your life with Pettr."

Glyde wasn't sure. He'd made his peace. He was ready for the rainbow and beyond. But he'd finally found the reason for all this, the one he'd left his home to find, and she seemed to need him to continue the quest. Was this the real reason for his journey?

"Bring my feather home," Soaria quietly implored.

"And where is home?" the petrel perched in purgatory asked. Glyde listened as Soaria spoke. He looked in the direction she described, the mist behind him, the sun on top of him, and he closed his eyes.

When he opened them, he was back in the burrow on the noisy little island that ricocheted from swell to swell. The island slowed, and the petrel wondered, had he just stood on the rainbow? Had he just met his great-grandmother? Had he actually spoken with Soaria? Glyde reached under his wing. Her feather was still there. Was it all a dream? Was it real? Could it have been a dream that was real? They said he had to make a choice, and he didn't remember making one, yet here he was back in the boat. It couldn't be real, Glyde decided.

The hands reached in and grasped him gently . . . for the last time. The weather conditions were perfect. They'd taken the petrel out to sea, where the large body of water would stimulate the pelagic bird to fly. Reach and Roe-shell were showing him their teeth again and making that human sound, the one that's in between a chirp and a bark, a bit more like clucking. They held Glyde, staring into his eyes once more. And then Reach released him into the wet air.

Although he was confused, Glyde didn't look back. He turned on a breeze and flew. The petrel knew where to go. Soaria had told him. When he finally got there, if it was actually there, he'd know for sure whether the encounter on the rainbow was real or imagined. It was time to find out.

Gonzo and Kwim had flown swiftly, silently, resolutely. They knew the destination. Returning to the swamp where they'd been before, where, for whatever reason, the pair failed before, they felt life would be different now. They were different. *They* was no longer plural. It was singular. They were one—one mind, one purpose, one life, one direction, one pair. They'd come to the place where the other matters more than the self. And when both partners arrive there together, in one sense, there is no self—that's left behind.

Yet in that moment, the death of the self is actually a birth, something Gonzo and Kwim hadn't anticipated but understood immediately. No longer ruled by their own selfish desires, whims, and impulses, they found a deeper joy, a greater meaning, in caring for the other. The pair appreciated that when you're no longer the center of your own universe, at times its sole inhabitant, the cosmos grows and expands. Life gets bigger and becomes more interesting, and a greater purpose emerges.

The ivory-bills returned to their swamp reborn. In short order, they identified a more permanent roost and crafted it into something that, for a woodpecker, could only be seen as spectacular. The roost was carved deep into the trunk, spacious yet snug. It was lined with moss, leaves, and feathers and safely situated high in a thick cypress with more water than soil around the base, allowing the swamp to wash away feathers and debris that might expose what lived above while rinsing scent before it reached noses that sniffed for meals. That same soggy soil would also deter other predators that climbed, crawled, or walked.

Bardus came to mind often. The great barred owl wouldn't be there to defend them. The ivory-bills would do that themselves. They'd done it before. They would do it better now—two birds, one life.

Gonzo and Kwim settled into a wonderfully satisfying routine. They foraged, they preened, they slept, they explored. They lived simply. The pair put no pressure on themselves to do anything other than exist as ivory-bills in the swamp. They became as much a part of their surroundings as any smell or sound. It was easy to do because this was where they belonged. And just when the whole "one simple life" reality became the new normal, everything changed, as it so often does.

Following a long, relaxing feed, the pair returned to the cypress. *I'm not as young as I once was,* Gonzo thought when his thigh cramped as he crawled into the nest. Kwim had aged as well. How could one not? To breathe is to age, yet Gonzo smiled. He didn't see the age in either of them. It was there, no doubt, but to Gonzo, Kwim was and always would be eternally young. When you soar into love in your youth, he observed, your mate never really ages. Kwim would forever be the *hot chick* he'd loved from the moment they met. Her eyes, particularly, were unchanged. There was a sparkle in them. It was her soul, her essence, and that was ageless.

This was one of the reasons Gonzo loved to make Kwim laugh. He'd decided long ago that everyone seems younger when they laugh. Kwim's eyes never shone so much as when she cackled, and Gonzo knew how to get her there. He hoped Kwim saw the same radiance in him, and when she laughed, he suspected she did. The pair preened, teasing each other. As they drifted off, dreaming the same dreams, Gonzo thought, *This is happiness. This is life.*

All that changed, in a manner of speaking, when Gonzo woke up. The first thing he saw when he opened his eyes was Kwim staring at him. She sat upright, stiffly, yet it seemed like she might not be breathing. Surely, she was breathing. When she blinked, Gonzo noted with relief that she was alive.

"What's wrong?" he asked.

Kwim just stared blankly and stepped to one side. On the floor of the roost rested four white eggs.

"Yours?" Gonzo asked, stunned.

"No, the squirrel laid them. Of course they're ours."

"How?" he asked. "You didn't know?"

Kwim nodded and shrugged her wings, saying, "Happens, I guess."

The pair smiled.

They decided who would forage first, because the eggs would never be left alone. Meals now had new meaning. There was work to be done. But when Gonzo flew off, two sets of eyes, eyes that had been searching for the ivory-bill for a very long time, were just on the other side of the tree.

Glyde flew northeast in the direction that Soaria instructed him to go. Whether the vision that had spoken to him was fiction, he couldn't say. But Glyde had her feather, had come all this way, and had to know. There was nowhere else to go, nothing better to do, so Glyde continued flying northeast.

As he drifted on, the petrel thought more about home than he had at any point since he left. It made him think that perhaps it was time to return, even though he was currently flying directly away from the Islands of Life, a term some used to refer to Galahope. Maybe Galahope was actually where he belonged. But if it was, why was he flying somewhere else? Regardless, when he finally did go home, he'd have a tale to tell.

The petrel decided he'd try a little harder to fit in. Maybe one of the reasons he felt like an outcast was because he tended to cast himself out before anyone else could. It was safer that way, a preemptive social strike, less painful than the alternative. But was it really less painful? It was painful to be rejected, not noticed, or undervalued by those you tried to fly with, but it was also painful to always be on the outside, alone.

Glyde considered that it might be time to stretch a bit, to put himself out there, to find a sort of middle ground. This journey had shown him that. He began to sense that the world was often richer when you were part of it. The petrel realized he could still be the master of himself, not only when he was isolated, but when he was among others, as well. He was reaching the conclusion that he needed more flavors in his life than a constant diet of Glyde.

The word *diet* caused the ponderous petrel to think of food. His hunger was deepening to the point of distraction, so for the first time since he left Reach and Roe-Shell, Glyde would feed himself. For petrels, a truly nourishing meal required flight, observation, strategy, risk, athleticism, and perseverance. All these elements needed to be in play for feeding to be genuinely fulfilling. At the moment, however, Glyde was prepared to settle for something well short of fulfilling. He was just hungry.

The meal appeared virtually on cue. In the distance, the petrel could see a patch on the ocean bubbling and churning where the rest of the sea was calm. He approached carefully. Glyde could see the fins of large fish breaking the surface as they rounded up and consumed smaller fish, anchovies perhaps. This was worth a much closer look. The petrel would have to be mindful of the predator fish. There was also competition from above. A host of birds plunged and plucked the shoal below. Somewhat apprehensive, Glyde considered just how rusty his skills were. This was full-on feeding in a strange ocean, not something for the faint of heart or for one who might be off his game. *Am I ready for this?* the petrel wondered.

Then Glyde spied something he didn't like. Drifting amongst the commotion was a floating island with man-flock casting lines from branches into the fray. They weren't interested in the little fish. They were hunting the hunters—tuna—and catching them. And birds, as Glyde well knew, weren't immune to the man-flock's lines.

He circled the commotion, contemplating his next move. Another bird pulled up alongside his flank, apparently doing the same thing. It was a beautiful bird, striking, white like the tip of a freshly broken swell with black slats on the upper tips of its elegant wings and a diagonal black band on each of the upper inner wings. A black slash of feathers raced through its eyes. The bird's face was tipped with a pointed orange-red beak. But wings down, the bird's defining feature was the flowing tail that stretched behind it, two elongated white plumes that were almost twice the length of Glyde. This was a pelagic bird that the petrel had never seen before.

Even with all the other birds feeding on the fish below—and there were many—not one was like the creature flying next to Glyde, and, of course, there weren't any like the petrel. Both seemingly rare birds sized up the situation. The other intimated that it had a plan. The bird nodded below, to the humans. Glyde wanted nothing to do with what was happening on the small floating island, nothing to do with those gangling sticks and those almost invisible lines with the shiny claws on the end reaching out into the water, dragging in huge fish, one after another.

The bird nodded a second time toward the man-flock, but Glyde didn't respond. The bird shrugged. While all the other fowl cascaded into the sea for the tiny fish that eluded the tuna, this one plunged as if he was going to dive into the hard little isle that the man-flock stood upon. He plummeted to the rear, behind the man-flock, away from the fish, diving in a direction that would drop the bird directly into the loud, smoking beast that propelled the island. The beautiful bird would die for sure.

But at the last moment, it pitched its wings and veered forward into an open, red den of some sort. On one side, it was filled with what looked like pieces of squid. The other side was stuffed with small fish, a type Glyde had eaten when he traveled with Sunny, Wilbird, and Piper. These were the lifeless little fish that the man-flock would sometimes impale on the claws at the end of the lines, yet these weren't on any lines at the moment.

The bird with the long tail landed on the red den and quickly swallowed a fish, then another. He grabbed one more in that orange-red beak and flew off, never even noticed by the man-flock, who looked the other way the entire time. The bird returned to Glyde's side, grinned, and swallowed the remaining minnow. Then he dropped down and did it again. As soon as the strange bird seized a fish and flew from the tiny islet, Glyde landed on the red den and joined the sneaky feast. The two birds took turns filling their bellies while the preoccupied birds, fish, and man-flock all looked in the other direction.

Having gone through the entire meal, the entire experience, without actually saying one word to each other, Glyde decided, now that he'd eaten his fill, he'd go with the flow and flew off with the breeze, continuing somewhat aimlessly in the general direction he hoped Soaria had sent him.

As he soared on, he noticed that the silent bird was still just off his flank, flying in what appeared to be the same direction. Glyde glanced over. The bird with the grandiose tail nodded. The two flew on. Eventually, the long-tail swerved toward the petrel. When they were within a flap of each other, Glyde couldn't decide what to say, so he blurted out, "Quite a meal back there. Great idea."

"Yes, quite a meal," the other repeated genially.

They flew on a bit farther without speaking until the long-tail said, "Shouldn't be long now."

Glyde glanced over at the bird, perplexed. "What?"

"Getting close," he replied matter-of-factly. "We're almost there."

The petrel stared at the long-tail. "Where?"

"The island . . . Nonsuch. I know where you're going."

Glyde grimaced. "I don't even know where I'm going, but you do?"

"It's not hard to tell. I knew the moment I saw you."

"Really?"

"You've got family on Nonsuch. It's the most logical place you'd be going in this ocean."

"Family . . ."

"Well, if not directly, in a general sense at least, your flock." The long-tail disappeared. He'd spied something on the surface and swooped down without warning to pluck the morsel. He swallowed and then returned to the petrel.

While he was gone, Glyde wondered . . . *Flock?* Soaria had also said flock, just as the long-tail did. *Could it be?*

As the birds flew on, Glyde had a touch of indigestion. *Ah, the squid and those little fish,* he thought. *Delicious even the second time.* And after reflecting on his repeating meal, the petrel's deliberation returned to his journey. Even though it wasn't over yet, Glyde couldn't help wondering whether it was worth it. For a moment, he considered the flightless cormorants back on Galahope, who, for their entire lives, never really traveled more than the distance they could comfortably hop because all they needed was right there, all around them: great nesting sites, mates, and the cold currents that delivered their nourishment to the surf just beyond the rocks.

Yet the more he contemplated the cormorants, the more he understood that even these flightless birds refused to be limited by their stunted wings. They hopped, indeed, but they weren't grounded. They hopped right into the ocean and entered an entirely new world. Dangerous, bizarre, and yet they had to explore, had to escape.

Would it have been better to have just stayed home on Galahope? Glyde was still unsure, although he doubted he would've found at home what he found in his travels.

And even though he'd concluded earlier that isolating himself wasn't really the answer, he still had no desire to be the life of the flock. The whole notion of the social butterfly repulsed him. So, why was he now considering less isolation and increased contact with others? Why did a way of life that made perfect sense to him before he left Galahope suddenly make less sense now?

Glyde was changing—not growing, not shrinking, just changing. But why? The journey, this journey had showed him that life is more interesting, more fulfilling when it's not always predictable and safe. "Think outside the nest," his mother, Sirka, had peeped more than once. New places, new faces ultimately made him feel more alive. And now—particularly while he was young, strong, without obligation—now was the time to fly. *Later, when I'm old like my father,* he thought, *that's when I'll land. That's when I'll nest. Young petrels are meant to fly often and far.*

On Galahope, tasting a new crab, a different fish, an unknown clam was fun—exciting, even—but uncommon. Eating the same food at the same time, gathering it the same way, always alone . . . that was kind of boring. That was existing. Living, the petrel concluded, was quite another thing. For instance, presently, he was flying with a seabird at his side that he'd never encountered before, which was exciting, yet Glyde was still alone in his thoughts. Aloft yet aloof, he saw that even with other interesting creatures around him, he could keep parts of himself isolated if he chose to. It wasn't an either/or equation. He could have both involvement *and* isolation.

On Galahope, Glyde could pretty much guess where his life was going, how the day would play out, whom he would bump into. One day was more or less like every other day. But out here, flying across an unknown sea with a stranger at his side, on his way to Pettr-knows-where, per*flaps* an island with birds like him, petrels he'd never encountered before waiting in the wind . . . this was why he had wings.

The irony made Glyde smile. By getting off the island, by encountering the unexpected, by interacting with diverse beasts, even Wilbird and Sunny, Glyde not only had learned about them, but he'd learned about himself, which was infinitely more important to the petrel. *What could be more interesting than me?* he wondered, tongue-in-beak.

Many of the birds on Galahope, especially the ones who teased him, loved their games. They played them day after day, although never really with Glyde. But now, at this moment, Glyde wasn't playing a game. He was living the game, and he liked it.

Flight, he decided, wasn't just about flapping your wings. Flight was about transporting yourself, your body, your mind, your senses to new places, to new creatures. Flight was about widening your world. Glyde drank in the thick, warm, salty mist from a corner of an ocean that was refreshingly unfamiliar. He turned to the tropicbird, its long tail streaming majestically behind it, a feathered creature he'd never encountered, never imagined until earlier this day. Glyde grinned and guessed his traveling companion was feeling something similar . . . but he was wrong.

The tropicbird returned the grin and nodded to the horizon. His beak smiled, yet his eyes didn't quite agree. *Is there something else in them?* the petrel wondered. With the black feather bar running along both sides of the bird's face through each eye, it was hard to read clear meaning in their expression. The petrel returned the nod. The tropicbird gestured again, this time with more emphasis, as if he was pointing something out. Glyde had to focus to see through the mist. Off in the distance, he could see it. Little nests of land split the sea. Over a hundred were sprinkled across the ocean. The tropicbird nodded again.

As they approached the southern rim of the islands, it became clear that the man-flock was well established. All the trappings of their existence were evident. The likelihood of this place being some sort of island paradise didn't seem good.

The pair of birds swung around under the lower tips of the archipelago and then turned north, flying up the eastern extreme. They crossed over inlets, a large bay, and a long stretch of beach. Glyde wondered where the bird was taking him and if this was the place Soaria came from. Soon he would know.

Once they crossed the beach, Glyde could see them, a patch of diminutive islands. He counted ten, but it looked like the last one, the northernmost islet, was the one that attracted the tropicbird.

The island was deep green, fringed with sand and a rocky tail, surrounded by clear, pale shallows and deep blue where the ocean reclaimed its dominance. A burp of land, ringed by water, days from the continental coast would have been the perfect place for a petrel, if only the man-flock weren't so close and so abundant. Glyde grimaced. Here, he thought, in the middle of the ocean, even here, the man-flock abounds. Strange, this far from any real land, a place where the man-flock clearly doesn't belong, and yet they thrive. But petrels who were created for this place and likely colonized the islands thousands of years before the man-flock ever saw them have to fight for a tiny piece of it. Strange world, indeed, he concluded. Yet on this one island where the tropicbird was headed, there were bushes, trees, open shorelines, unspoiled habitat.

Perhaps this was a natural sanctuary, Glyde thought, a gift from Pettr, holy land.

As Glyde descended, even before his legs emerged to touch down, he could see them. There were burrows, nesting burrows— forty, maybe more. Petrel burrows. The tropicbird nodded again, grinned, and flew off.

The long-tail traveled briefly until he reached a rocky rise. He slipped into a hollow the wind and sea had carved into the exposure and joined his family. Glyde was disappointed in himself that he hadn't properly thanked the tight-beaked long-tail, but the opportunity, he reasoned, hadn't really presented itself. It was a small island. Glyde figured he'd see the bird again and thank him then.

This island, this Nonsuch as the tropicbird called it, wasn't exactly Galahope. Still, it appeared there was a sizable colony of petrels. *Are they like me?* he wondered. *Are they Gwatta? Darum? Something completely different?*

Glyde gathered himself as he stood on the sandy soil. He rested. He thought. He surveyed. This was one island—not the largest, not the smallest—in what looked like an archipelago of over a hundred islands. This specific island, for its size, was one of the most undisturbed, so it was easy to see why the petrels, and the long-tail for that matter, had colonized it. As with most islands in the sea, however, this one was fragile.

Glyde noted that at its highest point, the soil stood less than the height of an average tree on the mainland. One angry wave could wash much of this oasis from existence. But the wave hadn't come, and the island was still here—for now.

The petrel waited patiently, yet none of the locals appeared. It was midday, and if these petrels were like his own flock, they'd likely be deep in their burrows, sleeping, avoiding the heat, waiting for the refreshing evening breeze to fly to them. Glyde considered the cool, moist sand in the dark dens, the comfortable nesting area, and was reminded how long it had been since he, a notorious late sleeper, had embraced a rejuvenating power snooze.

With the bare sun beating down on his feathers, Glyde found himself casually strolling into the closest burrow. The moment he stepped into the shadows, the temperature dropped deliciously. After a few more steps, it was even cooler, darker. In a soothing trance of comfort, the petrel shuffled on.

"No further," the words whizzed by. "*NO FURTHER.*" And they took hold.

Glyde paused.

"Not *this* burrow," the voice demanded. "Turn around. Fly on."

"I'm a petrel," Glyde reassured. "No nee—"

"GO! There's nothing here for you but trouble. Move on."

Glyde wasn't sure if *here* meant in this burrow or on this island. Then he heard them and understood. Muffled peeps. Clearly, this was a mother with young.

"I'm not here to harm you or your young. Like I said, I'm a petrel. I've flown a long way."

"So, keep flying," the darkness commanded.

"I'd like to do that, but I'm on a little bit of a quest here. I'm looking for petrels who might know one named Soaria."

"How do you know her?" the shadow responded. "Where is she? *How* is she?"

Not long ago, Azul had concluded that however it turned out, coming back to the Caatinga was worth the effort. He had, in fact, voiced the opinion to both Aura and Nipiklee. And now, there were almost a dozen sky parrots from the man-flock structure flying and feeding with him in the bush. So, given that result, his proclamation rang true. To be part of an actual flock—to, in effect, be leading one—was more than Azul thought he'd ever see in his life.

But had he known the actual cost, something Azul always assumed *he'd* be called upon to pay, he might've come to a different conclusion. The macaw was prepared to suffer. He wasn't so accustomed to comfort that adversity scared him. If his own hardship led to the return of the Spix's flock, it would be well worth it. However, as fate would have it, the sacrifice came not from Azul, but from Aura.

Azul hadn't seen his mate for many days. She hadn't left—he was sure of that. Yet while he, Nipiklee, and others had searched high and low for Aura, they couldn't find so much as a feather. In one sense, that might be good news, for whenever a hawk claimed a parrot, there were always feathers, lots of them. Still, there were other threats, areas of the bush where the man-flock had hung long, thick, dead, black vines that seemed to connect leafless, branchless trees that were planted in far-reaching, widely spaced single rows. Too often, especially at night, parrots would be cut and sometimes killed by the hard-to-see vines as they flew into them. But whenever that happened, even if something scavenged the carcass, there would be feathers. Yet there were none.

With Nipiklee at his side, Azul passed the time tending to the blue flock, always looking out of the corner of his eye for a hint of Aura. Part of him perpetually thought about her no matter what else was happening, yet the macaw was lucky to have something as important as the new flock to keep him occupied. It grounded him at a time when he might've drifted off into the emptiness that Aura had always filled.

The little green parrot reminded her friend that he believed he'd lost Aura before and was wrong. The soft blue macaw nodded, nuzzled Nipiklee, and waited. He knew how to wait, so he'd do that. Knowing that, now or later, on this side, or the other, he'd see Aura again, and that at least for the moment, the Caatinga would see pale-blue macaws in its trees once more, Azul would persevere, as he'd always done.

Nipiklee nodded to the tree directly across from their perch. Orsi sat on a branch. He watched the pair, wondering, perhaps, whether he should approach or not. Azul nodded in his direction, and his nephew glided to them.

After a moment of silence, Azul coaxed, "Yes? Is there some special reason for your visit? Or are you merely here to share a branch?"

"Which is fine with us," Nipiklee added.

Orsi moved his head from side to side rhythmically as if summoning something. "There is a parrot you should speak to."

"A problem?" Azul asked reflexively.

"I wouldn't say that."

"Well, what would you say? Bring the parrot here."

"It's not that easy. She's here, but not among us. She's with the man-flock. She's one of those who were taken, like many of us, and then somehow brought back, but still held by the man-flock."

"Is it about Aura?" Azul asked, hopeful and terrified in the same breath.

"Yes, in part. She hasn't told me everything. Maybe she'll tell you."

Bobby returned to the swamp. It was the story of his life. You could take him out of the bayou for a spell, but you could never take the bayou out of him, not for a moment. He and Tim had gotten a tip. It was just a few lines mentioned somewhat casually at the end of a field report a local naturalist posted in a bird watchers' newsletter, describing a strange woodpecker he'd glimpsed while paddling through the swamp. Bobby watched the postings almost as carefully as he watched the trees. He shared the passage with his buddy, and two days later, they were packing Dinty Moore beef stew, StarKist tuna lunch packs, Slim Jim jerky, Snickers, Mounds, Baby Ruths, and Mountain Dew into their canoes—a regular bayou buffet—as they prepared to paddle into the swamp.

Camoed up like they were special forces, they also fitted their boats with trawling motors run by small car batteries for times when they didn't want to paddle. It was quieter, stealthier. There was less movement, less disturbance in the water. Actually, their access point wasn't very far from a highway that passed close to the swamp. Ironically, it was one human noise, the sound of the cars and trucks speeding by, that helped to cover much of the noise the other two humans made entering the swamp.

Bobby and Tim watched everything, everywhere, as they moved along the water. A beaver slapped a warning, letting them know they were trespassing. A thick cottonmouth lounging on a log opened its mouth wide so they could see the telltale patch of white inside, advising the pair to keep moving. Bobby and Tim weren't there for the snakes or the beavers, yet the presence of the beaver was a good sign. Its felled trees that were too large to be dragged into the swamp would rot and eventually host beetle larvae. That could be useful.

A red-headed woodpecker landed on an old elm tree. It watched the humans while Bobby scanned the tupelos and oaks, searching for strips of bark hanging from trunks or scattered at the base. Mallards and wood ducks paddled off in the distance. Drifting in from the west, Tim could hear the chuckling laughter of pileateds. He was hoping to hear something else, the *kent-kent* call, or the *BAM-bam* double rap. But all Tim heard at the moment was the laughter of the pileateds. One of them flew closer, curious. It landed on a dead red maple and pecked at insects on the tree.

The bird that interested Bobby and Tim, however, wouldn't be intrigued by the humans. These birds would flee. Curious ones had disappeared long ago. The ones that survived, if any, had learned—perhaps evolved—to be stealthy, cunning, and distrustful of man. There was no other way for them. They'd become phantoms. They had no choice.

Bobby and Tim worked the water for the entire morning with nothing to show for the effort. It was a result they were quite used to but not one that either man was willing to accept. They paddled past a 120-foot bald cypress, its two rows of needles transitioning from the summer's yellow-green to the fall's red-brown.

They heard it at the same time. Their heads snapped simultaneously to the east as if they'd practiced the move. The canoes turned slowly. They heard it again. Tim reached for a recorder and snapped it on, frustrated that he hadn't done so earlier.

Keeey-eeent, keey-eent.

The high-pitched call drifted out from a nook in the swampy forest where an oak had fallen long ago. Sun streamed to the ground through the hole it left in the canopy.

Yes, the dead oak would be a grand buffet, Bobby thought. It would only need a sneeze guard and a stack of serving trays to be perfect. He glanced at Tim. His partner nodded, clearly thinking the same thing. Drifting closer with a video recorder mounted on the bow, they heard the call again, like a shrill, laughing trumpet.

Keeey-eeent, keey-eent.

A branch on a bush bobbed. Something fluttered behind it, then landed square in the ray of light that illuminated the fallen oak and perched on the horizontal stump. The bird stood proudly, defiantly looking back at the two men—a blue jay, not the ivory-bill they anticipated. But the woodpecker was in there. They knew. They'd heard it.

Floating closer to the sound, a squirrel scooted in front of the oak. Behind them, an otter broke through the surface. When the canoes struck the shore, an unseen white-tail buck snorted in the brush. Undaunted by the humans, the blue jay remained on the log. It pecked at a centipede, swallowed the insect, and confidently cried, *Keeey-eeent, keey-eent!*

The men grimaced, climbed out of their canoes, and consoled themselves with the ultimate comfort food, Dinty Moore stew and Snickers. Sitting on the same log the blue jay had claimed, Tim smiled. It certainly wasn't the first time a blue jay had fooled a birder. Their ability to mimic other birds was well documented. It was common for jays to impersonate hawks, clearing all the other birds and small mammals from a feeding site so they could sneak in and take advantage.

Suddenly, mid-Snickers, Bobby and Tim began to smile and nod at each other. Yes! They might not have heard an *actual* ivory-bill, but there was a great chance that the jay had. How else would it have learned the call?

Knowing his partner had come to the same conclusion, Tim warned, "Some are going to say that the jay could easily have picked up the call from another jay who heard it from another jay, and it was passed down."

"Heck," Bobby added, "I bet we'll hear that the jay learned the call from the recordings they played the last time they searched for the birds. But what are the odds?"

"I *know*."

Bobby walked over to his canoe, mumbling, "Decoys. Let's hang `em." He rolled back a tarp and bent low into the boat. "I'll mount the birds, you set up the cameras."

Tim nodded.

They were done in about thirty minutes. Three exquisitely carved ivory-billed woodpeckers—one female and two males, perfectly painted works of art, hatched during Bobby's free time— were affixed to the upper trunk of an ancient cypress, a small family dining together. The two men took a deep breath and stared admiringly at the foursome, wondering if they'd ever see the sight for real. Tim loaded fresh batteries into the cam . . . *Foursome?* Bobby had only carved *three* birds.

A third male had joined the group. It hitched nervously up the tree. It pecked at one of the wooden birds, then another, and before either man could move, it flew off into the swamp. The scarlet crest singed their eyes like tracer fire in the night. Brilliant white plumage stretched from the narrow head down through the lower half of its back until it burst across the trailing ends of its wings. The black feathers had a glassy sheen to them, like coal in the sun. This was a clean, healthy woodpecker. Without thinking, Bobby slumped to his knees, eyes glued to the fleeing bird.

The men focused on the distinct crimson crest, brazen and re-curved. The woodpecker flew with its head and neck extended, not tucked like a great heron or a snowy egret. It flew fast, straight, much more gracefully than the more frenetic pileateds. The ivo-ry-bill kept its wings flat, stiff, half bent on the upstroke, without that panicked, frenzied flapping so many other birds depended on.

The entire sighting was over in an instant, yet for Tim and Bobby, time had slowed to a crawl. They could replay the entire scene in their minds, freezing on any moment. Every detail of the event was immediately, indelibly seared into their memories.

"Is she OK?" the voice asked. Then, a petrel took a step, and one more until it barely breached the veil of the shadow. A young female, a Gwatta apparently, stared back at Glyde. "What can you tell me about Soaria?"

"Not much. I never really met her, I guess."

"You guess? Did you meet her or didn't you? That makes no sense."

Glyde nodded. "You're right. And yet, here I am."

The other petrel's eyes scanned Glyde's face, then worked their way slowly down to his webbed feet, contemplating the one who stood across from her. "You're a Gwatta."

"As are you?"

She bobbed her head. A chick popped its tiny beak beyond the safety of the shadow, examining the intruder, and was gently pulled back behind its guardian while it wriggled to break free.

Glyde introduced himself. He explained that he'd flown in from the southwest, pointing in the direction as if the other bird didn't know where southwest was. When he gestured, the single feather fell to the floor of the burrow.

The instant it touched the cool sand, the little chick raced out and retrieved it, then rushed back behind the female. A moment later, she emerged and approached Glyde slowly, cautiously. She stopped when they were beak-to-beak and dropped the feather between them. "This is Soaria. If you never actually met her, how did you get *this?* How did you get *here?*"

The light that meandered from the entrance into the burrow disappeared. Another bird, a larger bird, entered.

"You're with *him!*" the female hissed, shooting hot oil on Glyde while she retreated with the chick to the deepest, darkest corner of the cavern.

"What?" Glyde asked. "With who?"

Then he was shoved aside by the larger bird who muttered, "Out of the way."

It was the long-tail, the tropicbird, the very same one that helped Glyde find this island. Yet it couldn't be the same bird. The long-tail glanced back at Glyde just to make sure the petrel had no intention of interfering. Then he disappeared into the dark. There was an intense, brief struggle. A moment later, the long-tail emerged with his beak clasped around the chick's shoulder, the youngster lifted off the ground. The chick strained to free itself, but it was futile, absurd.

It all happened so quickly. The long-tail trudged past Glyde. The youngster whispered, "Help me."

"Save him!" its vanquished guardian screeched as she dragged herself after the chick.

For the moment, Glyde was frozen, but a moment was all he'd have before the long-tail escaped with the young petrel. It was shocking, surreal.

The tropicbird glanced back at Glyde one more time, and the two exchanged expressions, one of terror, the other a thin grin. The larger bird shook the chick violently to subdue him, but the little one only fought harder, determined to escape. Glyde felt confused, betrayed. The tropicbird shrugged and turned back to the opening of the burrow, walking toward the light.

Out of all that had happened, it was the grin that got to Glyde. The long-tail was feeding himself. That could perhaps be understood, even if the way he did it left a lot to be desired. But that grin changed things. It made it worse. It made it *bird*sonal. The tropicbird took satisfaction in Glyde's horror. The petrel could see that in the grin. The brute, however, had miscalculated, as brutes often do. Glyde had seen this same horror before, only with different players. He was a petrel. His flock burrowed as well. And on Galahope, there were those who preyed upon petrel chicks. But on Galahope, it wasn't a tropicbird that descended from the sky. The Gwattas had to battle hawks, and as ferocious as this long-tail might be, it was no hawk.

Glyde had seen his father do it many times, although he'd never actually done it himself. The worst place to clash would certainly be in the burrow. The larger bird had too many advantages. Just as Lupé would have done, his son planned to allow the tropicbird to leave with the chick, but the instant he cleared the burrow, the real fight would begin, in the open, on the wing, where Glyde could fly rings around the intruder who would be trying to hold on to the captive chick. For now, he had to wait until the long-tail stepped beyond the hole.

The female petrel glared at Glyde, clearly disgusted by his inaction, which she attributed to cowardice. The petrel wished he could explain to her that he knew what he was doing, that it would be OK.

The long-tail was at the opening. He stepped confidently, arrogantly into the sunlight with the thrashing chick. Glyde took a single deep breath and raced toward the bird. At the end of the burrow, there was just enough room for the petrel to spread his wings so he could emerge in flight, an advantage. He flapped mightily, lifted himself off the ground, and tucked his legs beneath him.

Suddenly, there was nothing but darkness, and the petrel smashed into a solid wooden wall that came out of nowhere to abruptly cover the opening of the burrow. Glyde picked himself up off the ground and noticed a smaller hole carved into the center of the wood. Terrified that the chick would be taken away, the petrel squeezed through the cut, hoping he could still catch up to the long-tail. That, however, would not be a problem.

A human towered over the burrow. It held the long-tail in one hand and the chick in the other hand. He placed the little petrel near the opening in the wood, gently nudging it closer to the hole. He used his free hand to steady the long-tail, who clearly was not happy to lose his meal or to be held. When the long-tail settled down, the human carefully perched it on a rocky outcrop, stroking it several times to calm the creature.

The female petrel thrust her head through the narrow opening and called to the chick, "Quickly, inside!"

Before he could heed the command, the youngster glared back at the tropicbird, forgetting that the long-tail was just being a long-tail. It was hungry, no different from any petrel feeding itself. But that stark reality, that underlying imperative of eating always becomes *bird*sonal when it's directed at you, when *you* become the meal. The youngster cast a cold stare at the tropicbird that said, "I am little and powerless . . . today. And you used that against me. A time may come when you are old and feeble, and I am at the peak of my powers. I will not forget today. I will not forget *you*."

The long-tail would have none of it. As far as he was concerned, the chick would never see that day. All that mattered to him was today, right now, when *he* was the master. The tropicbird swooped down, past the human, wings spread, beak wide open, ready to pick up where he'd left off. The bird struck quickly, before the human or the petrel's guardian could react.

Glyde, however, was better prepared this time. He launched himself over the chick, landing between the two birds. The youngster used the momentary delay to dive for the opening, but the large long-tail brushed Glyde away like an ant on an anchovy, grabbing the chick by its leg, flying off with it before anyone could react.

Glyde pursued the bird into the air. He wouldn't be so easily dismissed this time. Although the petrel might've enjoyed mixing it up aerial style, he knew job number one was to save the chick. The best way to do that was to get the long-tail to drop his prize.

Glyde caught up to the larger bird easily. He slashed across his face, biting him as he passed. Since the long-tail's mouth was occupied, he couldn't return the assault unless he dropped the chick. Glyde tried to herd the bird over water, just in case he did release the youngster. The petrel climbed up underneath the bird and plucked a beakful of feathers from its sensitive lower belly. As he prepared for another assault, the female petrel appeared and ripped at one of the long, trailing feathers that inspired the bird's common name. Judging the meal not worth the effort, the tropicbird released the babe, letting him fall wherever gravity might

claim him, wherever his stubby, down-covered wings might angle him.

The little one flapped furiously, to no avail. He stretched his tiny wings and held them stiff while he prayed they might be of some use, realizing that even if he managed to touch down on the sea, there was no guarantee of safety. He could meet his demise just as easily there as he could have—would have—with the long-tail.

The long-tail, however, was by no means going to deny itself a meal. The bird merely skipped the appetizer and went straight to the main course—Glyde. It swung around abruptly and faced the petrel, the two birds flying directly at each other. If he could connect, the larger tropicbird believed he'd surely damage the smaller petrel. If he could knock Glyde from the sky, and he likely would, the battle was over. With the petrel grounded, the long-tail would eat.

Glyde knew what was coming, knew what the other bird was planning, but saw no reason to think he couldn't dodge the ploy easily. The tropicbird bet on its bulk, while Glyde counted on his dexterity. Neither bird would ever find out who was correct. Pouring out of a sunbeam that had obscured their arrival, several larger petrels appeared and attacked the long-tail. Mixed in with the stocky saviors were a few smaller Gwatta petrels. It was over in a flap, the tropicbird driven out to sea.

The chick! Glyde thought. He spun and flew back toward the island. The little one had already been fished out of the water and returned to its roost by the time Glyde landed just outside its burrow. The female stood at the entrance, smiling as Glyde approached.

"How is he?" Glyde asked.

"Fine. Grounded for not coming to me when I called him, but he's fine."

"That long-tail was the same one that helped me get here." The female nodded.

"But why would he help me find this island and then hunt a petrel? It makes no sense."

"It makes a lot of sense if you're Utak. Normally, the long-tails eat fish and squid. They particularly enjoy flying fish. But Utak is different. He has a mean streak. He's not like the rest of his flock."

Glyde looked puzzled, and then was reminded of a petrel on Galahope named Bog.

The other petrel continued, "He wanted you here, hoping you'd father more young . . . to feed him."

"That's why he helped me?"

"Can you come up with a better reason?"

Glyde shrugged, but when he began to speak, she raised a single wing, cutting him off. "There's someone who wants to meet you, someone you'll want to meet." The female pointed to a burrow a few flaps away. Three petrels, seemingly Gwatta petrels, were perched near its opening, waiting, watching.

"Go," the female nudged.

"There? Are you sure?" Unknown burrows were starting to leave a bad taste in Glyde's beak.

"You will be welcome." Then she gestured toward the burrow.

Glyde drifted slowly past the three watchful petrels, who nodded to him. He landed and paused for a moment as the sea behind him slid down the rocks that ringed this part of the island. Water soaked the rubble that glistened in the sun, then dripped back into the sea, only to repeat the process again and again. Even though Glyde knew exactly when the surf would arrive and recede, it was still mesmerizing every time it happened. The ebb and flow seemed like such a simple action, something Glyde had seen his entire life, yet he could still watch it over and over. The rhythm had a way of reaching deep inside, as if the planet were singing to him, as if its heart were pumping the water over the rocks.

Remembering where he was, the petrel shook out his feathers and climbed through the narrow opening in the wooden wall that covered the entrance to the burrow. The wood smelled of the man-flock. Like many of the contraptions that came from their hands, this one was perplexing.

As he stepped deeper into the tunnel, Glyde turned. He looked back at the opening. A small shaft of light penetrated the portal, reaching just where Glyde stood. The farther he went into the tunnel, the darker it became. But petrels liked the night. They were comfortable in the dark—more so, however, when they could see the stars. Glyde wondered if the wooden wall was a way to make the den darker. How would that possibly benefit the man-flock?

Glyde took a few more steps deeper into the burrow. He was uneasy, especially after his previous encounter with the fox on the beach. Still, this time, he was positive that he stood in a petrel's roost. A fox could never fit through that hole in the wood. He paused, wondering if per*flaps* he'd come upon the reason for the covering. But again, why would the man-flock want to do that?

After a few more steps, the petrel looked back once more. The hole seemed smaller. The light seemed dimmer. Glyde understood. The covering was there to keep anything larger than the petrel, like the long-tail, out of the burrow. It was protection. The man-flock was protecting the petrels.

That one epiphany led to a wave of questions. Glyde grinned at the irony, how an answer could lead to so many more questions. Why would the man-flock do this? He'd seen them help on Gala-hope. He'd seen them hurt. They were a confusing flock. And then Glyde realized that he was procrastinating. He was allowing his mind to wander from the task at wing. Someone wanted to meet him. The petrel pressed on.

After only a few steps, Glyde encountered a mature Gwatta petrel. He was sitting comfortably on the cool sand. The bird smiled and greeted the younger bird. "You have come to us from the west, I have heard."

"Well," Glyde responded, feeling an unexpected, uneasy connection to the other bird, attributing the sensation to nerves, "I've come from the west . . . the south. It's been a bit of a journey. I'm from an island called Galahope."

"Actually," the older one said, "we both come from the west, from an island called Guadalupé. And now, we're both here. How strange."

"Where exactly are we?"

"Nonsuch."

"That's what the long-tail called these islands. Nonsuch?"

"Well, he didn't really call all these islands Nonsuch. The name only refers to this island, not the others around us. I want to thank you for helping today. For us, every life—every chick, especially—is sacred. I'm sure you understand."

Glyde clenched his beak and nodded.

"I'm told you knew Soaria but didn't know Soaria. Which is it?"

The petrel told his story, most of it at least, once again.

When he was through, the older bird asked, "She's gone? Did you see her perish?"

"No, I didn't see it. I was told by Bubo."

"Yes, the owl. Not exactly a wise owl, as you've described him."

Glyde shrugged. *Wise is such a strange word*, he thought.

The older petrel sat quietly for a moment. "So, I see how you didn't meet Soaria. Now tell me how you did meet her. It was after she perished, wasn't it?"

Glyde's eyes widened. He nodded. He hadn't told the old bird this part of his story.

The older petrel looked off, deeper into the burrow, deeper in thought. He lowered his head, then looked up and said, "I knew this would happen."

"You knew *what* would happen?" Glyde asked cautiously, not sure where the conversation was flying.

"This . . . us."

Glyde laughed nervously. "That we'd meet? You don't even know my name. How could you know this would happen?"

The older bird stood and stretched, reaching one wing out across the burrow. The other wing didn't move. It was twisted. Half extended, the top part of the wing faced toward the ground, and the underside was twisted toward the sky. This bird couldn't fly.

He tucked his wings awkwardly to his flanks. "When you get older—sometimes just a little bit older—you begin to feel things, and sometimes you just see truths. At least you think you do."

"So, what truths have you seen?"

"Deep down, I knew that I'd see you one day. But I didn't really anticipate that it would be *you*."

"Now it's you confusing me."

"Look at me. Do you see it? I bet you feel it. I do."

"The wing?" Glyde replied tentatively.

"Look past that. Look at *me*. I can see it in you. You don't see it in me?"

Glyde scrutinized the bird.

"Do I remind you of anyone?" The bird's eyes shone.

The younger petrel took a step closer, then one more. He lifted his beak, changing the angle of his head. "Well, you're a Gwatta."

"Yes."

"I haven't seen many . . . but you remind me of my father."

"And what is his name?" But before Glyde could answer, the older petrel continued, "Lupé. Is it Lupé?"

Glyde was stunned. "How could you know that?"

"I see you. I see him."

"You know my father?"

"I know my brother . . . nephew."

"My father," Glyde said to himself as much as to the other bird, "had one brother . . . *had* one. He died a long time ago."

"And no doubt your father still blames himself for the death. But he wasn't the killer, and I'm not dead."

"So, if you're my uncle—my father's brother—tell me, what is *your* name?"

"Barau. I am Barau."

Azul, Nipiklee, and Orsi allowed dusk to reclaim the Caatinga. Once it had, they moved toward the man-flock structure. Nipiklee perched watch, as she had done many times before, while Azul and his nephew approached the parrots contained inside. The pair settled on a shrub that grew just beyond the mesh, yet several of its branches managed to reach inside. It was a spot Azul had used to speak to Aura when she was still being held.

The macaws on the inside took notice of the arrival of the wild duo. Orsi leaned over and whispered, "The parrot we seek is called Providente. She is friendly but can also be quiet, distrustful. The man-flock has given her good reason."

Azul nodded. "No doubt."

Orsi squawked. He whistled and squawked again. A parrot stepped out from behind a cluster of leaves and shuffled her way to the end of a swaying bough. She whistled once and tilted her head to the side, waiting for a reply.

Orsi grinned and flew off into the bush, leaving Azul alone on the shrub. The macaw moved forward, and the parrot on the inside flew to him, landing on a section of the same shrub, the man-flock mesh still between them. Again, the female tilted her head. "You are Azul?"

"Yes. And you?"

"My name is Providente. If you are my friend, you will call me Prov."

"Then Prov it is. My nephew tells me that he has spoken with you. He feels it is important that I do the same."

"He is right."

"Can you tell me about Aura? Do you know her?"

"Your mate—"

"Where is she? Is she well?" Azul asked excitedly. He'd waited so long.

Prov took a deep breath. She shook her head sadly. "I do not know. I cannot say."

Frustrated, disappointed, Azul asked, "Then what are we doing here? Why do you need to see me?"

Prov looked at him warmly and said, "Azul, I may not have the answers to those questions, and no, I don't know Aura, but I believe I know someone else who would be important to you."

"There is no one else," Azul said quietly, hopelessly. "There is only Aura."

Prov tilted her head. "There is your daughter."

"My what?"

"Your daughter. I knew her. I taught her."

"I have no daughter. You are confused."

"Perhaps you're the one who is confused. I saw them when they arrived. I saw Aura. I saw the eggs. Aura came and went before I ever had a chance to meet her. The eggs as well, except for one that was left behind. It was hatched without its mother. And I raised her."

Azul was *screech*less.

"All this happened long before I was brought back here by the man-flock."

"There is a daughter?"

"Yes. She is—at least when I left—strong, smart, clever even."

"What is her name?"

"I called her Aratay."

Azul didn't respond. He seemed lost. After a moment, he quietly said, "Aratay," without any expression.

"I'm sorry," Prov said. "I had to call her *something*. I'd never been anywhere but with the man-flock. I'd never been out there, like you. But when I was a hatchling, I met another sky parrot who, like others, came and went. She was beautiful. She was smart. She was kind. And she had a quality, a spirit that refused to surrender no matter what condition the man-flock held her in. She was from the Caatinga, and you could see it in her demeanor. It was always part of her. I loved her so much."

"Was that her name? Aratay?"

"Yes."

"I knew her. You described her well. You are right, it is a good name, a good name for my daughter." A small grin creased the corners of Azul's moist eyes. Then he nodded and continued, "Aratay was my father's sister." Azul nodded again to himself, to the memory, and continued, "Did Aura know about our offspring?"

"If she didn't mention her to you when you were reunited, I would think not. She must have been with clutch when they originally captured her. And after she laid the eggs, who would ever think one would hatch? Without its mother, no less."

"Or its father."

"Yes."

"And yet it did."

"It did."

"Where did you come from, Prov? I know you were with the man-flock, but *where?* Where did they keep you? Tell me."

"Far from here."

"I have been far from here. Where did you come from?"

"I'm not sure. My sense of location is not as practiced as other sky parrots. When you've been imprisoned your entire life, many skills, many abilities that one should have are just not there."

"Yes, I understand," Azul sympathized. "But I'm sure you can imagine what I'm feeling. My daughter is somewhere beyond the Caatinga and likely is not free."

"Perhaps as I grow closer to who I was meant to be, I will be more help. And I will do whatever I can, always, to make sure that Aratay meets her father, so that there will never be oceans or man-flock mesh like this between you."

Azul grinned. It was a bittersweet expression that acknowledged both pain and satisfaction. "There is more sky parrot in you than you realize, Prov. Aratay, my father's sister, would be pleased."

"You will meet your daughter, Azul."

"Yes, I will."

The two men, convinced beyond a shadow of a doubt that they'd just seen an actual ivory-billed woodpecker, pursued the elusive bird as long as the sunlight allowed, but they couldn't spot the phantom a second time. They dragged their canoes out of the water without saying a word. They hadn't spoken once the entire afternoon. The two sat on a long, thick log, each with a notebook and a pen, writing down exactly what they'd seen. Would their notes show that they'd seen the same bird? Bobby was sure they would.

When they were done, the pair sat in Bobby's van, eating the last of the stew and the candy bars. It wasn't necessary to see the other's notes. Tim and Bobby knew what they saw, knew that the notes would be identical. The words were written to convince others, not themselves.

Once they were done eating, done scribbling, Bobby asked, "What now?"

Tim shook his head. There were lots of choices to consider. Do they tell others what had happened? If so, whom should they tell? Would it be better to wait and gather more evidence? Both were aware of reputable, credentialed, respected birders who'd reported ivory-bill sightings and were quickly, completely discredited and shunned. Being the boy who cried ivory-bill could be a dangerous thing on many levels. For some, it had proven to be career suicide to claim a sighting, especially without ironclad visual evidence, which was something they didn't have.

Bobby and Tim had agreed, even before the sighting, that this would always be about the bird, never about the two of them. So, if it was necessary to take the leap into the credibility, career abyss, neither would hesitate, but only if they judged it was best for the bird. And that was really the question, the only question: What was best for the ivory-bill?

If the wrong people knew about the discovery, it could also lead to the woodpecker's demise. Masses might flock to the swamp, disrupting the bird's behavior and, perhaps, damaging its fragile habitat as well. Certainly, there were people—lots of them—who shouldn't know. Were there those that should know? If so, it appeared to be a short list. And the more they discussed it, the shorter the list became. Other than their wives (Bobby and Tim weren't stupid), they decided to tell no one except for one person. Best if this remained a secret, they felt.

Even though people—the right ones, at least—could help the woodpeckers, when man had known about its existence, from Texas to Florida, from the Carolinas to Arkansas, and possibly as far north as Indiana prior to 1800, the species suffered a steady, tragic decline until the present. Now, most people in the know viewed the ivory-bill as extinct, and with good reason.

Yet there were some like Bobby and Tim who felt differently, and now those two *knew* differently. It seemed to them that the bird had managed to hang on against all odds. So, if humans believing that the ivory-bill was nothing more than a memory had resulted in the bird's survival, it seemed foolish to alter that perception. But to ignore the fact that the bird was still here and could likely use some help seemed foolish as well.

The friends agreed that they'd share their finding with only one other prominent person in the birding community whom they first met a conference at Cornell's School of Ornithology. They hadn't spoken to him in quite a while, but they thought the I-BIRD director, Vicente El Real, should know about the woodpecker. Surely, he could be trusted to do the right thing. Tim would track him down and set up a meeting.

Bobby continued to return to the swamp in search of the ivory-bill while Tim reached out to El Real. Eventually, the erstwhile director, no longer associated with I-BIRD, was located at a Spix's macaw reintroduction project in Brazil. Tim reached him by phone one evening.

"You have important news for me?" Vicente began. "I do remember you and Roberto from Cornell. I believe you and I met again at Monmouth University, as well."

"Yes, we did. I also heard you speak at Clark University, but we didn't get to connect personally."

"Regrets. Those were busy days. Before you speak, Timoteo, I remember well your research interest. I'm guessing we're going to talk about the ivory-bill. You believe you've seen one."

"Not just m—"

"Please, my friend, let me finish."

"Of course," Tim replied, perplexed.

"You and Roberto want to tell me what you've seen. You believe you've seen a specimen in the wild? You want to make plans to support this bird? And you believe I'm the man to help you, the one to help the bird."

"Yes, exactly. As I wa—"

"Don't."

"What?"

"Don't tell me. Take your findings to Cornell. The director of the lab is a good man, a man who can keep a secret and still get things done. There's another woman running a lab at Penn State who might also help you. Tell one of them. Don't mention my name or our discussion. It will be better for you and Roberto and the bird if I'm not involved." And then, Vicente El Real quietly hung up the phone and returned to the macaws and the Caatinga.

"How can you possibly be Barau? How can you be here?"

"My grandmother, Pakeet, your great-grandmother, that's how. Your father might not have mentioned it to you, but he's been to the other side. He died and was returned."

"What?"

"I saw him. I was there. He had choked on some man-flock waste, thinking it was a jellyfish. He suffocated on the beach and came to the other side." Barau looked at Glyde. In truth, he looked into Glyde. "Perhaps you know what I'm saying. Perhaps you've perched on the rainbow that bridges this world and the next."

Glyde stood silently. His uncle knew.

Barau continued, "Pakeet roosts in the burrow of Pettr. She has power and offered your father an opportunity to enter the other side or, if he chose, to return. But if he did come back, it could only be to serve the flock. And if he didn't do that, if he didn't fly the good flight, he would not pass to the other side when he returned, even though he would have passed at that moment." Barau looked at his nephew carefully. "His decision to father you with a mother from another flock . . . Well, Pettr will decide whether that was flying the good flight or not when your father returns to the other side."

"I'm not sure he had a lot of options," Glyde countered.

"To be certain," Barau reassured him. "I'm sure I would have done the same."

"If all you've said is true," and Glyde was sure it was, "that doesn't explain who you are and why you're here."

"I'm your uncle, Barau, as I've said. Do you know how I died? Did Lupé tell you?"

Glyde nodded.

"Good. Then let me tell you how I returned to this world, how I was reborn. I watched your father arrive after I had left this life, when I was on the other side. My big brother was coming back to me. And then he wasn't.

"Our grandmother returned him to Galahope. I wasn't jealous. If it was what Lupé wanted and it was best for the flock, then it was good. But I began to think . . . if my brother was allowed to return, if his presence was important to the Gwattas, why wasn't mine? Why couldn't I go back? So, I asked Pakeet."

Glyde glanced back at the small opening at the other end of the burrow. His stomach was unsettled. He was nervous, nauseated. Still, he stayed and listened.

"After some thought, Pakeet told me that she could send me back *once*. I would have to make the same agreement that my brother made. And I would have to accept wherever, however I returned to this life. I have to admit, I wasn't really sure what that meant. It didn't matter, really. I was about to get a second chance. I took it."

"From what my father told me, you never really had much of a first chance."

Barau flashed an empty smile.

"So, how did you get here, to Nonsuch?" Glyde asked.

"I took the offer, and this is where Pettr sent me. When God sends you somewhere, you go. And this wing," Barau held out his twisted limb, "came with me as well."

"So, you could never fly off this island?"

"Never have, never will. But strangely, the Gwattas came to me. First, a female. She could fly. She flew for the both of us. We made a family. You saw my offspring on your way in. Other Gwattas trickled in. We became a small flock. The other petrels, the larger ones you saw are cahows, cousins one might say. We've done well together. Believe it or not, there was a time not that long ago, really, when half a million pairs of cahows nested on the islands surrounding Nonsuch." It was another story that the two flocks had in common. Barau stretched his twisted wing awkwardly and paced for a moment. "I thought I would be sent back to Lupé, but I wound up here. Strange, but if you think about it—and I certainly have—it sort of makes sense."

"Not to me. I can't imagine why Pakeet didn't put you with my father, didn't send you to the Islands of Life."

"I felt the same way. She did what Pettr wanted. She did it for the Gwattas."

"Father on Galahope, you on Nonsuch, on two different islands? It could make sense, but on two different *oceans*?"

Barau smiled. "Two flocks—one here, one there. We might be smaller flocks, but if something terrible happened to one of us . . ."

"There would still be another," the younger petrel completed the thought.

"Yes, it kind of makes sense."

Glyde shook his head. "But there's a difference."

"What's that?" Barau questioned, intrigued.

"Here on Nonsuch, you have pure Gwatta petrels. Pure. On Galahope, we're mixed with the Darums, the dark-rumped."

"Well, maybe now that we know about each other, that will change. Maybe we'll all change."

Glyde shrugged and nodded.

By nightfall, Glyde had met Barau's mate and all his offspring. He had learned, among other things, that Soaria was actually Barau's daughter, his cousin. Perhaps that was why he felt so drawn, so connected to a petrel he'd never met. He'd also spoken to the larger cahows and heard the history of their modest colony, a history not so different from the Gwattas. It was a good time for the petrels of Nonsuch. The island, more than any of the others in the region, seemed to be for the birds. The man-flock made efforts to treat the petrels, the tropicbirds as well, with care. With respect, even.

But there was one threat that surrounded the precious island, closing in on it incrementally each day . . . the sea. It was impossible not to see it. The ocean was slowly, persistently rising. In Galahope, where the islands were much larger and much higher, the change wasn't as apparent. On Nonsuch, however, where the island was more or less flat, a clam could see it.

High tides were higher. On occasion, a burrow would flood. When the tides receded, they often drew valuable soil out to sea, holding on to a bit more of the shoreline than before the water arrived. Should a large hurricane strike, accompanied by a more eager tide, the birds' entire habitat might be washed away. It was a menace that neither man-flock nor bird seemed able to do anything about. The petrels could see it was coming and considered where they'd go if—or when—it struck. For Barau, who couldn't fly, the other side seemed likely. But at this moment in their lives, all was relatively well, so for now, the flock flourished.

The next day, Glyde rose with the sun and said his goodbyes. After talking with Barau, who reminded him so much of his father, he decided to return home. Whether he would remain on Galahope, the petrel wouldn't know until he got there, but he was going home. It was time.

He said one last farewell to his uncle, waved to his newfound aunt and cousins, and took a moment to watch the north wind rise. Then he climbed into the soothing salt breeze and headed south, down into the warm current. At midday, with the sun overhead shining through the clouds onto the gentle waves below, it occurred to Glyde that he'd been flying somewhat mindlessly, wrapped up in a haze of prayer, meditation, and thought that made time and distance feel like they stood still. It was surprisingly satisfying.

Glyde reflected on his journey, how far he'd flown, the different birds he'd met. Was it worth it? Would he do it again? Yes, the petrel concluded. As wonderful as Galahope was—something Glyde had gained a greater appreciation of—it was nonetheless rewarding to spread one's wings and get off the island. The petrel hung in the air, buttressed by a buoyant thermal, and grinned. He hadn't accomplished what he'd set out to do, hadn't even met Soaria before her passing, and yet he had accomplished so much that he never intended. He was a different bird, a better bird. The petrel imagined his mother, Sirka, cackling sarcastically to him upon his arrival home, "Who are you, and what have you done with my Glyde?"

The word came to him unexpectedly. It slipped out of the thin clouds. *Seamore . . . Seamore . . . Seamore . . .* It was another link in his *birdtra*, the words that only Pettr could send to you when you were worthy, words that carried prayers to the other side. *Seamore . . . Seamore . . .* The word rained down on him.

The petrel laughed at the irony, that this sacred, *bird*sonal word would actually be his own name, a name that he wasn't particularly fond of. Did that mean something? Was there a message there, or was it merely the Creator's sense of humor? He heard it again, *Seamore.* Or was it . . . *See more?* Glyde wasn't sure. Was it either? Both? Glyde would have to pray on it to know for sure. He would have plenty of time to find out, plenty of time to pray during his journey home. Perhaps the bequeathal of a third word for his *bird*tra was Pettr's way of telling him that he'd made some good decisions. Maybe Pettr was telling him that he was about to be faced with another.

A word kept coming, but now it was a different word. *Glyde . . . Glyde . . .* Suddenly, *Seamore* was gone, replaced by his nickname, *Glyde . . . Glyde.* It seemed to be growing louder. *GLYDE, GLYDE.* Soon, it was deafening, as if the name were being shouted into his ear. Then he realized it was.

"GLYDE!" the bird called to him. It was the young mother of the chick, the youngster whom the long-tail had attacked. She was flying beside Glyde, shouting his name into his ear. Glyde looked at her, baffled.

"You left," she said, huffing and puffing after racing to catch him. "You never said goodbye."

"I . . . I didn't know I was supposed to. I mean, we never really said hello, not in any normal way."

Slightly ruffled, she countered, "Well, we still met."

"Hey, I don't even know your name. That seems pretty basic to *meeting.*"

"You never actually asked. Are you asking?"

Bewildered, Glyde said, "Sure, seems like the thing to do."

"So, you're asking?"

"*I'm asking.*"

"Why, because it's *the thing to do?*"

"No, that's not why," Glyde responded, not quite sure what was happening.

"So, why? Why do you want to know my name?"

"Ahhh, because you're here?" And when the female looked back at him, unresponsive, Glyde thought for a flap and began to understand. He gathered himself and said calmly, "I would like to know your name because you are very interesting, and I would like to get to know you better." He had to be careful not to phrase the statement as a question, which he knew would annoy the other petrel but, in truth, would reflect the fact that Glyde was kind of guessing.

"Then do it," the female insisted.

"What?"

"Do it. Ask me my name."

"What is your name?" Glyde mumbled, never one to enjoy being led by the wing.

"Liv. My name is Liv."

There was silence. She was waiting for something. The puzzled male, as dense as an outcrop when it came to females, pondered. Then he said flatly, "Nice to meet you, Liv."

The other petrel smiled, almost triumphantly.

Glyde continued, "Why are you here? *You have a chick.*" Glyde's demeanor changed abruptly, and he asked urgently, "Is he OK?"

"He's fine. And I have not abandoned the chick," Liv pointed out, eager to dispel the notion that she was unfit as a guardian.

"It kind of looks like you've abandoned him. Maybe you should get back to the little nest rat, I mean the little egg of joy. Can't imagine what he's getting into without his mother around."

"I don't need to get back to him."

"All right, but it sure looks like you've abandoned your chick."

"Have not."

"I think you have."

"He's not *my* chick. Never was."

"Really?"

"You would have known that if you'd talked to me."

"Yeah, well . . . I kind of flew into an uncle who I didn't know really existed, and a few other things were sort of going on. That whole tropicbird abduction thing . . . You do recall? But what do you mean he's not your chick?"

"I was chick sitting. His parents flew off to feed together. Maybe your flock doesn't do that, but they asked me. That's why I was so frantic when the long-tail showed up. I couldn't let him die on my watch. And you're right. He is a bit of a nest rat."

"So, no chick?"

"Nope."

"Eggs?"

"None."

"Nest?"

"Not really . . ."

Suddenly, even to the naïve male, it was beginning to make sense. "Soooo, how'd you know *my* name and where I was going?"

"Barau."

"And you came all this way just to collect your goodbye?"

"Not really." The female looked into Glyde's eyes. It was the first time that their gaze truly met. Liv stared at him for a moment as they flew together. He stared back at her. "Do you want me to fly back?" she inquired. "Should I return?"

This time, it was Glyde's turn to say, "Not really." Then his expression changed. He seemed flustered. Glyde asked, "We're not like cousins or anything like that?"

Liv shook her head no. "I'm not one of Barau's daughters, if that's what you're pecking at."

"I'm just making sure. There aren't a lot of us. It could happen."

"I know, but it's not happening. Let it go."

"OK," Glyde agreed while they both crowed a relieved yet nervous chortle. Then, in an effort to let it go, Glyde banked the conversation in a different direction, saying, "What's with those tropicbirds?"

After discussing the tropicbirds, the rambunctious hatchling, and one or two other random topics, the pair flew on quietly.

The wind shifted, and a gusty breeze caught their unfurled wings, nudging them toward Galahope, toward the future. *Their future, per*flaps*.*

The End

Flocks of One—as if a flock should ever consist of *one*. And yet that appears to be the case, or at least the destiny of many species on the planet today. While this is a sad reality, the situation is not without hope. Humans can—and do—make a difference daily, whether it be positive or negative. This story attempts to shine light on several sides of the issue. Indeed, individuals themselves are often neither exclusively good nor bad, right nor wrong. Vicente is a case in point, a character who was inspired by actual events. Truth is stranger than fiction, if you will.

As I write this final thought, there is a murmur of exciting news for the ivory-billed woodpecker. The ghost of the swamp seems to have allowed us to catch a fleeting glimpse, a whisper that they are not gone, a plea that we might leave them a little corner of the planet to build a nest.

The Spix's macaw, generally believed to now be extinct in the wild, is still breathing and breeding, albeit in captivity. At the time of publication, there are at least two serious efforts to build a flock with a healthy genetic diversity. To my knowledge, neither of these wonderful efforts are taking place in the Caatinga of Brazil. My hope—and I think it's safe to assume that I am not alone—is that at some point, these birds will be introduced into the wild again, if a sustainable sliver of their world is allowed to remain. The dark irony is that the habitat is as imperiled as its fauna, a scenario repeated in every corner of the world. It would seem that it's just as vital to protect, to preserve habitats as it is to provide for those who live within the environment, which often includes humans as well as animals and plants. These are complicated issues, so beware of individuals with simple answers.

Nonsuch Island in Bermuda is a testament to what can be done, what should be done. Cahow petrels, once thought to be extinct, are making an impressive comeback due to their indominable tenacity and some meaningful help from the man-flock. But if we make well-meaning, sustained efforts to help these birds, and yet, as a world—or nation, as the case may be—refuse to seriously consider the full breadth of scientific research in areas of pollution, climate shifts, disease, deforestation, and so many other areas, the best efforts of the Bermudans and the cahows could easily be swept away as tides reach farther inland and islands like Nonsuch disappear.

As parents, whether you are one, whether you might become one, and surely whether you've had one, are we not custodians of the future? Are we not stewards of the present? Do we not do all that we can to prepare our children for life without us? We nurture and educate them. We try, to the best of our ability, to provide for their security, emotionally, materially, in any way we can. Is not our world part of this equation? Are we not bound to leave our descendants water they can drink, air they can breathe, a sun they won't have to hide from, an ocean that won't poison them, a forest that actually has trees, birds that sing, coral that blooms? What is more important than this?

Thank you for turning the pages of *Flocks of One*. I hope you enjoyed meeting new characters and reuniting with former friends from the series. While extinction and habitat depletion are serious matters, dire situations, they are far from hopeless. They contain stories, characters, settings that are beautiful, unique, unknown, funny, and touching, things I've tried to share on these pages. Thank you again for sharing your time and your interest. I hope you will join me again in another Eco-Adventure.

Connect with John

EMAIL: morano@monmouth.edu

FACEBOOK: www.facebook.com/EcoAdventureSeries

WEB: www.johnmorano.com

About the Author

John is Professor of Journalism at Monmouth University in New Jersey. He studied at Clark University, Penn State University, and Adelphi University. John began his writing career in New York at *Modern Screen Magazine*, the nation's oldest movie magazine, where he served as lead film critic and managing editor. From there he moved to Los Angeles to become the founding editor-in-chief of *ROCKbeat Magazine* before returning to New York to become senior editor for *Inside Books Magazine*.

After years of covering the entertainment industry, as an academic John became interested in environmental issues and penned his first novel *A Wing and a Prayer*. With the success of his first book, *The John Morano Eco-Adventure Series* was born, and several more novels ensued, including *Makoona* and *Out There, Somewhere*, and *Flocks of One*.

John's work has been endorsed by The Nature Conservancy, World Wildlife Fund, Ocean Conservancy, ASPCA, and other world-class environmental organizations. He has been cited for making complex environmental issues accessible to a wide variety of readers in an entertaining, uplifting way. Professor Morano is also the author of *Don't Tell Me the Ending!*, a popular how-to textbook for aspiring film critics.

John lives in New Jersey on the northern tip of the Pine Barrens in a log home with his wife, two sons, and two rescued Australian Shepherds. When he's not writing or in the classroom, John can be found hiking streams in the woods and collecting Cretaceous fossils or, when his knees let him, running up and down the basketball court.

About the Illustrator

Sarah E. Anderson is a visual artist practicing primarily in acrylics and pen and ink. She has contributed the illustrations for each installment in *The John Morano Eco-Adventure Series*.

Sarah received her bachelor's degree in fine arts from Carnegie Mellon University with a focus in 2D media such as painting, drawing, and printmaking. She has also studied at the Pennsylvania Academy of Fine Arts in Philadelphia and the E'cole nationale supe'rieure des Beaux-Arts in Paris, France.

She currently resides in Columbus, Ohio and is attending Ohio State University, pursuing a doctorate degree in occupational therapy. Her other interests include playing video games, going to museums, running half marathons, and reading books, when she has the time.

Sarah would like to thank John Morano for writing such a wonderful story and inviting her to contribute to it. She would also like to thank her parents and friends, as well as Grey Gecko Press, for their continuing support.

Connect with Sarah

EMAIL: seandersonart@gmail.com

WEB: seandersonart.com

Out There, Somewhere

Book 3 of the Eco-Adventure Series

When Maputa is caught in a fishing net off the coast of the Comoros, neither she nor the fishermen believe she will survive. But rather than meeting the Spirit-fish, the ancient coelacanth finds herself on display as a living fossil at SeaTopia on the Florida coast. There she joins a motley crew of captive sea creatures and the man-tide who both confine and care for them—including Samantha, a neglected teen who finds purpose at the aquarium.

At SeaTopia, the sea creatures and the man-tide both must navigate the complex world of care, captivity, and conservation. When the man-tide destroys the ocean and its inhabitants, are Maputa and her friends better off in the freedom and danger of the wild or the protection and confinement of the aquarium? Or does the Spirit-fish have another plan in mind?

Featuring a special introduction by Roger T. Rufe, President of The Ocean Conservancy.

Recommended Reading

This bittersweet chronicle of a working horse finally gaining his freedom was inspired by a real animal and true events, yet its underlying theme is about the universal value of friendship.

**Horse
by Leon Berger**

The hero is a sturdy draft horse: old, eccentric, and irritable. His name, suitably enough, is Groucho. By day, he hauls a tourist carriage around the heritage streets of Montreal. By night, he goes home to a stable in a run-down, working-class district.

When his owner dies, Groucho feels the loss and is helped through it by the ancient stableman, Doyle, who is also set in his ways. This is the story of how they cope with each other, as well as the threat which endangers their entire way of life.

www.ingramcontent.com/pod-product-compliance
Lightning Source LLC
Chambersburg PA
CBHW032104180726
48284CB00002B/441